Snake Dance

Snake Dance

Ulf E. Lidbeck

Lidbeck Press

For information contact:

LIDBECK PRESS
Centerville, MA USA
lidbeckpress@gmail.com

To Liss

In Appreciation

As my native tongue is Swedish, I express my sincere gratitude to my friends and colleagues, and especially to my daughter, Christina, and my son, Dag, for their editorial assistance in guiding me through the language barriers.

Ulf Lidbeck

Foreword

THIS STORY WAS inspired partly on reports in the local newspapers about drug dealers' activity on Cape Cod, Massachusetts. Soon after the author moved to the Cape a considerable shipment of drugs was said to be confiscated by the police and stored by the police in a safe place until the suspected individuals were taken to court. However, when the evidence was needed in court the police discovered that the confiscated drugs had disappeared! Gone without a trace from the vault in the police station. Soon thereafter a series of gruesome murders took place and several very wealthy, well-known drug dealers, who so far had always succeeded to sneak away free from every police trap, lost their lives. The man here called Benny was found dead in his magnificent Centerville home overlooking the ocean. "Drilled" by his enemies. Uncountable two-inch drywall screws penetrated his arms, legs, knees and skull.

The heroine of this story is Michele Renard a scientist of Native American Indian origin, a descendent of the Cape Cod Wampanoag (pronounced wam-puh-no-ag) tribe. She leads us into this breathtaking, thrilling story about a lonely little lady's fight for revenge, justice and social responsibility. Her passionate search for love and her crazy, completely fearless interference with two factions of ruthless gangsters has its special reason and background and can only be described as dancing with snakes.

The Snake Dance was originally a ritual dance performed by several Native American Indian tribes, among them the Wampanoag in New England. Brave warriors danced, swinging poisonous snakes with their bare hands, juggling with them, throwing them high up in the air, and catching, cuddling, and kissing them while the hissing reptiles tried to strike them with their fangs. This narrative shows the brave and fearless warriors' superiority over any deadly dangerous, unwanted intruder. When the dance is over the dancers show their respect for nature and the snakes by letting them free. Michele, however, has her own way to handle her lawless, snake-eyed opponents.

Chapter 1

"MY HUSBAND, RICH, and I had been filming lions for almost a month and we got some great sequences of their behavior, entirely new to us. Our tapes with sounds from lionesses and their cubs are sensational! Very charming and very interesting."

Michele paused for a moment.

"We planned to film rhinos, too, before leaving Kenya. So we loaded our Land Rover and drove to a water hole nearby where we knew we would find some rhinos. We also knew this area was infested by poachers. We had seen rhinos killed by machine gun fire, their horns cut off with a chain saw.

"That morning we followed a path with footprints from rhinos to the waterhole. We noticed that a lot of blood had been dripping along their way showing the animals had been wounded. In a glade we found a rhino cow and her calf. The calf had been seriously hurt, bleeding heavily from gun shot wounds in its hind. Defending her calf the cow had probably attacked the poachers and chased them away. She was wounded too - in her leg. The calf lay down. It was a horrible sight that moved me to the bottom of my heart. I got some pictures. Rich carefully went closer. You never know with rhinos. He wanted to see if we could stop the calf from bleeding to death. If we could tranquilize the cow, take the bullets out and give them antibiotics, both animals would have a good chance to survive.

"Suddenly three men came out of the bush. Without saying a word they went up to the rhinos, aimed at the animals' heads and fired several rounds with automatic weapons.

"'Stop the shooting for God's sake!' Rich shouted.

"Bending over the cow he looked at the poachers and shouted at them: 'What the hell are you doing? Don't you know they are protected,'

"Can you imagine what those men did? They simply raised their guns at him and fired several rounds. They shot him in the head! Right in front of me! Can you believe it!"

Michele leaned forward, hid her face and sobbed silently. Looking up, tears were spilling down her cheeks. "They murdered him. They murdered my Rich in cold blood. He was one of the world's most brilliant zoologists. He knew more about these animals than anybody. The men killed him just like that." She snapped her fingers.

Speechless, Ingrid and Ted Hallberg stared at the distraught woman who with trembling hands was drying her eyes with a small, lacy hanky.

"Poor you..." Ingrid slowly stroked her new neighbor's hair in a friendly gesture of sympathy and poured her some sherry.

Michele took a sip and went on, "I was sitting at the wheel of our Land Rover and I screamed at them. Then they took aim at me and fired. I had my FN carbine handy and fired back. That was such a surprise to them they got nervous and couldn't aim right. I hit all of them in their legs before they ran off and disappeared into the bushes. I ran over to Rich. He was fatally wounded. I called for help on the radio.

"With my rifle ready to fire I sat there all day with his head resting in my lap. I talked to him, comforted him and myself, too, I guess. We both knew this was a final goodbye. I knew he heard me even if he didn't respond. You know, our ability to hear is the last sense to go when life is over. I sensed the contact with him fading away. Finally I realized I was talking to myself. He died in my arms.

"I don't have many friends. Never had. Never cared much for socializing. My whole life was my husband, our daughter and our research. They were my only close friends, really. I felt so darned lonely and miserable when I lost him. I still do."

She blew her nose, took a deep breath and continued her story, as if talking to herself.

"At sunset the area supervisor and some of his men arrived in a Jeep. They were very kind to me and very upset. They took us to the research station and helped me make arrangements to send Rich and all of our equipment home to America.

"I stayed in New York for a while with Marianne, our daughter. She lived on Long Island. She was the sweetest girl. She married a super wealthy guy and her future seemed bright and secure. But, she told me she wanted to leave him. He was a crook, she said. By pure accident she had learned that his office was just for show. According to Marianne he was a big wheel in drug trafficking.

"One day," Michele continued, her voice shaking, "I heard him arguing angrily with Marianne. The quarrel ended with a gunshot. I ran to see what was going on. He met me in the doorway and asked me to call an ambulance. Marianne had shot herself, he said. I remember his eyes when he told me she was dead. I'll always remember his eyes—those cold snake eyes.

"I rushed in to see her. She lay on the floor shot in her head, like her father. The bullet wound seemed so unreal in her beautiful face.

"She killed herself!" her husband shouted.

"Oh, No! She never would have killed herself because she could always find a way out of trouble. I knew right away. She'd been murdered. How could any human being sink so low as to kill such a lovely creature, so kind and intelligent, so strong in her values, such a wonderful reliable friend?

"A police officer came, asked questions, made notes and said it was no doubt suicide. I had seen that policeman several times before. He was a close friend of Marianne's husband, probably involved in the same gang of drug dealers. So, what could I do? That's how I lost our only child. A smart, beautiful and intelligent girl."

Michele was silent; her gaze fixed somewhere far away. She was talking to herself and to her dead daughter: "You were only 25 years old, my darling. A few years ago we were such a happy family, with such big plans and such great expectations, and, now, here I am sitting all alone and feeling so darned miserable, pitying myself, with people I don't even know.

"Sometimes I regret I didn't kill those three poachers. I had them in the cross hair of my scope. Why did I lower the aim and hit their legs instead? God knows. And why didn't I shoot Marianne's murderer. I would have gone free had I invested in a good lawyer. If I had ended up in jail, I could probably have done my research from there as well as here at home."

Michele sat wrapped within herself. She lowered her voice and whispered: "We shouldn't allow things like this to happen; we shouldn't allow Justice to stand there with her blindfold off, seeing it all, doing nothing."

Then she spit out the words: "But I'll get my revenge! I'll find Marianne's husband and I'll make his life a living hell. I'll fight him and every drug dealer. And I'll see to it they'll end up behind bars. Never again will I meet uncivilized behavior with civilized awkwardness. I swear I'll search for them; I'll find them and I'll fight them until they crawl on their bellies begging for mercy. But there'll be no mercy! Next time I'll shoot to kill! And nobody will ever know who did it!"

For a brief moment fury and anger seemed to push aside her sorrow. Then she managed a smile.

"I am sorry, I lost control. I don't know why I'm telling you these things."

"That's alright. I'm glad you did," Ingrid said.

"But I don't even know you and never before have I told anybody about Rich and Marianne and how I lost them... I really hope I'll be able to control my anger and desire for revenge, and return to a normal harmonious way of living."

Ingrid looked at her and said: "Ted and I are the kind of people our friends always feel free to talk to. It's their way to express trust in us, I guess. They know we don't gossip."

"I came to Cape Cod," Michele continued, "because that was Rich's and my original plan. Both of us have Indian blood in our veins. His grandfather belonged to a Canadian tribe. My ancestors were Wampanoags, a Cape Cod tribe I'll contact to find out more about my roots. I have such a strong feeling this is where I belong. This is where Rich and I were going to spend the rest of our days organizing our notes, films, and photos, putting them together into books, films, and lectures, TV-programs and articles for magazines and newspapers. As soon as I get my things in order I'll write my memoirs and let people know about the wonderful things we saw, those magnificent, wild animals, and the beauty of our earth. How precious this little planet of ours is!"

Michele had moved into the house next door to the Hallbergs on a May morning bringing a small truckload of beautiful antique furniture. She drove a small, old and rusty car. She was a petite, fragile looking woman in her mid-50s. Her hair was white, cut short, and her alert brown eyes were framed in a network of tiny laugh-lines. Her smile was open and so heartwarming one got the feeling she was an old, close friend. She would soon add a dash of spice to the Hallbergs' lives, opening new doors not only to a stimulating friendship but also to thrill and terror.

Familiar with the hopeless feeling of standing in the middle of a mess of unloaded, disorganized furniture, rolls of carpets, trunks and boxes filled with all sorts of belongings, Ingrid and Ted had offered to help Michele unpack and move the furniture. They invited their new neighbor to their favorite dinner from the old country: Swedish meatballs with boiled, "woolly" potatoes, cream gravy, and lingon-berry jelly.

She accepted with a surprised smile and after preparing her bedroom for her first night in her new home, she walked up the brick path to her new friends carrying a colorful bunch of spring flowers from her garden: tulips, iris and narcissus. Over drinks Ingrid and Ted wished her a warm welcome to Cape Cod.

Michele Renard had the kind of beauty that doesn't change much over the years. A few more wrinkles simply added character to her face. Her husband, Richard, had been a zoologist, academician and scientist, like herself.

"We had a wonderful life together," she said. "We traveled a lot, did scientific research, filming and camera shooting, studying endangered species especially the big cats. We worked for years in Africa and India. But, as you know now, during a trip to Kenya it all came to an abrupt end."

***

On that first visit Ingrid and Ted talked late into the night with their new neighbor. After Michele left Ted observed: "She's a very lonely woman desperately seeking new contacts, telling us all about herself. By pure instinct she knew she could trust us. I like her."

"I like her, too," Ingrid agreed. "I found myself on her wave-length right away. That's very unusual! But, her need for revenge scared me. I believe in forgiveness and putting bad memories behind me. She should try to go on with her life, trying to make the rest of it a good life. She cannot bury herself in old injustices and self-pity."

***

Throughout the following summer and fall the three friends met almost daily. During the winter they often spent evenings together, sometimes in front of Michele's open fireplace, sometimes at the Hallbergs'. Michele was a most pleasant, witty and knowledgeable acquaintance. She knew a lot about animals' behavior, about plants and birds and environmental matters, and she knew what the public and decision makers had to be told to limit pollution and save remaining, endangered flora and fauna.

Ingrid and Ted had moved from their native Sweden ten years earlier. She, originally a brunette, now all white-haired, fifty and something, was a talented fashion designer. She was slender with a thin sensitive face and friendly blue-green eyes. He, not quite sixty, was a tall, sturdy, blue-eyed Scandinavian with silver-sprinkled temples. Retired, he had turned his artistic talents to designing and printing T-shirts for the two fashion shops and a very lucrative mail order business he and Ingrid ran in Newport, Rhode Island and in Osterville on Cape Cod, Massachusetts. They introduced Michele to her new neighborhood. They told her about places of interest on Cape Cod: unique walking trails, the best places for bird watching and all the ideal spots for viewing the sunsets, the best specialty stores and where to shop for good food at the best prices.

Life on Cape Cod slows down in winter and Michele spent most of her time organizing her scientific research material putting it together into a book. Ted's experience from years in advertising made him expert at helping her write copy as well as doing layout and editorial work. Ingrid's skills as a fashion photographer were put to good use in selecting illustrations and cutting or masking Michele's pictures.

Spring came early to the Cape that year. Like all Cape Codders they found this lovely time passing much too quickly! Regularly they took the car and drove along Route 6A watching the buds of the oak trees gradually growing larger, eventually spreading out, forming a sort of transparent tunnel over the picturesque road called The King's Highway.

This road follows the north shore of Cape Cod, winding through a landscape of well-trimmed lawns, gardens and old houses with facades of cedar shingles. Driving 6A at dusk in the spring with the headlights illuminating the light green buds contrasting with the dark violet-blue sky always provides a visual experience of great beauty.

Ingrid often said: "There is no place like Cape Cod in spring, it's sort of a Garden of Eden."

Unfortunately there were snakes in this Eden too—men with cold, snake eyes. Drug dealers, not seen but feared and frequently mentioned in the local press. Very little was said about the work of the FBI and the police. It seemed obvious somebody had leaked to the local media the agency's fear that this area was going to be one of the big, new markets for drugs. During the coming tourist season hundreds of thousands tourists would be visiting the historic sites, enjoying nature and the miles of beaches including the National Seashore, the great restaurants, and the pleasant accommodations of plentiful inns and motels.

Ingrid and Ted owned two Scandinavian fashion and gift shops, one in Newport, RI., and one in Osterville on the Cape. Every day during the summer and a few days a week during the slow, quiet season they commuted to Newport stocking their waterfront store in Bowen's Wharf with goods, mainly Scandinavian gifts, souvenir T-shirts and sweatshirts, which Ted designed and printed in the garage of their Barnstable Harbor home.

In the summer Ingrid's Newport store was open from ten o'clock in the morning until ten at night. When the weather was nice they sometimes opened an hour and a half earlier and didn't close until around midnight.

Chapter 2

THERE WERE THREE homes facing the open stretch at Barnstable Harbor: the Hallbergs', Michele's and the Sprenglers'. The Sprenglers had been there for several years. Ingrid and Mrs. Sprengler had talked a few times when they met outside in their common parking area. From their conversations Ingrid knew that Arnold Sprengler grew up in a good, solid middle class family. His parents had sacrificed a lot to give their gifted second son a university degree which neither of them ever had a chance to get. During Arnold's years at college he had worked in restaurants and in the summer as a golf caddy and lifeguard at a beach. When he graduated from law school in Boston his future was golden. He dated Sara, a doctor's daughter from New Jersey. They had met at an Italian restaurant where they were workings to earn some extra money, he for his tuition and room, and she for her trips home, which her father thought unnecessary, but she needed. She was the cutest, brightest girl Arnold had ever met. He adored her. She promised to stay away from other boys when he joined the Navy, became a pilot, and was sent to Vietnam.

He was a highly skilled pilot when he returned. But, the war had made him bitter. He couldn't forget the cruelties, the killed and mutilated innocent old folks, women and children, butchered civilians and soldiers, and the thousands of body bags with dead American boys being sent home. He had lost his respect for Washington. It was not his war; not a war serving the American people. He had concluded it was "their war"—Henry Kissinger's, Pentagon's, the weapons industries' and the politicians'. Everyone opposing the war was labeled a coward or being soft on commies—or both. Not until TV journalists following American troops documented American service personnel being ordered to commit atrocities against civilians did the American people realize what was actually going on.

He felt strongly that American decision-makers responsible for this war and its ultimate outcome had broken most rules of ethics he learned in law school. He believed they should not have gone unpunished for what he called their "dirty war", their crimes against humanity and the spirit of America in order to satisfy the lawmakers' and the Pentagon's flirtation with a money-crazed weapons' industry greasing the hawks in Washington with political contributions.

Kissinger, he thought, should be sent to the international tribunal in The Hague, and condemned as responsible for crimes against humanity for the 1.2 million civilians, who died in the bombings he ordered.

Sara kept her word. Arnold's dream girl was waiting for him when he returned. She never thought he had wasted his time in a meaningless war. She gave him a deep feeling of being welcomed home after doing his duty. Sara and Arnold had a small wedding. She took a teaching position in Cambridge and he joined a well-known law firm in downtown Boston with more responsibility than his salary indicated. Sara and Arnold were happy.

In due time two baby girls arrived and Sara gave up her career to stay home with the children. Both girls were bright and quick to learn and she was determined that they have the best childhood and the finest education possible and early on planned to send them to school in England and later to Oxford University.

Arnold worked hard. He needed Sara's "ground service" to reach their goals and to make his career take off, he said. They grew apart and she became lonely. The good night kisses were rare. She found him clumsy and egotistical in his approach to her. She explained to him that after giving birth to their two children, she had a need and a right to rest and be by herself and think of herself.

They spent every summer on Cape Cod and the girls had a wonderful time there. Sara used some inherited money to buy a home in Barnstable Harbor Square on Cape Cod and they moved from their rented apartment in Cambridge. Arnold made the daily commute to Boston and when friends told him the Cape was growing into a booming market he fell into the trap and opened his own law office with their help. Business, though, was slow and he finally had to go to Boston to find jobs. His former employer and all other law firms he tried had no place for him so he was forced to take any kind of work he could get. He drove a taxi at night and came home exhausted after a 16-hour shift. Still the money he made could not cover expenses for the office, his secretary and the girls' schools. Both his and Sara's savings were exhausted and there was no relief in sight.

He felt ashamed and useless and couldn't perform sexually. Although he was welcome to sleep with her he wanted to show Sara he could live without having sex with her. But despite his self-imposed abstinence, he'd lock himself in a room and masturbate thinking of her.

Sara saw him gradually reach the limit of his capacity and recognized the signs of approaching depression and a nervous collapse. Talking common sense to him she suggested they take a mortgage out on the house and get their finances back in order.

She knew he was sincere when he whispered there just weren't enough words to tell her how much he loved her when, for the first time in two years, he came to her bed where he was welcomed warmly and tenderly. He caressed and kissed her lovely full breasts, her smooth soft belly, and her exciting furry part. Suddenly tears poured down his cheeks. He tried to hide the fact that he was crying and overwhelmed by a feeling of inadequacy and helplessness. But when she comforted him and made love to him all his problems and doubts disappeared and he fell asleep.

For a time their lives seemed to turn into something near harmony. But reality is brutal. Cape Cod was not the place for a young professional wanting to go out on his own and build a career...not like New York or Boston.

The Cape's highly profitable tourist season lasts only 14 weeks plus a few weekends while business during the winter months is devastatingly slow. A large part of the population consists of elderly people who have already been through most tribulations of a normal life. Their wills are prepared, they have collected a lot of wisdom and experience as to how to stay away from trouble and lawyers, except for the pleasure of playing bridge or golf with them—and trying to wheedle free consultations out of them. So more and more unpaid bills piled up on the desk of Arnold Sprengler, Esquire.

Then one day along came a businessman from New York, recommended to Arnold by a friend and needing help. His problem was that he had too much money! Too much cash in bills! This first wealthy customer brought others with the same problems, and Arnold was able to help them! He created new companies. The companies bought other companies forming a maze of ownership. The new companies invested in stocks and bonds, in real estate and land. Arnold understood that all this cash, which the owners did not want to show, had to be illegal money, but he had no reason to ask or to bother.

Most lenders accepted cash as collateral for personal loans without mentioning the real collateral. The borrower's good name was security enough. He was fully aware that these phony companies were created to show income from transactions that never took place.

Arnold was encouraged by his clients to write invoices and charge for expenses he had never dreamed of. He traveled all over the continent making deposits to hundreds of accounts. He had always dreamed of having his own airplane and now he could afford to buy a Cessna in good condition. Banks welcomed him. Politicians started to call him asking for advice and some "little contributions... Maybe they could do him a favor or two in return?" He went to Boston to do business with The Bank, where a "friend" helped him invest and make all transactions look like regular, legal business.

A new law against laundering of drug money forced banks to report all transactions over $10,000. Arnold knew instinctively that he had to get out of this financial chicanery and he informed his clients that he wouldn't be available much longer for this kind of services.

Chapter 3

HIS CLIENTS, IN need of "laundry service," left him and the slow pace returned. A few months passed. One day a former client, Joe Cavallo in Chatham, called and asked for a personal favor.

"Arnold, I have an aunt who needs a ride from Florida to Cape Cod. Could you drive her? Would you do that for me?"

"Of course!" Arnold quickly accepted the offer. He certainly wasn't too busy and all he would have to do was to pick up this woman in Sarasota at an address not too far from his own mother's place.

"You will be well paid," Cavallo said. "Just send me a bill!"

Arnold told Sara he had a business meeting in Sarasota and a customer, an elderly lady, wanted to consult him while he drove her to the Cape by car. Sara found it a bit odd, but big customers often asked for the strangest things.

From Boston's Logan Airport Arnold flew to Sarasota. There he rented a car and drove to see his mother. She had grown smaller, he thought. They had a wonderful visit talking about past happy days." And do you remember when you gave me that beautiful bunch of flowers? And do you remember that Christmas…That summer on Cape Cod… That time Dad and you and I went to buy your bike…"

She laughed and her eyes sparkled with happiness. For her there were no boundaries between memories of the past and present-day reality. It was all a happy mix. He took her out for dinner and they talked late into the evening.

The next day he met with the woman he was to drive to Massachusetts...a reserved old lady who treated him like a footman. She had a lot of luggage, a big white Lincoln and a Puerto Rican maid in her twenties. Arnold helped the little maid pack all their trunks and cases into the car and they began the trip north. The lady wasn't at all talkative. She just sat, smoked cigarettes and watched soaps on the Lincoln's built-in TV.

The little maid though was remarkably pretty and well shaped. She talked about her home in Puerto Rico, how beautiful it was; how poor people struggled there and how fortunate she was to get into the United States. Miles and hours sped by. Every now and then there was a knock at the glass slider to the back seat and the old lady whispered instructions to her maid. Martinis were to be served or coffee or snacks.

When night fell Arnold checked them in at a hotel where they had reserved three separate rooms. The car had to be emptied of all luggage. The older woman had dinner in her room but Arnold and the Puerto Rican girl had supper together. Later that evening when he was in bed reading there was a knock at the door. When he opened it there was the maid asking to be invited inside. She wore a lovely silk dressing gown, which she slipped off and revealed a most appealing naked body. He did not know what to say. He raised a hand in a vague protest when she snuggled into his bed and turned off the bed light.

"Please don't be mad at me," she said. "I hate to be alone."

He stayed in his half of the bed, thinking of Sara. He was tired and not in the mood for this kind of game.

"I'm tired," he said, "and I want to sleep."

"Of course," she said. "I just want to feel someone near me."

15

She bent over, kissed him and said good night.

"Damn," he said to himself, and tried to fall asleep. She was a nice kid all right, full of fun. An entertaining companion when he was driving. But why the heck couldn't she leave him alone? He felt her soft hands around his penis but he didn't protest. Her grip was firm but pleasant. She felt him grow and his blood pulsing. She held firmer, pulled and caressed him. After a while she sat up, straddled him and bent forward. There was no way out for him.

"Why can't I stop this", he gasped. "Why do I let her seduce me? Why do I let these rich drug dealers make me dance to their tunes? I know what's the right thing to do, still I don't object..."

"Please lie still," she said, "please don't chase me away! Just relax and enjoy me."

Time stood still. She knew how to intensify his passion...his excitement. He closed his eyes, thinking...At home he had the best woman in the world. Why was he doing this?

He didn't want to be here in the first place, and he didn't want to be seduced by anybody. He wanted to be the aggressor and call the shots. The girl sat there on him in the dark. He felt her spasms and his body couldn't resist answering them.

"You are so good to me," she said and began to move slowly. He felt the culmination approaching. Their sexes communicated and he responded to her as their passion united in their anticipation of an explosive climax to their togetherness. She turned wild as she rode him in a frenzied gallop. Her ecstasy did not end but lasted and lasted.

"Please kiss my breasts. Oh! Please suck gently! Oh! Please!" She held her velvety, firm breasts to his lips and he thrilled with the sensation of being a baby boy nestled contentedly at his mother's breast and a man making love at the same time. As if under her spell he obeyed her.

"Oh," she whispered. "You are a perfect lover."

They lay there beside each other in the dark and he fell asleep breathing her fragrance…exotic, flowery, lightly spicy.

When he woke in the morning she was gone. Why had he let her come in? Why had he been so helpless doing everything she asked of him? This could ruin his marriage to Sara, his closest and best friend. He really didn't want to hurt her and he couldn't think of living without her. He was ashamed, convinced that nobody could really trust him ever again, not even he himself.

The two women had already had their breakfast when he ordered coffee, toast and cereal.

***

He was aware that the Puerto Rican girl was radiant and in good spirits. Soon they were on their way again. The car traveled without a sound, fast and comfortably. Late in the afternoon they arrived in New York. The elderly woman wanted him to stop at Hotel St. Moritz, but he didn't want to risk the same temptation again, so he insisted on just a quick stop for a bite.

A good and experienced driver, Arnold chose Hudson Parkway out to the New England Thruway and joined all the other drivers chasing each other out of New York. He saw more Connecticut police cruisers than usual so he kept to an almost legal speed. He felt more and more jittery about all the cruisers. Was this old lady a drug courier? Maybe she was Mr. Cavallo's aunt. He had his doubts. She did not invite conversation. The girl didn't reveal any secrets but talked and smiled joyfully all the time. The moon followed them in a cloudless dark blue sky.

"Did you sleep well last night?" He nodded.

"Was I good?"

"Yes and no."

"Glad you said yes."

He noticed more and more police cruisers. One tailgated them all the way through Wareham to Bourne. He felt his heart in his mouth when the red signals from a State Trooper flashed him to stop at the big parking area overlooking Cape Cod Canal.

Arnold pressed a button and the window slid down.

"Yes, is there a problem?" he asked the policeman.

"Sorry to disturb you, Sir. This is a routine control. May I see your license, please, and the registration."

He reached for his wallet. It was gone. How on earth? He could have sworn he had it in his jacket last night! When and how had he lost it? At the hotel, of course! The girl. He found the registration in the glove compartment.

"Albert, what is this about?" the old lady asked from her back seat. She opened the glass slider and leaned forward.

"Albert! Here is your wallet."

She handed him the wallet. The license was there in its little pocket. The policeman scrutinized it, looked at him over and over again. Then he nodded and gave it back. He saluted Arnold making a V-sign as he touched his hat.

"Thank you! That's fine, you may continue. Good night. Have a safe trip."

Arnold heard one policeman saying to his partner in the cruiser: "No it's not them. It's an elderly lady, her nurse and her chauffeur, Albert! I guess we'll have to wait till tomorrow. After all, we didn't expect them to leave the St. Moritz until tomorrow."

Arnold turned out from the parking area. He could see the brightly illuminated Sagamore Bridge about a mile up the canal. He was very, very tired, but the sleepiness he had felt earlier was gone. He leaned back, opened the sliding glass behind him and asked:

"Excuse me, Ma'am, but why did you call me Albert?"

She lit a cigarette and leaned back puffing out a thick cloud of French Caporal tobacco smoke.

"I don't take any chances, young man. You did OK! We'll soon be there, won't we?"

"Yes Ma'am, another 15 minutes and we'll be at the Hyannis Regina!"

"That's good! You're an excellent driver. I like you!"

He closed the slider and opened his window to let the strong tobacco smoke escape.

At the Regina the night porter was apparently half asleep at his desk. A TV with a ball game going on blared away from underneath and when Arnold hit the night bell the clerk jumped to attention with a jerk.

"Good evening, Mr. Sprengler. Welcome. The ledger here says that you are booked in for tomorrow night, Sir. But we've always got room for you, Mr. Sprengler. No problem! I'll take care of your luggage."

Arnold went back to the car and helped the elderly lady out. It was chilly and she kept a throw blanket around her shoulders. He reached in to pick up the little white cushion, which she left in the seat. There was something heavy inside. He could feel it was an automatic gun with a short pipe and a long butt. Nobody had noticed his discovery so he put the cushion with the gun back on the seat.

The Puerto Rican girl asked if he was staying.

He shook his head. "No, my friend. I'll drive home. It's not far and I think I need to sleep!"

"What a pity," her voice was soft.

Arnold noticed she clutched the little white cushion under her arm. "A pleasure meeting you, Albert," she smiled. "Thanks for the ride, I really enjoyed it!" and with a what-the-hell shrug she disappeared into the hotel bar.

Arnold found his BMW in the parking lot and, leaning back in the seat, he took out his wallet and looked at his license. It was his all right, his picture, his social security number. Everything seemed

OK! But he noticed that the name said "Albert Springer"! He took it out of its compartment. It was a perfect counterfeit. Behind it he found his real license. In the bill compartment there was a thick bunch of hundred dollar bills and a check for $5000.

"Oh, I get it! My wallet was the real reason for her amorous show last night," he smiled to himself.

He felt good about the money, but he had an uncomfortable sense of being a puppet manipulated on a string without a chance to follow or get out of the dance.

"Can I, a well-educated, intelligent man who enjoys hard work, and has a nice family, really not get off this treadmill?" he asked himself while driving home.

Chapter 4

SARA SPRENGLER WOKE up when her husband entered their bedroom. She sat up in bed holding her arms out to him.

"Oh, darling! How nice to have you back home again! How was the trip? Did you see Mom in Sarasota? How was she? Who was that lady you drove all the way from Florida? Why on earth didn't she take the plane? You look so miserable! Has anything happened?"

"Hi, dear!" Arnold answered in a tired voice. "Nice to be home! I'm deadbeat! Yes, I saw Mom. She's fine. I took her out to dinner. She sent her love to you and the girls."

He changed into pajamas. In the bathroom he studied his face in the mirror. "Good God, is that me!" He looked mean. His eyes looked cold and his mouth had become thin and insensitive. He didn't like what he saw. "This", he said to himself, "is what Dorian Gray discovered when looking at his own portrait hidden in that attic." It was no surprise that Sara didn't like the change. Tonight, though, he felt welcome, or did he? He swallowed two sleeping pills and went to bed. He lay on his back staring at the black ceiling. Sara, he knew expected him to reach for her. She wanted him to make the first move. But he was too exhausted and didn't want to talk about the trip

After waiting a while for him—just a kiss or holding her hand—she felt the barrier between them building. She thought he could just as well have stayed away one more night or even two or ten! Every time he came home from one of his trips she was happy again. The walls between them seemed to disappear and she felt close to him. But lately when he came home it took only a few moments for him to make those walls rise and she cared less each time. She tried again:

"Why don't you tell me everything that's bothering you?" she asked. "You have changed so much lately and I don't like the new you! Why can't you be the nice person you used to be?"

There was silence. Arnold knew every word she said was true, but he didn't answer. He would have liked to have told her but he didn't want to talk, or to say anything about the trip. The less she knew the better.

Once again, Sara was the one to break the silence.

"I think we should move away from here. You could get a job easily, and we could settle down somewhere else. I don't like those new, so-called important clients of yours. That Joe Cavallo has the eyes of a snake and he is ordering you to do the strangest things that are not a lawyer's responsibility! You can live without him. You can find new clients. I could support us with my teaching."

"You don't understand, Sara, business is business," he said. "Why do you worry? I can manage all right. Have you heard anything from the girls?"

"No, I haven't," she answered. "I know you better than you do yourself. I can read you like a little book, my dear. And I understand very well that you cannot manage or solve the many problems you have created for yourself on your own. I could help you, but only after you fully understand your limitations and what it is you need to function. Why is this Cavallo business so darned necessary? You are not a ruthless man! We do not need a lot of money! I don't anyway! I do not like it when our friends say you are a tough lawyer, cold and heartless. That's not you! And if that is really what you've made yourself, then I don't want such a man as my husband!"

"I'm sorry, dear, but I'm too tired to quarrel."

"Most marriages break up because people are too tired to solve their problems," Sara went on. "Most of the time it isn't the marriage that's the problem. Your ambitions are killing you, Arnold, and your excuses that you are tired are irrelevant. You could at least manage enough strength to accept my open hand when I stretch it out. I want to know the truth about what's bothering you. I can see there is something very wrong going on, and the only way for you to let off some steam is to talk to me about it."

Like so many times before Arnold tried to shrug off his uneasiness. He downed two sleeping pills and an antacid to numb his innate reaction. He blamed his rich, important customers for his own unlawful and heartless behavior that he knew forced some families from their homes and into poverty and lawlessness.

"Obviously you can fool yourself," Sara spoke sharply, "but you can't fool me. If you don't want to talk, that's up to you. Good night! By the way, the police called yesterday and they also came here this afternoon."

"What did they want from me? What was it about?"

"You know why they came here, my dear. You have already put together a good lie you hope they will swallow, haven't you? Good night, I need to sleep."

His heart was beating harder and faster. He wished the sleeping pills would work quickly but he also knew that it would probably take a while for him to calm down enough to fall asleep. There was a sudden forceful, hurting sting in his chest. He recognized the warning signal from his heart. He didn't dare take more pills. A good jolt of whiskey might help, but now it would only make things worse since he had taken those pills.

"The cops, of course," he said to himself, "wanted to know about his traveling and bank deposits. I was acting in good faith though. They probably also knew something about this last trip from Florida. I only did what a good client of mine wanted me to do. I better remember to hide the fake driver's license and some of the money..."

He was thinking of the Puerto Rican girl and the night she came to him and her soft breasts hanging over him touching, caressing his face. He fell asleep around 3. He had a nightmare and woke up an hour later soaking wet with sweat.

He dreamed he had an argument with Sara and she told him to get rid of that customer because she knew it was drug money. She shouted accusations at him that he helped make kids, sons and daughters of their best friends, drug addicts; that he helped spread misery and death. He dreamed he got so angry he smashed her in her face over and over again. She was bleeding. His ring had broken her beautiful front teeth and blood poured from her soft, wounded lips. Her friendly, honest eyes looked questioningly at him. He wept and could not understand how he had been able to hurt her. She was the only one he ever loved and the only one he really ever trusted. How could he do a thing like this even in his dreams? He switched on the light and bent over to look at her. Thank God, it had only been a bad dream. She was sleeping soundly and her lovely face was as beautiful as ever. He did not want to lose her. He bent over her and kissed her and whispered:

"I wish I could tell you, but I don't dare yet, but it won't be long. I promise."

He fell asleep and slept until 8:30. She was gone by then—gone to work. Why was she so stubborn about keeping her part-time teaching job? He was doing well enough now so she could stay home! A horrible thought crossed his mind: was she planning to live alone or to leave him?

She had brewed fresh coffee for him, and there were pancakes in the warming oven. The morning paper carried big Page One headlines about increased drug traffic on the Cape. The police, it was reported, had some clues including names.

His phone rang at 9 sharp. It was the police. They wanted him to come to the station as soon as possible. Could he be there at 10?

"Yes, of course," he said."

He put the false driver's license and Cavallo's check in an envelope and fastened it with duct tape to the back of the oil tank in the basement. The police would have to crawl in under the tank and search with a flashlight to find it. The odor from the oil would protect it from sniffing dogs.

The hearing at the police station was almost unprofessional, he thought. They asked about his deposits.

"Everything is in our computers," the policeman said.

Arnold said nothing. None of the banks he was working with had an on-line system. He knew the cops could not know.

He was queried about his trips and about his relationship with Mr. Cavallo in Chatham. The officer seemed embarrassed to ask so many questions. Obviously he didn't expect a lawyer like Arnold Sprengler to be involved in any criminal activity.

"We have to follow up on some tips we got last night. Thank you, Mr. Sprengler, you have been most helpful."

Once outside in the sunshine Arnold was glad they hadn't asked him if he was Albert Springer, the chauffeur, because he didn't have a clever cover-up story ready that could give him an alibi for the previous night. But what did the officer mean with "You have been most helpful"?

He returned to his office.

"Good morning, Mr. Sprengler, welcome back", his secretary greeted him cheerfully. "The police were here yesterday. They wanted to look around. At first I thought I should ask for a search warrant, but it sounded uncooperative, as though we had something to hide, so I let them in. Just for a few minutes, Mr. Sprengler, and I checked that nobody touched or took anything…"

"Or left anything."

"No, Sir. They didn't leave a message."

"Thank you, you did the right thing. Of course we shall always help the police."

After he had opened the mail he drove to Burger King and called Joe Cavallo. He reported on the trip, the police hearing and the police paying visits to his home and office.

"We were satisfied with your driving! Thanks! I need some more help right away! Can you drop by?"

"Yes, I would like to talk with you, too.," Arnold agreed quickly. "I'll be at your place in 45 minutes."

He needed an alibi and he wanted to know how come the cops were able to expect the shipment. In Chatham he stopped at Small the Florist and ordered a dozen yellow roses for Sara.

Chapter 5

JOE CAVALLO LIVED in a sprawling, beautifully landscaped villa overlooking the ocean and guarded at the entrance by a snake-eyed man in a stone booth watching a dozen TV cameras monitor arriving guests and surveying every inch of the high stonewalls enclosing the compound. With a meticulously clean hanky the guard wiped away non-existing dust from his favorite toy, a long barreled Luger.

He couldn't help but laugh as he looked down at all the "nobodies" working around the Chatham Fish and Lobster landing, scurrying back and forth like a colony of ants building an anthill. A fishing boat entered the harbor and docked. Screeching gulls flew in, diving for the fish guts thrown overboard. It was a hot day. On the horizon the aqua-colored ocean melted into the sky in light fog banks. Trawlers far out at sea could be seen disappearing in the deep troughs between the waves of the long swell, then slowly reappearing on the crest of new waves.

People were sunbathing on the sand reef that protected the inner coastline. A couple of trucks were parked there and some young men had set their fishing rods in steel pipes close to the water. They listened to rock music and drank from cans of cold beer stacked in iceboxes while waiting for the fish to bite. A family with small children was having a picnic on the beach. Their golden retriever lay cooling himself in the shallow water.

To the man in the booth all these people were just ordinary creeps doing meaningless, stupid things. A purring sound caught his attention. He turned around and recognized the car and the driver. Here was a man he considered worth admiring—a smart, successful businessman. It was Arnold Sprengler driving his BMW up to the heavy gates decorated with wrought iron ornaments of roses and leaves. The man in the booth smiled and nodded. When he pressed a button the gates swung open admitting the car and then closed when Arnold drove through and parked in front of the villa's ornate entrance.

A red-haired maid in a long black dress showed him in and asked him to wait in the round foyer. There was a small fountain splashing in the center of the room and richly upholstered comfortable armchairs were placed in groups of three around small tables with Tiffany lamps. The floor was marbled. Through a glass wall Arnold could see into the sunken living room and out over the ocean. A beautiful place. After a couple of minutes a man in a light gray three-piece suit came up to him.

"Welcome, Mr. Sprengler. Mr. Cavallo is having a drink. May I serve you a glass of whiskey or champagne?

"Thank you, a scotch on the rocks, please!"

"Very well, Sir."

Joe Cavallo was a big, bear-like man. Once, many years ago, women must have thought him very handsome and charming. Now his trade had marked him. His smile was artificial; his eyes were cold, reflecting nothing of the thoughts and the mood of the man behind them. His manners were still extremely continental however. He sat with his back toward the entrance, his interest fixed to a computer terminal. Every now and then he gazed out over the ocean and the beach. He was aware of Arnold's problems in trying to cover up what he'd been doing the last couple of days. Joe Cavallo already knew the police in Bourne had stopped Arnold and that he had slipped through thanks to some of Cavallo's own routine security measures.

"Good to see you, Arnold. Have a seat."

"How are you? What's up?"

"I want to know if you are interested in a job that would earn you half a million in a few days?"

"May I ask how and when?"

"Only after you have said yes or no! Think fast! Cheers!" They drank from their misty glasses. Arnold sensed a chance to make a big, fast hit and then get out. He was thinking of what Sara would say when this was over and he told her that he was ready to leave the Cape and start again anywhere—her choice. He would take only one more risk, and after that he didn't want to have anything more to do with Joe Cavallo, ever.

"OK, Joe, let's hear it: A. The purpose of the business; B. How we are going to organize it; and C. That I am in charge of everything where I am at risk."

"I knew I could count on you. You're my kind of guy! You're sharp and gutsy. You can control your nerves and I know you're a good pilot. This is the idea: I want you to fly down to Colombia, pick up a load of coke, fly it in to Florida, drop it there and then fly to my place in Texas to pick up your money in cash, in bills. If you figure out the right way of doing this you could make half a million a month."

"Sounds pretty risky to me! I'm not that familiar with the geography there, so I'll have to make some reconnaissance trips. We have to find out if they have AWACs down there. What I mean is, do they have radar monitoring the borders from the sky by airplanes patrolling the area.

"Good point, I'll find out about the AWACs. Maybe we could make those AWAC planes stay grounded for the critical hours."

Arnold realized that once informed about a project like this, he had to play by the rules. If he wanted to quit, it had to be when they were satisfied with him. And then there was only one way— disappear completely. It would have to look like an accident or he would have to disappear without a single possibility of tracing him. He had thought of several ways, but right now there was no way out. He had to be in command, so he said: "My Cessna has enough room for four people including the pilot, plus about 100 pounds of luggage. I need equipment for instrument flying: a first class navigation radio, an autopilot, spare tanks, and safety equipment for flying over the ocean. Also my plane needs a pro checkup and I don't want it done in New England. This cost has to be in addition to my payment—and my payment must be relative to my risk. A big load, more money."

Cavallo nodded. "It's a deal! The safer we can make it the better. Go ahead, you'll get all you need! Also, you will be paid per pound shipped goods, never less than $500,000 for each shipment plus costs. That is a very fair deal, but I want you to be satisfied and I have a contract here ready for you to sign. So, why don't you fly down there and find out where you can pick up goods and look for places where you can drop it off."

Moving over to a beautiful tapestry on the wall he pressed a button and with a humming sound the tapestry rolled up uncovering a detailed map of Central America extending from Colombia in the south up to the southern part of Texas in the north. He pointed and said: "This is where you go first. You might have to pick up the load at two different places. Here and there. We deal with several small suppliers fighting each other for the best deal. You take this route over Florida. South of Sarasota there is a place called the Rotonda where you can make a fast stop and hand over goods to my people. They will be waiting for you. The unloading has to be done in a flash. Then you head for my place in Texas. What do you think about that scenario?"

"Sounds like a piece of cake, but I know it's not! I have to check things out. I'll go to Sarasota and have a look at the Rotonda. I want to look for alternative landing strips and ways of escaping and tricking pursuers."

"Go ahead," the big man agreed. "Order all the equipment you need. I'll pay for it."

"I want to take my plane to the Cessna plant, and let them do the check-up and installation of the best equipment available. Then I'll fly along the coast to Mexico and cross over to the Gulf here, OK?" Arnold pointed at the map.

"What do you think about the cops and the DEA?"

"We have a mole among our people," Arnold explained. "My trip from Florida was leaked. They knew about the time of our arrival, but they didn't know I changed our plans or that my passengers were an old lady and her maid.

"When I start working on this new project, I'll insist that nobody but you and I know anything more than is absolutely essential to do the job. That means no training that could reveal strategy or details. The only info given out would be concerning precise orders on short notice."

"I like your military approach to our plan. Get in touch when you're ready. By the way I have some good tips on where to put the money you're going to make on this. I have a friend on Wall Street. With inside information you can double your money in no time at all."

Arnold smiled all the way back to his office where he started preparations for the long flight. For a moment he thought about taking Sara with him. It would be fun, and he enjoyed having her sitting in the copilot's seat. On several occasions when he was very tired and she was afraid he'd fall asleep, she had unzipped his fly and with her soft hand reached inside wrapping her fingers around him firmly, then beginning a rhythmic pulling, stoking, fondling. It never failed.

The first time she did it, he was really shocked that his sweet little Sara could do such a thing. When they got home and he asked her she simply said "I had to...to keep you awake. It worked, didn't it?" and then with eagerness and devotion she welcomed him to her.

"Yes, she's a great girl and the best of copilots," he reflected, but he decided not to ask her to come with him on this trip. She was sharp and would understand right away the reason for the flight. So he did what he thought was the wisest thing to do—tell her he was going to see a customer in Texas and take that customer to Aruba for a conference.

Chapter 6

BOTH SPRENGLER GIRLS were little beauties. Cathy, the stable, intellectual type, earned top grades in any subject she chose to study. She was 21, tall, slim, with chestnut hair, wore designer eyeglasses, and was always properly dressed. She was studying law and business at Oxford, England. Her sister, Maggie, 19, was a tiny, slim and well-rounded, redheaded combination of energy and reckless mischief. She did quite well at school when and if she found the subjects interesting. She could easily become enthusiastic about something but had difficulty maintaining her interest for any length of time.

The two girls arrived at Logan with British Airways. Sara and Arnold met them and for the first time in many months the Sprenglers were happy together. It was as if a fresh friendly summer breeze was blowing through the big Cape Cod house. In his library Arnold Sprengler was sitting in his over-size, soft leather chair listening to the news when Maggie, his favorite daughter, rushed in, spinning around the room so her wide cotton skirt flew around her like a big white flower. She threw herself in his lap and hugged him.

"Oh, Dad, I'm so happy to be here with you again. I love you, Dad! You're just the kind of man I'll be looking for when that time comes! And Mom! Isn't she the best of all Moms? You must be very happy together! She remembered I love sweet peas and she put a big bunch of them on my desk." Maggie rumpled his bushy hair with her slender, well-manicured fingers.

"You're much grayer than last time!" she said. "Do you have problems? How could you have any problems? You have everything a man needs. Is there another woman? Or is there a man flirting with Mom? She is so beautiful. Or is business slow? I wish that you didn't have any problems! But, anyway, you do look great with those gray temples!"

He smiled. "When your clients want you to take care of their problems you have to live with problems, especially when they're into big business."

Sara set the table with a linen tablecloth, sterling silverware, the best china and put tall candles in crystal holders. She served duck breast with applesauce, potatoes and green beans for supper. Arnold opened a bottle of Mouton Cadet and they toasted to good health, good luck and the joy of being together again.

The following morning Arnold came downstairs and found breakfast prepared but nobody there. Looking out the kitchen window he saw Sara and Cathy walking arm in arm up the brick path. When Cathy came in she kissed him and said:

"Good morning, Dad. Mom and I had a nice long walk and talk on the beach. I really do

think you and Mom should come over to London. It won't take you long to get a consulting job for a British company working on the US market. The British are not as tough as the Yankees, but they're smarter and they're expanding their influence much more than people in America are aware of. Please, Dad, think of what I'm saying. Cape Cod is a dead end business-wise. Just think of the fact that Cape Cod Hospital is the largest employer in the whole area; then probably the newspaper and some banks taking care of all the oldies money and ripping off the poor underclass of people dependent on the biggest industry here, the tourism, by treating them as if they had money... Then here come insurance agencies for people afraid of taking risks.

"Here we see luxurious looking houses or condos constructed out of junk material, slab, plywood and sheet rock, most of them with inadequate insulation making heating costs skyrocket in the winter. How about inadequate fire safety and septic systems polluting the groundwater... But all over the place we see eye-catching features like golf and tennis or country clubs for the better off. What happens when these people get old and can't drive, can't go shopping, are afraid to be alone, or need to have things repaired? Who cares? Lots of service people are ready to rip off old folks! Why don't you get out of here! Live in a real world with the style and pulse of London?"

Arnold was silent for a moment. Then he said: "The Cape is changing, dear Cathy. We have commuter buses to Logan Airport every hour. We have The Breeze, which shuttles people from one end of Cape Cod to the other. We have condos with excellent service. We have Senior Citizens' service centers doing an excellent job, 'Meals on Wheels' we have AARP and several others. Our American society is not especially helpful to retirees or low-income people, I agree, but people are safe here in Massachusetts and on Cape Cod, safer than in most other places in the US. However, Mom and I are considering moving. But first, I have some important business to take care of. After that we can think of turning this place into a weekend retreat or summer home for all of us. That way you'll always have a nice place to come to when London gets too foggy and dreary! The climate here is excellent and we still have lots of beautiful nature left. We have free horizons, clear blue skies and unpolluted, fresh air"

"Did you hear that, Mom?" Cathy called out to her mother in the next room. "Dad says he's not bound to this place year round and may think seriously of coming over to London."

"I promise you that Mom and I will come to London and check out possible opportunities, if Sara wants to," Arnold hugged his daughter.

"By the way," he said, "I have to go to Kansas, Texas, and Florida for a couple of days at the end of next week. After that I'll take a few weeks off so we can have a great time together - all of us. We'll go fishing and whale watching. We'll have picnics or go shopping in New York and Boston."

Sara came into the kitchen and looked at him with raised eyebrows. She couldn't believe what he just said. It was Sunday and Sara wanted everybody to go to church with her. Cathy agreed right away. Arnold said he needed to make a quick trip to the office, but changed his mind for the sake of peace in the family, and Maggie was willing to join only if her father did.

St. Mary's Episcopal Church in Barnstable is a beautiful little church with an absolutely charming garden filled with memories from members of the congregation.

Everybody at church seemed to know Sara. Arnold had to shake hands with a lot of people. There were two families he recognized andt didn't want to meet. He couldn't remember their names but he did remember their faces. Arnold had foreclosed on their oceanfront homes, which he now owned. Of course, it would have been possible to solve their problems so they could have kept their homes, but they were too stupid to see how, and their lawyer wasn't much help, he recalled Sara was happy having Arnold and the girls with her that Sunday.

Early Monday morning, Sara, Cathy, and Maggie drove him to Barnstable Municipal Airport in Hyannis. He got the weather information he needed and they all walked out to the plane on the tarmac. His mechanic had warmed up the engine and checked everything.

When Arnold kissed Sara goodbye, she said: "Yesterday was the happiest day I've spent with you in a long, long time. Let's have more days like that! Goodbye, darling, and take good care of yourself."

"That's my gal!" he said and climbed into the cockpit. "I guess nobody wants to leave the Cape for Kansas a summer day like this?" They all shook their heads and blew him kisses.

Arnold, with characteristic thoroughness, did all the necessary preliminaries—gas, oil, oil pressure, starting the beacons, the gyrocompass and getting the barometer reading to set the altitude meter. After being sure the coffee thermos and the icebox with soda were within reach, he got clearance to taxi out. He waved and put on his pilot's hat Then the tower gave him clearance to take off. He gave the Rolls Royce engine full throttle. The humming became a roar and off he went.

Arnold loved to fly! When he started the powerful engine and the propeller became a transparent circle in front of him, he felt like the power let loose and the vibrations became his own power and energy. And, when he took off, the wings were his wings, and he was a bird—free, independent, and strong. He felt able to think great thoughts and achieve great goals. Flying to him was the best recreation imaginable and very relaxing especially between moments of intense concentration.

It was a sunny day and excellent weather for his 1700-mile trip to Wichita, Kansas, where the plane would get a complete overhauling and new equipment installed. The flight took less than 10 hours in the air, interrupted only by brief stops for fuel. His secretary had notified the Cessna Factory. It took them two days to install the new equipment and while the plane was being serviced the Cessna PR people took him on a tour of their extensive facility. Arnold's secretary had also booked a reservation for him at a comfortable inn, a favorite stopover for pilots, sales reps and mechanics from all over the country.

Before leaving the Cessna Factory Arnold made a short test flight with an instructor and had a final lesson in operating the new instruments. Important details had been fixed, replaced or upgraded, all dents were gone and every square inch was cleaned. It was like flying a brand new aircraft. The bill was already taken care of, they told him.

He flew to Sarasota, got a rental car and drove over to see his mother. They went out to dinner at the Crows Nest in Venice, and she insisted he stay with her overnight. She had prepared her guestroom for him and wanted to enjoy every possible minute with him. Her eyes filled with tears when he left and waved good-bye.

Arnold was thinking of his women. They represented everything that was good, true and honorable in his life. How come he could not make a good, honest living without compromising his principles? He was ashamed of himself. His ambitions and egotism fueled by some misfortunes had made him insensitive to other people's problems. In a sentimental way he felt sorry for people with bad luck. But maybe they, like himself, had only themselves to blame.

He drove down Route 775, passed Englewood and spotted the "Rotunda" sign on the left. It was an amazing place. Originally designed by a developer for hundreds of small homes, the streets, town water, telephone lines and electricity were all in place, but there were no houses! Even the street signs were there. Straight asphalt-topped streets were in flawless condition, making excellent landing strips for a small aircraft like his Cessna. He spent more than an hour there, making notes of street names. Using a Silva pocket compass he marked his selection of landing strips with a cross so he could land and take off regardless of the wind direction.

There was but one road leading into the area. Cavallo's pick-up crews had to use Off Road Vehicles in order to leave unnoticed along a path eastward to Route 771 or Route 776. Headlights from two or three Jeeps could supply enough light together with the powerful halogen lamps of his Cessna to land and take off. There were no power lines or other obstacles to complicate the operation. This was an ideal place - not a single house anywhere and there was no reason for anybody to be there at night.

He called Joe Cavallo, who informed him that some business friends in development and banking wanted to rent the plane and have Arnold fly them to Colombia. They would meet him at the Sarasota Hilton. Arnold expected some shady Mafia type characters but instead he met three well-dressed gentlemen looking like British country squires. He had a few drinks and supper with them.

Early next morning they took off from Sarasota-Bradenton Airport, crossed over Florida to the East Coast and flew over the Bahamas to Haiti. From there they headed straight to Curacao and followed the coastline to Colombia. After the long flight they landed at Medellin.

Two men, friends of Joe Cavallo's, drove Arnold up to the mountains in a Land Rover. The trip took one full day across a beautiful landscape still virtually untouched by civilization. The inhabitants in the countryside lived in simple, poor houses and were miserably dressed. This was the heart of the cocaine country. The US authorized and financed repeated military and police raids on coca plantations but the information network of local supporters of dealers and coca growers worked more effectively than any official law enforcement. Arnold met farmers and their families who harvested the leaves. Coca was their main source of income. Of course, they knew about the problems their product created in the US. But, it seemed arrogant to talk to these poor people about pitying American drug addicts for their self-inflicted misery. After all they had used coca leaves for generations and learned to cope with it, especially to keep hunger away.

"I'll fly a different route back", he said to himself. "This new instrumentation makes it possible for me to risk flying northwest across the sea straight to Honduras".

He crossed the Honduran Gulf to the Mexican peninsula of Yucatan and over the Mexican Gulf to Corpus Christi in Texas where he phoned Joe Cavallo.

They met near Galveston at Joe's small, elegant villa on the water. Cavallo was enthusiastic about Arnold's report and eager to start new shipments right away.

"Sure, but only you and I will know of it, nobody else, OK? And no Puerto Rican girls..."

"OK." Joe smiled. "But you didn't mind her, did you?"

"Yes, I did and I don't want anybody mixed up with my private life. I want my instructions to be followed exactly as they are given. If I get into trouble I want to be alone. I'll keep you informed one way or another. When it comes to shipping this stuff I'm the boss, OK."

They discussed every detail and decided that Arnold would leave for Colombia the following morning. The Cessna's new extra gasoline tanks were filled. This time he headed straight across the Gulf for the Yucatan peninsula in Mexico, passed over Honduras to the Pacific, along the coast down to Costa Rica and then across the water to Colombia. He filled up with gas in Medellin where he found a phone and made an appointment for picking up the load. At ten o'clock the same night he flew up into the mountains and found the little landing strip lit up by several trucks and cars. Five big parcels, about 250 kilos, or about 550 lbs. were taken on board.

Everything went smoothly. Minutes later he was in the air again. The instruments glowed green in the dark. The sky above him was deep blue and the steep mountainsides to his right and left looked threateningly close. He flew north along a pitchblack valley following a winding river reflected by the sky. He crossed the plains and swampy areas close to the coast. When he left the South

American mainland flying over the Caribbean Sea he switched to auto pilot and relaxed with coffee and sandwiches.

He turned off his radio and radar knowing that his aircraft would shine like a Christmas tree on the US Coast Guard's radar screens or to the Air Force or Navy if he sent any radar signals or radio waves. To make it hard for the radar to detect him, he flew low, less than 100 feet over the water. He wished he had a faster or a twin-engine plane.

At 4 o'clock in the morning he finally spotted the West Coast of Florida and continued flying low several miles north of Tampa. He called Cavallo's man and said he could meet him in 15 minutes as planned. After the expected answer "OK, Pedro," he began a maneuver to confuse the coastal radar. First he turned almost 180 degrees and flying in the opposite direction he followed the coastline to the southern end of Gasparilla Island. There he made another 180-degree turn and then suddenly plunged down to just 20 feet above the waves of the Gasparilla Sound. It was almost light now. The woods seemed closer at high speed. He flew up the Coral creek and in over the Rotonda. He knew the map well and set the plane down where he saw two Jeeps waiting. Two men came up to him.

"Welcome! How was your flight?"

"Fine, thanks. Here we go."

He opened the door on the other side and after helping the men unload the packages he rushed out and stripped off the stickers with the fake identification letters on the fuselage. The men poured gasoline on the stickers and set it on fire while Arnold gave full throttle and took off. The whole operation didn't take three minutes. His next stop was at a small local airport near Sebring. He was expected. A teenage girl in a golf cart guided him to a hidden glade where two other business planes were parked. She drove him to the clubhouse and showed him a guestroom.

"Whenever you feel like it, come into the kitchen or the bar and I'll get you something to eat and drink. I've been told you had a tough flight all the way from Texas, so you must be exhausted. Relax and feel at home. There's a small red sports car for you in the parking lot. Here are the keys. See you later!" She disappeared. A black and white police chopper approached and flew in over the golf course. It made him uneasy. After a shower he dressed in fresh clothes and found the kitchen where the girl was baking.

"Hi again!", she said. With the back of her floury hands she wiped away some strands of long blond hair from her eyes. She was pretty. He couldn't help staring and smiling at her. He liked this type of woman.

"Want some fresh bread I just took out of the oven? Some policemen came and looked at your Cessna. They had a dog sniffing around in it, but they left."

"Oh? I wonder why?" He had swept the storage area with gasoline and hoped they didn't know that would tranquilize the dogs' sense of smell.

She served him coffee, jam and cheese with oven fresh rolls. It was delicious. After the meal he called Cavallo:

"Hi, I'm back!"

"Great job, great job! My people just reported they thought the police were on their way so they took the back roads out of the Rotonda. Call me again tomorrow."

Arnold spent the rest of the day driving around with a map, looking for good alternative landing spots. He talked to Cavallo and agreed to pick him up in Galveston. Cavallo met him with a limousine. His only luggage was two briefcases. The forecasters promised fine weather all the way to Cape Cod. Cavallo handed over one of the briefcases. It contained Arnold's payment in bonds and cash, all together over $500,000 for his first flight to Colombia.

Chapter 7

IT WAS JUST before midnight when Ted parked the Ford Fiesta in front of his home.

Yawning, unfolding himself out of the car, he stretched his long legs. It had been the first real busy day of the season. With a feeling of satisfaction he gripped the lunch-basket where he kept the store's cash sales stuffed in a brown bag. Finally, money was beginning to roll in after the long, slow winter and spring.

The night was chilly, crisp and beautiful. He went into the kitchen, picked a cool beer from the fridge and went back out to the wicker chair on the porch where he sat and watched the flickering of the full moon on the calm, dark water of Barnstable Harbor. Ted was always in high gear after these night trips, fighting sleepiness and finally overcoming it, It took him at least half an hour to wind down to a normal pace. He felt good sitting down, relaxing, enjoying the still of the night, listening to the hoots of the great horned owl living in the grove behind Michele's house. He heard a car turning off Route 6A driving down their road. It could be Michele's car. It was—with no lights on!

"A blown fuse could have made her lights go dead. She must have eyes like a cat," he said to himself. He saw her automatic garage door open, her car disappeared into the dark hole and without a sound the door closing. No lights were turned on in her house.

Then he heard some activity from the harbor entrance. A big, dark fishing boat, probably at least a 48-footer, entered the harbor, gliding slowly and silently. The only sound was the soft purling from the bow and the lapping of some lazy waves washing against the pole work along the docks.

It was obvious that the skipper knew his way through the hard-to-follow, narrow, dredged channel leading into Barnstable Harbor. The marine engines purred hollowly as only the big, powerful ones do, and the exhaust pipes hissed out cascades of cooling water during the skipper's skilled docking maneuver. A disturbed gull screamed and flew up to find a new pole for spending the night. Ted heard whispering voices from the stern deck and he noticed three men dressed in dark sailor's gear leaving the boat.

Carrying big bags over their shoulders they walked straight up to the big villa close to the dock at the Sprenglers' home. The men were expected, because somebody opened the front door even before they reached it. Light from inside fell on the brick walkway and clearly showed the silhouettes of three men entering.

One of the windows in Michele's studio was open and Ted got a glimpse of her face and her white hair. She seemed to be holding a camera or binoculars. She waved at him and he waved back. Finishing his beer he went indoors and up to the bedroom where Ingrid was sleeping peacefully. He undressed in the dark and went to bed.

The following day began with one of those superb Cape Cod mornings—a clear blue sky and a salty, gentle breeze slowly moving the branches of the oak trees in the Hallbergs' back yard. Ingrid and Ted were having breakfast on their back deck and listening to the early morning news when the doorbell rang. It was Michele dressed in white and wearing a big, wide-brimmed hat trimmed with pink roses and tied with a gossamer coquettish face veil.

Ted greeted her at the door. "Good morning. Come in! What's up? In a few minutes Ingrid will be ready to take off for Newport."

Michele was in top form. "Hi, everybody! Could you possibly take a freeloader to Newport? I'm off today! And I would like very much to be a tourist in America's Cup Town on a day like this! I doubt my poor old Toyota would make it all the way to and from."

"Of course," said Ingrid, "but please don't expect me to be your tour guide around the mansions, the beaches or the bars along the waterfront! I have a very busy day today. I would love to take you out for lunch at The Black Pearl or The Clarke Cooke House."

"Sounds terrific! Thanks! I'll rush back home and pick up my camera and binoculars. Be back in a flash!"

Ingrid checked off lists of merchandise Ted had packed in her car.

"Don't forget to print the shirts I have piled up in the garage," she instructed her husband. "There are directions on top of each stack! And don't use the conveyor dryer until the laundry is done, or you'll most likely blow a fuse. And don't wait up for me tonight. We'll probably be late. I might show Michele what Newport's like at night!"

"Forget about that night life stuff! You gals better be home before one or I'll call the State Police to search for you!" he shouted as the car backed out of the driveway.

"I love those handsome troopers. Don't you, Ingrid?" Michele laughed.

They waved goodbye through the open sunroof and the small car disappeared towards Barnstable Village. They passed the Courthouse with its Greek pillared facade and the Sturgis Library, one of the oldest in America. Soon they were on the Route 6 Mid-Cape Expressway heading for Sagamore Bridge. Morning fog still hung low over the water when they crossed the Cape Cod Canal.

Ingrid was silent. She enjoyed Michele's company. Michele was open-minded, full of fun and creative ideas, and she enjoyed sharing the memories and experiences of her interesting life

"Michele, I know you have something special on your mind. You are up to something you want me to get involved in. Right?"

"Yes, of course you could guess that. I need some advice and help." She followed the scenery as it passed by. But she didn't say anything more and they were quiet the rest of the way, each busy with her own thoughts.

Chapter 8

INGRID STOPPED OUTSIDE her Newport store, unlocked the door, and hung the two flags she always kept flying outside, the Swedish one to the left and the Stars and Stripes to the right. Opposite was the Candy Store, the greatest and one of the most popular of all Newport bars, which would be opening soon for hungry and thirsty tourists already strolling around checking menus and prices of all the restaurants along the waterfront.

There was no doubt that the Candy Store was the best place to hear really good sailor stories and fascinating lies about life at sea. In the winter a big wood stove spread a friendly warmth attracting frozen dock workers and test sailors and maybe a few lost tourists who stopped in for Australian beer, real English stout or Irish coffee.

A handyman was washing the restaurant windows and brick terrace. He set out small café tables and two chairs at each table. The bartender, an amazing, super efficient little man with a friendly smile and an enormous memory for names and faces, was sponging off the bar and wiping all the glasses. He called out a greeting to Ingrid and Michele as they carried in one box after the other piled high with newly printed shirts and various other merchandise into Ingrid's store.

"Did Ted tell you what he saw last night?" Michele asked.

"No, I was asleep when he came home and we only talked business this morning. Why?"

"I see you're busy," said Michele, "so why don't we have lunch at the Candy Store around one and I'll tell you something very interesting. I'll make reservations. I have some work to do. I hope to find a certain yacht in the harbor, so I'll go for a stroll and be back for lunch OK? Ciao!"

A small line of tourists was already waiting outside Ingrid's store when Michele left, a sure sign it was going to be a big tourist day. Along the docks skippers and sailors on the big, chartered power cruisers had the day's first iced drinks ready on the quarter-decks and the nearly-nude bodies of raisin-skinned women aboard had been carefully protected with sunscreen lotions—on some boats their own women, while on others young playgirls "invited" to come aboard to make the day at sea more exciting and enjoyable.

For the true sea-loving sailor or boating enthusiast this menagerie represents a peculiar breed of sailing human beings. Most of them cannot handle a boat if their life depended on it and need captains and crews to do the simplest things. But that's never a problem because crews are included in the lease.

Newport has a beautiful harbor and it's easily understandable why America's aristocrats chose to build their "summer cottages" there.

Michele walked slowly out to the end of the concrete pier and looked out over the big harbor where hundreds yachts of all kinds were anchored. She gazed over the glittering, sun-drenched bay, framed on the west by Goat Island and on the south by Fort Adams' 18th century casemates and granite walls near the Ida Lewis Yacht Club.

She let her camera focus on one big power cruiser after another, scrutinizing them from stem to stern. She put on a set of earphones wired to her video camera. She knew one specific yacht was out there somewhere, because several days earlier, with the same listening device, she had overheard a conversation between her neighbor, Arnold Sprengler, and a man onboard a power cruiser in Barnstable harbor mentioning the name of this boat... And there it was! Her telephoto lens zoomed in on the gilded signature sign with sculptured figures of Neptune and mermaids. "*SNOWBIRD, New York,*" she read.

Her camera looked just like any ordinary video camera, but the parabolic microphone attached to it was much longer and so was the telephoto lens. Michele and her husband had used it for filming and taping shy songbirds, lionesses with cubs and other animals that would not let a photographer, come near. Now she could see close up and listen clearly to activities almost half a mile away. This was really a lucky strike! She tried to look like any ordinary tourist watching and filming some vacation views. Here she had a chance to get vital information. But the men mostly told dirty jokes. But all of a sudden the conversation changed: "...last shipment to the barn went fine, very smooth," one voice said.

"Our boys got 100 kilos ready to pick up. All we're waiting for now is your dough. The price is still the same, but next time I'm afraid we'll have to ask for five or ten percent more. The cops are getting smarter and the Coast Guard is on the alert, so we have to be much more careful. Also, the new equipment my pilot invented cost an awful lot to develop."

Michele was enjoying the salty balmy breeze. She heard every word as clear as a bell and her little video recorder registered it all. She looked around. Nobody seemed to pay any attention to her. The conversation on the *SNOWBIRD* continued, "...some fancy new device...we've been to Boston and got it all in hundreds and twenties, mixed numbers, no series, used bills Come to the barn tomorrow night around ten."

The man paused, then said: "Personally I prefer Chatham, but I understand you like Newport."

"Newport is the ideal place for my business. All these tourists and sailors make it easy to stay anonymous here. Nobody around can see or hear anything. I get great tender service, too. An Irish fellow brings all kinds of deli stuff in his small boat and the harbor's tender boats have the nicest little sailor girls at the helms. With our speedboat I can pick up business friends and take them back without anybody seeing or knowing about it.

"Newport has excellent restaurants, great bars, lots of kids and lots of young girls in need of dope and money all the time, and willing to pay no matter what! Cape Cod is too slow for me, but I know the market there has a tremendous potential."

The other voice continued, "...my car was smashed the other night by a little lady. Her car was hit in the front and she had to drive home without lights. She got so shook up she blamed it all on herself. The fact is it was my fault. I had a few drinks for the road, three or four...too many! If she had called the cops I would have been in trouble. Anyway, she said a friend of hers would take care of the repairs at her cost. That friend is known to run the best auto body shop on the Cape, so I accepted gladly."

"You walked straight into my trap," Michele smiled to herself. "I'll get you, I'll go after you and I'll make your lives a miserable holy mess. I'll rob you and make you two blame each other. You will regret you chose the drug trade to make money. This is no longer a Christian society. Egotism and revenge are accepted... even hailed, and I have every right in the world to demand justice and punishment...and you better believe it! I'll find a way!"

Satisfied with her investigation so far, Michele walked along the pontoon docks just behind The Treadway Inn. More beautiful boats were docked there, some small and simple ones, some large elegant oldies and many new luxurious ones. The appetizing smell of fried onions and beef coming from the galley of a ritzy ketch reminded her it was time for lunch with Ingrid.

Chapter 9

IT WAS A perfect Newport summer day. Michele walked hastily across the cobblestone Market Square of Bowen's Wharf where hundreds of tourists flocked outside the stores, which offered colorful clothing, trinkets and souvenirs. Along the docks parents with little kids were taking photos of each other in front of the beautiful boats or with the huge restored 100-year-old anchor in the center of the open square. The well-supplied outdoor bar at The Black Pearl was filled with guests sipping drinks and having lunch under green and red Cinzano umbrellas. Ingrid was giving instructions to her sales girls when Michele popped through the door of the shop with a cheery "lunch time!"

Ingrid joined her and they crossed the street to the Clarke Cooke House, where a tall blond man in a tux welcomed them. A hostess guided them to a table on the second floor and they were seated on a comfortable sofa with big soft cushions covered in a cool pastel blue and green floral print on a white background. Protected by a blue and white canopy they had a magnificent view of the harbor. Each ordered a Dubonnet on the rocks and a chef's salad.

"Ingrid, I have some interesting things to talk to you about and also some questions you probably can help me with." Michele began, looking around and noting with satisfaction that nobody was sitting close enough to overhear their conversation.

"You know the people living in that big colonial across from mine in Barnstable? The one with the private pier and a big dark blue fishing boat. What kind of people are they?"

"You mean the Sprenglers? He is a lawyer. Some years ago he opened a law office on the Cape. To start with he had a tough time. He commuted to Boston and worked late every night. But they seem to be doing well now. He owns several properties on the Cape and even has his own airplane. Ted has met him at the small airport in West Barnstable. They say 'hi' to each other, but Mr. Sprengler doesn't seem to be very sociable.

"Mrs. Sprengler is a darling! We chat every now and then when we meet on the street. Apparently she has everything a wife could ask for, yet she still appears to be unhappy. But she never talks about her problems. She was away for a long time and I thought they might be going to divorce, but she returned. Ted and I have never really felt like inviting them to our place."

Ingrid sipped her Dubonnet and continued: "I have heard them arguing saying pretty awful things to each other! He seems to be the macho type and she seems to dislike his business. Also, his choice of friends is not hers or ours, sneaky-looking, snake-eyed guys. Somebody told me he is seeing customers in Texas and Florida. Ted says Mr. Sprengler generally flies alone." Ingrid paused having some salad then went on "The Sprenglers have a big powerboat. Every so often they go out fishing, but they never bring in any fish. If we had a boat like that we'd go out for weekends and stay overnight on board. We'd go out just to watch the sunset or to set lobster traps. I've only seen Mrs. Sprengler on board that boat a few times! She probably doesn't like the sea. Maybe she gets seasick!

"They have two teenaged daughters going to school in England. I've not seen much of them lately, but they are very attractive and well-mannered young ladies and they speak beautiful English. I love that British accent! During the girls' vacations the family seems to enjoy being together."

Ingrid paused for a moment. "I really don't have much more to tell you about them. We simply don't know them."

"Oh, you have told me quite a lot! You see, I think Mr. Sprengler is a crook! Quite an important crook! I happen to know a little about him, not much, but enough to have second thoughts! I'll tell you more about that on our way home. It would be great if you and Ted could help me. You see, I have a plan…"

"But, Michele! If you think he is some kind of gangster, why don't you contact the police or the FBI or whatever?"

"Because… Because there are several reasons. First of all, I have a feeling somebody is leaking police information to these guys, warning them. If I told the police what I know, my own personal safety would be in jeopardy and the crooks would be warned in time to change their plans. Secondly, as you know, my husband, Rich, and our daughter, Marianne, were both murdered and no justice was done to stop the killers or make the killers responsible. I feel a moral obligation to intervene against crime, especially when it comes to drug running."

"I am sorry, Michele," Ingrid said, "but I can't think of a way to help you. Anyway we can talk it over with Ted tonight. He is good at coming up with new ideas. Maybe we could keep an eye on somebody or tailgate them… I'll try to get the girls to take the store tonight, so we can go home a little earlier. Meet me at my shop around 5:30, by then the rush is over and business will be slow until 8. See you! Thanks, I enjoyed the lunch!"

After Ingrid left Michele paid the check, finished her drink, passed by the noisy crowd in the bar and went out into the blinding sunshine. Bannister's Wharf is the heart of the busy Newport waterfront. Brick walkways, antique gas lanterns, fanciful, old-fashioned shop signs and old buildings create such a picturesque atmosphere that you actually think you'll meet that "Moby Dick" character, Captain Ahab, face to face round the next corner.

The Clarke Cooke House is an old building; a former inn, which was moved to its present location when the waterfront was restored after the Navy left the area. Behind the building is a small dock where the harbor's tender boats pick up and drop off people from yachts anchored in the bay.

Michele boarded one of the tender boats and told the helmsman, who actually was a helmsgirl, she just wanted to go for a little trip around the harbor. Other passengers came on board carrying baskets of supplies, groceries and bottles of liquors and wine, loaded shopping bags, all sorts of paraphernalia, sails and sailor bags. When the boat passed close to the *SNOWBIRD* Michele aimed the video camera towards it and got some close-ups of the two men on board and their two female companions.

Going ashore at Goat Island, Michele asked to be picked up in two hours. Then she walked to an outlook point to keep a close watch of the *SNOWBIRD*. Once again she zoomed in the men on board. Their conversation wasn't very interesting at first. She couldn't help but hear the men's raucous laughter as they jockeyed with each other making generous bids for the ladies' scanty bikinis. After considerably large sums of moneychanged hands, she saw the women stripped of their bikini panties sit astride on the nude and waiting laps of the two raunchy guys. It was at least an hour later before she could tape what proved to be an interesting conversation.

In order not to seem too interested in that specific yacht Michele walked around and along the docks for a couple of miles. Her feet weren't used to so much exercise, and the cool, salty air made her a bit drowsy. She was content with her day and felt perfectly relaxed sitting in the sunshine waiting for the launch boat to come by and pick her up.

Chapter 10

INGRID SMILED, WELCOMING Michele. It was just a half-hour or so before sunset when Michele returned from her final investigating boat tour around Newport's harbor and ended her walk outside Ingrid's shop. A raw evening fog was beginning to roll in from the sea. "Typical sweater weather," she said, stepping down from the store's doorway onto the brick walk. "That means good business! I don't have to stay in the store tonight! You can't imagine what a relief it is to quit now. The girls are really sweet. They are always ready to take some extra hours. I'm sure one of the reasons is that handsome hunk at the restaurant across the street. I think he's especially interested in our blonde, well-endowed Linda. She's a rascal and very, very charming!"

They walked the America's Cup Avenue along the harbor basin towards Long Wharf to pick up Ingrid's car. From the bell tower of the small, white church on the hill came a brittle tune by Bach. In the west the skies were purple when Ingrid drove slowly through downtown Newport. The tourists swarmed all over the road on their way to find the restaurants with the right menus, prices and har**bor** view. She passed the Bellevue crossing with the old red

Tennis Hall of Fame, where some of the world's big tennis stars had just finished a match and the fans were pouring out.

"I have been thinking things over and I'll help you with anything you ask me to do." Ingrid looked very serious and continued, "I'm sure it won't be difficult to talk Ted into it, too. "Great!" Michele enthused. "You're certainly the one I hoped would help. I filmed some interesting videos and got some good tapes of a conversation on board the boat called *SNOWBIRD*. But let me tell you about this case starting from the beginning. For quite some time Mr. Sprengler has had guests every evening. Last night, before midnight, his fishing boat came in with a good-size shipment of drugs. It was loaded into a car that left soon after. Lately, the same people have come and gone regularly, so one night when their boat entered our harbor, I aimed my bird watcher's microphone at them and listened.

"You see, I still have all the equipment my husband and I used. With my parabolic microphone you can hear birds several hundred yards away singing undisturbed as if nobody was watching them, and as clearly as if they were sitting in your hand. For several nights I've been listening to the men on board Mr. Sprengler's boat. My suspicions were finally confirmed. A bell rang when I heard them mention the name of a man in Providence—some retired organized crime boss. Suddenly it made sense when they said they expected snow! I mean, snow in June? It's cocaine, of course!

"They mentioned a boat's name, the *SNOWBIRD*, a yacht docked in Newport, and a meeting that was to be held on board that yacht today. So, walking along the docks, searching, watching in my telephoto lens, listening with my parabolic micro... Bingo! There she was, the *SNOWBIRD*! When we get home tonight we'll listen to a most interesting conversation, and plan our strategy!"

"There is one thing that amazes me," Michelle paused. "I don't understand this Sprengler guy. Can't he see that his whole family, his wife and daughters, are sitting ducks and easy prey if his gangster friends are getting tough. A man like Sprengler with a nice family is definitely no match for the hard-knuckled guys in the drug trade. I hope nothing happens to his wife and those girls. I hope what happened to my daughter won't happen to their girls. I'll keep my eyes open. Mr. Sprengler is really taking stupid risks."

In Wareham Ingrid stopped at a snack shack and picked up some freshly fried clams. The smell was wonderful and whetted their appetites!

"A glass of chilled white wine and a toasted roll, to go with the clams, that's what we'll have when we get home," she said.

Ingrid felt drowsy and kept up a flow of talk to help stay awake.

"Have you noticed how the fragrances of the night are changing as we drive along this route? It starts with the strong smell of salty air in Newport, and then we pass the beach with its pungent smell of seaweed and low tide. Then we hit the choking exhaust fumes from the heavy highway traffic out of Fall River. After that nature takes over again with the subtle smell of the woods and reeds along the ponds lining the road. A couple of miles before we join Cranberry Highway we're hit with smells from Wareham's French fries and pizza places. After Wareham, along Cape Cod Canal, there is often smoke from passing container liners or from the power plant in Sagamore mixed with raw mist rolling in from the bay.

"But the best is when we've crossed Sagamore Bridge—the smell of Cape Cod hits you. It's a honey-sweet fragrance from the roadside heather alternating with the clean smell from pine resin and honeysuckle. The sea breeze quickly removes all exhaust gases from the truck traffic.

"And when we turn off the highway and drive along our own 6A road with all its quaint stores, I feel, maybe only in my imagination, the musty scent of old antiques and historic treasures," Ingrid said as they pulled into her driveway.

They could see Ted working at his desk in his studio. When they entered they heard the music from Prokofiev's "Romeo and Juliet..."

"He needs to be in the right mood when he's creating. He needs Bach, Beethoven, Brahms or sometimes Prokofiev even if he is just creating a cat design for a sweatshirt print," Ingrid laughed.

Chapter 11

IT DIDN'T TAKE long to set the table, glasses filled with cool Chablis and plates heaped with fried clams and toasted rolls. Ingrid gave Ted a detailed report of her day in the store and then Michele explained her detective work on the docks and the reason why.

Ingrid noticed that Ted looked both amazed and troubled.

"We have to do something," she said. "We have to help put these people behind bars! Think of all kids and families those goons will destroy and all the misery this drug business creates for everyone it touches."

Michele plugged the video camera into the TV. There it was, the glittering harbor in Newport, the sounds of flapping sails and rippling waves, power boat engines, the docking fishing boats, lobsters being unloaded and ice loaded, water streaming over wooden tubs filled with crawling lobsters. The sound effects made it all so alive. Several boats were zoomed in; private conversations meant only for the people involved could be heard distinctly. The telephoto lens caught a big white cruiser. At first the picture was a bit fuzzy, then it became crystal clear and the close-up showed a sign with golden mermaids, hovering gulls and King Neptune sitting above the name, *SNOWBIRD, New York*.

"This is where it starts," Michele said.

They watched and listened and not a word was spoken until the TV screen turned to black and the show was over.

"Those guys are not the kind you play games with," Ted stated, "so we have to plan our method of action well. First let's hear what you suggest, Michele, then let's watch the video once more to be sure we haven't missed anything."

"We could hint to the State Police that someone in the local police force is leaking information," Michele suggested, "or we could steal the cocaine and leave it to the troopers. I know how to sneak up unobserved close to animals, and I don't think these human beasts can smell and hear as well as the wild ones. We could overpower them, handcuff them and call for help. It would be wise to change our appearance though—dress up in some fancy clothing, wear a wig or something, so they can't recognize their innocent neighbors!"

"Now I'm completely convinced that you are really crazy," Ted declared. "I had my doubts before, but this confirms my suspicions! How on earth would we be able to overpower them? To them killing is routine! They are at least three ruthless men, most likely well armed!"

"So are we! I have all the guns you could ask for. My hunting equipment is the best money can buy. We even have things they probably don't have!"

"What for instance?"

"My infra-scope for example! I can see them in the darkest night from a distance of up to 400 yards and I can hear them even farther away. We can videotape them and everything they say long before they have a chance to find out we are even watching them."

"But what if they fight back?" Ingrid broke in.

"Bang! Bang! We take the initiative. We shoot first! No killing! My tranquilizer shots for lions or rhinos will make them defenseless. We handcuff them, put duct tape over their mouths and call the police!"

Ted laughed at Michele's enthusiasm and unconventional suggestion. "Yes, but the shooting will wake up everybody in the neighborhood. People from all around would show up and the gangster's henchmen would come after us before we have a chance to sneak away."

"I have some really good silencers so we can work without interruption provided we can surprise them," Michele explained.

Ingrid's eyes opened wide and she asked: "How can we avoid being recognized and pursued and retaliated against? If they have a leaking source in the local police force they will easily get a house warrant and find enough evidence in our house to be convinced we are the ones who interfered."

"No problem," Michele replied. "I have a friend who runs an auto body shop, a former policeman. I know we can count on him to fix us up for a little fancy dress show! He can supply police uniforms and a car for our disappearing act! We surprise them. I put them to sleep for half an hour with my tiger tranquilizer! We grab the dope, snatch the money and walk away…singing!" Michele smiled!

"It's been a long time since I was in the military and practiced shooting, but give me a good gun and a reliable scope and nobody will be able to get us," Ted interrupted.

Michele went on: "I have just the gun for you, a nine-millimeter, semiautomatic rifle with a silencer and a Zeiss scope. Rich and I always took it along with the cameras on our hunting trips. We have never used it except for target practice and the time I shot at the poachers. It's a terrific weapon—it's Belgian."

"I think it could get pretty complicated," Ingrid said, "especially if there are several people. We can't just walk up and ring their doorbell! Let's see if we can come up with several different ways to get them and work out details."

They thought of several alternative plans, some fanciful and crazy, others quite realistic and practical. To start with Ingrid offered to alter the police uniforms to fit, and Michele said she would keep track of what was going on in the Sprengler house.

When they were too tired to continue a meaningful, productive conversation, they walked across the little Harbor Square to Michele's house. She gave her two friends a quick demonstration of her unique hunting equipment explaining:

"To be well informed and for watching activities in the darkest night we simply switch on the infra-scope and watch. We put the earphones on and aim the microphone at the Sprenglers like this."

In spite of the darkness Ted could see and hear that the Sprenglers had visitors.

Mr. Sprengler was outside talking to a tall man. Michele switched on the tape recorder. Staying away from the open window, hidden in the dark, they listened and watched.

The men were discussing a new shipment. Something was going to be picked up by Sprengler's boat at sunrise and Mr. Sprengler could expect it to be landed the next night around eleven in Barnstable Harbor

"I'll call and tell the buyers to come and pick it up at midnight," Mr. Sprengler nodded.

Only moments ago Michele, Ingrid and Ted had been so weary they could hardly stay awake. Now they were fully alert.

After giving some final orders to his companions Mr. Sprengler walked up to his house, and smoked in the dark on his "farmer's porch" before going indoors. Michele and the Hallbergs saw Jack, captain of Sprengler's boat, sitting on the quarterdeck having a nightcap before going to his cabin below and turning out the lights.

"This is a bit much!" Ingrid said.

"I have a plan," said Michele and in a whispering voice told them: "Let's meet here tomorrow night. Shall we say at 8 o'clock?"

They agreed without question. She was no doubt bold and fearless but also clever! Hopefully the police uniforms would help command the proper respect and create confusion.

The next day flew by. On her way home from Newport Ingrid tried to visualize how the coup could work out. The plan was simple, bold, cool, and daring!

Chapter 12

"YOUR NEXT FLIGHT will be in about a month," were Cavallo's final words when they split in Newport. Arnold was content but still he had an unpleasant feeling of being trapped.

The Sprenglers spent most of the next few weeks together. Sara was happy that Arnold finally took some time off to be with the family. They had a terrific summer. Arnold checked in with his secretary several times a week and went to his office just to pick up the mail. When it was time for Cathy and Maggie to go back to school in England Sara and Arnold flew to London with them.

He visited several law firms and at one of the major ones a senior member of the firm said: "We have a client making large investments in the US and they'll need advice from a skilled Yankee lawyer. I'll mention your name. Generally they do what I suggest they do."

The Sprenglers enjoyed their stay and Sara and Arnold returned to the Cape a few weeks later. On his first day back Arnold heard from Cavallo.

"I need a new shipment, and I want you to fly straight to Miami, pick up some passengers and repeat the previous trip to Colombia, load the cocaine and fly back to Florida."

He followed Cavallo's plan and a few days later he landed at the Rotonda and threw out the load in no time at all. He took off again as quickly as before remembering to rip off the false ID letters on the plane. He flew along the Wyakka River, lower than the treetops all the time so no land-based radar could keep track of him.

Joe Cavallo had contact persons all over Florida and everything was arranged for Arnold wherever he needed to land for fuel or sleep. When the trip was completed, Arnold landed safely at Barnstable Municipal Airport in Hyannis on Cape Cod.

Another month passed without any news from the London law firm. Arnold kept trying to find out new ways to get away from Cavallo but couldn't come up with any ironclad, workable ideas.

His third tour to Colombia started out from Galveston. He used the same route and again he unloaded at the Rotonda. He landed and dropped the load in record time, but the Air Force or the Coast Guard radar must have spotted him. Cavallo's men were leaving with the cocaine in their Jeeps, when Arnold saw the police helicopter coming in from the west. It was dark, but now he knew the terrain well enough to take off without lights. Once again he chose the escape route up along the river. Flying so low the plane almost touched the water he was hidden by the tall trees. The helicopter was slower and soon lost track of him, but Arnold chose to use one of his alternate escape routes. He landed on a highway and taxied into a protected parking area where a crew of Cavallo's men was waiting for him. They dismounted the wings and winched the plane into an enormous moving truck.

Arnold sat in a van next to a burly, black man, who was singing "Swing Low Sweet Chariot" in a rich, deep baritone. They hit the road with the rig hauling the Cessna following a mile behind.

"What do you do if the cops stop us?" asked Arnold. The man kept singing as if he hadn't heard. After several minutes the song was finished and the driver was quiet for a while. Then he said:

"I never stop singing until I have sung the whole piece to the end. You must respect Saint Cezily! Yessir! If the cops stop me? I stop. But I do not stop singing, until the song is finished. Nosir! But when I have stopped singing I ask the officers: 'Yessir, how can I help you?' That's all I do! But, of course, I have to warn my brother in the rig driving behind us with your flying machine! So if I see the cops ahead or a police helicopter up there I simply press the transmitter. When I am singing on the radio, my friends know there is red alert, you know!"

They arrived at the small airport near Okeechobee without problems and the plane was unloaded, put in a hangar and stripped of its false identification signs. A rented sports car was waiting there for Arnold so he drove to Miami and boarded a plane to Boston. Back on Cape Cod he went directly to Joe Cavallo's home in Chatham where he was introduced to one of Cavallo's New York business friends, Luis Bolivar, a tall, smiling, balding man in his upper 50s.

The pretty red-haired maid in the long black dress served a delicious luncheon of oysters, halibut marinated in Tequila spiced with orange and anise accompanied by a vegetable melange. For dessert they enjoyed a Savarin with plums in rum topped with ice cream and a dollop of whipped cream.

They had coffee in the living room overlooking the ocean. The doors were closed but the figure of the butler was visible through the glass wall as though he was standing guard.

"Luis is working on the New York market. Can we guarantee him one shipment a month beside ours? That's my question," stated Cavallo.

"That can be arranged," Arnold replied, "but I'm not willing to fly it all by myself, the way I have been lately. It's exhausting and it's getting more and more risky. Last time the 'Smokies' almost ripped my pants off."

The men laughed but Arnold was serious and went on:

"A police chopper was there only minutes after the last drop and I just made it! I had to take off in the dark and flee like a rabbit. The cops in that area are too alert for me now. Other importers probably use the Rotonda, too, so the police most likely are keeping the place under observation. If a cop lives in the area, he could easily watch and report when our pickup crew arrives. Or, we might have a little squealer among our own people. I have a new, better plan."

"When can you start to fly for me?" interrupted the New Yorker.

"I'm not interested in working for a lot of people," Arnold went on. "My job is getting more and more difficult because the DEA are gearing up! And they're damned good. They've got choppers, AWACs, and F-16s from the Air Force working with the Coast Guard. We need more sophisticated equipment. Joe Cavallo and I work great together and I don't want to change a winning team. I want fixed rates and only one person informed of my plans. You have to cooperate. OK?"

The two gangsters nodded to each other. Luis pointed out that in New York he had a big market with tough competition, so he needed "import assistance without middlemen". But Arnold just laughed at him and shook his head. The New Yorker stood up and thanked Cavallo for his hospitality. The men shook hands.

"I wish you were my man," Bolivar said to Arnold.

"I am," was Arnold's reply. "My guess is that you have already decided that the two of you are on the board of directors of a new import and transport company. Am I right, Joe?"

Cavallo grinned and taking Luis Bolivar's hand asked: "Partners?"

"Partners!"

The men slapped each other's shoulders and Joe Cavallo gestured to Arnold to sit down while he accompanied Luis Bolivar to his waiting car. Returning, Cavallo poured a double whiskey on the rocks for himself and one for Arnold.

"Now let's hear about your new ideas."

"I want to build a device we can drop at sea. First, it will sink to the bottom, like the mines we dropped in the Navy. After a specified time it will release a small sonde with a radio transmitter and an antenna, attached to the anchored mine by a long thin wire. A computer in the mine will be programmed to respond to radio commands. We will make it disappear if the Coast Guard is near, or we can haul it up when we want to.

"There is a company in New Bedford manufacturing emergency radio transmitters for fishing boats, life boats, rafts and offshore racing yachts. I'll ask them if they could build such a device. I have seen similar machines used by scientists at the Woods Hole Oceanographic Institution for marine exploration. The idea is to fly along the coast and with the help of GPS drop our bomb exactly where we want it. Some time later, we could go out there and pick up the goods. Under water we could use a long wave radio to communicate with the sonde, so it can stay on the ocean floor until we think it's safe to pull it up. A device like that can be used many times if serviced as carefully as an airplane. What do you think?"

"I don't like the idea of dropping $5,000,000 worth of goods in the ocean..."

"We could start with smaller shipments. But I assure you that flying for 10 hours 10 feet above the surface of the Mexican Gulf is not very safe. This new tool will pay for itself quickly! You have to think of the life of the pilot, too...that means a lot to me!"

The two men decided to invest $100,000 each in the development of the "coke-mine". When Arnold left his brain buzzed with construction details for the new device that would make his trips practically police proof. But, he didn't pay any attention to a little lady getting out of a rusty old car. She looked just like a tourist, with a big video camera walking around filming the beautiful view, the beach life, the trawlers out on the ocean and, as if by mistake, she had aimed at the houses along the beach.

Arnold got the names of a small engineering company and a weapons specialist, who could build the coke-mine. It took six months to produce the prototype and in the meantime Arnold made two more trips to Colombia. He took the route over the Bahamas, landed at different places and changed the ID of the plane to confuse anyone who might try to track him. He said he was heading for Jacksonville, but flying along the East Coast, he suddenly dove to zero altitude and disappeared from the radar screens. He changed course, landed at the Rotonda, dropped his load and returned to the coast continuing his trip towards Jacksonville. Such tricks he knew would fool the police and Coast Guard if they weren't on top alert. Joe Cavallo had friends at all airports. They made the puzzle even foggier by giving incorrect information leading pursuers off on the wrong track.

Chapter 13

IN THE EARLY spring the coke-mine was ready. At the same time Arnold Sprengler ordered a twin-engine aircraft, a Beech Craft Baron, which seated four passengers very comfortably. The Baron's sleek and elegant lines are a delight to a pilot's eyes. It is a fast aircraft, easy to handle. Arnold needed less than a week's training with the supplier and a young instructor to get licensed to fly it.

The plane felt much bigger than the smaller Cessna. The powerful engines purred until he gave full throttle and was firmly pressed back in his seat by the incredible acceleration during the takeoff. Arnold, like every pilot, loved that feeling! With its spare tanks his new plane had an operation range of more than 3,000 miles, making it possible to cross the whole continent nonstop.

After flying his new Baron to Cape Cod, Arnold drove home to Barnstable Harbor. Sara had just come in from her work looking happy and relaxed and gave him an affectionate hug. His decision to close the Hyannis law office and go to London for a few years had given her a real lift. Their improved finances made it clear to her that moving to England wouldn't be a foolish decision. Also, she anticipated the opportunity to spend more time with their daughters, and the thought of being together shopping or attending concerts and theater with them, rejuvenated her.

Arnold had told Cavallo that he needed a copilot to make the long trips. Flying from Colombia to New England and dropping the coke-mine east of Cape Cod was too demanding for one man alone. He had been looking around for some time, and finally found just the man he wanted.

He met Michael Soames in Galveston. Mike, a former Air Force captain and flight instructor from California, had been laid off by a defunct airline. Mike proved to be the right choice. He was a skilled pilot, daring, humorous, easy going and reliable. He understood what the flights were all about, but found no reason to ask questions when he saw a chance to make a bundle of fast money.

With Mike in the copilot's seat Arnold flew to Medellin in Colombia, where they loaded the mine packed with half-pound plastic bags. To make it look like a taxi flight they also picked up two businessmen bound for Boston. Arnold understood that they would be monitored and followed by the coast radar, AWAC radar or by satellite. The first part of the trip was no problem at all.

Approaching the New England coast the risk of getting caught gave them a real case of the jitters. Arnold and Mike didn't say a word. South of Martha's Vineyard they descended to 1000 feet. It was a beautiful night, ideal for their plan. The wind blew from the southwest at about 10 miles per hour and the sea was not too rough with waves about three to five feet. Arnold had chosen alternative places for dropping the mine out of sight of the Coast Guard and away from common fishing grounds. The first spot was east of Monomoy Island.

No boats were visible in the area, so when the GPS indicated they were at the right spot, they dove. The aircraft swept only feet above the waves when Arnold pushed the mine out through an over-size door in the rear of the fuselage. He couldn't see the splash and continued the low level flight until they were north of Cape Cod. Approaching Boston, the Logan tower told them to stand by before landing.

Arnold, Mike and their passengers had to pass customs and a group of officers boarded and checked the aircraft with a police dog.

Arnold's fishing boat was anchored in Chatham with three men on board and the next day he ordered them out to the exact spot where the sonde was to appear. The coke-mine had an inch-thick foam coating making it impossible to detect with an echo sounder. Captain Jack and his men watched the waves in silence, and exactly at the right time, at precisely the right place the buoy suddenly popped up! It looked like a fishing rod standing upright in the water. Through an open well in the middle of the boat, they could reach the wire leading down to the cocaine container and the anchor. They hauled the sonde on board. After pressing a button on a remote control, a nylon rope came up along the wire to the sonde and the container with its valuable load could be hauled on board.

Captain Jack grinned and said to himself, "That Arnold! He sure in hell is a smart guy!"

When it lay on the floor in front of them Capt. Jack pressed a second button on the remote control and the anchor started to pull in the rope that wound itself up into the container like an eel. The men watched in amazement and smiled.

They closed the bottom of the well and placed a big load of crawling and kicking lobsters on top of the hidden drug container. Only a very thorough inspection by custom officers would reveal that the big catch really wasn't just all those lobsters but several million dollars worth of cocaine.

They landed the lobsters in Chatham, but it wasn't until after sunset that the vessel set out to round the Cape Cod peninsula on its way to dock in Barnstable Harbor. They arrived around midnight, a beautiful, dark night, and nobody seemed to be around when Arnold's men carried their catch of cocaine, loaded in sailor bags, up to the Sprenglers' house—nobody, that is, but an alert little lady watching them in her infra-scope, and taping their conversation with the help of her bird watcher's parabolic microphone.

Arnold didn't waste any time calling Joe Cavallo to tell him their first try with the new equipment had been a phenomenal success. The next trip they agreed would be a repetition a few days later. Arnold couldn't possibly dream of having a neighbor listening to this conversation, but Michele's microphone registered every word of it.

After lying at anchor for a few days in Chatham, Arnold's fishing boat docked in Barnstable Harbor.

Chapter 14

THE THREE FRIENDS had supper in Michele's kitchen. She served a delicious quiche with fresh tossed salad and cold Perrier.

"I got the police uniforms. Ingrid's and mine are a bit large and Ted's is a bit too small, but what the heck, nobody will see us anyway. Here is a wig for Ingrid and one for me, and this is just for you, Ted!" and she handed him a full, black beard.! "My uniform is already hidden on board your boat. From there I can watch them land and walk up to the Sprenglers' house. Also, I borrowed a car that I parked outside here. The license plate is phony so I hope the real cops will stay out of this area tonight."

They tried the uniforms on. Ingrid's was so big she had to put two big pillows in her pants to fill them out and she had to use suspenders so they wouldn't fall down. Her uniform cap was so big and it kept slipping down over her eyes, so she put on a black wig and fastened the hat's chinstrap to keep things in place. A sweater with thick shoulder pads filled out her jacket.

"I can't say I look too bad!" she said, examining herself in the mirror. They all laughed when she pointed at Ted and remarked: "You look like Long John Silver or Captain Blackbeard! You could scare the socks off anybody!"

Ulf Lidbeck

They all laughed but became serious when Michele gave them instructions.

"You two have to take a walk around the wharf to the rear of the Sprengler house. Cover your uniforms with these black raincoats and hide in the bushes between Sprengler's pier and the house. I'll be hiding in the cabin of your sailboat. We can talk on our walkie-talkies, but we have to use the earphones so nobody nearby can hear us. Keep one of the earphones in place, unplug the other so you can hear what is going on around us and listen to the radio as well."

In front of her she had two weapons. "These are loaded and cleaned of all fingerprints so don't touch them without wearing gloves."

Ted had brought two pairs of black silk gloves he had used when he held the office of master of ceremonies in his Odd Fellows lodge. Michele nodded her approval and said: "Ingrid, you take the Walther pistol and Ted, you know how to use this," and she handed him a rifle with a silencer and an infrared scope.

The sun set and the skies in the west changed from purple to mauve to dark blue to black. Sprengler's big fishing boat was on its way.

Michele wearing a black jump suit walked down to Ted's sail boat and hid in the cabin. It was still warm in there after the hot, sunny day. She saw Ingrid and Ted walking together and disappearing in the shadows. A raw haze drifted in from Maraspin Creek and the marshes. She sat in the darkness no more than six feet from the cabin's opening and had a perfect view of the pier and the walkway leading up to the Sprenglers' beautiful colonial. She noted it was impossible to observe most of the path from the house because of the thick bushes lining both sides, which at the same time created a perfect hiding place for Ingrid and Ted. She noted the slow movement when Ingrid and Ted sneaked in under the bushes and hid there.

"Those two move through the darkness just like cats, she thought"

The warmth soon disappeared from the open cabin. The air was chilly and raw and made Michele shiver a little. Finally she was alerted by Ted's voice in her headphone: "OK! We're at our stations! We can see you when you blink your eyes! This is an excellent location, over."

"Great! Everything is fine here, too. Over and out."

Time passed slowly. All three waited and waited. The silence was intense.

They noted a small boat gliding into the harbor. The men on board had obviously had a tiring day, but they seemed happy, so the catch must have been good. They flushed their boat deck with buckets of water and scrubbed it thoroughly. Flashlights swept around when they checked the moorings before leaving the boat. Heavy steps were heard on the gravel. Car doors slammed and their pickup truck drove off.

"Hey, I can hear the boat...now I see her."

It was Ingrid's voice that first alerted them. All three could hear the other's breathing in their earphones. They even heard their own excited heartbeats, but it was hard to tell whose heart was pounding loudest.

The exhausts of Arnold Sprengler's big powerboat swooshed and hissed closer and closer, then docked slowly and elegantly. Two men jumped from the boat and tied thick nylon hawsers to the moorings. The engines went silent. The men talked in whispers.

The night sky was cloudy but the moon often peeked out making it easy to see the three men unloading several big sailor bags and carrying them on their shoulders up the pier and along the brick path closer and closer to the bushes.

"We're ready," Ingrid's voice whispered.

"Wait till I say GO," Michele whispered back. She picked up the clumsy tranquilizer gun and aimed at the man walking in front.

"Poof"! A muffled sound was heard from the dock. The man turned around and wheezed angrily at his companion just behind him. "What the hell are you doing? This is no time for games!"

"Poof!" A second sudden hollow sound was followed by a third "poof"! The three men stared behind them. They dropped their big sailor bags. They touched their backs with one hand, dropped to their knees and fell to the ground.

"What happened?" two voices asked in the radio.

"Let's wait 30 seconds," said Michele. "I got them with the tranquilizer gun! They should be out by now. GO!"

Ted and Ingrid crawled out from under the bushes and Michele went up the path taking quick steps and bending over the last fallen man. He stared indifferently at the moon with glazed eyes.

"We better just leave them like that. They'll sleep for about 45 minutes. I have to find my syringes. Help me! Light here! I got them, let's grab the bags and leave."

"No, let's pull them in under the bushes so they cannot be seen from the house or from the parking area. Our three friends pulled the three sleeping guys in under the dense bushes.

A car turned around the corner. The powerful headlights swept over the harbor and stopped at Sprengler's parking lot. It was a white Lincoln.

"Darned," said Ted. "We better hide and get set for some shooting."

A car door opened and three men stepped out. The light from the old-fashioned street lamp fell on two big gorillas in light gray Italian-cut suits and one slim man in a dark three-piece suit wearing a soft fedora. He was carrying two briefcases. The men started towards the Sprengler house. Passing the dense rhododendron bushes close to the entrance, they were out of sight of the men in the parked car.

There was a new "poof" from Michele's tranquilizer gun. The syringe hit one of the big guys in his back. Michele wasted no time to reload. In a few seconds, before the second gorilla was even aware of what had happened to his companion, he got a syringe in his shoulder. The effect was immediate. Without uttering a word the two big guys leaned against each other before slowly sinking down like inflatable Donald Ducks with the air let out. They went down on their knees holding onto each other for a few seconds before collapsing to the ground.

When the man with the briefcases reached the brick path leading from the pier to the house he saw the three sailors sprawled on the ground beside their canvas bags. He stopped and looked around. Michele stood frozen, hidden in the rhododendrons. He probably never noticed her half-closed eyes behind the large caliber, double-barreled rifle aiming at him. "Poof!" Suddenly a well-placed lion's tranquilizer syringe was firmly planted in his shoulder emptying its content into him.

"Hell! Who's there?" he whispered. Then he discovered his two gunmen piled on top of each other like one big hump in the middle of the path. Michele, Ingrid and Ted stood dead still. He must have seen them. He put down his briefcases, reached for his gun in a shoulder case with one hand and pressed his other hand firmly around his hit shoulder. It hurt. Then his legs folded and he sat down like a tired boy after running home.

"OK! Ted, please hide these two bags under your slicker, and Ingrid, can you put one in your wide pants?"

Even though the canvas bags were heavy Ted easily hung one from each shoulder under his slicker. Ingrid was so nervous they had to help her push a bag into her wide pants. She looked like she was expecting a big, overdue baby.

They walked up to the sleeping gangsters. Michele searched the ground and picked up the last of the syringe projectiles that had knocked out all the men so successfully. She grabbed the heavy briefcases from the sleeping man and put her slicker around them. Then the three friends took the brick path through the bushes to the parked Lincoln. Michele rapped on the black tinted window. The driver's surprised, pale face appeared. At the same moment Ingrid tapped on the window on the opposite side. It was partly open. She pressed the button to the tape recorder Michele had provided, and a harsh, raspy voice shouted: "Freeze! Police! If you move we will shoot! You are surrounded, so just stay calm."

The man behind the wheel raised his hands.

Michele rapped again. "Please open the window, Sir!"

He opened it without argument.

"Sorry to disturb you, Sir. We're investigating a tip we got. Have you seen anything suspicious around here."

The man shook his head and asked somebody in the back seat, "Have you seen anything suspicious?"

The answer came in a deep rattling voice: "Hell no! Tell 'em we're waiting for some friends. We're going to that restaurant with food for sailors and horses."

"That's on the other side of the harbor, Sir," said Michele, "Sorry to disturb you. My partner on your other side always suspects everybody! Forget it! Good night, Sir! Come along. Let's go back to the station!"

Ingrid and Ted were a bit astonished but marched after Michele over to the car she had parked in the dark shade under the elm trees earlier in the afternoon. Michele took the wheel and drove towards the bay and the beach. At a crossing they saw the sign for the Mattakeese restaurant announcing in gilded letters: "Food for men and horses...and transient sailors."

***

Luis Bolivar had sent some of his toughest goons to Barnstable carrying the huge sums of money to be exchanged for the goods they were ordered to pick up. Since Arnold had arranged for Sara to visit her girlfriend in New York he was home alone waiting for his boat to come in with its valuable load of drugs and for Bolivar's men to show up. He heard his boat dock at the pier and expected his men to knock at the door any moment. He gave them time to clean up the boat, having directed them to be especially careful handling the cargo so that no bloodhound could sniff around and find anything.

Arnold heard a car stop in his driveway and a car door close. Still nobody came to the door. He waited a few minutes then looked out the window. He saw the white Lincoln parked in the driveway. He felt his scalp tingle in terror and his forehead break into a cold sweat. He stood like frozen. He could not imagine what was going on when three police officers approached the car, talked briefly to the driver and then the policemen went over to a car and drove off.

He had heard somebody moving outside the house. My men, of course, hiding from the police, he reasoned. Still, why didn't they come to the door as agreed upon? He got even more upset when he saw the Lincoln silently drive off.

Arnold rushed out to talk to his men. He found all three of them lying on the brick path leading down to the pier hand cuffed and groggy. He helped them into the house, grabbed his loaded automatic and a flashlight and went outside to look around. Nobody there! But when his light beam hit the harbor basin it picked up something floating on the water. It was a body, the body of a man with a fedora hat jammed down over his face.

***

When Michele had passed the Mattakeese restaurant she turned to the right and switched off all lights. Driving slowly in total darkness she took the road eastwards parallel to the beach. Nobody could have seen them. After a mile or so the road turned south where it joined The Old King's Highway. Only there did she turn the headlights on. On winding back roads they finally made it to Hyannis, and parked outside the auto body shop of Michele's Finnish friend. The canvas bags with the smuggled goods and the briefcases were transferred to Ted's and Ingrid's Ford Fiesta parked nearby.

"If I drive straight home," Ted said, "we'll be there about the same time we generally get home from Newport. Nobody will suspect us."

"I think we should get rid of this luggage first," Ingrid suggested. "It's stupid to ride around at night with 200 pounds of cocaine and maybe a few million dollars in the trunk. And it's pretty silly to keep it at home. If they have police connections they can get warrant orders to search every house in the immediate area. So, why don't we drive to our Osterville shop and store it in the basement until we can get rid of it."

"Good idea, Ingrid," Ted agreed. "Let's head for Osterville! But first let's take these uniforms off."

He started the car and Michele leaned back and sighed: "Good thing the show is over. It was fun wasn't it!"

The traffic was heavy in spite of the late hour. At the Centerville traffic lights they turned left and passed the dark cemetery. A police cruiser was tailgating them! Ted checked that the headlights were on and that he wasn't driving faster than 35mph speed limit.

They came to an intersection with a stop sign and proceeded through Old Centerville Village. The cruiser stayed right on their tail!

Ted turned right. The police car turned right, too, and kept on tailgating them all the way to Osterville along the road which wound through the beautiful garden landscaping marking the entrances to the secluded waterfront estates well hidden from public view. Ted stopped outside the "Sign of the Owl", their favorite bookstore. It was closed and dark, of course. The cruiser pulled up beside them. They noticed there was a dog in the back!

"Right on time," Ted muttered under his breath.

"How on earth could they have found out?" whispered Michele.

But the policeman at the wheel smiled recognizing them and nodded before continuing down the road.

"It was the sheriff, he lives in the house over there!" Ingrid explained with a sigh of relief. "He had to follow us. He couldn't pass because there are double yellow lines all the way!"

Ted unlocked the rear door to the store. They carried the canvas bags filled with the drugs down to the basement and put them into thick plastic trash bags, sealed them well so no drug dog could sniff anything suspicious. They hid the bags under the staircase.

When they opened the briefcases they just starred at the contents for a long time.

"Must be more than a million dollars!" Ted gasped.

"Probably about five," said Michele. "That's what they said on the video from Newport, wasn't it? I feel terrific! What a night!"

"We must find a good place to hide all this stuff," said Ingrid. "I don't want it here for too long. Now, let's go home and get some sleep!"

Chapter 15

JOE CAVALLO WAS sitting on the deck outside his villa in Chatham looking at the dark blue night sky. He was thinking of the positive turn his business had taken and how easily and smoothly this Arnold guy got hooked up. For a few thousand dollars this first class guy was his! Bad times really are good times!

The butler coughed discretely, knowing that Mr. Cavallo was not to be disturbed when thinking. He almost whispered:

"There is a phone call for you, Sir."

It was a terrified Arnold Sprengler.

"Luis Bolivar seems to be playing games with us. His men were here. They disappeared with the goods and all their money as well! They drugged my three men, knocking them out. One of their own guys was left behind, too, floating in the harbor. He is dead! What are we going to do?"

"I don't believe it!" Cavallo roared. "You mean you landed the goods, they stole it and then they ran away with it and the dough as well! For Christ's sake why did you let them?"

"I didn't let them! You should never have talked to Luis about our new way to land it! Or when! The robbery took only a few minutes. I was in my library doing some paperwork and heard the boat dock and Bolivar's car park outside. I expected the men to come in as we had agreed, so I went on working. Moments later when I looked out the window I saw some cops talking to Bolivar's men!"

"I'll call Luis and ask him what the hell is going on! I didn't tell him that our merchandise was coming here tonight. Are you sure it was a white Lincoln?"

"Positive! Who could it be if not Bolivar's guys?"

"You or me, of course, and it's not me!

"And it's not me! I don't make risky flights and create sophisticated equipment and then blow it all to hell!"

"You better not play games with me, my friend, because I can be pretty damned nasty to people who do!" Cavallo warned.

"Do you think I'd still be here talking to you if I had just cheated you out of several million big ones? Not even my men knew they were going to land it here today. They were out fishing when I gave them the order to come here and they can't use the radio on board without my knowing it!"

"OK! Shit! This is what we're gonna do. Clear the boat of anything that could be considered evidence. It has to be so clean that you can invite all the state's K-9 dope sniffers on board for a look around...and get your guys out of there! Give 'em a story they can stick to. Then call the police and report that you think you saw a body floating in the harbor."

"OK, will do! Who the hell did it? Who knew about this?"

"Sooner or later we'll know. Now, get going and do as I told you! Good night."

Joe Cavallo hung up. He took a handkerchief from his pocket and wiped sweat from his forehead. He had been through some major blows before and he could handle a $5,000,000 loss, but it made him fighting mad that he couldn't think of who might have robbed him.

It had to be Bolivar's men, he thought, who came with the money to pick up the bags. When they saw the goods were unprotected…or it had to be Arnold. That cold-blooded character was just sitting waiting for goods worth five millions to come to his place at the same time as five millions in cash. He could have killed the man and grabbed the money, kept the goods and is now blaming the buyer. To a new man in the game, like Arnold, 10 mill is still a big sum.

Cavallo poured himself a big glass of Chivas, turned on the TV and watched a golf tournament so exciting he forgot the robbery. Funny thing, the best golfer's name was also Arnold! What's the difference—Luis or Arnold? He knew he would soon figure out who was responsible and how to get the money and goods back.

The following morning Arnold called Cavallo. Neither of them had slept well. Both were jittery, tired and irritable. "OK, Joe, somebody just ripped us off big time! Giving us a big-time rip-off. If it's Bolivar, we'll be accused and he'll play tough with us. We have to find a way to replace the lost goods. The suppliers might have known something. They have to help fill the gap when a shipment gets lost like this."

"Sounds good to me," said Cavallo. "Why don't you come over here for lunch? How about 1 sharp?"

"I'll be there," said Arnold. They hung up.

Chatham Bars is not only a very well-known inn with its own golf course, its own private beach, a splendid view over the ocean and an excellent kitchen, it's also the name of a sand reef or bank with great beaches east of the town of Chatham. On the east side of the bank is the Atlantic Ocean. On the west it is separated from the mainland by a 500-yard wide waterway with some piers and the Chatham Fish Landing where tons of fresh lobsters, cod and flounder are landed daily. The Coast Guard's patrol vessels are often docked there.

It took a lot of guts for the captain of Arnold's fishing boat to dock next to the Coast Guard boat. But Captain Jack was a cool character with a flair for the dramatic. Like a pro actor. Often he invited crews from the Coast Guard vessels to come on board for steamed lobsters with butter, fresh, warm rolls and iced beer.

From the deck of his house, Cavallo could watch all the fishing boats in the harbor and at the landing. He recognized Arnold's boat. Seeing the Coast Guard people on board made him panicky knowing that his multimillion-dollar shipments might be stored right under their noses. He feared the Coast Guard. Their men were much too smart and alert to let themselves be fooled easily.

Cavallo watched an elderly gentleman parking a small Japanese car on the beach and carrying a big video camera on a tripod to one of the inn's speedboats. A muscular, young Scandinavian looking man helped the old man on board and minutes later the boat sped off throwing cascades of foam over the mirror-like water and landing on the white beach of the sand bank.

The old man was dressed in a blue sailing jacket and blue pants. He had a short well-groomed beard and a white walrus moustache that gave him a sad look. His long white hair under a Greek sailor hat flew in the wind. But Cavallo could not see that behind the sunglasses peered the lively eyes of Arnold's neighbor, Michele Renard.

She set up her tripod with the camera and the parabolic microphone and put on the earphones. Aiming at Cavallo's residence she heard Arnold's voice and his conversation with Cavallo. She heard how the two men grew more and more suspicious of each other, and how they tried to avoid blaming each other for the loss of cocaine and money she and her friends had snatched the night before. Cavallo not only respected his New York colleague, Luis Bolivar, he feared him!

"Luis is a big shot. He's so big and has made so many millions by now that he probably believes he can get away with anything,"

Cavallo pointed out. "There is rivalry among his top men. We have to play it cool and let him get his goods. Our next shipment can pay for this loss. I'll just raise the local prices."

Michele taped Arnold and Cavallo's conversation and filmed a panoramic view that ended at Cavallo's house. A light gray service van with the blue and yellow horizontal stripes of the telephone company stopped outside the wall surrounding the well-guarded villa. A man with pole-climbing foot holds was sitting high on a utility pole nearby. Michele saw him installing a small black box the size of a bar of bath soap on the wire leading to the Cavallo compound. Moments later the man descended and stood on the ground taking off his yellow hard hat. His forehead was wet with sweat, which he wiped away with the back of his hand. The wind hissed slowly in her earphones, but even so she could hear him talking:

"Done," he said to a man sitting at the wheel of the van. "Let's get the hell out of here before we run into trouble!"

Michele switched her lens to telephoto and got a close-up of the repairman before he drove off. She had a strong feeling somebody was watching her so she stroked her old man's beard, scratched her head so the cap's visor slipped down over her forehead. Then she aimed her camera along the beach and got some shots of beach strollers in direct light. But her supersensitive microphone was still aimed at the house.

Her time on the sandy beach was up and the speedboat came to pick her up. The young man was talkative. He said his name was Russell. "Did you get some good shots?" he asked.

Her mask was perfect. She nodded so the moustache flipped up and down. "Flowers," she said with a voice that really sounded like that of an old man, "and beautiful, reflections on the water," she added

He docked and carried her bags and camera to her car.

"Do you know the people living in that house?" She pointed at the Cavallo residence.

"Sure! He's a drug dealer! Everybody knows it, but he outsmarts everybody. With all his money he can do whatever he likes. I think he was even on the town council at one point! No, I don't know him, I just know what people say about him. I think it's a very good idea to stay away from him."

From an old-fashioned purse Michele picked out a 20-dollar bill, folded to twice the size of a stamp. "This is for you, Captain," she said. "Take your girlfriend out for dinner and have fun!"

She sensed she was still being watched by Cavallo's men so with the characteristic gesture of an old gentleman she took out a bent Peterson pipe and stuffed it with tobacco from a leather pouch. She lit the pipe with shaking hands. The man watching with binoculars was convinced that the old man down there, relaxing with his pipe, was not a threat.

The man holding binoculars was sitting in his small glassed-in booth at the beautifully decorated wrought iron gate guarding the entrance to the Cavallo estate. Michele parked her car and walked up to him. With the pipe gripped firmly between her teeth and her hands deep down in her pockets, relying on her meticulously applied mask, she looked straight into his eyes and asked: "Who lives here?"

"This is the Cavallo residence and Mr. Cavallo is not expecting you and he does not want to be disturbed!"

Michele bent closer. She saw there were five TV monitors beside the man. TV cameras were surveying the walls surrounding the compound and the steep stairs to the beach. The man with the binoculars was carrying a gun.

"There are some rare flowers along the stairs from the beach up to this house. Do you think Mr—what was his name—would mind if I came and shot some pictures there for my film about seashore plants?", Michele asked in her old-man's quivery voice.

"Why don't you give him a call and ask. If you were a woman," he laughed, "and in your 20s, I guess he'd say yes—no question about it—but to an old man like you...I don't know!"

"Ah! I see, thanks anyway. Take care!"

Michele returned to her car. It had been a rewarding day. The man in the booth shook his head and switched one monitor to a local TV channel and a soap opera.

Chapter 16

CATHY SPRENGLER WAS cool, intellectual and reflecting, Maggie was fire…emotional, high-strung and outgoing with an incredible memory but she was lazy always waiting for others to make things happen.

Cathy and Maggie's favorite place was Guido's, one of the hot spots in the Hyannis area, with the right music, the right atmosphere and all the right people. That's where Maggie met Michael (Mike) Soames one Saturday night. Cathy, too, met someone that night, a friend of Mike's, who thought he was a comedian and cracked jokes all the time. But she didn't find him at all attractive or even amusing. So Cathy left early and Mike promised to drive Maggie home later on.

He soon realized that the red-haired girl, full of whims and madcap ideas, was the daughter of his boss and chief pilot, Arnold Sprengler. He admired Arnold, who was the most skilled pilot he ever met. Mike had realized right away that Arnold was involved in the drug traffic on a short-term basis, and that he wanted to get out of it once he had made enough money. Mike also understood that Arnold's daughters didn't know anything about the real reason for their father's wealth and his frequent trips to the Caribbean.

Mike and Maggie had a great time together that evening. After midnight they went for a walk along the beach enjoying the balmy summer night. They felt as if they had known each other for years. Walking hand in hand they listened to the waves and the sound of the wind whispering in the lyme grass and singing in the low, stunted pine trees. They didn't talk much, just walked. Finally they sat down and watched the reflection of the moonlight dancing on the water. Neither could think of anything much to say, so they didn't bother really. Both were content with the silence.

The two of them were realistic enough to understand that their sense of comfort might simply be caused by a mutual desire for trust, togetherness and the kind of real honesty and unselfishness they had not met outside their families or close friends. An amazing feeling of well-being filled them both as well as an unspoken awareness they were to meet again soon.

He drove her home in his old, ugly VW Golf and when he said good night he hugged her hard and long. He didn't want the night to end. They exchanged their first kiss. She took a key from her purse and opened the door. When she turned around to be kissed again he said:

"Oh, Maggie, I had a great time tonight."

"I'm glad. I like you a lot." She didn't want her feelings to run away as they so easily could do. She felt in control and liked it.

Their lips barely touched in a gentle embrace. She held him to her—she didn't want to let go of this new friend, who was like no other boy she had ever met. To look into his smiling eyes seemed a bit silly, but was in fact very, very nice.

"Good night, Maggie!"

"Good night. I had a terrific time."

She closed the door slowly so nobody would hear it, but the house was full of ears. Her mother heard her and so did her sister. Only her father didn't hear a thing. He slept deeply and snored lightly. He had complete confidence in Maggie. She was his kind of girl, felt like him, acted like him. She could always take care of herself.

She tiptoed up the stairs and into her room. She didn't turn the light on while she undressed and made her way to her bed in the dark. There she found Cathy waiting eagerly to hear what her little sister had to tell.

"You're late," she whispered. "Did you have a good time? Where did you go?"

Maggie smiled. "He is the nicest boy I've ever met. Isn't he cute?

What do you think of him?"

"Yes, he sure is handsome."

"I had the best time! We went for a walk and sat talked. Then he drove me home. Cathy, I can't wait to see him again! Oh, my God, do I feel terrific! And, besides, he's a real gentleman!"

"Tell me more!"

"That's it! That's all there is to tell! And he's a real gentleman!"

"You mean he didn't make a pass at you, or even try to?"

"You got it right! And I didn't come on to him either! I didn't even think of it. We just had a good time together. He gave me the best hug I ever got! Strange, isn't it, to judge a date by his hugs. Never thought of that before. He definitely knows how to treat a woman."

"I'm glad you had a good time. Glad you met a nice boy! Good night. Sweet dreams."

Cathy bent over and kissed her little sister on her nose. She suddenly felt a wave of deep affection for Maggie. She was delighted to see her uninhibited sister so seriously happy. Cathy went back to her own room balancing on a narrow beam of moonlight on the floor. A saw-wet owl was whistling in the tree outside her window.

Summer passed quickly. Mike and Maggie met every day, making plans and dreaming together like young couples do when they are in love.

Sara left for New York to visit friends and take a closer look at several antique pieces she had seen the last time she was in the city. She enjoyed mixing contemporary and antique pieces of art and furnishings in pursuing her own home decorating. She had definite opinions about what she liked and didn't like. Her excellent taste and remarkable flair for combing things tastefully made the Sprengler home very charming. Now Sara was going to stay for a few days with a girl friend on Long Island, who ran a small antique shop on Madison Avenue. She was looking forward to browsing through art galleries and museums, and a couple of fashion stores for a change of pace. She was particularly interested in some early Spanish-looking armor and weapons to decorate the big white-walled entrance hall in their home. Also, during a previous visit she had seen two paintings she thought might be Chagalls and she wanted to have another look at them. She loved dining at the city's gourmet restaurants and taking in a couple of Broadway shows.

She was in high gear when the girls and Arnold drove her to Hyannis Airport and waved her off on the morning plane to New York.

Arnold hadn't told anybody he was going to make a quick trip to Colombia. He merely said he was going back and forth to Texas with some people and that he had to meet with a customer. He would stay in touch with the family by phone.

During the night the coke-mine had been loaded on board the Baron without attracting anyone's attention. Cathy and Maggie were at the airport saying goodbye to their father when Mike arrived in his VW Golf and walked up to Maggie. She was surprised to see him there. After a quick hug and kiss he entered the cockpit and took the copilot's seat next to Arnold.

Arnold wondered at the warm-hearted goodbye Mike had given his daughter. He smiled when Mike tried to explain: "We just... And I think Maggie is the nicest girl I've ever met," he said after a while.

"You bet! And you better behave!" Arnold replied.

"Don't you worry!"

The two girls waved until the plane disappeared in the sun-drenched veils of clouds in southwest. Maggie had tears in her eyes and a big lump in her throat. Cathy sensed her sister's emotional reaction recognizing the signs when Maggie overreacted because she was disappointed or left alone.

"Mike will be back soon, Maggie. Anyway, you need a few days on your own to think things over and give your relationship a chance to develop without rushing into anything."

Maggie hid her face in her hands for a moment and then looked up. "I knew he was leaving today, but I didn't know he was flying with Dad. And I didn't expect to feel this way. You know I want things to happen. I don't want to wait. I know he is the right one for me. I don't want him to leave me! I have so much to talk to him about. I want to be with him." Maggie took a deep breath and tried to blink the tears from her eyes.

"You are too hyper, Maggie," Cathy scolded softly. "Don't worry. Dad said Mike is super—the best pilot he ever met. Nothing will happen. Come on, now, let's drive over to that new place and have a cup of coffee and talk."

After a few minutes they parked outside one of the busy, new restaurants on the Cape. Cathy ordered coffee and blueberry muffins.

"I need something stronger than coffee," Maggie suddenly said and went over to the bar, which was closed this early in the morning. Then she disappeared into the ladies' room. She returned calm and smiling. Cathy noticed the glazed look in her sister's eyes, but didn't want to believe what she feared, and she wasn't about to discuss right now. It was obvious to her that Maggie was doing cocaine.

A couple of friends joined them joking and talking mostly about life on campus, about their summer jobs on Cape Cod and how little was left of their paychecks after they had paid for room and board. Five girls shared one room, sleeping on the floor in their sleeping bags. Those working in the restaurants were lucky because most owners let them eat for free. All problems blew away when someone suggested going over to Kalmus Beach. Maggie was in the center of the attention, laughing and joking with everybody. Swimsuits and surfboards came out of nowhere. Chilled beer and sodas were stored in iceboxes in every car and truck.

The lonely days Maggie had feared flew by and Arnold and Mike returned. Maggie and Mike met daily. They took long walks along the shore. They drove to Provincetown for lunch. They went jogging together. They flew to Martha's Vineyard and spent the day. They took the early morning ferry to Nantucket where 18th century houses originally built by wealthy whaling captains are maintained with loving care.

They had dinner in one of the restaurants on the water…oysters with stout, baked lobsters and for a dessert fresh Nantucket strawberries and real whipped cream. When the sun set the gas lamps in the streets were lit. Maggie wanted to stay overnight at an inn, but Mike knew it would cause tensions between him and Arnold, so he preferred to return Maggie to her parents' home even if the idea to spend the night together was very tempting.

The next day they went whale watching on a big, fast tour boat out of Barnstable Harbor. After lunch on board a tour guide took them to well-known whale feeding places. Humpback cows with calves came alongside the boat with their big, watchful eyes staring at the crowd on board. Mike was thinking of the coke-mine and its multimillion-dollar cargo on the ocean floor only a few miles away. With a flapping of their powerful tails these animals could easily damage the sensitive sonde.

Maggie talked her father into inviting Mike for a dinner she and Cathy prepared: grilled swordfish with garlic-lemon-butter, mushrooms, squash, and small potato balls dipped in breadcrumbs and pan-fried. A cool Sauvignon Blanc was served in pale green glasses. For dessert they had boiled ginger pears served on an ordinary piece of plain pound cake drenched in the pear juice and Cointreau, which was superb. The girls followed their mother's rule that each meal should be well prepared, elegantly presented, and absolutely unforgettable.

Arnold liked that. After dinner he poured snifters of his finest California brandy, which he said only needed just one more generation to be in class with the best French cognacs.

When Mike was ready to leave Maggie joined him for a short walk. All the small fishing vessels were docked for the night and not a sign of life could be seen. The moonlight was reflected on the calm dark water.

"You know, Maggie," Mike said holding her by both shoulders. "You must stop using dope." His blunt remark caught her by surprise. Shocked, she stopped and stared at him.

"What makes you think I'm on drugs?" she asked almost belligerently.

"I see it in your eyes. I have used it myself and I recognized it right away, so there is no point in trying to hide it from me. I'll help you quit!"

She was embarrassed. She couldn't say anything and stared down at her feet as she continued walking along slowly. "It's nothing serious," she said. "I don't need help."

"Listen, Maggie, I have a very good job. I love it and it would be crazy to jeopardize it with the use of crack or coke or even marijuana. If we are going to be together it has to be without crack or coke or any of that shit. Because if I let you, it won't be long till

I'm back using it. I've quit once and for all, and I'm not going back! That's it! It's up to you. You can quit. I'll help you!"

"You're exaggerating, Mike! I'm not addicted. I have everything under control! I promise. I snort a line once in a while, and that's it."

"Sorry, Maggie. I know what I'm talking about. I don't want you to use any kind of drugs. You have to quit.

"I know it's not that easy. I'm in love with you and I want you. But, I don't want you if you're gonna use that crap. Because I don't want a junkie, and I mean it!"

"Aren't you being a little too serious, Mike?"

"No, I mean it, really! This is serious business!"

"OK, I will!"

They walked in silence. She could not believe that he really would leave her just because she did a line sometimes, now that everything had started out so perfectly.

To Mike it was OK to make money on drugs but the idea of Maggie using it terrified him. He knew that if the urge returned for whatever reason he wasn't sure if even he himself could resist. Damn this whole thing! He wanted her. He wanted her spirit, positive and strong, lively and creative. Whenever that wretched dope came in, it left helpless, irresponsible wrecks!

"Stress, solitude, sorrow, difficulties, and depression are the main reasons for starting to use drugs. Together we can fight all that, can't we?" he said trying to cheer her up.

Their serious discussion hit Maggie hard. She knew he meant what he said. He really was serious in his ultimatum! She knew, too, she wasn't about to let him down. Of course, she told herself, she could stop if he absolutely wanted her to. He said it would be difficult, but if he could do it, so could she. They kissed good night and when they hugged she heard him whisper into her hair: "Don't go away from me. I want you. I love you."

"What did you say, Mike?"

"I said that I love you. To hell with this damned dope! I want you to call me as soon as you start to crave it and I'll be right over. We'll have a great time together without dope. Good night my love!

She found her key. Then she hesitated and put it back in her purse. He seemed so genuinely concerned about all this drug business she felt he really must sincerely care for her. She liked the feeling. She didn't want to think things over as Cathy had suggested. She was already convinced that this relationship would become strong and durable. She didn't want the evening to be over.

"It's not that late yet," she said pulling at his arm. "Let's go to the beach and watch the jazz boats sailing by on their way to the Canal."

She put her arm around him and pushed him onto the little path leading around the house. Behind the yacht yard the path wound through 10-foot-high reeds. The gentle wind whispered softly and its sound blending with a concert performance by hundreds of crickets.

They sat down on a small skiff turned upside-down in a little secluded glade overlooking a narrow section of the beach. A whippoorwill sang nearby. Its clear tunes and the music and singing from the passing boats and the slow purling of lazy waves along the beach edge were the only sounds. They didn't talk. They were completely content just sitting there together.

They kissed, long, intense, passionate kisses. She ran her fingers over his lips He responded by gently kissing her eyes, her cheeks, her ears, her neck. She was sure he loved her. She was lulled by the fragrance from the honeysuckle behind them and he was sensuously aroused by the fragrance from her body. Was it a perfume? No, it was simply herself. He wanted her for the rest of his life! Nobody else. Just this girl. For the first time he really felt she was no more a girl but his woman. He wanted her to be part of his future.

"I'll promise to stay away from drugs if you absolutely insist," Maggie whispered. After a long comfortable silence she asked: "You said you wanted me?"

"Yes! Yes!"

Another long pause and then she said: "I want you, too! Now!"

It sounded so simple and she said it so naturally. Their eyes met. They lay down on the bed of warm, dry grass behind the skiff. Only the man in the moon saw them and he probably smiled when they took off each other's clothes.

She caressed his chest and his face and kissed his eyes. Her breasts hung over him round and soft. She offered them to him, cuddling him up to her as if he was her little baby boy. He let his hands explore all of her from her neck down to her firm round hips. He felt her soft belly as she separated her legs inviting his whole hand to touch her there while she fondled his masculinity. It was big and warm and pulsing. She talked to it: "You are the funniest thing, so smooth, so hard, so full of life." She held it firmly and nuzzled it with her nose, her cheeks and her breasts. This is mine now!"

"Yes, only yours. Nobody else will ever have it."

"I want it now, please."

"I want you to be mine. I want to be yours for ever."

"I'm all yours, from now on, only yours, until death separates us."

She was silky, soft and pulsating, wet and welcoming. It was not what he had expected, not a wild, crazy feeling. It felt calm and peaceful to be in there. It was like coming home after being away for years and longing to be back. There was the future. He thought of his father. He could hear the old man whisper: "This is a good woman, she is yours, always be good to her and she will be the best of friends, the best of lovers, the best you could ever wish for."

He looked at her face, a happy, contented Maggie…the most beautiful face he had ever looked into. There was perfect harmony between them. Their passion which had started almost timidly had risen slowly like a breath becoming a breeze, then a storm, then a hurricane, then a twister and then their egos became one in a furious crescendo. Only the moon and the stars watched. And the whippoorwill called. Time stood still.

"I've never been this wild in my whole life and never this thrilled," she said. "What about you? I didn't know making love could be like this!"

"I think we're made for each other. I'm so happy you are mine, and you...you just got me for the rest of my life. Do you really want me? Do you, Maggie Sara Sprengler, take this sweaty pilot, Michael Frederick Soames, to love etcetera, etcetera so help you God? So say 'I do.'"

"I do! I do! I do! And, do you Michael F. Soames, take this love-smeared, redhead, Sara Margarita Sprengler, to love and take care of for the rest of your life? So say 'I do!'"

"I do."

In the bright moonlight he stroked her back, scratched by the dry reeds and sharp grass. Their straw bed had felt so comfortable to him when they lay there. He was sorry for her, but Maggie shook her luxuriant red hair and laughed. "It was worth it!" she said and looked towards the bush where the bird was singing. "Little whippoorwill, thanks for your performance. You sound as happy as I feel right now!"

When they finally said good night and Mike walked back to his car he knew he could help Maggie deal with her drug problem. He would see to it that she was contented and kept under constant surveillance until her craving for stimulants disappeared.

The following day he left his motel room early for the airport to be sure the Baron had been serviced properly. He doubled checked every single point on the checking list! Nothing was left undone. There was a phone call for him in the mechanic's office. It was Cathy. She was very upset.

"Mike, I just have to talk with you. Did you know that Maggie is using drugs?"

"Yes, I learned about it last night and we had a long, heart-to-heart talk. I'm afraid she's not taking it as seriously as she should. How long has this been going on?"

"Only a few months, I think. I saw her kind of groggy looking in London, a few times, but I never thought of cocaine. Now I just found some envelopes with white, bitter tasting powder, a glass pipe, some razor blades and a tiny scale in a small box among her things. You must help her quit! Please!"

"She promised me to stay away from it, but it's not that easy. I'll do my best; I don't want her to be a junkie! She means an awful lot to me! "

Chapter 17

MICHELE LEFT CHATHAM behind and headed home along Old Queen Anne Road. She pulled into a rest area and removed the wig, the fisherman's beard and the moustache. With wet-wipes and moisturizer her old man's face disappeared. She shook out her short hair and looking at herself in the rearview mirror she had to smile. The deep wrinkles, the wart on the nose, and the scar under one eye were gone. She put on fresh lipstick. The old man with his pipe had vanished!

Stopping outside her home she recognized the service van from the phone company...the same van! The same men were installing the same soap-bar size black boxes on the telephone wires! She watched them work, not only on the Sprenglers' cables, but also on the ones to Ingrid and Ted's house and on her own.

"So," she said to herself, "some very cautious people are wire tapping Cavallo's, Arnold Sprengler's home and the neighbors'. The only ones interested in listening to these lines would be the drug dealers from New York...or the police."

Michele looked at her watch. It showed 4:30 p.m. She turned her car around and headed for Osterville arriving just in time to see Ingrid and Ted give their display window a last look before closing their shop for the day. They carried their briefcases and the lunch basket they always brought with them to work to their car and when Michele parked behind them they greeted her with weary smiles. She invited them for dinner at East Bay Lodge.

"Sorry," said Ingrid. "I just can't! I'm completely exhausted! It's been a busy day. Let's go home and have dinner at our place instead. We have some nice smoked trout in the fridge."

Michele shook her head and said: "No, we have to talk right away. It's urgent and I've had a tough day, too. I've found out something you have to know before you take a single step over the threshold of your home tonight. Come on, follow me. Let's talk and relax with some good food."

The Hallbergs weren't too enthusiastic, but followed Michele driving under the spreading branches of the giant, old trees lining both sides of Wianno Avenue. The hostess knew what her guests always ordered, and once seated Ingrid, Michele and Ted were served vodka martinis straight up with a twist, without even asking.

Michele told them what she had seen and heard in Chatham and finally about the bugging of the phones.

The chef recommended Wienerschnitzel topped with lemon, capers and anchovies. After dinner they drove to Barnstable Harbor. The Hallbergs opened several windows to clear the house of the heat left from the hot, sunny day. The setting sun spread a bright red light on floor and walls and the evening breeze filled the rooms with refreshing, pine-scented air. There was a knock at the door and Michele came in. She opened her briefcase and took out a small walkie-talkie.

"Come, let's go for a walk and watch the sunset," she said. Ingrid looked really tired, but said it was a good idea to get some fresh air. They walked along the beach.

"Use Channel 30 if you need to communicate and please leave the thing on all night so I can contact you if I need help," Michele said.

"If you are afraid and want me to come and stay with you tonight?" Ingrid asked.

"Thanks, but I don't think it's necessary. However, I would like you to keep the walkie-talkie on. We can't say if or when they want to take a closer look at us, but I'm sure they will. Nobody will walk into my house or peek through my windows or listen to us without realizing that they'd better be careful!"

A bright orange setting sun glowed in the violet mist over the mainland. Their walk ended at Michele's house where they sat on the back porch sipping chilled Rhine wine. They didn't talk. The fact that they were suspected had put a damper on their usually easygoing manner.

It was dark by now…a balmy night with a clear dark blue sky sprinkled with stars. Fishermen in their small boats entered the harbor and docked. The men on board didn't say much of anything but from one boat they flung several big plastic containers filled with flapping flounders onto the pier. From another boat they hauled up four big tunas. It took a crane mounted on a truck to get them ashore. Those tunas were a welcome catch worth between $2500 and $3000 each in cash.

A big, American car stopped near the telephone pole in the center of the Harbor Square. The windows and shutters of Michelle's studio were open. A thin voile curtain illuminated by the streetlights made it impossible to look into the room. From inside, though, the three friends had a good view of what might occur outside. Michele aimed her parabolic microphone at the car that just arrived. She handed one earphone to Ted. Two male voices could be heard whispering. Michele turned up the volume.

The men were talking about food and getting ready to eat. They had a cooler packed with sandwiches and beer, and were obviously prepared for a long, dull night. The microphone picked up crude burping noises as the men ate and drank, revealing their table manners.

Michele and Ted could hear two or three telephone rings and Arnold Sprengler's voice answering "Hello".

An agitated Mrs. Sprengler was heard saying: "Arnold, it's me, Sara. I'm still in New York. I'm finally convinced that you are involved with these drug people. And your youngest daughter shows all the signs of being a cocaine user."

There was a long silence.

"Arnold, are you still there?" Sara asked.

"Yes, yes, dear. Are you sure Maggie is using drugs?"

"Cathy said so and Maggie is in bad shape! One more thing. I will not return home to live with you if you continue to associate with these drug dealers. If your business is killing my child I'll never see you again and you and your rich friends will be in deep trouble. I promise you—I'll see to that!"

"But Sara, my dear, I just have to finish this deal…"

The click when she hung up had a definite final sound and Arnold Sprengler put his phone down with a heavy sigh.

"That lady sure meant what she said," commented one of the men in the car and the other one continued: "If Mr. Sprengler is on his way out, that means trouble for him and us. Now, these other people, the neighbors, they might know something about George's death and why he was unconscious when he was thrown into the water here in the harbor. We have to check them out. The two with the store in Newport are easy. They're away from home all day. Sneaking into their home to look at things and plant some bugs is a piece of cake."

"That little lady in the house behind us lives alone, so when she goes shopping one day I'll go in there and find out if she might have anything to do with all this. Bolivar is a fanatic when it comes to checking security. I mean, I don't think these neighbors are involved. Sprengler, yes. He's got a BMW. But these other ones— no, no! Just look at their junky old cars! Anyway, I'll follow

Bolivar's orders, damn it! He knows how to run this kind of a show!"

"Sure!" his companion agreed. "I'll go over right now and plant some bugs in each house so we can hear what they talk about. Honk if you see them coming."

A man got out of the car. He and his shadow seemed to float away in the pale light from the lamppost and he disappeared behind the bushes next to Ingrid and Ted's house. Ingrid stood breathless. She saw a dimmed torchlight move around in their rooms. It took only a few minutes. Then the jumping light from the torch went out and the man was seen walking back to the car.

"So what did it look like?"

"Nice home. Very European. Art and stuff and lots of books. I put one bug near the fireplace, one under a sofa, one under their breakfast table in the kitchen and one in their bedroom. The last one I hid in their library. Now I'll pay a visit to that lonely, little lady's house."

"OK. First we'll give her a call to see if she is in."

Michele whispered: "We can't let them in here! If they see my collection of arms and electronics I'll be in big trouble! I need time to hide my stuff. I have to stop him from coming in."

Michele's phone rang! Once, twice, three times…

"If you answer the phone now they'll postpone the visit," said Ingrid.

"I have a plan," said Michele. "The two of you stay here on the second floor and be ready in case I need help. In the meantime I'll go and get a bucket."

Her phone rang over and over again while Michele disappeared downstairs. She locked her front doors and sneaked into the garage. In her headphones Ingrid overheard the conversation in the car outside.

"Good. She's not home. Run over and see if you can get inside. I'll honk if I see her coming. OK?" The car door opened and closed with the clicks of a fine automobile. Michele was hiding in the dark kitchen, alone, waiting.

"He's on his way," whispered Ingrid in the walkie-talkie.

"I have a little surprise for him," Michele whispered back. She was a bit shaky. Now she saw him! A dark shadow was moving about outside. He tested every window. They were all locked. When he tried the French doors leading into the dining room he found them tightly bolted. In order to open them he'd have to break the glass, but knew it would be stupid to make any noise, so he went back to the kitchen door.

"Excellent," he whispered to himself when the screen door opened without a problem. "This lock's just too cheap for a home like this."

Suddenly the kitchen door swung open. And there was Michele with a cigarette lighter in one hand and a bucket in the other.

"What's up? Don't you know big bad boys should leave little old ladies alone?"

The intruder was so surprised he instinctively reached for his gun in its shoulder holster. But he was too slow. Michele threw the contents of the big bucket at him. It was gasoline! His eyes opened wide in amazement and his jaw dropped giving him a stupid, startled expression. He backed off a step giving Michele just enough time and room to reach out and hit him with the foot long lighter flame.

BOOOMMM...! Ingrid and Ted heard the hollow sound of an explosion, a man's scream of terror and Michele slamming a door shut. The next moment they saw a figure completely engulfed in yellow-orange and blue flames running across the open harbor parking lot and after a few enormous jumps throwing himself head first with a big splash and a hissing sound into the harbor. Blue and green flames flickered over the surface. After a while the sooty and burned face of the trespasser appeared a good 25 yards away, gasping for air after the long swim under water in his nicely tailored three-piece suit.

"All helpless little old ladies can go to hell," he croaked.

Michele sprayed the burning ground outside her kitchen door with a fire extinguisher. "I don't think he'll bother me for a while," she said grinning, going upstairs to join her friends. "You can go home now," she told them.

Ingrid and Ted disappeared in the dark shadows behind Michele's house, walking through neighbors' gardens in a wide circle so as to keep out of sight of the men in the car. Once they got home and to give the listening gangsters the impression they were returning from walk, Ingrid said in a loud voice: "That was a nice walk but it's good to be home again. Let's light some candles, sit down and relax."

A few minutes later Michele called on the phone. "I just had a burglar here. Can you believe it! But I frightened him off! I don't think he'll be back, at least not for a while anyway. When I came in through the back door I didn't put the light on because of the beautiful moonlight. That's when I saw a man sneaking around trying to open the windows before coming to my back door."

"What's going on in this neighborhood?" Ted asked. "First a New York mobster's found drowned here and now a burglary! I think we should call the police! Do you want us to come over?"

"I don't have any valuables or anything of interest to anybody! I'll just lock all doors and switch on the burglar alarm. Then I'll go to bed with a good new book. If he comes back I'll have more surprises for him," she laughed and continued: "Do you think this visit may have something to do with the drowned man?"

"No," said Ted, "I don't think so. Some other mobster probably killed the guy who was found in the water. It was simply a handy way to get rid of the body here in this peaceful corner of the Cape. I mean, we live off the beaten track and at night nobody's around here. He was probably killed somewhere else and just dumped here.

"We'll be right over, if you want us to. I think you should put all your outside lights on right away and call the police first thing tomorrow morning."

"OK, I'll have the phone right by my bed and I'll call you if he comes back. Good night!"

Ingrid grabbed the phone from Ted. She talked fast. "Are you sure he's gone and won't come back? I don't want you to be alone." She didn't wait for an answer. "I'll be right over," she said and hung up. "I'm going over to see her and I'll be back tomorrow morning," she told Ted.

"Good! Go ahead, dear."

Ingrid got her toothbrush and a towel and picked up her pajamas and a robe. She gave Ted a quick kiss good night and he watched her run across the square, knock on Michele's front door and when it opened vanish inside.

It didn't take him long to find the listening bug in the bedroom. It looked like a small, flat camera battery with a four-inch long tail of thin copper wire. With his pocketknife he cut it loose and dumped it into a glass of water.

He poured himself a stiff Scotch and went outside. Sitting on the porch in the dark he watched the open area and the car parked near the telephone pole. He saw a man walk out from the bushes at Sprenglers' pier. That guy looks awful, soaking wet; his clothes hung like rags and he could hardly walk. When the man reached the parked car the door swung open and Ted saw him fall backwards into the rear seat. Then Ted placed the tape recorder close to the bug on the mantelpiece and turned up the volume so any other sound would be drowned out by the most appropriate music he could think of to entertain his audience out in the car— Beethoven's Fifth, the Destiny Symphony. Ingrid and Michele had also registered what had just taken place in front of the house.

Every comment heard in the car was taped. "What the hell happened? You came storming out like the cannonball man at a Ringling show. I feel really sorry for you, but you know, you sure put on a great show! I saw you surface and crawl up soaking wet like a drenched cat. Later the phone rang and the 'little old lady' called her Swedish friends. I taped their conversation and it seems to me they don't know a blasted thing about our goods or the killing of George, or anything else of interest for us! How did you catch fire? How badly burned are you?"

The man in the back seat didn't answer. He was looking at his burned hands. He reached for the rearview mirror, which reflected his swollen, red face where big white blisters were starting to bubble up. His well-groomed moustache was gone along with his eyebrows and most of his hair. Harbor water was still dripping from the burned beard bristles left on his face. A strong smell of meat, forgotten on the grill, filled the car! He starred at himself in the mirror with horror but then he broke out into a loud laughter.

"Ha, ha, ha! I'll be damned! To hell with this stupid job! What a feisty little devil... exactly my kind of woman! If I knew her I'd give her a hug! That's how a lady should behave! She was fast, clever and gutsy. And, boy, was I stupid! I didn't suspect a thing! And she made raw meat of my face! I'll definitely stay away from her for a long time. But, when I've recovered, I'll call her! Yeah! She's my kind of female!"

Ingrid and Michele smiled at each other.

The voice from the other gangster continued: "Why don't we drive to the hospital and have them look at your face? The recorder can do the listening."

"You're right. Actually it doesn't hurt that much except when I laugh! Take the tape recorder to my Ford parked under the trees over there. We'll come back tomorrow and replace the tapes. I, too, am pretty well convinced these people aren't involved. Now, this Sprengler guy! He's smart as hell, but he's got problems."

The Lincoln drove off.

"I feel sorry for Mrs. Sprengler," said Ingrid. "She's a lovely person but that husband of hers seems bewitched with the idea of making money at any price."

Chapter 18

MICHELE HAD KEPT her eyes and ears open to everything Arnold Sprengler had been doing and saying. She knew a new delivery from Colombia was due and Arnold would fly the payment, nearly $5,000,000 in bills, to the Bahamas. A new, larger and lighter coke-mine had been built. It was to be stuffed with money, dropped in the ocean close to Nassau and picked up by a local crew. Michele met with her friend, the seven-foot Finn who owned Cape Cod's best auto body shop, and had put together a little story about visiting friends who might need a car for the weekend. He had gladly given her the key to his yard with permission to come and take any of the cars he kept for stranded customers.

Ingrid and Ted were informed of her plans to rob the money transport. The police uniforms from the first coup had been altered to fit. Michele was just waiting for the right moment to strike. Finally it had come. The narrow Route 6A just outside the Sturgis Library was the place they had chosen for their coup.

A helpless looking elderly couple was standing looking under the open hood of their Jaguar. Michele, dressed and masked as a police officer, smiled at Ingrid and Ted in their disguises as she stopped the traffic directing cars to pass in only one direction at a time. The big white Lincoln with the New York gangsters was the first to slow down. The old lady asked the driver for help.

"We are having problems with our car. Would you please give me a ride to the nearest pay phone just down the road so I can call our son?" she asked.

"Sorry, Ma'am, I'm not allowed to take anybody unknown in this car, I'm not even allowed to stop," said the uniformed driver in a heavy New York accent.

There was a "poofing" sound from the old lady's purse and the eyes of the driver suddenly froze in a blank stare. His jaw dropped, but his cigarette still hung stuck to his lower lip. Ingrid looked into the car. There were two more men in there. The one in the back seat leaned forward:

"Listen, my good lady. We'll call for a tow truck. Now, Peter! Back out of here and pass! Move it!"

There was another "poof" from Ingrid's purse and the hidden tranquilizer gun shook from the recoil. The man in the back seat sat back, grabbed his left shoulder with his right hand and leaned his head against the headrest. The man sitting next to the driver realized they were trapped. Ingrid saw his Uzi gun, ducked and escaped a fast round of bullets. The car door was swung open and Ted's voice thundered: "Surrender! This is the Barnstable Police. You are surrounded!"

The gangster moved as fast as a rattlesnake and Ted hardly saw the gun. There was a deafening bang like that from an elephant gun when Ted fired his double-barreled. The car's moon roof was blown into pieces raining down over the surprised gangster covering him with a layer of small crystals sparkling in all the colors of the rainbow. He dropped his gun and holding his hands up he came out of the car. Ingrid reloaded and placed a fast tranquilizing shot in his behind. He stood teetering for a moment as though balancing on a tightrope then he fell forward into Ted's arms who laid him back in the seat next to his sleeping partner. Two big suitcases in the back seat were quickly carried over to the Jaguar.

Keeping her nerves steady Michele checked the trunk of the Lincoln and found a third suitcase. She collected the syringe projectiles still hanging from the three men before resuming her role as policeman. She waved some cars along and rushed to the Jaguar.

"Hurry, let's get out of here! They'll wake up in five minutes."

With tires spinning and screeching they took off towards Exit 6 of the Mid-Cape expressway. The robbery had taken less than four minutes. Michele was pleased and smiled to herself thinking the caper was OK considering the robbers' inexperience!

"I noticed his CB was on channel 3." Michele said, "Let's listen to it. They might have company and some kind of escort."

The CB was silent for a while. Then a groggy voice said: "Bolivar, Bolivar! Are you there?"

"Yeah, I'm here. What's up!"

"Damn it, where have you been?"

"Just stopped to get a burger at Exit 6!"

"Ouch!" said Michele. "He's just in front of us, over there at the restaurant near the bus stop!"She sped up the ramp to the expressway heading down Cape towards Chatham.

The voice went on: "You gotta stop a black Jag with three people in it. One policeman, one elderly man, and an old woman. They got us into the world's simplest booby trap. They grabbed everything and took off!"

"Idiots! Did you say a black Jag? I just saw one pass heading east! I'll get the bastards!" The silver Lincoln with New York plates reached the eastbound lane in a matter of seconds. "I can see the Jag now!" said the voice in the CB. "That car is fast as hell but the traffic keeps him from driving at full speed. I can catch up with him!"

Ingrid watched the speedometer hit 140 miles per hour! Still the sound from the V-12 engine was hardly noticeable in the leather-upholstered interior.

"We're much faster than they are," Ingrid assured herself, and felt better when the distance from the pursuing Lincoln increased.

"Yes, this Jaguar is the unbeatable sprinter! I have arranged a little chase stopper," said Michele and let the speed drop. The Lincoln came closer, only 200 yards away, when Michele suddenly turned left off the expressway onto a narrow police path leading over an incline in a sharp bend across the median to the westbound lane.

"Oh please, Michele," whimpered Ingrid, "Step on it and get us out of here! They are close! I can see their guns sticking out the windows!"

High grass licked the belly of the Jaguar when Michele stopped just after the bend. She grabbed a steel wire hanging from a pole and pulled it while driving slowly a short distance before she let it go and accelerated up on the west bound lane.

"What was that?" Ted asked looking back. The Lincoln had stopped. Michele drove at almost legal speed to the next exit before answering the question:

"A couple of days ago I placed an farm harrow next to that path— upside down, so all the spikes are turned up. With the wire I just dragged it over to the middle of the path. It was virtually invisible in the high grass, so they have probably four flat tires by now!"

From the CB came a loud outburst of vulgar language and some newly-created obscenities when the "Silver President" called the "White Lincoln" and asked for help.

And help was on its way. Michele had already called the police and asked them to rush to the police path crossing the median between Exits 7 and 8 "because machine gun fire had been heard there only minutes ago. It seemed some men in a silver Lincoln had been firing wildly at another car."

Michele stopped outside the closed auto body shop. She parked the Jaguar and they loaded the "confiscated" suitcases into her own rusty old car. They changed clothes, took off their wigs, removed the makeup and were on their way to Osterville where the confiscated bags was hidden in the basement of Ingrid's store. A quick check showed that the three trunks were stuffed with bundles of used twenty, fifty, and hundred-dollar bills!

When Ingrid and Ted unlocked their small Ford Fiesta, Ted turned to Michele: "I wouldn't mind having that Jaguar we just drove."

"Yes! I would think you would! Guess what?" She giggled and with fiendish glee said: "It was Cavallo's Jag. I borrowed it!"

"Aren't you a little devil!" Ted laughed and Michele and Ingrid joined in until tears filled their eyes.

When Michele could talk again she said: "I think we have to keep our old cars for a while. It would be crazy to give the impression of sudden wealth. Let's lie low and make plans for using the money. Now, remember that your house is full of bugs, so don't say anything that could give them a hint!"

The mysterious car parked near the telephone pole was still there when Michele drove into her driveway. She checked the burglar alarm. Everything indicated that nobody had tried to break in. She felt less uneasy now, undressed and got ready for a relaxing hot bath.

Ingrid and Ted came home a few minutes later. Ingrid opened the mail looking for new or unusual stamps, which she cut out and dropped in a big brown envelope. "One day when I get the time, I'll sit down and sort all these through". She separated the mail into files to be entered into the computer.

"Eleven orders today," she said after a sip of the martini Ted had mixed for her. She couldn't stop thinking of the bugs transmitting every word she said to the men in the car outside. "Ted, you know what? I think it's awfully dusty in here. I don't think I've vacuumed this place thoroughly for a couple of weeks. Tomorrow is the day!

Anyway, I have been thinking of the burglar Michele had. She said that the man didn't look like a burglar. He looked more like a private investigator or something. Wonder how she managed to scare him away. Does she have a gun?"

"Oh no!" Ted answered quickly. "I can't imagine that. She often says that guns are just for violent, stupid people."

The men in the car were listening. One of them had his face smeared with a yellowish balm for burns and blisters. Still he grinned and took a big bite of a sandwich, swallowing it with hefty gulps of beer and sat, looking off into space, waiting for the inevitable series of loud burps. Then he nodded. "I don't think these neighbors are involved in our business. I think we can skip this surveillance."

Michele let herself sink slowly into the steaming hot bath water. She had a glass of iced Campari and a good book on the chair beside the tub. This was her favorite way to relax after a day of hard work, stress and thrilling experiences.

Refreshed, tranquil and very tired she went to bed. Her considerable arsenal of guns and hunting equipment had been placed in a vault, the size of a small room, installed in her basement carefully hidden behind a false wall with shelves filled with little jars labeled with Miriam's Cranberry-orange Jelly, Svea's Beach Plum Jelly, Babs' Rhubarb Chutney, Ingrid's Hallonsylt, Elderberry Juice and other products from her own or friends' gourmet kitchens.

She had, however, the feeling she needed some protection, so in her bed she had a six-millimeter FN Automatic, the Rolls Royce of small handguns. Every single part of that weapon was polished and smooth to the touch. It was exactly the right size to fit comfortably in her small hand. Only the silencer made it a bit awkward. She knew how to handle it and she could make any offender realize he had met his match.

***

Luis Bolivar had never experienced anything like this before. Nobody had ever dared play this kind of trick on him. The police cruiser behind his car would have been easy to get rid of. A quick round from his Uzi and they would have been gone, but his driver had whispered a warning: "Damn it! Look who's ahead of us!"

A State Police cruiser had just turned off the westbound lane in front of them. Two Troopers jumped out, with machine guns ready to fire and approached Bolivar's car.

"Gentlemen, will you please step out!"

The command rang firm but foolish in Bolivar's ears. He had hidden his weapon in the specially designed compartment under his seat but the driver was too confused to conceal his gun. Surrounded, Bolivar and his two men stepped out of the car, were handcuffed, and taken to the Barnstable Police Station. The Lincoln was searched, no drugs were found, but their guns were confiscated.

"I never shot a single cartridge, but we were shot at," lied Bolivar, and to himself he whispered: "Good thing we never had a chance to shoot. I don't have a Massachusetts gun license."

The Troopers did a smell check to see if the weapons had just been fired. Still they refused to make it easy for him. It wasn't until the next morning after a phone call to his lawyer that Bolivar was released. He wasn't used to such treatment. He had some Cape Cod policemen on his payroll but the State Troopers complicated things for him. For the first time in many years he felt helpless, but he had recognized it was Cavallo's Jaguar he had been chasing. "Damned bastards," he spit out, "damned bastard criminals!"

Next morning, vacuuming her house Ingrid found the hidden bugs.

"I wish they would transmit the smell," she said, dropping them at the Barnstable municipal dump.

Chapter 19

BECAUSE THE COAST Guard and the DEA were showing unmistakable evidence of being on the alert Arnold's direct flights to Colombia had to be cancelled. Instead one of Cavallo's connections took care of the transports from Colombia to the Bahamas where Arnold could pick up the shipments.

Earlier the problem had been importing the drugs while payments had easily been made to the seller or his representative in the US. But tough new American laws against money laundering forced sellers to demand payment abroad, or to accounts in banks outside continental US.

In the cargo area of Arnold's Baron there was the new, bigger coke-mine loaded with $3,000,000 in bills. There should have been five million, but since Bolivar hadn't shown up with his money as promised and he had been impossible to reach by phone, Arnold and Cavallo decided to put up one-and-a-half million each of their own money. Arnold's new bomb would be loaded with this money and dropped in the waters near Nassau. Arnold would have to explain to the new connection how to pick up the money. The sophisticated satellite navigation equipment on board his Beech

Craft Baron made it easy to specify the exact position for dropping the load.

Mike and Arnold enjoyed flying together. They talked about everything except drugs and drug traffic.

"Arnold, you have a great family."

"Thanks. Yes, I do."

"Maybe I shouldn't say this, but…"

Arnold thought Mike wanted to talk about leaving the drug trade when they had made enough money so he answered:

"You can trust me."

"Arnold, I'm in love with Maggie. We…"

"You are what!"

"It's mutual! With your permission, I want her."

"With my permission! You ask for my permission? Maggie would never ask anybody's permission when it comes to choosing her partner."

"Right! But I do. I know she's your pet, and you know what I'm working with."

"This is not a lifetime job, my boy, and you're a good pilot."

"Coming from you, that's quite a compliment. Do you think that later on you and I could…"

"Yes, I'll help you quit this business. All we need is time."

This was a risky conversation but Arnold liked Mike's frank approach and straightforward attitude. They watched the instruments in silence and checked position and weather information. Coming closer to Nassau they saw more and more ships, sailing yachts and big power cruisers below. The sun was setting and the ocean was calm. They were on schedule. The evening mist covered the eastern horizon and one star after another became visible—Vega, Orion and all the others.

They swept along the coastline of New Providence 300 feet above the water. Not a single vessel was in sight. Light evening dusk protected them from any observers when they dropped the money-filled "bomb" exactly where it was supposed to be anchored, just west of Eleuthera Island.

A little later they landed at the Nassau airport. Their aircraft was guided from the landing strip by an attractive girl riding a Honda scooter with a small sign on the back seat saying: FOLLOW ME! Outside a hangar and an air club, the girl signaled to them to stop and cut the engines. She welcomed them and said, "The customs people inspect every incoming plane. Leave your Baron right here; I'll look after it. Just park and anchor it for the night. Would you like me to call a taxi?"

"Thanks." Arnold handed her the keys. "Somebody's waiting for us," he said.

Two very British-looking gentlemen in knee-length shorts and tropical helmets greeted them and drove them in an old Bentley to a nearby waterfront mansion. They introduced themselves as Harry and Bertie. The conversation flowed so easily it seemed to Arnold and Mike that they had known them for years. They talked about flying. Harry Greycoat was a former Spitfire pilot and Bertie Brown a former skipper on a British destroyer stationed in the area during WW2.

While they were enjoying an excellent meal four beautiful "hostesses" joined them at the table. They were also available for a "private" party that evening. Harry looked questioningly at Arnold and Mike. Both men shook their heads and the girls left. Before parting Harry wanted to know about the next day's work. Arnold described the principles for the new coke-mine and the new payment routine. "I have a manual with detailed instructions. You'll get it tomorrow, when we pick up the money bomb," he said.

After saying good night to Bertie and their host Harry, Arnold invited Mike to his room for a nightcap. There was a bottle of fine Scotch and two crystal glasses on the mantelpiece and the two tired pilots poured themselves two good-size drinks and relaxed.

"I have a feeling somebody is following us," Arnold said. "I haven't seen anyone and I think those British chaps are OK, but I have this suspicion…"

"I hardly ever sense such things," Mike said, "probably because I don't feel that involved. I'm just a copilot with no business responsibilities."

"Oh, you're involved alright. In this game everybody who knows what's going on is involved. Are you armed?"

"No, I don't like guns."

"You ought to carry one, we'd be safer that way. I'll get you one tomorrow."

"Thanks, but no thanks. I'm no good with guns. Also," Mike added, "I'm going in and out through custom gates all the time. Where would I keep it? Not on me! Not on board the Baron! It means too much trouble and too many explanations, too much paperwork and too much wasted time! And guns are so noisy! I hate all noise except from aircraft engines! I love the humming from a Rolls Royce or a Merlin. And, I hate confrontations. I prefer a peaceful approach, but if somebody attacks me, I'll kick him down and out before he realizes what happened!"

Mike gave Arnold a quick demonstration of kickboxing. His rapid moves were so powerful one of his loafer shoes took off and skyrocketed straight through the French doors sprinkling broken glass all over the terrace.

"See?" He couldn't help laughing. "Sorry!" He limped outside to pick up his shoe. He surprised someone because he saw a dark figure dart from the shadows and disappear, jumping from the terrace down into the dense bushes below. Mike found his shoe and went back inside.

"I'm really sorry," he said. "You can have my room. By the way, I must admit I respect the warning signals from your sixth sense. Somebody was hiding outside, watching us. When I went out there he leaped over the balustrade and disappeared. I couldn't run after him with just one shoe on. Could I?"

Arnold smiled. "I have a feeling it's the New York people looking for revenge for the money they lost. Or perhaps it's the same people responsible for that robbery. There could be a leak. God only knows where! I have a feeling…"

Mike interrupted: "I think we'd better be careful. Let's change our plans."

"Yes, and they might know about our new equipment."

"Good night, Arnold." Mike stopped in the doorway. "Sure you don't want my room?"

"Positive! Thanks anyway. Good night!"

Mike was nearly asleep when there was a soft tapping at the door. He opened and Arnold sneaked in.

"Stuff your bed so it looks like you're sleeping in it! There are extra pillows in the closet over there and take that carpet, roll it up and put it in the bed."

"You had another feeling?" Mike asked with a smile.

"Yep!"

It really looked like somebody was sleeping in Mike's bed. Somebody who didn't snore…

"We'll sleep in the rooms across the hall," Arnold said and ushered Mike into a dark room with two beds. "They seem to be unoccupied! You take this one; I'll take the one next door! Good night, again!"

Mike chose the bed near the window and within minutes he was asleep. The sound of the door opening wakened him. Someone came in, closed the door and went straight to the bathroom. He heard running water and the flushing of the toilet. In total darkness that person slipped into the bed beside Mike's. He wasn't sure whether it was a man or a woman.

"Must be a lady," he thought. "It's her perfume. Better not tell her now. Better keep still. Hope her husband is in Africa! Damn it!

I can't spend all night messing around in rooms I don't know," he said to himself. The bed was comfortable. The girl over there was already asleep. So he just let himself slip into the arms of Morpheus.

The sun shone through the windows when he woke up, a bit confused about where he was. There was a woman in the bed next to his. She was still asleep. It was one of Harry's "hostesses". She was very pretty. He noticed the butt of a pistol sticking out from under her pillow.

"Oh! My God! She would probably have shot me if I had scared her! Hope she's a sound sleeper."

Mike bent over and slowly, very carefully pulled the gun out half an inch at a time. She moved in her sleep and turned over. Her black hair shone silky against the white pillow. Mike pulled carefully—two, three, four inches! How long was this darned thing? He knew it had a long silencer on it. Finally he got it out and looked at it. A nice little Beretta! For a moment he wanted to wake her up, but decided to leave and picked up his toiletries. Without making a sound he left the room closing the door after him.

Relieved, he took a deep breath. A man came along the hall. It was Bertie, their host's friend from the night before, the former officer of Her Majesty's Royal Navy. He stopped and looked inquiringly at Mike.

"Nice morning," Mike said and went into his room. Everything there seemed untouched. He brushed his teeth, shaved and had a shower, singing a foolish Danish drinking song about an old farmer who went out for beer.

There was a knock on his door. It was Arnold.

"What the hell have you been doing all night? I sneaked into the other room and you were gone, but I did notice an attractive young lady still asleep in there. If you're sincere about Maggie you shouldn't sleep around with other girls like this! I'm really disappointed."

Mike just laughed at him. "You probably won't believe me but the truth is that I fell asleep right after you left and woke up when this woman walked in and went straight to bed! Her own bed, that is, without even looking in my direction. Thank God! She fell asleep right away. So I thought why bother. I closed my eyes and dreamed sweet dreams—of Maggie! Look what that broad had under her pillow! When I saw it, I took it and sneaked out!"

"Well, well, what a nice little piece of business. Let me have a look." Arnold took the Beretta, handling it with his hanky and examined it. "Four shots have been fired recently! Still smells!"

Mike dressed and went over to inspect his bed. There were two bullet holes in the sheet covering what was supposed to have been Mike's head! There was gunpowder around the holes. The shots had been fired at close range.

"I think I can guess what my bed looks like," Arnold said. "Let's get out of here!"

He went to his room and his suspicions were confirmed.

"What a shame, on those nice embroidered sheets," he said and arranged the bed so it looked slept in. He and Mike went downstairs where a butler formerly attired in dark blue morning suit announced their breakfast was being served and that their host would join them in a few minutes.

"Let's keep calm and have a good meal to start the day," Mike suggested as they sauntered into the dining area where a lavish smorgasbord of delectable dishes was set out.

A balmy breeze swept in through the open French doors. They helped themselves to fruit salad, toast and jam and found an umbrella table on the terrace. The butler was pouring tea from a silver pot just as Harry, the former RAF pilot, appeared in the doorway. He gazed at the cloudless blue sky and smiled at his guests.

"What a delightful day," he said. "Let's have our cup of tea and then get going. Did you sleep well?"

"Yes, thank you, like a hibernating grizzly!" Arnold replied.

"Same here. Had an awful dream that somebody shot me, though!" Mike answered.

"How dreadful! But that's something you don't have to fear here. My security is first rate! Now, I've told the crew on board my fishing boat to expect us around nine-thirty."

After breakfast they got in the Bentley and Harry drove out through the magnificent gardens a long, beautiful marble clad pond with a mass of spraying fountains.

"I think we need to change our plans," Arnold said. "You see, Harry, we were actually shot and killed last night. It wasn't only as Mike dreamed. Somebody pumped bullets into the beds where they thought Mike and I were sleeping."

"You don't say!" said Harry as he drove slower. "How dreadful! Who would do such a ghastly thing and why?"

Arnold told him about their nocturnal experience.

"Yes! Time to change our plans," he said, "go to the airport and take the Baron for a surveillance ride. Harry, why don't you call your crew and ask them to set out as planned but without the three of us? Tell them they'll get detailed information at sea."

The Baron was fueled. Mike started the engines and taxied up to the tarmac where Arnold and Harry waited. They flew east and at ten o'clock sharp they could see Harry's Bertram cruiser leave its dock and head southeast. They also noticed a big Cerutto leaving a dock a mile from there. Through his binoculars Arnold studied the Cerutto and spotted two divers getting into their wetsuits. The powerful four-engine Cerutto was following Harry's Bertram slowly, keeping a distance of about a mile.

Arnold pointed at the speedboat. "It could be the same people who tried to kill Mike and me last night. They might try to steal our money."

"Yes," said Harry, "someone seems to know what we're up to. They need a lesson!"

Throughout the day the crew of Harry's power cruiser received changes in orders over the radio, new headings and new locations to go to. The Cerutto continued following the identical orders and kept the same distance. Finally Harry told his crew to return and dock. Because of technical difficulties, he explained, the operation had been postponed until the following day.

Early next morning they flew to a spot ten nautical miles away from where the coke-mine had been dropped and now rested anchored on the bottom. The chart indicated a depth of 50 feet where they dropped a new phony canister loaded with TNT. To it was attached an anchor with a long rope leading to a float with an antenna and a small radio transmitter sending beeps only.

Harry's crew set out early in the morning. The men in the Cerutto followed. From their high observation post Mike, Arnold and Harry watched the pattern of the prior day repeat itself. Arnold informed the crew that the equipment was working fine and they had located the goods.

"It's transmitting on frequency 32.9," he said and gave the exact longitude and latitude.

"Can you hear the beeps?"

"Sure!"

"OK. Go there and get it. It'll take you less than an hour to find it."

The message wasn't even completed when they saw the Cerutto pick up speed. Doing over 60 knots the big, sleek racer flew across the water throwing up cascades of white foam and heading in the direction of the floating antenna.

"Hey!" cried a voice from Harry's boat. "A speedboat is heading for it! We'll never get there in time! Please, give instructions!"

The answer came quickly. "Unfortunately we can't help! Try to find out the location of their docking place!"

The Cerutto circled the floating antenna. The men onboard started hauling in the canister. Harry held a remote control device with a trigger in one hand and his binoculars in the other, watching. Over the radio he heard excited voices from the men when they saw the container and hauled it on board.

"OK, we got it! It's supposed to be three mill in greenbacks. How do you think they open this thing?"

"I'll help you open it," Harry said and pushed the remote control trigger. A short, loud, scratchy noise was heard in the receiver and a 300-foot high orange fire pillar rose over the blue water. Various pieces of wreckage flew in all directions. The Cerutto was never seen sinking. It disintegrated.

"Gotcha!" said Harry with a malicious smile.

Mike registered everything. Harry, the gentleman, had turned into a revengeful, vicious murderer. There was a lunatic smile on his totally insensitive face. Mike had an intense feeling of disgust and was close to vomiting. Arnold seemed less disturbed by the brutal scene. He knew that cruel power creates respect. He knew, too, there was no way to come to terms with these unknown adversaries.

Harry called his crew and gave the correct destination. A long-wave transmitter signaled the coke-mine to send up a float, which was hauled up and hidden in the cold storage area under tuna, marlin, swordfish and sailfish.

At over 40 knots the big Bertram cruiser, a favorite of powerboat lovers, looked almost majestic when it glided into the harbor and docked. Seated in the Bentley with Harry at the wheel, Mike brought up the nighttime incident and questioned the security system.

"I'm sure happy they didn't succeed," said Harry. "I'm not only upset but I'm also confused because the leak couldn't have come from that many sources. The attempts to murder you and steal the money in the coke-mine could be ordered by the New Yorkers. I have only trustworthy men on my team. Only Bertie knew our plans, but he's my closest friend. I'll have a serious talk with him tonight."

Arnold and Mike met in the men's room.

"This is probably the only place where we can talk freely! Tonight we'll sleep in the same room. We can take two-hour turns. We'll go to bed early, OK?" Arnold suggested. Mike nodded. He was still greatly disturbed and told Arnold in no uncertain terms: "The killing of the crew in the speedboat was absolutely unnecessary! I don't want to be involved in such brutal violence. You must stop this madness, Arnold!"

Arnold didn't reply. In a way he saw his ruthless self as a second person he did not want to be responsible for. That evil self had to be stopped in some way. Mike was right; he had not yet been completely entangled by Mammon.

Mike listened outside the door to the room where he had spent the previous night. He heard sobbing from inside. He knocked cautiously. He knocked again but no answer. Then he opened the door and looked inside. His companion of the night before was sitting on her bed with her face hidden in her hands; wild sobs wrenched her shaking body.

"Oh, it's you!" she managed the words. "I thought…Thank God! You're still alive!"

"Why did you try to kill me?" Mike asked.

"I can't explain, but I had to obey or…"

"Or what? "

"Or I had to go…they said, but now it's all over. My only real friend, my husband, was killed today. He was on board a boat and they were all killed." She took a deep breath and continued: "That beast Bertie came here this morning. He beat me up and said I was a no-good damned whore! He said I had been sleeping with you! And he beat me and beat me!" Her eyes were not only red from crying, they were black-and-blue and almost swollen shut from bruises.

Mike felt a surge of sympathy and compassion for his would-be murderess. Seeing a beaten and abused woman always angers a gentleman. "I feel so bad for you, I am so sorry."

"You know, you have to be very careful. That old sailor is a very dangerous man. He's after you. But now, that they've killed my husband Dave, I'm not afraid anymore. He must have taken my gun. I wish I had it. I'm gonna get him. I'll not let him push me around any more and force me to do things..."

With his handkerchief Mike carefully wiped her tears. He filled a basin with ice water, dipped a towel in it, wrung it out and patted her face, holding one arm around her to comfort her. Hoping it made her feel better he stroked her hair tenderly. At least she could feel that somebody cared.

"Why don't you try to sleep," he said. He helped her to lie down on the bed and spread a blanket over her. He checked to be sure the windows were closed and locked. He wanted to comfort her, but he couldn't think of anything to say other than banalities.

Standing in the doorway he said: "I'm locking your door so you can rest undisturbed. I'll come back. Promise not to try to kill me again?

She looked forlorn, nodded and sobbed silently.

Chapter 20

THE MEAL HAD been excellent - the red wine, light and very dry; the medallion of veal with small balls of fresh fried potatoes and a variety of sautéed baby vegetables. The taste of the red jelly made you think of berry picking in a dense wood where the air was filled with fragrances from moss, resin and soil, and where a black bear or a moose might stand behind thick tree trunks watching you

"Harry, you certainly have an excellent wine cellar!" Arnold said, twirling his glass letting the liquid form the characteristic pattern of a fine, dry wine on the inside. He held it against the light from the crystal chandelier and admired its tawny color.

"He most definitely has!" said Bertie. "And he guards it like the dragon does the princess with the golden hair. What's so special about these wines anyway? You drink them, you like the taste, you drink more, you get drunk and that's it!"

"Fine wines express culture," Harry retorted. "That's why, my friend, I rarely waste any on you. Sailors like you should stick to rum and whiskey!"

Arnold still looking into his wineglass said: "I appreciate this marvelous, velvety wine. I raise my glass to thank our host for a delicious supper. Gentlemen." He nodded and let the choice beverage slowly into his mouth, moving it around so that every single taste bud could have an opportunity to fully enjoy it. "We had a busy day, and tomorrow Mike and I will have a long trip back to Cape Cod, so I want to get to bed early. Thank you and good night."

Mike rose, thanked the Britons and said good night. He had a bottle of Remy Martin X.O. in his room and, after pouring himself an uncivilized oversized drink into a cognac snifter, he went out on the terrace where he found Arnold sitting with his nose buried in a crystal snifter. "I talked to Harry," he said, "and he's going to have that coke-mine ready and loaded for us tomorrow morning. I guess nobody is that interested in killing us now that they can't get their hands on the money any longer. Also, they need us to bring the merchandise into the US."

"Nobody trusts anybody," said Mike.

The phone rang in Arnold's room. He went in and answered it. It was Cavallo shouting:

"Where the hell have you been? I've tried to reach you all day!"

"We ran into problems and had to change our schedule. All I can say is that we're doing our part OK. When we meet I'll tell you the whole story."

"Damn it, Arnold, the night before you left we got ripped off again. Bolivar lost five million! Be very careful! Harry is the only one you can trust. Bolivar's boys could be around where you are. They're mean, and I mean MEAN! So everything is OK! Good night, then," said the voice from New England.

Mike thought he would check on the girl to see how she was doing and to see what information she might have. He took the brandy bottle and a glass, crossed the hall and knocked on her door. It opened. The girl's face was a disaster - bruised and discolored. She motioned him to come in and close the door behind him.

"Can I do anything for you?" he asked.

"No thanks, I just need to rest although I would like to talk to Harry. He has always been fair to me, but now I don't know what to think. Why is everything turning so evil? Why did I ever get into this?"

Mike knew the answer, but couldn't say it: "Because you are stupid, because you thought you could trust bad guys, because you couldn't say NO, because you're not your own master once you're involved with drugs and the bad guys."

At first he had considered giving the gun back to her, asking her not to shoot the wrong men next time, but he changed his mind. Of course, she couldn't be trusted. She was probably on hard drugs and her need for them could make her do almost anything. He poured her a generous glass of the cognac. "Drink this and go to bed. You'll feel better tomorrow. Rest now, then talk to Harry. Also, you'd better call some close friend tomorrow morning and you should certainly get away from this house."

She took a big gulp, shook her head and made a face. She took another gulp and said: "Thank you, you're nice. I wish you could have met Dave; he was a good man, too! I can't really believe that he is dead. Bertie called and told me on the phone. He didn't even have the decency to come here to tell me in person that he was sorry."

"He was probably afraid you'd kill him!"

"He's weird and he's rotten. Thank God I didn't kill you. I hope your friend is OK, too!"

"Sure, we always wear bulletproof vests!" Mike lied. "Now, rest, we're leaving tomorrow. I'll have somebody from the kitchen bring you breakfast. Good night and God bless." He nodded and closed the door. Arnold met him in the hall.

"So, you can't stay away from that woman!"

"Poor girl, her husband was killed in that boat explosion. Bertie had ordered him to go on that job. Bertie is the one who ordered our execution."

"I can't feel sorry for people who try to kill me. I'll talk to Harry," Arnold said and went downstairs.

Harry was sitting at his Steinway - playing melancholy pieces by Schubert and Schumann. On the piano there was a bottle of Perrier and a tall glass of it with lots of ice. His eyes were closed and his head moved rhythmically to the music. Nobody else was around. Arnold stood quietly beside him for a long time. When he had finished playing Harry opened his eyes and smiled at Arnold.

"It's nice, isn't it? I wish I could play it like Horowitz. You know, making the piano sing, whispering quietly sometimes, thundering sometimes or dancing sometimes. I like the whispering the best!"

Arnold was amazed. What an extraordinary gangster! But he knew it didn't pay to judge a person by his weaknesses, nor by his nice sides, for that matter. Even the most evil of men can seem to be civilized. He recalled one vivid instance involving the man responsible for Auschwitz, the Nazi death camp in Silesia, Adolf Eichmann. The story went that Eichmann loved roses and would walk around his beautiful rose garden admiring the beauty and the fragrances of his exquisite flowers, which he fertilized with ashes from people he ordered killed and burned!

Speaking aloud to Harry, he said, "Aren't you being too hard on yourself? Playing like Horowitz? I think you play extremely well! By the way, did you know that Bertie sent the men out in the speedboat? And that he had ordered our execution last night?"

There was a long silence. Harry was both bewildered and stunned.

"No, I can't believe it! Who told you?"

"A man of yours, Dave, has a wife. She told Mike."

"Oh, Miranda! She's a doll. She often stays overnight here. She's a nice girl, but she is hooked on dope. There's nothing she won't do or hasn't done when she loses her high and needs a fix.

Her supplier owns her, even has her peddling her body. Where is she?"

"In her room, upstairs, third on your left. She's in bad shape. She was brutally beaten and has been crying. Bertie did a real job on her. She looks awful."

"Poor thing!"

The tall man rose, stroked his balding head, took his glass of ice in one hand and the Perrier bottle in the other and went upstairs. After a couple of knocks on the girl's door, it opened and he was let in. She told Harry everything and he promised her compensation and said Bertie would have to leave.

***

Sitting in big, comfortable chairs in Mike's room they talked about the flight home next day.

"We'll both sleep here tonight," Arnold said. "I have a bad feeling… You take the first turn sleeping. Good night!"

Mike didn't bother arguing about Arnold's suspicions and his exaggerated precautions to spend the night with one staying on guard while the other slept. He just said good night, lay down on the bed and went to sleep. Arnold sat in the dark room. The moonlight filtered through the open window drawing a narrow bluish path across the floor. Time crept by. Following Harry's example he served himself a tall glass of sparkling mineral water with lots of crushed ice.

His eyes adjusted to the dim light. He could see Mike turn over, taking long, slow breaths. He liked the young man, his courage and confidence and his disgust for this dangerous and stupid job. Arnold felt badly he had drawn Mike into this, but it was good to have him around.

After two hours Arnold should have wakened Mike, but his paternal instinct made him let the younger man sleep for two more hours. He believed in the old saying that one hour's sleep before midnight is worth two after. At 2 o'clock he alerted Mike and they changed places.

Half an hour later, Mike was alerted by a clicking sound coming from the electrical outlet near the bed and he saw it slowly turning. A minute later the cover of the electrical wiring box was wide open. He moved silently over to Arnold and shook him gently. In a few seconds Arnold was wide-awake watching as Mike pointed at the new small opening in the wall whispering: "They must have read Sherlock Holmes, I bet a poisonous snake will come slithering in here. Here it comes! It's a hose, a flexible transparent plastic hose."

There was a hissing sound. Arnold tried to detect a smell…no odor, but a very noticeable stream of air. He was sure it was some form of odorless gas.

"CO?"

"Could be as simple as that!"

After waiting a while Mike carefully bent the half inch-thick almost three-foot-long hose and let the dangerous, odor-free gas seep back into the neighboring room where it came from. Arnold had used his dark robe as a screen so a watching eye from the other side couldn't see into their room. He then turned on the air-conditioning. It didn't work! Slowly, without a sound, he opened the door to the terrace letting fresh air into the room.

Hours later the sun rose, the thrill and anxiety from the night was gone.

Arnold thought the game with the gas hose was over. He forced the whole hose back into the other room and re-adjusted the electrical outlet so nobody would ever know what had taken place. When he returned to his own room he found himself having difficulty breathing. He hurried to open the windows and rushed out to the terrace for fresh air. Then he walked over to Mike's room and showered.

At the breakfast table Harry joined them. "See! Our security system works fine."

"Sure, we're still alive! Did you talk to Bertie?"

"No, I didn't have a chance to!"

Harry took them to the airport in his Bentley. The coke-mine was loaded on a van traveling behind them. Harry smiled when Arnold asked him to let him have a look at the contents of the container.

"Everything is OK. This is fine clean stuff. Bring the same amount of money next week and I'll have a load just like this one ready for you."

There was a call on Harry's cell phone.

"They have found Bertie dead in the room next to yours, Mike! He was lying on his bed. No signs of violence," Harry relayed the message. "They think he might have committed suicide gassing himself to death or he might have tried to kill one of you. Strange fellow, Bertie. I was quite fond of him. However, he was always in a financial bind of some kind or other. We shared everything equally, but he always wasted his money on stupid speculations. I just wonder who or what made him deceive me? We were such good friends for almost 25 years. I'll miss him! I never could really trust him. I've often wondered what made him become a crook. Yes, I'll miss him."

Arnold laughed. "You ask that? You're a crook yourself! So am I and so is Mike!

"What has turned us into crooks? Each of us finds our own excuse to break the law. Money is like dope. It's very difficult to return to an ordinary life once you've become used to it. Can you ever rely on any of your colleagues now? Will you ever be able to trust anybody more than you trusted Bertie? And what do you consider dirty tricks?"

Harry answered: "There are only two really dirty tricks— blackmailing and squealing. I can cope with the rest."

"How about stealing five million from you? What do you do then?"

"I can do without five mill for a while! Then I'll just steal it back, of course! I have the resources and they know it, so generally they don't even try."

"But Bertie tried."

"He must have been threatened" Harry explained. "Otherwise he would never have done it. He would probably have cleared up the whole mess with me later. He was OK."

"But why would he kill us? He didn't even know us!"

"Somebody wanted the two of you gone! Maybe a competitor. Maybe they wanted to take over your transport business! You get a nice piece of the pie and if they had your coke-mine you wouldn't be needed."

Harry parked the Bentley and they walked together to the hangar, where the Baron waited for them.

"Mike, please check the Baron for any tampering. I'll have a look at the coke-mine."

From a small, leather wallet containing little tools, Arnold chose a set of hex keys and opened the container for the anchor line, checked and closed it. He opened the radio section, sniffed, scratched the gray insulation around some thick wires and closed it. Finally he opened the cargo-space. It was filled with plastic bags. He took a few out, palpating and examining each one carefully.

"General Cautious, I say," Harry commented, standing beside him smiling.

"Thanks for not walking away, leaving me alone if it would have blown up!"

"I like you, Arnold! We can do business together. I have known Cavallo for many years, and he says you're good. He's an old fox! But too greedy! That's his Achilles' heel. Greed deadlocks our thinking. Good risk management makes us survive."

Mike completed his thorough inspection of every possible hiding place.

"Two of my people are going to Boston with you," Harry announced, "to do a market research and to talk to Cavallo."

Arnold shook his head, but said nothing.

"No guns on board." Mike stated firmly.

Harry laughed. "Don't you worry! Your passengers are nice people, lawyers, by the way. Here they come!"

Two slim, young women in their upper 20s walked toward them. One was a stunning brunette in a blue pinstripe three-piece suit with vest cut in a country style revealing her nicely curved bust line under a white chiffon blouse with a soft small bowtie. Her companion had long, straight cut, blue-black hair. She wore a tailored white tuxedo-style suit with a light pink blouse, matching pink patent leather shoes and a carnation of the same color in the jacket buttonhole.

"Jenny, this is Arnold and this is Mike," Harry gestured towards the pilots. "This is my daughter, Jenny. Take good care of her!"

The two men did their best not to stare impolitely at the exceptionally attractive young women.

"And this is Miss Suzy Yang, Jenny's secretary," Harry continued. "Not only does this amazing girl possess a brain like a PC, she has a built-in mainframe!" She was unusually tall for a Japanese woman. She gave Arnold and Mike a pleasant smile and nodded.

"Thanks for your confidence. They'll be safe with us," Arnold said, helping the girls on board. Harry's men loaded the coke-mine into the cargo bay and Mike checked the mechanism for dropping it.

The engines started and spun quietly. Hardly any vibration could be felt in the fuselage and the cabin was comfortably silent. Harry waved as the aircraft rolled away along the taxiing strip.

After the routine conversation with the tower they rolled into starting position on the runway and took off. Mike was flying and Arnold was busy with the radio navigation. Mike had drawn the flight route on the map the night before and made notes along the track. They worked in silence.

"My Dad must know you well," Jenny said.

"He has to take risks," Mike replied, smiling at her.

"No", Jenny shook her head. "Dad never takes any chances. He has a built-in sensor telling him when he can go ahead or when he cannot trust people. This is the first time he has ever let me meet with his business associates, not even old, close friends."

Mike switched to autopilot and went over to the galley. He offered drinks and snacks. The conversation was light and sociable and they watched the ocean under them disappear in the dark blue-violet evening fog. Approaching the US mainland they could see the lights from the big cities on the horizon and Mike watched for the lights from the Cape Cod coastline. He was thinking of Maggie. Suddenly he became alert.

"I see a Coast Guard chopper on the radar. I hear him talking to Otis Air Force base. We're expected," he said and turned eastwards towards a protecting fog bank at sea.

Chapter 21

WHO HAD BETRAYED them? Arnold watched the ocean below. Then there was a call on the radio: "This is the Coast Guard calling Baron November sixty-six, sixty-six Mike Alpha. Do you read me?"

Arnold answered in an almost cheerful voice: "November sixty-six, sixty-six Mike Alpha here, you're clear as a whistle Mr. Coast Guard."

"Welcome back to New England!"

"Thanks, always a pleasure to see this coastline!"

"Tonight we have a special offer for you! Free lobster supper and coffee to all passengers on board aircraft from the Bahamas and the Caribbean. You're ordered to land at Otis for further instructions!"

Arnold replied immediately: "Changing heading from Boston Logan to Otis OK, but I have a request. Could we be searched at Boston's Logan instead? I have passengers expected there at midnight. Please grant permission to continue along original route!" Gaining time was crucial. Another minute would be enough. Time ticked away while they heard a mumbling conversation between people at Otis.

"Mike Alpha, this is the Coast Guard chopper ten sixteen. Sorry, your request was not granted. Please follow orders."

"OK, Mr. Coast Guard. I confirm change of heading Boston Logan to Otis."

Mike took the yoke and Arnold went astern to prepare dropping the mine. He ordered their two passengers to fasten their seat belts at once. Mike made the turn and at the same time a quick dive into the fog bank. The fog was not dense. He saw the water coming toward him and he almost touched the crests of the waves when Arnold dropped the coke-mine and they ascended again. Seconds later they shot out of the fog bank heading for Otis.

"Woops! Bumpy roads in New England. I spilled my coffee! Damn," Mike said into the radio, hoping the drop had passed unnoticed by the chopper. Arnold locked the cargo door and unscrewed the hooks and wires from the simple drop mechanism. He moved the suitcases from the cabin into the cargo space and said to his passengers: "Sorry, ladies. We'll just make a short stop at Otis."

"Good show," he whispered to Mike. "The chopper couldn't have seen anything, but the Coast Guard radar might have picked up the splash."

Otis gave landing instructions and an impressive landing illumination came on.

"It's beautiful," Arnold said to himself. "What a pity my guilty conscience makes my heart pound so hard it can be heard by anybody within 20 yards!"

The welcome was perfect. A white Jeep with a "Follow Me" sign guided them to a building where a group of men were waiting. The Baron was their fifth aircraft to be searched that night and the procedure, though thorough, wouldn't take too long. A female officer in a well-tailored uniform welcomed them and expressed apologies saying it was necessary to show authority against drug traffickers.

Mike realized Arnold tried to be as outgoing as possible, so he joined in. A table was prepared for them and on the menu were chicken or lobsters. Another female officer came up to their table. She hoped everything was OK.

"We have checked your luggage and your aircraft. Everything seems to be in order. We haven't analyzed the radar video yet. You made a funny maneuver and almost got your behind wet out there," she said looking at Mike.

"Yes I spilled my coffee and got hooked to the yoke. I'm afraid I must have lost about 40 feet."

"Sixty-two and a half to be exact," the officer smiled. "Ladies and gentlemen, you are free to leave. Thank you for your patience." She asked them to sign some forms. Then she said goodbye. An hour later they landed at Logan. They got two two-room suites at the Marriott.

After saying good night to their passengers Arnold turned to Mike. "No Don Juan tiptoeing tonight, my friend."

"I just followed your orders. Still nothing happened! I wonder why Harry's daughter needs to talk with Cavallo,"

"I think they're investigating the robberies. I can't figure out who's behind the Barnstable robberies if it isn't Bolivar."

Arnold called his fishing boat and a sleepy Captain Jack answered the phone. He was ordered to pick up the coke-mine and drop it at another site, where it would be safe from fishermen and the Coast Guard.

Chapter 22

THEY DROVE ALONG Route 6A passing through the picturesque landscape to the majestic tones of Beethoven's Pathetic Sonata. Ted was at the wheel with Ingrid beside him. In the back Michele lay diagonally across both seats comfortable on a pile of pillows. Her eyes closed as she absorbed the rich sound from the six-way stereo, something her car didn't have. The bass voice of the radio announcer at 'GBH in Boston informed them that the Beethoven concert would continue with The Leonora Overture and Symphony Number Four. That was the only human voice heard the whole way from Barnstable to Eastham on the Lower Cape. When the music ended the three friends sat in silence until Ted turned right at the National Seashore's Headquarters heading for Nauset Beach.

"This kind of music gives me a big lift," Michele said. "When I was in New York last time I saw one of those poor individuals nobody cares about, a woman wrapped in rags and plastic bags lying on the sidewalk. Her big woolen hat still showed traces of once lovely pastel colors, but it was soiled to an indescribable brownish gray and pulled down over straggling tufts of her greasy, gray hair. She rolled her head in waving movements, her eyes closed to her misery. There was a wonderful smile on her face when I bent down to put a five-dollar bill in her hand, and I heard she was listening to Tosca. She grabbed my finger, shook it, opened her eyes for a few seconds and whispered 'Thank you, sweetheart' and went back to her dream from the Met.

"Well, that's America. Our land of dreams, dreamers, and dream makers, where dreams save people from insanity. This is where greed is king and we are taught that you can't be bothered to help pay for the education of poor children or their vaccination or their medicine. This is where the 'in' thing is to think only about yourself, and only of your own children's education; where peopln with money select representatives for the common people; where we ignore all Christian rules—don't forgive, don't forget but fight back, and never, never turn your other cheek. Is this the America you thought you came to? Honestly?"

Every so often Michele felt the need to expound on her social ethos. For Ted and Ingrid it was a bit depressing to confront the cruel reality of the American society face to face. After all, they had chosen to leave the Swedish welfare state to live in the United States. To them the US had represented freedom, humanism and prosperity. Now they felt uncomfortable when they heard somebody criticize the land they had chosen as theirs. Also since America had opened itself and said welcome, it felt wrong to find fault instead of doing something to make it better. Ted and Ingrid rarely said anything when Michele let off steam from her social conscience. They knew she was right though.

At Nauset they walked down the long, steep stairs to the broad expanse of white beach. The slow swell from the Atlantic rolled in thundering over the sandbanks. Screaming gulls hovered towards the wind, looking for shells and mussels to be washed ashore. Quick little sanderlings ran up and down the brine, inches away from the waves, picking small shrimps in the wake of the retreating water. Carrying their shoes and socks the three friends let the cool, clear water wash over their bare feet, and every now and then a series of big waves made them dash back to the dry, warm sand. After walking half a mile or so, they found a perfect spot for their picnic. They sat on blankets and opened the basket filled with cool white wine, fried chicken, French bread, cheese, and grapes.

"I never serve a fine wine in plastic mugs," Ingrid said, placing tall-stemmed wineglasses on a piece of flat driftwood. Ted poured the chilled Chardonnay and they lifted their glasses, looked at each other the traditional way Swedes do when they drink. The glasses clinked as they drank a toast "to America".

"OK, the meeting is hereby declared open," stated Ted. "On today's agenda I have one report that we are still suspected and under surveillance, and a second report about Michele's eavesdropping. Finally we need to discuss two things, one for a third coup, and one for the use of our fund of confiscated drug money, which now amounts to about $8,000,000. Mich, the floor is yours."

Michele was munching on a chicken leg, and when she was finished she started talking. "I was on my way to Chatham when I noticed the car we saw parked beside our telephone pole. It was tailgating me so I had to change my plans. I turned and headed for the Heritage Plantation in Sandwich, parked and went in. The man in the car followed me. In the Carousel building I sat on a horse on the merry-go-round thinking of the best way to get rid of him. But, wouldn't you know! The guy jumped on and sat on the horse beside mine."

They drank some more wine and Ingrid cut pieces of Camembert, Brie and Swiss cheese to go with the crispy, freshly baked bread in the basket. They all ate with good appetite as Michele continued her story.

"He bent over and said something like: 'Ma'am, please excuse me! I might seem obtrusive but I'd like to talk to you.'

"I was a bit shaky so I replied: "'Sorry, Sir, I'm not interested.' But he didn't give up! He returned my angry glare with a kind and charming smile. 'I've been watching you every day for quite a while,' he said, 'because I have something I must tell you!'

"'Oh, really,' I said. The carousel reached full speed and its barrel organ music drowned out his reply. When it stopped he sighed: '...so now you know that...'

"'Know what?' I said.

"He looked lost and said: 'That I am madly in love with you!'

"'You are what?' I said and laughed at him.

"'I said I'm madly in love with you and I want to meet you. I have to explain....'

"'It's not necessary to explain insanity,' I said and when I got off I pushed him away from me. He looked at me but didn't expect or notice the classic gesture of a pickpocket. So, I succeeded in snatching his car keys I had seen him put in the right pocket of his jacket.

"I went back to my car ignoring him. He followed, but pushing against the stream of park visitors he had difficulty expressing his romantic feelings or amorous intent without making a fool of himself.

"'Can't you see I'm not interested. Please leave me alone,' I said.

"'I don't want to bother you. I just want to introduce myself. Let me invite you for dinner at some nice place. Please, let me call you,' he said when I drove away. In my rearview mirror I saw him frantically searching his pockets for the car keys I had in my purse."

"You must not meet him alone," Ingrid advised. "It's a trap!"

"Maybe they want you out of your house," said Ted, "so they can go in and plant some bugs. Why don't you make a date with him? We'll keep an eye on your house while you're out. You might get some information from him."

Michele nodded. She had more to tell.

"From my listening post I have found out that Arnold is on a new trip with Mike, his copilot. This time to the Bahamas. They'll be back with a new load this week. They are blaming the New York people for our robberies and the New Yorkers are blaming Arnold and Cavallo. That's exactly what we wanted! Now all of them are thinking of revenge! And I am the one who'll get it!" She laughed.

"I don't think it would be very smart to strike against them here on the Cape," Ingrid pointed out. "If the New Yorkers take over the drug business here it will be a lot harder for us to fight them. Just think how convenient it is for you, Michele, to go upstairs, aim your bird watcher's microphone at Mr. Sprengler and get all the latest news!"

"Why don't we trace them to New York and hit them there?" Ted suggested.

"A good idea, but dangerous," Ingrid agreed. "You know, if we are going to operate in New York, a motorcycle is much better in city traffic than a car, so why don't we buy a good, fast motorcycle."

"Right!" Michele nodded her approval.

Ingrid changed subject. "I'm not terribly thrilled about storing eight million stolen dollars in my store! We have to come up with a good way to invest that money. Eight million at ten percent interest makes over two thousand dollars a day! We can only invest if the money is clean, so it has to be laundered. Seems we run into one illegal operation after the other."

Michele smiled. "OK. This is how it works," she said. "We show my friend on Wall Street a briefcase with say five hundred and fifty grand in bills. We deposit it. That is the collateral for a loan he will grant us for five hundred thousand. Formally he gives us the loan because we have good credit. We use the loan to buy stocks, junk bonds or real estate or whatever generates a quick profit. Or we buy a store and make daily deposits pretending it comes from sales, but in reality taken from our unlaundered reserve hidden in the basement.

"When we repay the loan my friend returns the briefcase with five hundred grand, keeping fifty for his help, and we start all over again. The money is cleaned, earned almost tax free thanks to wealthy lawmakers who decided to call this joke an investment."

"Terrific idea. Where did you learn that?" Ted asked.

"Everybody in finance knows that most drug money goes to Wall Street and overheats the market. All but our government! Or they believe that a rising DOW is a sign of health. Stupid people think it's daring investment!" Michele explained.

"I like the idea of robbing gangsters," Ingrid said, "but this is unlawful activity and against my principles."

"Listen, you must try to forget the ideals, morals and ethics of your old indoctrination. That's history, thanks to our self-healing economic system! We have twenty thousand illiterates! Where are the morals and ethics of a president cutting education but giving a twenty or fifty thousand dollar pay raise to everybody in the government, and still having the nerve to let the minimum wage in this country remain below poverty level."

Michele shook her head. "No, my friends, let go of such scruples as long as we don't take advantage of poor, hard-working, honest people. Washington is the guiding star when it comes to ethics and moral issues in America!"

Ingrid and Ted were speechless.

"If Sweden is the paradise for the stupid, this seems to be the paradise for the unscrupulous. Why do I love America?" Ted said.

"Because it's dynamic and you can change it," Michele smiled at him. "Americans will listen to arguments that make sense, but they are blinded by respect and admiration for men making money, talking tough and waving the Stars and Stripes."

The sun was setting and the sand had cooled down. The wine bottles and the picnic basket were empty and the trio declared the meeting closed. Michele agreed to meet with the lovesick stranger in the New York car and see if he had any information about how to strike against the "Bad Big Apple Boys."

Chapter 23

MICHELE ANSWERED HER phone.

"It's me, Bill!"

"Who's *me Bill*?"

"Oh, don't say you don't remember the love sick idiot in Sandwich!"

"I just forgot him! Feeling better now?"

"I feel fine, thank you. Would you possibly consider having lunch tomorrow with yours faithfully?"

"Let me see...tomorrow, why not, but don't count on my catching the bug. I'm too old for charmers and I'm definitely immune to what you're suffering from. What on earth turned your head, poor man? When and where should we meet?"

"I suggest Antony's at one. I'll pick you up!"

"Thanks, but I'd prefer meeting you there."

"OK! Great, I'm looking forward to it."

"See you there tomorrow at one. Goodbye."

She found a parking space not far from the entrance and walked slowly towards the restaurant. A new white Buick passed her and she saw the smiling face of the Sandwich man. His window slid down. Driving slowly beside her he apologized for his shameless suggestion to see her, but he was sure they would enjoy each other's company.

A valet parked his car and they walked in together. Michele was stunning in an all-white, chiffon dress she had purchased in Paris a few years before. It was designed in mid-calf length, draped softly over the shoulders and falling in graceful diagonal folds to one hip. Every woman and most of the men in the restaurant turned and followed her with admiring eyes. It wasn't difficult to hear "Who are they?" in the hum of voices. He was very good looking, too, and they made a most attractive couple.

They were given a table overlooking Cape Cod Bay. He offered her the best seat with the best view. He pulled out her chair and pushed it in when she sat down. Michele opened the conversation with: "So, Bill, what's your real name and what do you do for a living?"

"My name is William Gordon. I am originally from Long Island. Stayed with my grandmother in Providence, RI, and got an MBA from Brown. Then I studied law in Boston for a few years, but quit and got a degree in computer science instead. For several years I was with Data General. Now I have a job collecting data for a New York company. Very well paid, but not exactly what I'd prefer to do. Oh, by the way, I'm divorced. What do you do?"

"I'm a writer. I have traveled a lot and studied animal behavior. I write about animals. Nothing too deep…mostly children's books and short stories for some magazines and articles for a syndicate that publishes them in several daily papers. I read a lot. I'm a widow and my husband left me a pension that makes me independent, if I take good care of my money."

Bill was obviously a well-educated and highly intelligent mobster. Michele had difficulty getting any vital information from him. He said his boss was visiting the Cape and they were to meet the next morning at the Hyannis Regal Inn. Bill himself would probably stay for another week or two before returning to New York.

He was a pleasant and courteous man and a good conversationalist. Michele was amazed how quickly the time passed. She enjoyed his company. It was fun to go out with a man again. She detected a certain bitterness in the way he talked about himself. His job had separated him from his wife and his son had chosen to stay with his mother.

"There is only one thing for you to do," Michele advised him. "Quit that job! No job, no money is worth making you ruin your life and do things you dislike."

"You're being naive, Michele, you don't know the hard realities of life."

"Maybe, but there's always a way out. Are you in their hands? Do they have some hold on you?"

"Yes," he said but the next moment he regretted his quick reply. "I mean NO, I have a long-term contract...difficult to break."

"What happens if you walk out on them?"

"I just can't do that! But why are we talking about my job?"

"Because it gives you problems. I might be naive, but I can see through your mask. I don't know why I should be concerned with your problems if you neither care nor dare to take the necessary steps to solve them."

Michele changed the subject. "My best friends are going to a fashion show in New York in a few days. They've asked me to come along. Maybe your work here will be done by then and you'll be back in the City. We could meet and you could show us around, go to a concert or to some nice restaurants, or take in a Broadway show. Nothing fancy. I like good artistry".

They were silent for a time after finishing a superb luncheon of grilled and striped bass, followed by a dessert of baked pears in caramel-wine sauce with whipped cream served with crispy, almond lace-cookies.

"I'd be glad to show you my favorite places in New York, maybe not the fanciest, but certainly the best! And, of course, your friends are welcome to come along…as long as I get to see you. Just let me know when you'll be in the City."

When they were ready to leave Bill took a card from his wallet and with a gold pen wrote down a phone number. "This is to my hotel in Chatham, The Dolphin. Call me any morning before nine to tell when we can meet in New York. Promise?"

"OK! I also promise not to set you on fire again!"

Completely dumbfounded he stared at her with his mouth wide open. Then he grinned. "You recognize me! When did you first recognize me?"

"When I saw you in that car parked outside my house. When you wire-tapped my phone conversations with my neighbors," she said smiling back at him. "My specialty is to notice little things like little black boxes on our telephone lines, a car with New York plates parked in a place where nobody ever parks and people sitting all night long with headphones on, eating hot dogs, and drinking beer. See what I mean? You forgot to blend in. But why should I give a hoot! I like you and we could have a real good time together in New York."

They went outside into the warm sunshine.

"You're smarter than I thought," he said.

Michele shook her head. "No, my friend. I'm not particularly smart, but you're not as smart as you think you are. It's illegal to wire tap telephones, so your job must involve illegal activity unless you're a cop. You say you're not comfortable with it? I've just one word to say about your job and that is… *quit!*"

He looked thoughtfully at the ground, kicking a small stone and biting his lower lip. He forgot to ask the parking valet for his car.

He walked beside her in silence, suddenly aware how pleasant it was just being with her.

"I'm sorry, Bill, did my outspoken opinions ruin our pleasant meeting?"

"Yes, Michele, and no. I guess there's a point in one's life when we have to choose and say 'I want to go my own way, I want out!'"

They stopped at her rusty little car. She got in and rolled down the window. "Why don't you sit in here and tell me what it is you really want to talk about."

"Oh, it's just simple loneliness I guess."

He got in and pushed the seat back to make room for his long legs.

"Now, Bill. Tell Michele why you wanted to sneak into her home with a gun in your hand!"

"It's a bit complicated."

"I understand that. But if this is a second attempt at getting some information from me or to look for something you haven't succeeded in finding out so far, then you're welcome to come and look in my kitchen or my library or wherever. I've nothing to hide from you. I'm a very uninteresting person with a very quiet life and only a few close friends. I have overcome my loneliness by working, reading, writing, and listening to music. When I write, I live with the personalities I create. To me that works the same way as drinking alcohol. It stimulates me and I push aside my problems and let a lot of unexpected, thrilling, amusing and happy things happen to me. In my imagination I've already met a lot of men, much nastier and meaner than an armed intruder sneaking around my house. So I invented a couple of simple ways of creating respect."

"I'm truly sorry about my clumsy introduction," he said. "I really am. One day I'll be able to explain…"

"I think today is a splendid day for doing just that. I'm well aware you're not working for the FBI, or the Drug Enforcement Agency! Your employers must be highly suspicious people with significant resources. They work out of New York and have business contacts here on the Cape. Anyone with a little common sense and logic could figure that out. I combine these facts with what I read in our local papers: There were two or three gruesome, drug-related murders here last winter and the police seized a shipment of cocaine. But guess what? It all disappeared from the police facilities without a trace! Stolen from the cops! Everything points to a well-organized drug business here."

Bill listened to her and nodded.

She continued, "Cape Cod has a long coastline, excellent for smuggling goods from passing ships. In the summer the Cape offers an enormous drug market, with millions of visitors and thousands of kids on school vacations working here. I understand that the dealers are really rough guys and tough to do business with and that helping hands might have difficulty explaining their real local occupation. Right? Yes, I think you are one of them! I feel sorry for you because it demands an awful lot of courage and determination, preparation and planning to build up a base that makes it possible to walk away. They scare you and at the same time they dangle a carrot at you."

"This is a horrible accusation! I..."

"Bill, if you value good friendship you have to be honest."

"But, how can you know all this?"

"Don't you see? I don't know anything! I just put observations together and assume. I have no intention of going to the police telling them what I assume: First, because they are not interested in the suspicions of little old ladies; second, because it's their job to do that kind of thinking and they don't want anybody to tell them how to do it; and third, because I think there are policemen on your company's payroll. If I knew anything and told them, it wouldn't take long until I had some serious accident, was found drowned or run-over or dead from an overdose or suicide. Your colleagues are very clever at   finding ways to make unwanted people disappear. But don't worry, I won't tell. After all I don't know anything for sure, I have no evidence, no proof and it's none of my business! Also, I see no reason for making things worse for you. I have more constructive and pleasant things to do."

He scratched himself carefully under his chin still tender because the blisters were not completely gone. His longing to be her lover had cooled, but he enjoyed talking with her. This was a subject he really wanted to discuss with an intelligent person. But he couldn't think of anything more to say because he didn't dare talk too much.

"If there is any way I can help, please let me know," Michele offered.   "Personally, I know that you, and only you, can do something for you. Right? Still, I can't think of one good reason for you to pay me a visit at night with a gun in your hand!"

She knew only too well he'd be in deep trouble if he said anything more. She was glad he didn't attempt to lie to her.

Chapter 24

MICHELE GOT A tremendous kick out of her masquerade performances. For this particular caper she chose a skintight white jogging suit, a red wig, an oversized nose with clear signs of too many Martinis. This plus a heavy exaggerated eye makeup and a dark plum-tinted lipstick transforming her face into that of a tough broad. The man at the Hyannis Regal's front desk couldn't tear his eyes away from her bouncy oversized bust and brushed his hand against it as he handed her a registration card to fill in. She didn't object.

She spoke with a heavy Texas accent: "Well, young man, my glasses don't go with my outfit so I can't wear them. Please do the writing for me? And please put me in a room close to 305."

Her long silver nails sparkled when she handed him a business card and a 10-dollar bill. He chuckled to himself recognizing the common excuse from women believing they look younger when not wearing glasses.

"Sure, Ma'am, 306 is just across the hall." As he wrote her name he read aloud: "Monica Haricot, Houston, Texas. Work: Neiman Marcus," then he looked up and asked:

"Your car, Ma'am?"

"Oh, a red convertible with white leather interior!"

"Brand?"

"Yeah. Sure it's brand new!"

"Of course, but what brand? What model?"

"A BMW, naturally!"

"BMW, what else!" he muttered.

"Texas plates of course?" he asked.

"Texas, of course," she nodded. He made a sweeping wave calling a young bellhop over to take care of her two bags.

***

Bill looked at his watch. He was scheduled to have breakfast with Bolivar in the Regal's tavern at 8:30. Michele watched them and sat down at a table next to theirs. She was sure Bill wouldn't recognize her. The two men had a hearty American breakfast loaded with cholesterol and calories: eggs, greasy bacon, and fat-soaked home- fried potatoes. Observing them as they ate Michele wondered idly why on earth is it called home-fried?

Why do people ruin perfectly good potatoes in such an unpalatable way? Our poor hearts! Maybe the Good Lord wanted these hardened hearts to beat only a few more years. She read the "Houston Chronicle" while enjoying her own simple breakfast of tea and toast with honey and cheese, and a glass of orange juice.

When the men were ready to leave, Michele rose and put her hand on Bolivar's shoulder. In a slow Texan drawl she asked: "Didn't you work for us in Houston, Sir?" Her nimble, soft fingers tucked a miniature battery-size bug under his collar and she continued: "Didn't we dance at that Wilson's party back in May?"

Bolivar showed an unexpected sense of humor when he patted her cheek and said: "Yeah, we sure did, didn't we? Your name was…?"

She enjoyed the game and wanted it to go on so she kept quiet.

"Yeah, now I remember," he said. "You're Betty! Betty Hog! Aren't you?"

"Hog! You gotta be kidding? I hate Betty Hog! No, my name is Monica. Monica Haricot, but call me Monique and I'd love to prance around the floor with you again. How about tonight if you're coming here for the dance. You'll find me in the bar around 9. Please come."

Bolivar squeezed her shoulder. "Sure, Monique, sure! See you then! Come on, Bill, we've got things to do." He smiled and smacked his lips and the two men went to his room. "What a hot chick, Bill! I'm gonna bounce her all over the place tonight. Wow! I had a chance to feel her butt. Delicious, my friend, and made to order for a full dose of my special sex aerobics." He rolled his eyes and laughed his best locker room laugh.

The men opened their briefcases and sat down at the table.

"OK, Bill, what's new?"

"I've kept an eye on the people around Arnold's place. That's a waste of time. They're not involved. We had their houses bugged and their phone calls taped. There isn't the slightest sign of involvement. But our friend Arnold has been busy. He's a smart sonofagun. He left for the Bahamas, as you predicted, with his own money! Our plans must have gone wrong, because last night he called home and talked to his daughter and said he would be back today. He called from Otis Air Force Base. Also, it was Cavallo's Jaguar the robbers used for the hijacking a few nights ago. We're bugging Cavallo. They probably know it because they play innocent and don't say a thing!"

"Cavallo is a damned backstabbing bastard! Here he has a chance to work with honest distributors and he cheats us one time after another and has the gall to go on with it," Bolivar snorted. "I had my connection in Nassau rig a little trick to get back the five mill they took from us last time. Four boys and a three-million-dollar Cerutto were in position and this Arnold character blew the boat and all our guys straight up to heaven! Not even their pants came down, but Arnold's money arrived alright!"

Bill took a big flat bottle of bourbon from his briefcase. He held it up for approval showing Bolivar the label. The big man nodded and Bill filled the glasses to the brim.

"If they have the nerve to try again, and they might, we've got to wipe them out and handle Cape Cod ourselves. What I want you to do is to find out about their local distribution network, which people they're working with and how much this district is worth. It's a good area because the people from Providence are working here. They are pros, you know, and big, very big, even by New York standards. They don't go for lean markets, but I don't want to start a war with them." Bolivar had spoken slowly. He sipped his bourbon.

"I met a girl!" Bill said, "and I want a few days off to see her in New York next weekend. Nothing special seems to be happening here anyway, and I'll give you the facts you need before then."

***

Ingrid and Ted sat with Michele in room 306. They had headphones on and listened.

"Now, Michele, you know what you can expect after the dance! Strange, I thought men like him liked big behinds not those cute little buns you walk around with," Ted teased.

"He loves anything and everything as long as it's a woman, It's exciting to fool these guys. I can't wait to knock them down and out."

"I think we have to stop them," Ingrid said, "…and Arnold and the Chatham people and get them all behind bars. Why on earth are you taking this risk going dancing with that creepy snake tonight?"

"I want to be sure that everything works out my way. Listen! He plans to be in New York tomorrow night and at the headquarters the following morning! My plan is taking form. I bought a Yamaha motorcycle and tried it yesterday. Fabulous! Now let's go. Our tape recorder can do the listening now. We aren't needed until tonight."

The Regal's bar was crowded that evening. Michele saw her reflection in the mirror and mused "What a bride!" She had been in her room and checked the tape recorder and packed her things, ready for a fast getaway. She found a seat at the bar and ordered a Smirnoff-martini straight up with an olive.

Bolivar came alone. "Bill couldn't make it. He was trying to call some girl he met the other day, but she was out. So..."

"Well, nice to see you again. Had a busy day? What keeps you busy anyway? Still working for Neiman Marcus? Or are you your own boss now?"

"Yeah, kind of. I have a company in New York. I'm here to check on some complications with a Cape Cod subsidiary in the lobster business, so I would like us to have lobster after the drinks."

She found out that he had his office on Fifth Avenue overlooking Central Park. He also had an apartment just around the corner, only a couple of minutes' walk from the office. He loved New York, he said. He earned enough money to do and have whatever pleased him...girls, shows, girls, dancing, girls!

"I fly to Atlantic City once a week. Generally I win more than I lose. I enjoy a smart opponent in poker," he told her.

"So do I," she said.

They got a table. He ordered champagne and lobster. They danced. He clutched her in a viselike grip and took turns squeezing her fanny and moving up to her bosom. Michele found him to be surprisingly humorous and playful and an excellent dancer. He obviously found her sexy because while dancing he pressed her close, so close his enormous erection almost hurt her. She held her arm around his bull neck and tried over and over to find the transmitter she had planted under his collar the same morning. She clung closer and searched franticly, but could not find the bug.

"You're a great dancer," he said. "You promise a lot and he bent down and kissed her neck leaving his mark. "Why so silent. Did I hold you too close?"

She felt confused. "No, no. I love it" she said and made another desperate attempt to get the bug. Had he found it? Did he suspect her of being out to get him? He was a dangerous man. She knew this was not just playing with fire; this was dancing with a poisonous snake...like her Native Indian ancestors. She was nervous for if he knew the truth he would kill her with his bare hands and with a fiendish smile on his face. Slowly a feeling of terror made her insecure and jittery. He was the kind of sex-crazy guy who thoroughly enjoyed rape.

Michele danced like a wound up toy doll. He did a terrific tango. She performed the turns and twists, but he was too excited to move and held her tightly pressing her against his erection. Michele was relieved when they sat down to a lobster dinner. He gobbled his food and consumed champagne by the bottle.

She excused herself, went to the ladies' room and called Ted giving him instructions. "He's a real bull; hope I'll come out of this alive," she said before she hung up. Returning to the table she walked around him diverting him by the provocative movement of her hips. Stroking his neck and shoulders she could feel the antenna! It was still in place. She ordered a double Scotch.

"This is the best with lobster and champagne," she said and poured the Scotch into her champagne. "Try this! I love it! A 'Texas Smoother', that's what we call it. Gives you an alcohol high! Taste how smooth it is! Like it?"

He emptied the glass in two gulps. They were on their third bottle of champagne when he had to go to the men's room again. His heavy drinking made his visits there frequent. Each time he left the table Michele poured her whiskey into his glass or into the flowerpots behind her. Each time he returned his face was redder than before and he was recharged with physical desire.

He was on his sixth mix of Scotch and champagne. She wanted to dance; she wanted to find the bug. And dance they did. Couples stopped to watch them do the tango. In spite of his enormous alcohol consumption he danced very well. People around them applauded. When the music finally stopped she embraced him. Hanging around his bull neck she pulled out the tiny little transmitter. She took a deep breath of relief.

"Gosh, Fred Astaire, you sure know how to turn me on!" she teased.

"Old and bold! But I can show you a good time."

"Oh, you're the best," she cooed. "It's time for some real fun, you know, just the two of us. Upstairs..."

His face lit up. She handed him his seventh "Texas Smoother" and he gulped it down with a big 'aaahhhh!'

"Let's go!" he said. He held his arm around her all the way to his door. Ted waited silently for them in the hall. As they passed him, he handed Michele the plastic bags he had hidden under his jacket. She held them behind her back. Bolivar unlocked the door and Michele barely had time to kick the plastic bags under the bed before he unzipped his pants, grabbed her roughly and kissed her with animal passion.

She let one hand slide from his bull neck down to his crotch. She took a firm grip around his pulsing erection and whispered to him: "Get this one ready for me. I have to run to my room to put a little hat in place, if you know what I mean! Why don't you undress and hold this one tight so it won't shrink. I don't like men in rubber suits, I want you as you are, so we'll go with just my little hat in place! OK? I feel super wild. I'll be back in a flash!"

She helped him untie his necktie and nibbled at his ear. Then she went directly to her own room where Ted was waiting ready to help. She tore off the wig and pulled on a dark blue sweater. They grabbed her bags and rushed downstairs. Ingrid was waiting in her car.

"You called the police?" Michele asked.

"Yes, I did, as you can see!"

With flashing lights three police cruisers stopped at the entrance. Several policemen and a policewoman ran into the hotel.

***

"When we arrived," the police officer reported, "his door was not fully closed and this perverted rapist was sprawled naked on his bed gripping his enormous…you guess what…with both hands! A real funny sight. And we found two pounds of cocaine hidden under his bed!" The policewoman blushed. "I was the first one on the scene", she said.

The officer in charge reported: "He's in custody, of course. This is the second time we have arrested this man. We have reason believe he's a major dope dealer! We'll keep him for a while and set a really stiff bail. His bags with dope are from the same shipment as the ones stolen from the police last year."

"What did he say in his defense?"

"He was pretty drunk, and blabbered something about a Texas redhead who wanted to seduce him. The person who called us said the lady involved had been too upset to make the call. She had reported that the man we arrested is a sex maniac and a well-known drug dealer, who forced her to use cocaine, then tried to rape her and threatened to kill her.

Chapter 25

"MELANCHOLY MELODIES CAN be like whimsical, sad butterflies, it seemed to Ingrid, as the crystal clear tunes of a flute shyly fluttered out from Michele's backyard. Ingrid was checking her mailbox when she first heard the fragile wafts of music. Reluctantly, she walked over to her friend's house feeling like an intruder when she found Michele sitting on her deck playing the flute. She repeated the melody, almost whispering, very sensitive, very moving, very lonely.

There was a silence and Ingrid said in a low voice: "Michele, are you crying?" Michele turned around with her eyes full of tears trying to smile. She nodded and looked down.

"Dear Mich, may I sit here with you for a while?"

Michele nodded again. Ingrid kneeled and embraced her friend touching the tear-filled eyes with her cheeks, comforting, kissing, and whispering: "My lonely little friend. I heard your flute saying: 'come and comfort me I'm so desperately lonely.'"

Michele took a deep breath and said: "It's tough to be tough all the time, when you really aren't tough at all! I miss my Rich so much. I'm so darned lonely and incomplete without him. And, I feel so lousy, so darned lousy, about what I did yesterday. It doesn't help that I keep telling myself Bolivar is an evil and rotten, ruthless, merciless murderer. He is killing thousands of fine young boys and girls, or turning them into helpless, hopeless wrecks with his damned dope. Few of his victims will ever be OK again. He gets rich selling despair especially to parents seeing their children crushed and broken and destroyed. He is the symbol of everything I loathe—degeneration, viciousness, selfishness and greed.

"Yesterday I double-crossed him, I played with him like in a crazy snake dance. I am ashamed of myself. I behaved in such a mean and calculating way that I scared myself." She paused, sighed and continued: "It was a real snake dance. You know there is a ceremonial American Indian dance performed by my ancestors, The Wampanoags, where the brave warriors dance with live, poisonous snakes, juggling with them throwing them high up in the air, kissing them and treating them disrespectfully, while the hissing reptiles tried to stab their fangs into the dancer. A symbolic way to demonstrate superiority over a calculating, intelligent and unpredictable killer and an unwanted intruder or dangerous enemy, but I wasn't sure of the victory. I was so scared.

"How could I behave like that! Revenge is no excuse for uncivilized behavior. I didn't know if he was playing with me the same way I was playing with him. He got so aroused he kept pressing me against him in a tight grip. His big thing was so hard it hurt. It was disgusting! Going to his room was really lunacy. I'm relieved everything went as planned. And did I ever get him drunk! He must have a heck of a hangover right now!"

They laughed.

"I planted the dope under his bed and I accused him of rape and drug dealing! The police locked him up because of my lies. I sure got him into a sticky jam! But could he dance! People applauded when we did the tango. There were moments when I forgot who he really was and let myself go wild and it made me happy, happy. A man is so good to have - not only as a lover but also a true friend.

I'm hungry for a really good man. Sometime I wonder why life has been so cruel and freakish to me.

"This Bolivar is a funny weirdo in a way. Boy! Was it a thrill to find out I still can turn a man on and light his fire! I'm so glad you came by Ingrid." She sat quietly, then asked: "You must be happy, aren't you?"

"Yes, I am. I'm very happy, but most of what I experience as happiness is not wild exaltation, but more the feeling of living a richer life than most people do, thankful for my few friends with whom I share a feeling of togetherness—friends intelligent and sensitive enough to express themselves in words or deeds and taking their time to find ways to work out their problems. I'm happy doing a meaningful, creative job, but also doing little things like baking a good cake, knitting a new sweater, or planting bulbs in the fall and watching them come up in early spring. I'm happy I have a friend like you, Michele, with whom I can talk about anything, serious or crazy, real or dreamy, smart or dumb. And I have a husband I've loved since I was a girl, a man I know like a book. Yes, we are still crazy about each other. Yes, I consider myself a happy woman."

"Sometimes when I'm alone in the dark, I think of you and Ted," Michelle sighed. "I wish I could do as you can—just stretch out my hand and touch the man I love, surprise him with a big bear hug and get one in return. Just holding hands would make the loneliness and the demons in the shadows go away. Because they get real sometimes. Branches from the big tree sweeping the walls and roof create sounds like evil intruders, sneaking around killing people just to satisfy sick minds."

Ingrid noticed Michele's melancholy returning while talking about her loneliness. "Please, play something for me!"

"I will. I love this. It's my favorite. Mozart."

It seemed as though the notes from the Flute Concerto began as tiptoeing out of Michele's flute, then jumping out, and finally emerging in a dancing stream bringing harmony and contentment to both player and listener.

After finishing the piece Michele was stimulated, full of energy and ready for action. She and Ingrid listened to the tape from Bill's and Bolivar's conversation. They discussed Bolivar's plan to go back to New York early Friday afternoon, and Bill's free weekend to see his girl. Bolivar instructed Bill to drop by the Fifth Avenue office on Saturday morning for breakfast.

"We'll have to tail them to find out the address," Ingrid said. "That weekend we're going to the fashion show. Why don't you join us?"

Ingrid's friends usually got excited when she talked about fashion shows. They didn't realize there is very little glamour but mostly hard work at shows in Paris, Milan, Florence, or New York.

"The first day," Ingrid would explain, "we walk through the whole show taking notes about things we like. When we have seen it all we take a break and discuss what to buy. We visit the interesting booths and have a close look at prices and things. The second day we do the buying. It's hard work. Miles and miles of walking, decisions, calculations, and projections. We buy only what's 'us', ignoring pushy salespeople. You're welcome to come along, Michele. There are lots of nice clothes to see, especially from Europe and California. Sometimes we don't buy anything, just check that my design is on the right track."

Michele decided to go along. She wanted to do some shopping and she wanted to see Bill.

"By the way", she said, "this morning I burned the red wig. If Bolivar ever found out that I was his redhead Texas doll, I guess he'd lose his sense of humor in a snap. Don't you think so?"

Chapter 26

SITTING ASTRIDE THE motorcycle Ted watched Bolivar leaving the hotel. Ingrid and Michele in the Fiesta were parked five miles ahead and were to start driving only when they heard Ted tell them over the radio that Bolivar was on his way. Keeping in radio contact they alternated the tailing in order not to be noticed. Ted saw the limo stop in Seventy-first Street, a man get out carrying a big trunk and Bolivar's Lincoln continue around the corner down Fifth Avenue. It stopped in front of an impressive entrance with a canopy awning and a uniformed doorman. Minutes later Ingrid and Michele parked a few hundred yards down the Avenue. Michele didn't waste any time. She jumped out of the car, rushed into Central Park and set up her tripod with the listening gear.

She watched the skies in the west become wine red. An orange sun was sinking in a bank of purple and gray over New Jersey. People coming home turned on their lights and TVs and in the dark silhouettes of the New York skyline thousands of windows lit up looking like small greenish stars. In Bolivar's building few apartments were lit up but Michele was able to find the window she wanted with little difficulty. She envied people leaving the steaming city on such a weekend. A gang of rowdy kids interfering with her filming in the dark forced her to return to her friends.

At the St. Moritz they took a two-bedroom suite with a great view overlooking Central Park. Michele aimed her parabolic microphone at Bolivar's rooms and through the telephoto lens she got a good idea of what was going on in there, but the street noise made it impossible to hear anything. Her phone rang. It was Bill. She asked him to join them for dinner at the Russian Tea Room a few blocks away.

"I never had dinner with a gangster!" Ingrid said when Michele told he was joining them. "Exciting isn't it!"

Bill, splendidly attired in a dark blue tux, was waiting in the bar. They had martinis before walking to the restaurant. The night was balmy and the hectic pulse of the big city was a stimulating contrast to the sleepy pace of Cape Cod. For dinner Bill suggested blinis with caviar and vodka, then borscht, followed by genuine Polish duck breasts. His conversation was casual and full of interesting and amusing stories from an adventurous life. He paid Michele every possible attention, which she enjoyed tremendously. She told him her schedule for the next day: Early morning, jogging in Central Park before noon, some shopping, and then lunch with him, if he had the time and felt like it. She hadn't been to the Museum of Modern Art for years and would like to go there if he'd join her.

"… And", he suggested, "I could try to get four tickets to 'Les Miserables'."

It was almost midnight when they finally went back to the hotel. Bill left and sauntered down Central Park South whistling.

"Charming man, Mich!" Ingrid raised her eyebrows looking at Michele.

"Yes, isn't he? He's part of my plan for tomorrow."

The following morning Bill was walking up Fifth Avenue when he ran into Michele jogging out of Central Park. She slowed down, turned and walked beside him, following him to Bolivar's. They decided to meet at the St. Moritz around noon. She gave him a quick hug and at the same time managed to pin her little bug onto his jacket. He disappeared into Bolivar's house and she walked over to a parking lot where Ingrid was waiting in a rented car. They activated the radio receiver and the tape recorder, locked the car and left.

"Don't you feel bad playing sly games with Bill?"

"Nope! I'm not hurting him. I'm just letting him help me get some information. Or do you suggest we let them go on with business as usual? No way!"

Ted and Ingrid took the commuter bus to the fashion show at the Javits Center while Michele went to her room, showered and did what ladies do when they get ready for a heavy date—putting nail polish on her fingernails and toenails, blow-drying her freshly shampooed hair and spending a lot of time in front of the mirror applying a perfect make-up. Shortly before noon Bill called and announced he was downstairs. Michele gave herself an approving nod in the mirror. She was sure her well-cut English suit with a smart, small hat a la '30's were just right.

Bill met her at the elevator, took her outstretched hand and kissed her on each cheek. She tingled at the feel of his smoothly-shaven skin against hers. They had coffee in the hotel cafe and decided to go to the Museum of Modern Art.

After hours of art walk and talk they spent another full hour in the museum's gift shop during which she managed to unfasten the bug without Bill noticing. She bought a couple of art books and was extremely pleased with her day. They walked towards Fifth Avenue.

"Tired?" he asked.

"No, happy!"

"Let's go shopping. I'll carry your MOMA books."

They took a taxi to Saks. She found an English trench coat for the winter, went over to Lord's, saw a coat there she liked but returned to Saks deciding on the one there. He paid.

"Tired?" she asked.

"No, happy!"

She couldn't resist patting his cheek. He was a great guy to be with, no doubt about it. What a pity he was a thug!

"Where are you staying?" she asked.

"At the Penta, should we go there?"

"You are a darling, Bill."

"I love you, Michele, I do."

"That's fine, I like you too. Let's get to know each other a bit better."

"The reply I hoped for! You're wise and tough!"

"Much, much tougher than you think, my dear, and I ask a lot of a man."

"So what are the requirements?"

"A gentleman, intelligent, compatible, creative, honest. A man with class and a heart."

"That could be me."

"Ten or 20 years ago, maybe."

"I was nothing then, come on!"

"I would love to love you, Bill! The good, honest you."

They walked by the Penta. She said a definite no thanks to his invitation to go in for a drink.

"You certainly are in charge of yourself."

"Always will be. Love being with you though."

"Really?"

"Can't you feel it?"

"I'll boost my feelings tonight!"

He stopped a taxi, gave the driver a ten-dollar bill, and asked him to drop Michele at the St. Moritz. Well in her room, she threw the box with the new coat on a chair and herself on the bed, kicked off her shoes and gratefully accepted the martini Ingrid offered her.

"Been shopping?"

"Yes, open it up and have a look."

"Great! Oh, I love it!" Ingrid said and swept the coat around her admiring herself in the mirror.

Ted had picked up the tape with the conversation between Bill and Bolivar. Michele started it. There was Bolivar's voice and Bill's. Bolivar was angry. He swore over a red-haired police tart and was so mad at himself for walking straight into her trap. The judge had demanded $75,000 in bail!

"Seventy-five grand! Hear that! And I was the victim! Completely innocent! She planted that cocaine in my room, but they didn't believe me! She said I had raped her! Can you believe it! They didn't believe me! I regret I didn't rape her! That damned bitch, she outsmarted me!

"Nobody knew anything about her. Nada! She just vanished into thin air. Which shows she's a cop. It took me till Tuesday to get out of the slammer. Hear that! For the second time in my life— the second time in one week! Bill, you take over the Cape distribution. I'll never set foot there again."

They heard Bill saying he was sorry to hear the dancing ended in jail, and couldn't help asking: "Did she dance well?"

"Yes dammit. But don't you get hooked like that. Have a good time with that broad of yours. See you Monday."

"She's not a broad. She is very much a lady."

"The best are the worst and the worst are the best!"

"She's a good woman and I need the company of at least one decent human being."

"Buy your needs for God's sake! I pay you enough to pay for 10 bimbos."

"Don't you tell me how to handle women!"

"Get lost!"

Some movements were heard. A woman's voice announced that Tom and Ben were waiting. Then Bill's voice said: "Be careful boys, he's sour today. He stepped on a mine! Ended up in the slammer. If you laugh he'll kill you!"

"Ouch! Now he might get the pitch that bad things could happen to good people! What are you doing tonight?"

"I'm off, seeing some lawful people."

"I didn't know you knew any."

Bolivar's voice came closer.

"I expect you back tomorrow morning for our usual breakfast meeting at 10, OK? Now, hit the road and come back with a nice bunch of orders."

They heard a door slam, Bill's steps, the escalator, steps, and street noise, honking cars, horses clopping along Fifth Avenue, Bill whistling. The sound died off when the bug was too far from the receiver. Michele, Ingrid and Ted listened a second time to the tape and destroyed it.

Bill picked Michele up at seven and they started the evening with dinner at "Le Coque au Vin," where Madame La Patronne suggested goose breasts fried in butter, spiced with fennel and garlic encircled with brandy-fried mushrooms, and hazel potatoes. For dessert Madame served her homemade carrot cake and coffee with a snifter of pear brandy.

After the theater Bill took Michele back to the hotel where in a laughing and joking mood they kissed good night and Bill walked away whistling happily. He was in love.

Chapter 27

THE COMMUTER BUSES to the fashion show stop at the big hotels picking up people in the rag trade from all over the US, and shuttling them to the Javits Center, New York's Expo Center. This complex of steel tubes, glass and concrete "should never have been built," Prince Charles of England probably would have said...if asked.

Ingrid and Ted went to work, observing the new fashion trends, asking prices, making notes of interesting things to buy. Meanwhile Michele left the hotel and headed for Central Park which is at its best on Sunday mornings with fresh, still unpolluted air, greenery sprinkled with dew, children playing, families walking and joggers sweating, huffing and puffing. Scattered groups of exhausted young people with hangovers are in no condition to bother anyone.

Michele, dressed in a jogging suit, was carrying her big tennis bag with the video and listening gear. She found a quiet spot and zoomed in on the upper level and the corner windows of Bolivar's main office. She listened.

There he was, ordering his secretary to bring in coffee and apple cinnamon muffins. Michele couldn't see Bolivar sitting in his chair, but she heard his secretary announcing Tom and Ben, and moments later new voices. It was hard to hear what they said. They were too far from the window. But Bolivar spoke in a thundering voice.

"OK, boys, how was business last night?"

Some mumbling. More mumbling.

"OK! I want you to come to my private place at 3 sharp and bring this week's money from the whole district along with your orders. Capito? And Tom, tomorrow around 4:30 you'll take the afternoon plane to Nassau and find out exactly what happened down there. Four of our guys were blown to hell when collecting money from the New Englanders. Report back Thursday. Bunny has your tickets. Ben, you work in the Village and report back to me if you have problems with competitors. No credits OK? This meeting is over."

Michele quickly folded the tripod and walked closer to the entrance with the tall uniformed attendant. She watched Tom and Ben coming out, two young men in striped, gray three-piece suits and soft felt hats. They looked exactly as if cut out of a Mafia movie. Both wore scarlet buttonhole carnations. A black Lincoln stopped, the doorman opened the door and the two gangsters disappeared into the limousine. Michele got their pictures on the video.

"I need to talk to Ingrid and Ted about this. A fast strike, just a good jab, but psychologically a pretty heavy punch in Bolivar's solar plexus," she said to herself as she walked through the park back to the St. Moritz. In the hotel room she studied the videotape to make sure she'd recognize the two men. On her way out she left her bag with the video camera in the deposit booth in the lobby and took a taxi to the Javits Center. She rushed up and down the aisles looking for Ingrid and Ted. She finally spotted them at a display featuring California clothes, but they had to complete their ordering before they could listen to her.

"We have a quick job to do right away. You have to come along. We have to be at Bolivar's place before three."

To confuse and discourage any possible pursuers they left by a back door, got a taxi and walked the last block entering by a rear door through the hotel's garage.

Michele asked Ted to get the motorcycle and drive over to Bolivar's private place. "You park outside and try to get in through the door. Two gentlemen will be coming there at exactly three o'clock carrying a suitcase that I intend to snatch! Ingrid and I will escape on the motorcycle while you, Ted, walk away."

Ted parked outside Bolivar's entrance. The license plate on the motorcycle had been changed. Michele had taped a New York plate over the registered one! A lady with a poodle walked up to the entrance, Ted followed her and held the door open. She looked at him. He said good afternoon and she merely nodded. She entered the elevator. He waited, thinking this is crazy. How on earth would two women manage to rob two ruthless gangsters?

Precisely at ten minutes of three he watched his women coming. Without any sign of recognition he opened the door for Michele. Ingrid waited outside, holding a large, empty shopping bag with a Saks logo.

"OK," Michele whispered, "Ingrid is coming in with them. You, Ted, wait in the elevator and when they enter, you walk out. I'll be here."

"Yes, I understand, but this is crazy!"

"It will work O.K., Ted. Stay cool. If we run into trouble, your job is to cover us when we drive off. Stop them if they follow, or shoot."

"I don't have a gun!"

"So! Find out some other way to stop them!"

Time passed slowly. A couple of minutes before 3 Ingrid picked up her purse and looked inside.

"That's the signal," said Michele.

A big black limo pulled up outside. Ingrid moved toward the entrance. Two men got out of the car and walked up to the door passing her. Each carried a briefcase. They pressed the bell to Bolivar's apartment and waited for the buzz. It came. The door opened and the men let Ingrid enter first. Ted walked out from the elevator, held the door open for Michele, who went in followed by the two men and Ingrid. The door closed. Ted waited. Sweat was pouring down his forehead and along his spine. His innocent Ingrid and this crazy Michele together fighting those mobsters!

When the elevator finally came back down Ingrid walked out carrying a large shopping bag. Michele followed, stepping quickly over two men lying on the elevator floor with glazed, unseeing eyes. Ted reached in, pressed the top floor button, backed out and closed the door. An elderly man approached the elevator, which had not yet started. Ted pressed his foot against the steel door while pulling the handle pretending to open it.

"There is something wrong with this door," he said

"Who are you?" the old man asked, scrutinizing Ted.

"I'm visiting Mr. Bolivar."

"Mr. Who? There is no Mr. Bolivar living in this building! Now let me try that door!"

At that moment the elevator finally decided to start, moving slowly upward with its sleeping load. The elderly gentleman shook his head, nodding to Ted as he left the lobby. The limo was waiting outside. Ted saw his two women on the motorcycle turn the corner, and he heard the high-powered sound of the Yamaha speeding down Fifth Avenue. He tried to walk slowly in the opposite direction but after 200 yards or so he started to run. He flagged a cab on Madison Avenue and got to the Javits Center, where he caught up with Ingrid and Michele. They were sitting on a low concrete wall licking ice cream cones! Tensions slowly eased and they all laughed.

"That must have been your first hit without a false nose! Wasn't it, Michele?"

"Yes! I wished we had worn some kind of disguise."

"How did you knock them out?" Ted asked. "I couldn't believe my eyes! They were completely zonked!"

"They didn't have a chance! We stunned them. We each had a stun gun and we simply put those things to work on their necks from behind. They fell like butchered bulls. To be sure I gave them a minor tranquilizer shot. They looked young and in good shape. Hope they have strong hearts!"

She smiled and licked her ice cream.

The phony license plate on the motorcycle was removed and a couple of minutes later Ted stopped at a garage and paid the parking boys to keep the motorcycle there for a week. He found a place nearby where they could pack the briefcases and send them by UPS to the store in Osterville. He took a cab back to the fashion show. To avoid the crowd at closing time they left the show early. When their taxi turned the corner some hundred yards from the hotel they saw Bill leaving the entrance. He looked around as if checking to see if he was being followed, then he walked away rapidly.

"I guess his visit wasn't that all unexpected," Michele said when they headed straight for the bar and ordered three very dry martinis.

"He probably went through all our things!" Ted commented. Sipping her drink Michele said: "Everything compromising has been removed. He couldn't have found anything!"

Ingrid turned to Michele. "I feel sorry for you. You wanted Bill to be very special to you. I don't think he is. He can be quite dangerous to us."

"You know, Ingrid, I think I understand Bill. He's like an alcoholic. Only a few strong people manage to get out of the mess he's in. He's like Arnold. And I'm pretty sure that Mike, the young pilot flying with Arnold, will end up with the same disease unless some miracle girl changes his life. Circumstances, desires, weakness and greed get a tight grip on them and they get carried away. Criminality, or 'social maladjustment' if you will, is sometimes like an illness.

"Prison terms or fines don't help. We treat them the same way we treated lunatics a hundred years ago. We protect ourselves from them and don't give a damn what happens with them! Often they're also alcoholics or on drugs. Their egos won't accept minor roles or low positions. They're not part of our society. They believe they are superior to others and predestined to make big, fast money."

Ted and Ingrid were still uneasy about Bill's visit to their rooms. But the martini had relaxed Michele and relieved any feeling of danger and so she continued her monologue on social responsibility:

"Everybody involved with crime isn't a hardened criminal. Most first-time offenders will stay away from crime if they're put on probation and given the right opportunities. That's a fact in other western countries. Programs providing jobs, housing, education and childcare would prevent most crime in the US. We say we cannot afford it, still such programs would cost society less than we're now paying for imprisonment.

"I feel sorry for Bill," Michele went on. "He's smart and tough but he'll find out that I'm a tough cookie, too! I don't fall for hugs and kisses and soft talk even though I might enjoy them! You don't have to worry about me."

Ingrid nodded and said: "In our society fear is big business. Insurance companies and their agents or stockholders have no interest in preventing crime-lowering insurance rates because it's their income. People's fear makes probation an unpopular solution to crime prevention. Most people doubt that criminals could be productive taxpayers."

Ted slid down from the bar chair. "Why don't I leave you two here to solve the problems of our society. We're thieves, too! Every thief can rationalize his behavior. In India we would probably have been high-ranking members of the thieves' caste! What about dinner? Michele, why don't you call Bill?"

"I'd prefer not to."

"It might be a good idea to show our innocent faces."

"That's true. He's suspicious but he's not a big problem. I sure hope the two tranquilized guys won't remember our faces," Michele said.

Ted wanted something light and tasty for supper and made reservations at the Jockey Club next door. They changed for dinner and Michele phoned Bill. He sounded upset.

"My boss called about a serious incident. He asked me to stay here in New York for a while to work on a new investigation. I've already started."

"Sorry to hear. I had a very busy day and must have walked about 10,000 miles at that fashion show! Now I'd like to relax and have dinner with you. Please come over and join us in about an hour."

***

Michele, Ingrid and Ted met Bill in the lobby and they walked over to the club. They sat down. Bill seemed eager to talk. "Two of our men have been robbed. It was two robbers, probably two men dressed like women. There was a witness," Bill said, "an old man who seemed to have everything mixed up. He said he didn't have his reading glasses on, but he had talked to a man who's name was Bolivar, which my boss found strange. I was sent out right away to check the situation. The robbers escaped on a motorcycle. This town is full of gangsters."

"Most crimes are committed within the criminal society," Ted said. "Prostitutes get murdered, gangsters shoot gangsters, drug dealers steal from other dealers, and so on. The victims could have some connection with the robbers."

"This was a money transport that nobody else knew about!"

"What do the police say?" Ingrid asked Bill.

"They don't understand a thing and we don't have much confidence in a corrupt police force anyway."

"I think the theory about the transvestites may not be that crazy," said Ted. "Two women would hardly speed away on a motorbike. The police should check places where transvestites meet. Can the victims identify the robbers?"

"No, our men were stun-gunned. Doctors say the electric shocks erased part of their memory and they'll probably never remember what happened in the elevator."

"Oh, was it in an elevator?" Michele asked. "I don't like getting into elevators with people I don't know." Then she added: "I wish I could ride a motorbike."

"Good God! No! That's insane! You're too vulnerable, too exposed and totally unprotected. I can't think of a more stupid vehicle!" Ingrid said seriously. She felt less nervous after hearing Bill's story.

Bill and Michele followed Ingrid and Ted. Bill felt lonely, he said. He wanted Michele to stay a few more days. The short time they spent together had been so nice. He felt like a new person. It was like the first time he fell in love, she had a positive influence on him, he told her. Michele could sense his desire when he put his arm around her. And she didn't find it unpleasant at all. When he leaned over to kiss her she made quick and coquettish toss of her head so the kiss landed on her cheek rather than her lips.

"That was quick," he said.

"Yes, I am quick! I can see your moves coming. I'll let you know when I want to be kissed. I still think you should leave your job. It stands between us. Quit it and I'll consider..."

"You demand a lot!"

"I'm worth it!"

Chapter 28

NEWPORT WAS LIKE a boiling pot. In restaurants, bars and shops along the waterfront the ringing sound of cash registers was heard from early morning until after midnight. Carloads of people dressed in seagoing outfits carried sailing bags stuffed with clothes and provisions down the narrow lanes to the docks where suntanned crew members welcomed them on board waiting charter boats. The launch service was busy ferrying sailors to and from their boats around the clock. People from all over the United States came to see the former capital of the America's Cup races. A five-car caravan from Cape Cod with young people in shorts and tank tops moved slowly along the America's Cup Avenue in the bumper-to-bumper line from Long Wharf to the Ida Lewis Yacht Club.

The Sprengler girls and their friends spent the whole day at the beach. After sunset when the cool, damp evening fog rolled in from the ocean they shopped for sweatshirts. Maggie and Cathy dropped by Ingrid's shop to say "Hi" before they moved on to The Black Pearl outdoor bar. After burgers and beer Cathy missed Maggie. She was gone…no one had noticed when or where. It was time for the crowd to return to the Cape so Cathy and a couple of her friends asked around but none of the waitresses or bartenders had seen Maggie. Cathy became worried when someone finally told her she had seen a red-haired girl leaving with a man.

Cathy and Maggie had a room at the Treadway Inn and intended to stay overnight but their friends wanted to drive home around midnight. Cathy grew more and more concerned about Maggie. She was nowhere to be found and Cathy returned to the hotel to see if her sister had been there. But no. It was getting late. Cathy was tired and while waiting for her sister she fell asleep. She woke up around 2 o'clock in the morning and Maggie still hadn't come in. Cathy got up and walked over to the wharf area where crowds of people were still strolling around with drinks in their hands. In vain she asked if anybody had seen Maggie. Now Cathy was really upset and had a chilling premonition that something terrible had happened. People tried to calm her. They invited her to join them. She was bombarded with proposals for spending the night with her as she hurried through the crowd. She was crying. Tears smeared her mascara. Back in her hotel room she called Mike. It was 4 o'clock by then.

When Mike answered the phone and heard a woman crying he assumed it was Maggie.

"Maggie, is that you? What's wrong? Are you OK?"

"No, Mike, this is not Maggie. It's Cathy. Maggie and I are in Newport and Maggie has disappeared. I can't find her anywhere. We were in a bar with several friends and suddenly she was gone. It was around 9 and we were on our way out to Ocean Drive for a barbecue."

"That's odd. Maggie and I had planned to meet in Newport tomorrow. I'll come right away. Where are you?"

"At the Treadway. Room 505. Oh Mike, that's really nice of you. I'm terribly worried. Maggie seemed jittery and I have a feeling she went to look for coke. Oh, please hurry."

It was five-thirty when he knocked on her door. Cathy looked terrible, red-eyed and panicky. She was dressed and together they started the search immediately, beginning at the launch service. A tired-looking blonde sat in her tender boat holding a mug of steaming coffee with both hands. Yes, she remembered the kids from Hyannis and she remembered Cathy and her redheaded sister, but the sister hadn't been on board her boat going out to any of the yachts.

They woke up teenagers sleeping in their cars. They asked if Maggie had been seen at the Wharf Deli or the Raw Bar. No! They walked around the docks and called out her name. They drove to the Sheraton and asked people there. Everywhere, the same negative response. It was past 9 in the morning and they had been to all hotels in the area.

They went to the Candy Store to have breakfast and there they heard the horrifying news: A young woman had been found dead floating behind the bulwark under the Lobster Landing. Neither Mike nor Cathy could believe it was Maggie. Mike didn't say anything and Cathy gasped for breath and tears streamed down her face.

An ambulance and a police cruiser stopped at the Lobster Landing. Mike ran over. On a stretcher under a gray felt blanket was a tiny body. Mike asked the fire fighters if he could take a look at the victim. "I'm afraid it may be my fiancée," he explained.

"It's just a little girl," the man said.

He lifted the cover and Mike saw the face. It was Maggie looking as if she were asleep. He had never realized how incredibly beautiful she really was. With trembling fingers he slowly touched her forehead, her closed eyes and her mouth. His eyes filled with tears.

"Yes, she is my fiancée," he whispered.

"Hey, officer! This man knows the victim!"

A policeman turned to Mike and at the same time Cathy came up to him. He took Cathy in his arms and held her tight. "It's Maggie. She looks like she's sleeping. What have they done to my Maggie!"

A fisherman came over to them. He stood silent until the policeman asked him if he knew anything.

"I found her! I found her when I was going on board my lobster boat over there. She was floating in the water. Her red hair was like a halo around her face. I got a rope around her and lifted her on board. All she had on was this little shirt. I tried everything to resuscitate her. I poured out all the water and I tried mouth-to-mouth, but she'd been in too long. I know how to do it. I saved one of my crewmen once after he'd gone overboard and drowned. He'd been dead for half an hour. I blew life in him. His heart began to beat and he started breathing. But this girl…if I'd just found her earlier."

The fire fighters didn't want anybody in the ambulance.

"She's my sister and I'm going with her," Cathy insisted and the Rescue Squad men didn't stop her. She sat crying alone with her dead sister on the way to the hospital. She held the cold little hand in hers and wanted to warm it. She looked at the face she remembered since it was a baby's. She had seen it develop into this beautiful, young woman's face.

Mike told the police everything he knew of what had happened the previous night. The officer took notes. At the hospital Mike found Cathy in the emergency room. They waited. A doctor came out looking tired and distressed. "The girl died of an overdose," he said. "She has been sexually molested. We found particles of human skin scratched from a suntanned person under her nails."

Cathy and Mike couldn't believe what they heard. They were stunned.

"Who would do this to her?" Cathy asked.

"I'm sorry, Miss. In the summertime Newport is not an innocent little town. At night this is like New York! Girls shouldn't roam around alone here! Scum bums—rich and poor—from all over the country come here. I can guess what has happened."

"Yes? What?"

"Sir, your fiancée was probably looking for drugs. She found a supplier. She went along with him and before she knew it she was given an injection. When she protested she was most probably given some more to calm her. Then she was raped. When it became obvious that the doses had been too strong she was simply thrown in the harbor. It probably happened on board a boat. She died around 11. A small boat must've dragged her body to a dark spot of the harbor.

"She left us one little clue," the doctor said. "In her fist she held a paper napkin with the name *SNOWBIRD* on it."

Chapter 29

"I'LL STAY HERE another day," Mike said when they returned to the hotel. "You have to call your folks. Or do you want me to call them?"

"Mom is in New York. She won't come home until Dad stops working for the drug people. She also said you were involved."

"Yes, Arnold and I flew coke together. We had decided to get out, but big sums of money were stolen and we were accused. Arnold is trying to clear things up."

"How could you do such a thing? Maybe the cocaine that killed Maggie was smuggled in by Dad and you!"

"Cathy, we wanted to quit! I hoped to make some fast money, and I did, like Arnold. He's made millions and millions!"

She shook her head. "I know Maggie loved you but I hate you for this."

"I love her. We had promised each other...she was my happiness. I'll find out who did this."

He called Arnold. After Mike had finished his story, Arnold was silent for a long time

"Are you there, Arnold?"

"Yes, yes!" said a bewildered voice. "Is Cathy there?"

Mike handed her the phone.

"Yes, Dad."

"Is it true that Maggie is dead?"

"Yes Dad, I saw her. She looked as if she were sleeping. She was murdered. It must have happened before midnight. She held part of a napkin in her fist. It said *SNOWBIRD*. Why? But why have you been doing this kind of business, Dad?"

"I have done something horrible to all of us! One day I hope to tell you why. I'll call Mom. Let me talk to Mike."

Mike took the phone. Arnold talked and Mike repeated, "OK, I will. OK, I will," several times before he hung up. Then he sat down and covered his face with his hands. He heard Cathy sobbing silently. He asked her if she felt up to having dinner. Shaking her head she lay on her bed and put her hands over her eyes trying to stop the tears which ran nonstop down her cheeks.

"I want to go home," she said.

"I understand." he said. "I'll stay until all formalities with the police and the hospital are taken care of and arrange for bringing Maggie back home." He rose. "I need some fresh air. I'll go for a walk and find a sandwich or something. Want to come along? I'll get a room close by."

"No, I'll stay. I'd appreciate if you stayed here tonight and talked to me," she said.

After a while he returned. "I got one ham and one cheese sandwich. Let's split them. I also got some orange juice and a bottle of Scotch. Want some?"

He poured one glass of juice and two of whiskey. He handed her the Scotch first and she took a big swallow and made a face. She wanted to talk about her sister, about the wonderful unforgettable moments they had shared…skiing, skating and going out dancing together in Europe. Maggie, Cathy said, was the best of friends. The liquor made it a little easier for Cathy to face up to reality. She asked for another Scotch and he poured out half a glass. She bit into the ham sandwich, ate half of it, and then took the one with cheese he had left for her. She had some juice and fell asleep while eating. Mike woke her gently and helped her into her bed.

He slipped out a back door. In Bowen's Wharf he took up his cell phone and called a number Arnold had given him.

"Bolivar?"

"Speaking."

"I'm Mike, the pilot flying for Cavallo. I'm interested in making a deal with you. Flying for you, no middlemen."

"Where did you go last time?"

"Familiar with Nassau, Bahamas?"

"OK."

"Familiar with a little welcoming committee at Otis?"

"Oh, yeah!"

"Good joke, Bolivar, good joke! But I already smelled a rat in Nassau. So I took precautions. That's why I'm calling. I want to see you tonight."

"Tomorrow will be better. Be here at 9 for breakfast!"

"Sorry, but if you want to stay in control of this area you better see me now!"

"Meaning what?"

"Pick me up at the end of the pier at Bannister's Wharf in 10 minutes, and I'll explain." Mike hung up and walked down the lane past Ingrid's shop and the Black Pearl and all the little stores on the pier. He moved through the crowd like a zombie. The night was balmy and people were noisy. He was thinking of Maggie. He had met other girls, but Maggie had really meant a lot to him. She was the only one for him and now, suddenly, she was gone, peacefully sleeping on that stretcher, never to wake up and come back. When he had bent over her and kissed her she had been cold. His feeling of solitude was now mixed with anger.

"I just need one small piece of evidence and I'll let them know they'll have to pay a very high price for what they did. An eye for an eye won't be enough," he mumbled to himself opening the gate to the outer pier restricted for guests and crews only. He waited, listening. Wires slapped against masts. The lazy wind sung in the rigs. Waves rippled slowly as if whispering to him from below: "Not a soul around, not a soul around, not a single witness..."

***

In Barnstable Harbor Square, Bill sat in his car listening to a tape with all phone calls to and from the Sprengler house when the call from Mike and Cathy in Newport came in. Bill listened carefully. Mike was going to try to board the *SNOWBIRD* to clear things up and get revenge.

"We have to warn Bolivar," he said to his friend and associate, Frank. Before Arnold hung up Bill had found his cell phone. It was dead. The batteries were dead! Damn! He had to find one nearby! There was one in Barnstable Village. It was out of order. With spinning wheels he continued to the restaurant at Exit 6 where he found a phone booth. A teenage girl was having a lively and detailed conversation with someone about her terrific new boyfriend. Bill knocked at the window trying to make her understand he needed the phone in a hurry. She answered by shaking her head and mouthing a big "NO".

***

A high-speed rubber raft approached and docked in front of Mike. The man at the big engine asked: "Are you the pilot?"

"That's me."

"Jump aboard!"

They sped out and boarded the big white yacht. Bolivar sat on the stern deck watching a ball game on TV. He nodded and two men came up to Mike. One held him and the other frisked him checking to see if he was armed.

"I don't carry a gun when I visit friends, I'm counting on your protection. Besides, I fly, I don't shoot."

"Sit down! Want a drink?"

"Please, Scotch if you've got some aboard."

One of the men went over to a bar and held up two bottles.

"Chivas or Black Label?"

"Black Walker, please!"

The man filled a glass with ice and placed it in front of Mike together with the full bottle. Mike noticed deep, fresh scratch marks across the suntanned face! Four parallels lines...possibly from a woman's fingernails!

"You should stay away from cats!" Mike commented.

"Oh! Ho! She won't claw me again!"

"Shut up and get out! We need to talk," Bolivar snarled.

The two men left. Mike threw his ice overboard and poured himself some of the expensive whiskey. He and Bolivar were alone now. "Too nice for ice," he said, smiled, lifted his glass and they drank to each other.

"Cavallo wants me to fly once every two weeks only," Mike opened the conversation. "He can't sell more than that and he wants to keep the prices high. I know this route by heart now and I'm willing to fly two or three times a week for you if you can sell that much. I have some money myself and I want to do business in quantity. I want 10 per cent of the gross plus expenses."

"Too much!" said the New Yorker.

"Less than you pay now!"

Mike rose and walked around the spacious deck, looking up at the stars and sipping the amber drink. This was the place. Bolivar had obviously believed his bluff because he smiled and leaned forward to grab the bottle. This was the moment Mike had been waiting for. With the speed of a professional karate teacher his flat hand cut through the air and hit the big man over his neck. With a cracking sound Bolivar's big, bald head flung backwards in a grotesque position. Mike bent over him, lifted and carried the heavy man across the deck and eased the body slowly and silently into the black water. The hairless head slowly popped up and down while the stream carried it under the bow where it disappeared. Mike's heart beat heavily. He forced himself to remain calm. A few minutes passed. The man with the scratched face appeared in the door.

"Want anything, Sir? Where's Bolivar?"

"Some more ice, please. He's up there!" Mike pointed towards the fly bridge indicating that Bolivar was up there and asked: "You want some ice, too?"

Somewhere in the big power cruiser a telephone was ringing. Mike looked at Bolivar's empty glass and noticed there was no ice, so he rose, shook his head and handed his own glass to the man. "Did you have a red-haired girl here last night?"

"Who told you? It wasn't just me. All of us…"

This time the karate hand hit the side of the man's neck breaking the spine with a loud crack. He was dead before he hit the cabin floor.

***

When Bill could get to the phone and dialed *SNOWBIRD'*s number he heard it ring over and over again. He waited and waited till finally one of Bolivar's men answered "Hello!" in a groggy voice.

"Is Bolivar there? I need to talk to him right away!"

"Sure, he's watching the ball game. Just a sec."

"Telephone for you, Bolivar! It's Bill. It's urgent."

The man went up the stairs and stopped in the doorway. Mike stood with his glass in his left hand, bent over the dead man in the corner.

"He fell," said Mike. "Let's help him up!"

The man took a step forward, but realized something was very wrong. He reached for his gun and Mike's precision kick hit him on the jaw with such tremendous force it knocked him unconscious while he was still standing on his feet. A millisecond later the edge of Mike's right hand hit the man's neck breaking the spine. Mike looked around and threw his glass and the whiskey bottle with his fingerprints overboard. He didn't feel well. He was dizzy and wanted to vomit but all he could manage was a bad case of dry heaves.

"An eye for an eye is not enough for scums like you. This is the ultimate price and you knew it." Mike surprised himself talking to himself. He felt like he had been sleepwalking and now he suddenly woke up realizing what he had done. "I know it's not worth it. How could I do this? I really disgust myself."

He was shaking when he sat down in the raft, started the engine, untied and drove almost noiselessly at low speed passing several boats where people had turned in and let themselves be rocked to sleep by the lapping sound of slow, lazy waves. He reached Long Wharf, tied the raft to the dark landing under the oil tanks and walked slowly along the quay back to the hotel. The moon glittered in the black water; raw fog from the ocean rolled in hiding the yachts. Minutes later only a few high masts were visible over the dense mist. He didn't care if anybody saw him. He felt he deserved to be taken to justice, but there was nobody around. Newport was at rest.

***

Meanwhile in Barnstable Village Bill was waiting, still holding the phone to his ear. He heard the man at the other end lay down the phone. He heard steps walking towards the aft deck. He heard the ball game commentator on TV. He also heard two heavy bumps and somebody moving around. Nobody seemed interested in talking to him on the phone. Minutes went by. Bill emptied his last coins into the slot and finally had to hang up. Boliver was negligent and nonchalant, but he had always treated Bill with respect. Something must have gone very wrong. He had an idea what it might have been and he was shaken by the thought. He went back to his car and decided to call back again later from the hotel.

"We came too late," he said to his companion, Frank, who was waiting in the car. Frank shook his head in disbelief.

***

Back at the hotel Mike opened the door without a sound. Cathy was sleeping peacefully. He undressed and went to bed. He was exhausted, overwrought, but couldn't sleep. He lay on his back, looking at the ceiling where reflections from passing cars flickered. He had done something he knew would haunt him the rest of his life. This was not at all like on TV or in films when crooks were killed, and that was the end of the story. This was not the end of this story. Killing a human being was not like stepping on an ant. He didn't sense any remorse, but a feeling of guilt and shame and insecurity grew and grew. The girl in the bed beside his turned over and opened her eyes.

"Do you have you any aspirin?" Cathy asked.

In his bag he found two pills, filled a glass of water and sat down on her bedside. With his hand that less than an hour earlier had killed three men he stroked her hair gently, handed her the glass and lifted her head so she could drink comfortably.

"Thanks, Maggie always said you were a gentleman."

"Among monsters I become a monster," he murmured.

"What did you say?"

"Oh, just sleep well, sweet princess" he whispered kissing her forehead.

They didn't talk much in the morning. She showered first and when she was ready she came out of the bathroom completely nude as if she were all alone. She looked at herself in the mirror, examined her breasts and dressed slowly while he shaved and watched the voluptuous young woman, self-confident in her femininity and beauty. She was just like Maggie, but she was not his. He never had a sister. He would have liked one just like Cathy, thinking: "It must be like this to have one…to watch the beauty of the female body without desire, just having this feeling of being full of admiration for life itself."

He called the hospital and a funeral home. He called Arnold, who was still groggy after popping sleeping pills with several whiskeys. "I did what you suggested. I'm bringing Cathy home now. See you in a while."

He hung up, carried Maggie and Cathy's bags to his car and checked out. The ride to

Cape Cod took almost two hours. He really didn't want to go there. He wanted to sit beside Maggie's sister as long as possible. He had been dreaming about himself and Maggie, about buying their own home, about going places—maybe to Europe. He had never been in love like this. In such a short time she had become a vital, necessary part of his life and future. Now Maggie was gone and he was not only a criminal and a drug trafficker but a murderer, too.

He frightened himself. "Oh, God, help me!" he whispered.

"What did you say?"

"I said I think I need help to get this over with…

Chapter 30

CATHY AND MIKE arrived at the Sprengler's home in Barnstable Harbor around noon. The house was silent and Cathy stood in the hall, her arms hanging limply at her sides.

"Dad! Are you home?" She called and called again. She had never realized there was an echo in their house. It had always been a home filled with friendliness, joy and laughter. Mike put their luggage down and together they looked around—in the kitchen, in the living room and finally in the library.

There was Arnold sitting at his handsome Winston Churchill desk. Beside his clasped hands was his small, elegant, blueblack Walther pistol. He looked at Cathy with empty, hopeless eyes. There was a tear-stained photo on the table near the desk—Sara, Maggie, Cathy and himself laughing into the camera. His chin quivered and he shook his head slowly. Suddenly he looked old, very lonely and very tired.

"Dad, I'm home," Cathy kissed his forehead and covered his trembling hands with hers. She turned to Mike and said: "Will you please pour me a whiskey. Better still, make it three glasses." She pointed at the bottles on the bookshelves behind Arnold and sat down in the club chair opposite her father.

"I don't want to live any more," his voice was a hollow whisper. "What have I done to you all? I don't deserve to live. How could everything have gone so wrong?"

"Even though you made some terrible decisions, Dad, I still love you. Now you have to turn things around. You're not a coward. There's a solution and you'll find it. Get some sleep so you can think clearly. Please, don't do anything right now. Maggie was in love with Mike. Mike will help you."

Mike tried to catch Arnold's vacant gaze. Reaching for the Walter he asked: "May I take this?" Arnold nodded. Mike picked up the pistol and emptied the magazine. Carefully he pulled the jacket and caught the last cartridge. He put the cartridge back in its plastic box in the drawer where he knew it was kept, and put a glass of whiskey in Arnold's motionless hand.

"We need to get out of this stupid business," Mike told Arnold. "We must take charge. Together you and I will find a way to straighten things out and get ourselves rid of this damned mess. OK? Let's drink to our success", and he raised his glass.

But Arnold sat as if in a trance mumbling half under his breath, "I can't undo the harm I have done. I never understood in the first place why people are dumb enough to use cocaine. To me it was just business—business where stupid people paid big bucks for a high. I can't understand what Maggie needed it for. I provided the *SNOWBIRD* with cocaine. I killed my daughter. I loved her more than you can imagine. I called Sara. She doesn't want to see me, ever. She has good reason not to."

"Let's have some coffee" Cathy broke in. She went to the kitchen, made some coffee and returned to the library.

"Mike", she said, "will you please stay here tonight? The guestroom is ready for you. Please stay."

***

Bill didn't hear anything from Newport, nor did anyone answer the phone when he called, so he drove down to see what was going on. When he couldn't find Bolivar's yacht the girls at the tender service told him the *SNOWBIRD* had been confiscated by the DEA. All on board had been found dead.

"On my first morning trip," one girl said, "I found a body floating in the harbor. I towed him ashore and called the cops. A doctor said the man's neck was broken. When the police boarded the yacht they found two more men killed the same way. It's a drug related crime, the cops said."

Bill bought a newspaper. The whole story was already in there, including hints that the death of the girl the day before had something to do with the *SNOWBIRD* murders. This was the situation he had never dared hope for. The nightmare was finally over for him. He was free. Bolivar could no longer threaten or blackmail him. The sea gulls screamed and Bill enjoyed the balmy wind from the ocean as he walked back to his car and told Frank, who had accompanied him on so many of these trips, what had happened.

Frank's face was expressionless when he said: "Bolivar thought he could boss everybody around. There are gangsters and gangsters. These dead ones were really evil guys. That killer did us a big favor. I feel relieved. Don't you?"

"Yes, Frank, I feel free. But there aren't good or bad gangsters. We're all bad…the drug dealers are the lowest. I've had enough. I'll quit. I think you and I should split and never meet again. We should forget this chapter of our lives, OK?"

"You're 100 percent right, Bill, but I want to remain your friend."

That same day they drove to New York and went to Bolivar's Fifth Avenue office to get some money. When they arrived, the secretary had everything prepared. It was up to Bill to decide if the office was to close. Bolivar had left written instructions on how assets were to be used in case of an accident like this. Bill was mentioned as the new boss and a generous starting capital had been deposited to a Swiss bank account in Bill's name. All the employees had been taken care of and substantial funds were given to the church Bolivar attended and to a home that once had taken care of his elderly parents.

Bill made his own evaluation of the situation: an evil empire was broken up, and hungry hyenas were eagerly waiting to grab the leader's role and the unprotected market. He called Michele, told her what had happened and invited her to spend a week in New York. She hesitated briefly. But then, Bill was fun. He had class and he knew how to behave—so why not! She agreed to spend a week with him in New York.

***

Arnold and Mike were sitting quietly in the library when Mike asked: "Why don't we go over to Cavallo's and just tell him we're fed up with this business?"

Accepting the inevitable Arnold replied: "It's not that easy. He doesn't trust us. There are only a few things he believes in: One, himself: two, the almighty dollar, and three, threats from powerful, rich people. We are none of those, so we can't just quit! If we started our own air taxi business in California, he would come after us—first blackmailing us then killing us because we know too much! If we moved to London or anywhere on earth he would never stop tracing us and finally tracking us down. Buying a new identity would be the only way!"

"I'm not going to become somebody else just because Cavallo can't accept the fact that I'm in control of myself," Mike asserted, "and I've washed the Devil out of my soul."

"Cavallo is a small-time dealer compared to those in Providence, New York, Miami and Houston and, of course, L.A.,"

Arnold went on. "But he is growing, because he is tough, efficient and ruthless. He'll try to take over some of Bolivar's markets."

Mike expected Arnold to mention the killings on board the *SNOWBIRD*, but Arnold didn't say a word about it then and he never would as long as he lived.

That afternoon the Newport Police called wanting to ask Mike some questions. "Tell them they are welcome anytime," Arnold said, and shortly two police officers arrived, one civilian dress and one uniformed. Cathy asked them to wait in the library.

"Mr. Sprengler, we're very sorry about your daughter's tragic accident," the officer said shaking hands with Arnold. Turning to Mike he asked: "You were in Newport early yesterday morning and you left today between 9 a.m. and noon?"

"That's correct", Mike said. "Cathy, that is Miss Sprengler, called me the other night around 4 in the morning and told me that Maggie, my fiancée, was missing. She asked me to come and help look for her sister. I met Cathy at the Treadway Inn just before 7 AM."

"…and you identified Miss Sprengler's body and talked to the police and the doctor. That's all in order," the officer interrupted.

"So what is it then?" asked Mike.

"Does the name *SNOWBIRD* mean anything to you?"

"Yes, my Maggie held a paper napkin with that word on it in her hand. I guess it could be a restaurant or bar where she met a drug dealer. We knew she had a weakness for dope."

"The *SNOWBIRD*," the policeman explained, "is a yacht anchored in Newport Harbor. The owner was found dead this morning and two of his crewmembers were apparently killed also. One of them is tied to the death of Maggie Sprengler. Will you please tell us your whereabouts last night, hour by hour, Mr. Soames?" The police officer's tone was sharp and his question came like a whip. His intense expression made Mike uncomfortable.

"I can't tell the hours exactly, but I was with Cathy. She was so upset I didn't want to leave her alone, so I stayed with her at the Treadway."

Arnold looked up at Cathy, who stood in the doorway, hands on her hips.

"Yes," she said, "He went out and got juice and sandwiches, which we had for supper. I was very depressed and we talked until we fell asleep. I asked him not to leave me alone. He slept in Maggie's bed."

"We have witnesses, Mr. Soames, saying they saw you last night at the wharf."

"That's correct, I was there. It was late, around 10 or 11, when I picked up the sandwiches from the Wharf Deli. Also, I got myself a bottle of whiskey at the liquor store near the Mooring."

Cathy nodded and said: "You mean that three men were killed on a boat named *SNOWBIRD*, and Mike is suspected of going on board and shooting them? Isn't that a bit much for one man alone?"

"Yes, it must have been quite a performance, because they were not shot—their spines were broken. Two of them have been identified as ruthless professional hitmen from New York. The reason we're here is that you, Mr. Soames, have a good motive!"

"If those men killed Maggie, they got what they deserved and I'll be the first to thank whoever did it. But how could anyone have known they are the ones to blame? When did the killing take place, by the way? I was out of the hotel for less than an hour."

"You are doing business with a certain Mr. Bolivar don't you?"

"No, I don't do business with anybody! I'm employed by Mr. Sprengler. We fly a private air taxi. I don't know anybody by the name of Bolivar."

"We found a note left by Mr. Bolivar with your name on it and there was a phone call from the Wharf area to the *SNOWBIRD* around midnight. Are you sure you didn't make that call, Mr. Soames?"

"He was in my room, it's the truth," Cathy interjected. "I swear on the Bible! I woke up in the middle of the night and we talked."

Mike took advantage of this opportunity to establish an alibi and added: "I think that was around one o'clock."

Cathy suspected that Mike could have, indeed, taken revenge while she slept. She watched him. Their eyes met for a brief second and she broke the contact and looked down at the floor.

"...Was he alone capable of killing these hitmen with his bare hands? Was that why Dad had hired him?" she asked herself as she listened to the policemen's questioning.

Mike knew at once they were trying to trap him and he was especially careful with his answers. "Why don't you go hunting for Maggie's killer instead of looking for the ones who killed a bunch of drug dealers? Isn't killing of gangsters done mostly by gangsters?"

"We are 99 percent sure who killed Miss Sprengler. We want to be sure no lunatic is around killing sailors in our harbor. Even criminals have the right to be protected by the law. Nobody is allowed to kill anybody."

"Of course! I'm sorry but I'm very upset," said Mike.

"You are right, Sir, saying most murders are committed by criminals killing criminals. We are also pretty sure about the identity of the killer on board the *SNOWBIRD*," the uniformed officer said as he and his partner concluded the questioning and left.

"Bolivar and his thugs got just what they deserved," Arnold said to Mike "I don't think the police will bother you again. It was good of you to go to Newport and stay with Cathy. I appreciate your consideration."

Chapter 31

MICHELE WAS SINGING as she burst into Ingrid's kitchen. "I'm going to New York. Guess what I'm up to?"

"It's not very difficult to guess," Ingrid laughed. "Could Bill possibly be involved?"

"Women understand women!"

"Of course you should see him. You need to know more about him. Will you redeem him, or are you back on the warpath?"

"Both."

"I wish you luck! But aren't you complicating your life unnecessarily!"

"Maybe. Am I awful?"

"No! It's tough to be alone when you've lived with a good man for years. Life has to be a little old, a little new, a lot of fun, a little blue—so why not try a little new!"

Bill met her at La Guardia in his new Buick, which already showed signs of the merciless New York traffic. "Having a car in New York is stupid," he said.

"I won't go so far as to suggest you to change it for a motorcycle," Michele laughed.

He didn't react to her joke.

"Do you want to stay at the Penta as my guest or would consider trying my humble den. I just moved into a newly-renovated townhouse on the Upper East Side."

"I'm curious to see your home."

He parked under the plane trees and opened the gate's electronic lock with a magnetic plastic card. The five-story town house had a small walled-in garden and a fountain with dolphins splashing water into a big shell. The heavy, cast bronze door opened to marble floors, white marble walls, a brass and crystal chandelier and a brass elevator door. The interior of the elevator was all brass, mahogany and mirrors. It was silent and fast. He slipped the magnetic card through a slot. The sculptured mahogany door swung open to his all-white living room. There was a big bowl with fruit on a glass table and several big contemporary paintings on the walls.

He helped her off with her coat and said: "Welcome to me!"

"…said the spider to the fly!" Michele added.

"'No!'…said a bumble bee," he laughed and seemingly from nowhere he produced a bottle of Rhine wine and two green hock glasses. A glassed-in bookcase covered one wall of the room and Michele read some of the titles including old school books from college years, books on law enforcement, on economics, about politics and lots of fiction plus, and she could hardly believe her eyes, poetry. A complex character, this Bill! She was glad he didn't kiss her right away. She was glad he didn't serve her champagne. The wine was so much nicer.

"Cheers! Welcome to my humble dwelling and a great week in the Town of Towns!"

"I thought that was Rome."

"Yes, it was!" He helped himself to a handful of salted nuts and said with his mouth full:

"Come, let me take your suitcase and I'll show you your room."

He opened the door to a closet, another to an all-white bathroom and in her bedroom a small fridge a couple of bottles of sparkling mineral water. No touching, no kisses, nor hints towards the bed with the chintz bedspread. She was relieved. He simply left her there, walked out, switched on the TV and sat down to watch the news.

"Have to have a look at news and weather so we can plan a few days ahead. Sorry, but it won't take long!"

She didn't hear him. Still in her room she freshened up and changed into a raspberry red ultra-suede skirt and a navy shantung blouse, accenting her ensemble with a double pearl necklace and a simple Danish silver bracelet. She smiled at herself in the wide bathroom wall mirror. "OK, this is me, and I'm quite good-looking, aren't I?"

"Watching the ball game?" she asked joining him in the living room.

"No! News and weather. This week looks to be nice. I have tickets to the Met. I also have some to the City Ballet and to Carnegie Hall. What do you think about that?" He shut off the console and they sipped the cool wine.

"I have to tell you how great it feels to be free! My boss passed away and he left me a boodle of money. And the company, too! He wanted me to take it over. But I dissolved it. Everything has been split up among the employees. I have enough to do whatever I'd like to."

"How did he die? Was it an accident?"

"Yes, he was in an accident." He nodded.

"In Newport?"

"Yes, in Newport! How did you know?"

"On board his yacht?"

He looked amazed but didn't answer.

"His name was Bolivar, wasn't it?"

"Why should I lie?"

"Am I good at guessing?"

"Well, what do you know!"

"There is a lot I don't know or care to know, but I found out all I wanted to know. I talked to my neighbors, the Sprenglers. I read about the killing in Newport and did some thinking. Now I have it confirmed. I'm glad you got Bolivar off your back. I hope you have the willpower to stay away from his business for good."

"You bet I will! Do you know who killed him?"

"My guess is probably as good as yours! I think there's only one person with a strong motive, who was in the area at that time, but I only read the papers. I haven't seen any police reports. They did you a great service! So forget the Sprengler girl and that young pilot."

Silence.

"I'd like to make reservations at the Waldorf for a late dinner tonight, or do you have another idea?" he asked.

"No. Whatever you arrange is fine. But, Bill, what did you do with all the dope Bolivar kept in stock?"

"Do we have to talk business?"

"I think we can discuss anything now that the whole thing is finally over. It will be much better between us if we don't have any unanswered questions."

"OK. Inventory is inventory, if you don't lock it up and count it and hold somebody responsible for it, and you turn your back...it's gone! I simply ignored it! And a couple of days later it didn't exist!

"If I had asked for it, the answer would have been that somebody borrowed it. I didn't want it. I wanted to get rid of it. If I had tried to give it to some honest person or an institution it would have complicated my life a lot. They would have traced it! And who would like to have some thousand pounds of cocaine in his basement? You can't very well go to the police and say: 'Hey, look what I found in Central Park!' Not with these quantities." He laughed and she couldn't help laughing with him, thinking, but *not* saying: "I know how it feels to have a basement filled with cocaine."

"What do these drug lords do with all their money? And, what are you going to do with your millions now that you intend to retire from this rotten business and become honest and legitimate?"

"Why do you ask?"

"Because if I'm going to get involved with a man again, I want to know a lot about him. That's all."

"The 'Big Boys' never touch the money. They turn it over to experts who take care of it, investing it, making it grow. It becomes spec houses and condominiums. Most of it goes to banks as collateral for loans invested in Wall Street, one reason the Dow keeps reaching new heights.

"That's exactly what Bolivar did. He knew the right people. They trusted him and he paid them in advance. That's all! He reinvested huge sums in new drug projects. He invested in stocks and bonds. He also owned luxurious homes in four different places around the world. And he loved to travel. Also he had an expensive payroll with high-ranking people on it, not only in this country but abroad, too...people he needed, politicians, police officers and customs officials, probably military men in the radar information units and a whole army of distributors and bogeymen. Bribes were a considerable expense account.

"Most of the big shots have a weakness for luxury and the *dolce vita*, spending fortunes on stupid things. Bolivar was not that keen about putting on a show. He was realistic...nice to the few he trusted; totally ruthless to the rest. Obsessed with making his fortune grow, he was worth more than four or five billion dollars. He was also completely sex crazy. He was almost insatiable. He could have sex with five women in one night—one right after the other. When one girl asked him to cool down because she'd had enough, he wanted a new one to take over right away and after her, another and another. Afterwards he would sleep for 30 straight hours.

"Bolivar liked Newport because of the young girls he could get there. He was very generous, not only with dope if they wanted that but he paid them very well for indulging in his love games. But, while having sex with them he treated them brutally. It must have taken them a long time to return to a normal sex life or any intimate relationships with boyfriends or husbands after having been used by him.

"He liked me for some reason. I really don't know why. I became his idea man. I thought up new business, suggested new combinations, new people to work with and sometimes I did some detective work. After our meetings though he only said: 'Good idea, good idea.' Mostly he did something similar to what I had suggested."

Talking about these things was a relief for him and Michele understood it.

"Are you afraid of anybody, Bill?"

"No. You see, I never was more than an adviser and fact collector. I never did any dirty work and I always treated everyone involved well. I never wanted to know who did what and I never recommended violence or blackmail."

"You don't think you will have to move for safety reasons?"

"No. But the gangsters know who I am and they might try to get me back in the business again."

"What kind of business are you looking for now?"

"I don't know, I haven't been thinking about that yet! The closest to being a crook I think would be a smart investor!" He laughed.

"Or a banker!" she filled in.

"Good idea, good idea, and invest the money in the third world, 'loose it' to a Swiss account and then be repaid for the loss by US tax money.

"Yes, or start a Savings and Loan and have the FDIC bail the company out when the money is 'lost' by high wages or to companies filing for bankruptcy. Wasn't that what some president's son found was a smart way to get rich?" Michele went on: "Or start an insurance company for hospitals and doctors, and accept only customers who graduated among the top five from a specific list of Med Schools and have 10 years of irreproachable duty because I think there are qualified doctors who suffer for the malpractice of those who never should have become doctors in the first place. Or you could consider a position as a police detective!"

"Not such a good idea. I can't switch sides!" Bill pointed out. "The most lucrative, of course, would be becoming a politician, a lawyer, or a doctor, but my experience in law is too specific for an honest job and I could never be a doctor. I'm too old for that, and besides, I can't stand the sight of blood!" He shuddered. "No, I have to do something I like. Once I watched a TV program about a Canadian guy who bought a bakery in the Caribbean. I'm a pretty good chef and I wouldn't mind having an inn with a restaurant somewhere in a warm, pleasant place!"

"You said you had enough money to do what you want."

"More than enough for both of us."

"Would you consider fighting drug traffickers?" Michele asked.

"You mean that a retiring old devil like me ought to join a monastery? No, I think that coming out of this business alive is a miracle. I will not have anything to do with these people ever again. So, just forget about that."

"OK, I think a baker or an innkeeper sounds perfect for you."

"Then I'll need a woman to help me."

"You've already got one, haven't you?"

"Yes, I love you, Michele!"

"But what about your wife? I understood you truly loved her."

"Yes, I did love her. But she left me."

"Because of another man?"

"No, because of me. Because I wanted to earn big money, even if it was dishonestly and because of Bolivar. We both knew him before he became a big shot. She disliked him. But she's a finished chapter. Couldn't you and I...?"

"We could try, but I'm very serious about love and especially old love."

"I'm old, and in love!"

"If we're going to have supper at the Waldorf tonight, why don't we have just a small bite now," she suggested. "I could do some shopping? I noticed you have a deli and an old-fashioned butcher's shop around the corner."

"Too late, my dear. I've already prepared something for a light lunch. Hope you'll like it."

In the kitchen he put on an apron and a chef's hat. They laughed. From the refrigerator he took out a bowl with two chilled duck breasts and several plastic bags with an assortment of crisp salad greens, onions, tomatoes and green, yellow and red peppers. Small rolls of French bread dough went into the oven as he began to prepare the salad and the fowl.

"Please open another bottle of that wine. I like it very much, don't you? It will go well with this salad," he suggested.

Michele found a corkscrew and went to work. He arranged the salad artistically. He cut the tomatoes and shaped them into two birds, which he put on top of the salads. With the bread he served Camembert, Gorgonzola and Swiss cheese in bite-size cubes decorated with parsley and peppers. He worked quickly and his fingers did exactly the right things to make the simple salad a work of art. When the bread in the oven was ready, so was the meal. Michele served the wine. When they ate they realized they could talk and talk forever enjoying each other's company.

The sun set and the twilight called for candlelight. His two leather sofas were soft and cool. He stretched out on one she on the other. The candles flickered on the glass table between them. The blue hour in New York with purple skies in the west and stars lighting up one after the other is an unforgettable experience for New Yorkers and visitors as well. Bill's choice of music disclosed a love for the classical. They listened and enjoyed.

"My Gosh, we have to rush!"

They went to their rooms to change. Michele wore a full-length skintight silver lamé sheath and a matching, small pillbox hat. Bill put on a white tux. When they met in the hall they gazed at each other, and liking what they saw, laughed and applauded one another with an unanimous "Wow!" As a final touch Michele flung a luxurious silver fox fur over her shoulders and Bill hummed "Putting on a Top Hat" as he picked up a hat and a slim black cane with a silver top.

At Waldorf people from the first seating were leaving to continue their evening at theaters, Broadway shows and concerts. Bill was welcomed by the maitre d' with a recognizing smile and an admiring nod to Michele, who no doubt was one of the most elegant women in the Waldorf dining room. The meal was superb as was the big band, chosen especially to please this audience of silver-haired ladies and tanned, half-bald, white-templed gentlemen slowly dancing cheek to cheek alternating with swings in a modified jitterbug tempo and occasionally a lively jive step.

For Michele and Bill this was their music…right out of the late 30's and 40's. They moved smoothly over the floor, he the perfect partner catching her firmly when she would spin around like a ballerina. They never lost contact and smiled continuously, fantasizing with joy that their youthful spirit had returned for just a little while.

Michele liked dancing with Bill. He did a neat tango and they whirled around laughing at their passionate panther moves. They were of the same dance generation. They had listened to the same records on their portable phonographs. They had danced to favorite records so scratchy they could hardly detect the tunes of

"Stardust" and "Opus One". Their favorites were still The Dorsey Brothers, Basie, Ellington, Louis, and Ella Fitz. It was like then when they danced away the evening and their feet were aching so much they had to take off their shoes walking home!

Later they strolled up the silent street. Fall was in the air. Her new silver fox had been a success. She had received so many compliments.

"You were the queen of the night, Michelle. You introduced the real foxtrot. It was fun."

"You were the best jitterbugger. You should have had that hat and the cane when we danced."

When they entered the apartment she said: "Bill, please hug me. I'm so darned happy! This was the most wonderful day I have had in ages." She kicked off her shoes and sank down in the soft leather sofa.

He took off his jacket, got a club soda from the fridge and took a bottle of Grand Marnier from one of the bookcases. He served it in cut crystal glasses. He took his shoes off and sat with both feet up in the other sofa leaning back looking up at the dark blue sky visible through the glassed ceiling. It made him feel as though he were sitting in the open air. He liked this apartment.

"This was a great evening, Michele. To think that we are going to have one full week together. Terrific!"

She lit the candles, turned off the lights and snuggled comfortably in his lap.

"There is the Bull," she pointed at the stars.

"Don't even mention the name Bull…Ivar the terrible! Or was it Ivan the terrible!"

"OK, there is always a snake in paradise! But I'm talking about stars! There is Perseus. He was a Persian king. He wants Andromeda, the constellation over there. Look, can you see his pointed hat and how he stretches out to reach Andromeda's foot? Look over there! There is Cassiopeia. She's Andromeda's mom."

"Aren't you a funny girl!"

"Yes, please unzip my dress a little. It's so tight I'm almost suffocating…just a little," she said when he pulled the zipper all the way down to her waist.

"I wouldn't want you to suffocate."

She leaned back and lifted her face to be kissed. His hands found their way under her dress and bra. He fondled both her breasts in his big warm hands. The upside down kiss lasted and lasted. He waited to see if she would pull back. She didn't. "She's so terrific," he mused. "I am so happy to have met her, happy to sit and desire her and there's no doubt she responds."

"I love the feel of your warm hands. You thrill me. We danced nicely together, didn't we?"

"Yes, Michele, we did. Did Perseus reach Andromeda?"

"Yes. They had a wonderful time together."

Michele lifted her bosom in pleasure. It was so good to be with a man who knew just what to do and how to do it!

"Did they stay happy together for the rest of their lives? To me it seems he is still trying to reach her!"

"That's how they stay happy. He reaches out and asks: 'Please, little princess, come to me.' She says: 'Do you seriously love me? I'll come only if you are nice to me and behave like a gentleman!' And he is gentle and a real man!"

She could feel his manhood erect. He didn't hide it. She smiled and reached for another long kiss. They sipped from the mandarin-flavored cordial. They watched the stars; they caressed and kissed.

He removed her bra and she slipped out of her tight dress. She stood up and offered him her breasts running her fingers through his hair. He lifted her and carried her to his bed. His eager hands caressed every part of her. Her beautiful face, her graceful neck, the square shoulders and the fine still firm, round breasts. He had to kiss them again and again. His hands wandered farther to her soft belly and he could not resist tickling her navel. She laughed and quivered and kissed him. His hand continued down. There it was warm and silky and he touched her ever so gently. She parted her legs welcoming him to her.

She held his face and kissed him over and over again and he gave her pleasure.

Later she watched the New York sky through the glassed ceiling. Between the stars an airliner headed northeast. Was it bound for London or Paris or Rome? She missed Europe. She missed the far away places where she once had been so happy. She and her man. It was strange how wonderful it was to be together with this new man. She had always thought the only one she could be happy with was her Richard.

They lay, her head on his arm, his hand on her belly.

"Did you enjoy it?" he asked.

"Yes! Yes!" She bent over and kissed him. "I did when you did."

"I'm sorry I didn't meet you 30 years ago."

"Be glad you didn't. I was madly in love at that time and my husband was a tall, strong, very decisive man, very capable of defending his interests, intellectually and physically!" She laughed. "No, Bill, be glad we met now."

Soon they slept, amazed they could still be totally carried away by love the same way they had been many, many years ago; now, perhaps, with even more appreciation, intense feelings of harmony and gratitude.

Chapter 32

STROLLING DOWN FIFTH Avenue Michele and Bill stopped to window shop at Tiffany's. One display was all emeralds, another amethysts, a third, rubies, and a fourth, diamonds. Tiaras, bracelets, necklaces, and rings for millions of dollars sparkled behind the thick armored glass. Michele looked at each window, wishing.

"I want to give you something. Let's go inside!"

She tried to stop him. She didn't want to have anything from him, but he steered her through the entrance and together they looked around at the beautiful jewelry and the staggering numbers on the price tags.

"No rubies, no pearls. They don't bring me luck."

"I want you to have that one." He asked the sales assistant to show them a beautifully cut five-carat sapphire in a simple but magnificent platinum setting.

"Sapphire is the sky, eternity. It means freedom, yours and mine. Try it on, please!"

He put the ring with the big blue stone on her finger. It came alive. It hypnotized her. The blue became the sky over Cape Cod. The darker shades of blue became the ocean. She imagined she could hear the sound of the roaring waves along the long beaches she loved. The blue changed and became the sky over Africa, where she had spent the happiest years of her life. There she had lain looking up into the sky, watching the dark blue night become purple, red, amber and finally light blue like the shimmering stone. There was music in this blue stone! She heard the adagio of Mahler's Tenth. It came closer and closer, and it brought memories of happy, happy days, when she was not alone and never had to worry about anything. Her eyes misted and the stone shot flashes of sky blue light through her tears.

This is weird," she thought, "why am I reacting this way, why does my imagination run away with me like this. "Bill, what an amazing stone," she said.

"You are crying, Michele. Why?"

He handed her his hanky. "You like the ring?"

She dried her tears and nodded.

"How stupid to start crying for no reason," she thought. "Men always ask why, when women cry. Don't they know there isn't always an answer?

"But Bill, $15,000! That's crazy!"

"Crazy or not. Do you want to keep it on or should they wrap it?"

"I'd like to wear it, but I don't dare to. You can't walk around in New York City with $15,000 on your hand. Someone could steal it or I could drop it!"

"Nonsense! Have you ever walked in the street and lost a ring that fits this perfectly? And, you know, nobody will ever believe it's real anyway. Because people in this town adore 'lookalikes' and nobody walks around with fifteen grand on!"

She flung her arms around his neck. "Thank you, crazy Bill! How can I ever thank you?"

"You don't understand, you already have! I'm free and I'm young again. I'm back on the right track thanks to you. You're the first normal human being I've talked to in years. You know who I am and you're still with me. Isn't that worth celebrating with a little thank you! Let's go out in the sunshine."

She kept the ring on and walked out the door without noticing the smiling, amused police guard who must have overheard the conversation. She hid the ring with her other hand, but she had to glance down at it over and over again. She had never experienced anything like this. A ring with a stone that made her see heavens and oceans and hear music from strings! She bumped into people, she didn't hear the buses or taxis honking or notice traffic lights changing. Bill had to grab her and hold her arm.

"What an extraordinary woman!" he reflected.

They went shopping. They got him a light blue necktie and her a light blue silk blouse to match the new ring. Back at his apartment over a cup of coffee she slowly felt the hypnotic effect of the exquisite sapphire change into a sense of reality. She had an overwhelming feeling of peace and harmony when the blue hour dimmed all details of the view. One New York went home for a rest and another New York prepared for a hectic night. The sky was purple over New Jersey but clear blue above. The first stars became visible. Blue-violet clouds with orange halos sailed in from the southwest. This magnificent scenery was all for free! For the homeless out there and for them in this dream apartment.

Michele could not let go of the idea of influencing Bill to do something for society by way of compensating for the problems he had been part of creating. After a while she asked: "You have seen this drug business from the inside. What steps taken by society to fight it did you fear the most? What could have ruined your business?"

Bill thought for a moment before answering: "In India and China and in Cuba they took all addicts off the streets to treatment centers. We could do that. We could stop dope entering the prisons rehabilitating all addicts in there. Drug use and addiction is a consequence of stress and frustrations. Lack of hope, lack of possibilities, lack of money and jobs, lack of education. Society could provide jobs rebuilding deteriorated infrastructure, erasing the ghettos, building decent homes, and free education on the net.

"Only education will make a new generation understand that drugs destroy them. Only education will give them a chance to qualify for better, honest earnings. Today we have over 20 million illiterates here in the US simply because kids are brainwashed into believing they can talk themselves into being the best and do whatever they really want to without a basic education. Our schools are financed locally, which is lunatic. All American kids, rich or poor, should have the same basic education and the same good schoolbooks wherever they live in our 50 states. All ghettos must be cleaned up.

"The people's representatives in Washington represent only their contributors and themselves, not the voters. That has to be changed to create a society that cares for its people, not

only for the ones who contribute to politicians. Nowhere in our Constitution is it written that companies and institutions or other entities with no voting rights should have any right to influence the outcome of our elections."

Not waiting for Michele's answer he continued: "Uneducated people with no hope for the future are expensive to society. The cost of basic education would soon be repaid by better tax revenues and better productivity. Using education money for stimulating industry or to strengthen war power like we have permitted for years is simply economic degeneration."

"What you say makes sense, but we cannot afford all these social reforms. Where is the money?" Michele countered.

"The money is here, for heaven's sakes!" Bill stated without hesitation.

"You can't say that! We can't force people to pay for things they don't like or expect people to hand over their hard-earned money to those without money!" Michele argued.

"That is the standard excuse for not taking responsibility in relation to their capacity and the profits they make from society. Society provides the environment for moneymaking people. Society has the right to charge for their use of this environment and infrastructure.

"Society provides licenses to TV and radio stations. Most of those companies don't give anything back for the rights and the enormous power they are granted by society. They should pay more than taxes. They are allowed to air subversive, stupefying commercial indoctrination instead of meaningful, useful, educational information. Every radio and TV station should be obliged to help our nation's most qualified educators reaching into every home, to every child every day. Providing basic education today is a federal duty. They should be forced to send political debates for free. Instead of charging millions for political commercials paid by tax-free pressure groups or companies. Local home owners and local school boards cannot be responsible for our international competitiveness or the local drug problems."

This harangue was not what Michele had expected. Bill certainly was a thinking man. She sat silent a long while. Bill had some more coffee.

"Could we return to the drug question?" she asked.

"Sure! There is a parallel between alcohol and drugs. Ask people 'who should pay society's costs for the misuse of alcohol'? Some say the consumer and others say the distiller. Both are right. But nobody wants to pay the bill. Representatives of the industry say higher booze prices will hurt the industry! Hear that? Hurt an industry that creates more misery in our society than any war has ever done. Consumers say it becomes too expensive! My objection is if it's too expensive, you shouldn't buy it. Booze prices should include a tax, covering its cost to society, paid by the consumer and collected by the distillers' distributors, the liquor stores. Same thing with tobacco."

"What about legalizing drugs?"

"Don't go down that road! That would be like the alcohol situation. The authorities would give licenses to the big importers or manufacturers or important friends. High taxes would probably 'hurt the industry'! Now taxpayers and medical insurance are paying the costs. Letting drug users kill themselves is inhumane, immoral, loss of productive people, loss to society by loss of income from taxes and a sign of degeneration. Allowing drugs to stop chronic pain is OK, but the lawyers in Washington cannot give doctors that freedom because they know it would be misused. They know that federal laws cannot police such misuse.

"Each human being is, if treated right, an asset to society. There really aren't that many asocial individuals! Most of our locked up criminals are victims of petty crimes, a substandard education and a neglected environment. We have more locked up people per capita than any other civilized nation. We care less about each other than do people in any other western societies. We waste our human capital the same way we waste our natural resources."

"You are a good liberal, aren't you, Bill?"

"No, I'm a bad Republican! I think our Constitution needs to be updated. But more importantly, I think that every member of society should be encouraged to become better informed, better educated every year. Stagnation is decay. We have the knowledge and the means to distribute the education. But since it demands long-term investments not only in our own school districts but in poor ones, which cannot afford it on their own and no private enterprise can make it a profitable fast enough, it doesn't happen."

"Why don't you become a politician?"

"Actually, you might well say I am an amateur politician! Stupidity and weakness made me get involved with Bolivar. Stupidity and weakness would probably get me involved in new Watergates, Iran-Contras, HUD or Savings and Loans scandals! More and more I have come to understand that 'common man' is a fine title. And, I like the idea that 'Fanfare to a Common Man' could have been written to someone like me. A good boy who turns bad and turns good again before returning to dust!"

"What about the money you got from the drug business. It represents addiction, lost hopes, sorrow, crashed families and the death of thousands of young people and their parents' dreams. Doesn't that bother your conscience?" Michele asked.

"Yes! "

"Give one million to a center for the homeless!"

"They would trace the gift and get me!

Michele smiled and said: "A camel cannot go through the eye of the needle and a rich man cannot come to heaven unless he gives away all his belongings!"

"The Eye of the Needle' was the name of a gate somewhere in the Biblical country. The opening in the wall was so low that the camel had to go down on his knees to crawl through the gate. So, I'll have to kneel, OK! But when it's time for me to meet Saint Peter I won't be a rich man!"

He dropped the subject. "We're due at the Met pretty soon. It's "The Tales of Hoffman." Let's get dressed. Why don't you wear your new blue blouse!"

"Your extravagant gifts make me feel guilty!"

"Me, too! 'Guilty, but not responsible!' as a late president said…or was it 'Responsible but not guilty'!"

She put on her white ultra suede skirt and the new blouse, a perfect match for the ring. Her only other jewelry were her pearl earrings. Even though the night was warm she couldn't resist sweeping the silver fox over her shoulders instead of a white jacket. Hoffman was great. Kathleen Battle's singing was celestial, Placido Domingo incredible and Olympia (the doll) was darling and amusing. During the entr'acte Michele noticed many very elegantly dressed people, wearing tons of jewelry but nobody wore a ring like hers! Some ladies had eyes like hawks!

"Bill, did you know, that a hawk can fly 500 to 600 feet above the treetops, and a little mouse scurrying along the ground is sure the leaves protect him from predators in the sky. But a hawk can focus its eyes like a camera and see clearly under the protecting cover of leaves, and spot the little mouse. The same way some women here are focusing in on my ring. I have the

feeling they know the ridiculous price because they know every price of everything at Tiffany's!"

Bill laughed. "It's not the ring, my dear. They envy you—your style and beauty," he said and hugged her. She noticed the scrutinizing eyes and heard the whispers: "I don't recognize that couple. Do you know her? Did you see her ring?"

Michele arched her neck, preening like a peacock. She knew she was beautiful. It was a perfect evening!

Once at home Bill served cognac and she sat in his lap talking about the opera performance. "You were the most beautiful of all the women there tonight!" he said, "you really were...you were radiant".

They sipped the cognac, kissed good night and he walked her to her room and kissed her good night again. She undressed and put on her long, white nightgown with gold ribbons outlining her round breasts, then she went over to his room. He lay in his bed wearing a light blue pajama.

"The blue pajamas matches my new ring," she thought. He was reading a book. He really looked like a dad! Or a granddad! She stood in the doorway and asked:

"May I come and lie in your bed?"

He looked over his glasses and smiled at her. She was magnificent.

"Yes, of course."

"May I lie in your bed without being seduced?"

"Isn't that a bit risky?"

"I want to be with you without being seduced."

"OK, I promise!"

"Even if I tempt you?"

"I'm not so sure about that!"

"Then I won't come."

"OK, I promise."

With a girlish giggle she jumped over him and in under the cover beside him. Leaning on her elbows she kissed him. Her breasts touched him softly and pleasantly. She lay back and closed her eyes. He continued reading until his book dropped to the floor and he turned off the light

***

The sun shone into the bedroom on a new, glorious New York day! She was still asleep when he got up and put on the coffee. He put small crispy Italian rolls in the oven. He went in to her with everything on a breakfast tray. She woke up and sat shaking her head smiling at him. This was the joy of normal life he had been longing for years!

"Today is Metropolitan Museum Day! We're off in an hour or so," he said. "You slept well, I see."

"Yes, I did. You resisted my tantalizing! Now I feel safe with you." She paused. "The woman in that photo, is that your wife?" He nodded. "She is beautiful. You didn't take it away when I came?"

"I thought of it, but decided not to."

"Didn't you think I might get hurt?"

"Thought of that, too. But, if I came to your home, would you hide the picture of the one who was your best friend? Isn't he part of you forever? Why hide that?"

"But my husband is gone forever."

"Not true, he will always be with you. You meet him in your dreams. You like to see and touch things he used and loved. To you he will never die completely. What you say and think now is part of a database the two of you created together. The older we get the more we live in our comforting memories. That's OK. Dreaming is all right!"

Days flew by…Carnegie Hall, the Art Galleries, the Ballet, the Dance night on board the jazz boat on the Hudson. He took her to the airport. They kissed goodbye.

She passed through the security checkpoint and waved to him. He stood there motionless for a long while thinking how his life had changed. He liked the new turn it had taken. It had been stimulating to talk with an intelligent woman about things that mattered.

At first she smiled to herself; then she laughed. She thought of all the crazy, funny things they had done during this wonderful week. She laughed at his quibbling when it came to social issues.

Chapter 33

MICHELE TOLD INGRID about her New York adventure. Ingrid's smile changed from astonishment, to supportive, to indulgence. The two were having coffee on Michele's back deck. The sun was warm, pleasant and summer-like. A hummingbird searched the garden for red, trumpet-shaped flowers and found the salvias.

"I have thought things over," said Michele. "I have to stop running away from sense and reason. He is nice in many ways. But there is something very alien with him. Bill is not the right guy for me and I am not the right girl for him. I have to break up with him."

"I think you did the right thing," Ingrid said. "I, too, am skeptical as to the wisdom of your future life with him. You need a man with a firm sense of ethics, an intellectual, who can share your interest in science. A man you can tell everything to. Go hunt for one! Send Bill back to his wife!"

They admired the fantastic sapphire ring. "Sapphire is the symbol of loyalty and trust!" Michele commented.

"Loyalty and trust are things to dream of. Will you ever trust Bill 100 percent?" Ingrid asked. "There are probably lots of things he can't ever talk to you about. Bolivar's closest adviser can hardly be totally innocent? The man found dead in our harbor was a victim of a power struggle among Bolivar's men. Bill came out a winner."

"But, Ingrid, the killer could be one of the gorillas in the Lincoln or the driver or one of the guys we robbed in the elevator," Michelle reasoned. "Bill said Bolivar used the other guys for dirty jobs. You don't think it was Bill, do you?"

"Are you clutching at a straw?"

Michele shrugged. And changed the subject…

"You know, your Swedish Tosca cake is the best cake I've ever tasted. I have all the ingredients we need. Why don't we make one, right now! Let's distract ourselves with something that's fun and productive. Rational thinking", Michele continued, "needs an injection of excitement, creativity, or physical work."

"And something good to munch on," Ingrid added.

They sang together and talked as they prepared the batter and the caramel. When the cake was finally in the oven Michele looked at her watch and said: "I've got it! I'm going to send him a letter!"

"What time was it when we put the cake in the oven?" Ingrid asked.

"Eleven-twenty! The police work we're trying to do is dirty work. Maybe we should stay out of it?"

"It has to bake for half an hour before we spread the caramel-almond topping on it and then it will take another twenty minutes. I think anything we do to stop drug dealers is good. It won't take long until somebody takes Bolivar's place. The local market will feel the impact of our work. Maybe they won't find our area appealing if they run into such devastating jokes like the ones you played on Bolivar's dance evening or the hijacking of five million bucks!"

They laughed. Michele said: "Bill had so many good points of view. I don't think he killed George, the dead man in our harbor. He was Bill's friend. I hope he didn't."

They finished the Tosca cake. It came out perfectly. Ingrid went back to her own house and was sitting at the kitchen table with bills, books, tax forms and bank statements when Michele walked in and handed her a letter. This is what I'll write to him, she said:

> "Dear Bill,
>
> Thanks for a wonderful week. We could do well together in many ways, but there are rules of ethics we cannot neglect. Hugs and kisses heal. You deserve a good woman. Please forgive me for taking your wife's address and sending her the sapphire ring you gave me today. I enclosed a letter saying: *Dearest, Please keep this in memory of a man who loved you and only you and now has finally followed your advice and broken all ties with crime. Please, my love, call me if I may come back to you. I don't deserve you, but I ask you to forgive me for not standing by you and being loyal to you. Signed: Bill, Your address and phone number*
>
> Michele"

Ingrid was silent for a while.

"You're something special, Michele! This is the right thing to do. It hurts, doesn't it?"

"Bill and I really had a good time. He even gave me moments of contentment. He made me aware of the fact I could actually be happy with a man again."

She looked relaxed and smiled a little foxy, mischievous smile.

"I've never thought about men since Richard died. He often said we had many sympathetic colleagues and good friends in our field, but I never got to know them. What Rich and I found out

230

about tranquilizing, anesthesia, and the dosages has never been published. He said we should apply for a patent and it could give us a good income for our retirement...

Soon there will be a zoologists' conference in London. I should go!"

Chapter 34

MIKE ENTERED THE kitchen on his way out for a jog. Cathy dressed in a pink jogging outfit was making coffee. "I want the coffee to be ready when I return," she said. "Why don't we run together? I'll show you a good trail!"

He agreed. She kept a good pace. He had a problem keeping up with her. She was quiet. They followed the beach for 20 minutes before she stopped.

"This is where I turn. I do some aerobics here and let my heartbeat calm down. Then I return through the woods."

They did some push-ups and sit-ups. Afterwards, lying on their backs they looked up at the white cotton clouds lazily sailing across the Indian summer sky. Suddenly she asked him:

"Did you kill those thugs?"

"I think they killed Maggie and I think they got what they deserved. Do you think I killed them?"

Did she really want to know? She might become afraid of me, he told himself. He had hoped she wouldn't ask. He did not want to lie to her. He wanted to be her friend, wanted to be trusted. She didn't answer his question.

She was light, slim and fast. He was tall, heavy and muscular and would have preferred a slower pace but found it humiliating to fall behind. He was totally exhausted when they finally reached the Sprenglers' white gate. She served coffee and called for her dad to tell him breakfast was ready, but he didn't answer. He was nowhere around. His BMW wasn't there. Cathy called his office and the secretary said he was expected back around noon. She hung up and turned to Mike.

"He's too depressed to be left alone," she said, "A few days' rest isn't enough. Where do you think he is?"

"I think he is seeing Cavallo. He might try postponing or canceling scheduled flights."

***

Mike's Volkswagen rolled up the driveway to the Cavallo residence stopping at the gate. Mike honked but the man in the booth shook his head indicating he didn't intend to open the gate. Mike got out his car and with a jump stood with one foot on the hood and the other on the roof of his car looking over the wall. Arnold's BMW was parked at the main entrance.

"Hi there! I'm Mr. Cavallo's pilot and this is Miss Sprengler. We need to talk to Mr.Cavallo and Mr.Sprengler. Please open the gate!"

The man behind the bulletproof glass shook his head.

"Please tell Mr. Cavallo we're here. Tell him Miss Sprengler wants to see her father. See! No guns on board!" Mike turned and made a few funny jumps to show that his tight-fitting clothes could not possibly conceal a gun. He parked his car and they walked through when the gate slowly swung open. The butler met them and asked them to wait. Arnold was sitting with Cavallo on the glassed-in veranda. There was a stack of papers on the table between them.

Mike signaled the butler that he wanted to talk with Arnold and Cavallo. The butler shook his head. Mike laughed and nodded. The butler kept shaking his head. Mike walked towards the door. The butler blocked the way.

"Please, Sir. I have orders to let you wait."

"I don't like to see Arnold talking alone with Cavallo," Mike whispered to Cathy. "This unwillingness to let us go in makes me mad." He raised his voice and said: "Will you please tell Mr. Cavallo that I'm not used to being forced to wait and Miss Sprengler needs to talk to her father now! Understood! Get going, Fatso! Tell Mr. Cavallo NOW!"

"Please, Sir."

"Come on, man!"

"Mike! Please wait!" Cathy interrupted.

The butler signaled. Two men came blocking the door.

"Why don't you ask Mr. Cavallo before you start a fight you might loose?" she asked.

The butler picked up a phone and through the window Cathy could see Cavallo answering. He nodded. The butler opened the door. Cathy and Mike entered. Mike noticed a Newport newspaper on the table nearby. Passing the butler he whispered: "Read that paper and consider your situation, my fat friend."

Cathy did not recognize her own father at first. This was a tired old man. Her father's energetic spirit had disappeared. His shoulders drooped and his usually alert eyes were empty. Cavallo looked up at his two new visitors. Cathy thought: " Mom was right. This man has the eyes of a snake." She went up behind her father's chair.

"Mr. Cavallo, my father is not well. He needs a doctor and I want you to end this meeting right away so I can take Dad home with me. The death of my sister came as a shock to him and he is severely depressed."

"Dear Miss Sprengler, your father and I are talking business. We have a contract. I want him to fulfill his part of it or else he'll have to take the consequences. That's all. Your presence here doesn't change a thing."

"I told you my father needs a doctor. Please be reasonable, Mr. Cavallo. When my father has overcome his depression, he'll be ready to go back to work. Can't you see that he's unable to make any long-term decisions in his present condition? Nor should he fly in his condition. OK, come along, Dad! Let's go home. You need to rest and I'm here to take care of you. Goodbye, Mr. Cavallo!"

She took her father under his arm and helped him out of the chair. Arnold squeezed her hand and smiled at her.

"So, so, so! Now, please sit down and let's finish. You two have to wait out there." Cavallo said.

He lifted the phone and asked the butler to come in right away, "and bring some more coffee, will you?" he added.

Cathy looked at Cavallo.

"Why should my father stay here against his will? I'm a partner of the Sprengler law firm and I won't allow my father, in his present condition, to negotiate with a client like you without my presence. Is that clear? What on earth makes you think he has to follow your orders! Come on, Dad, I'm afraid we just lost a client! Mike, please help me take Dad home."

The butler hastily put a tray with a coffee carafe and some mugs on the table then blocked their way out.

"Mr. Cavallo has more to say to you. Please, wait a minute," he said.

Cavallo stood up. His face was red with fury.

"We've had severe losses lately and my investigations show that Arnold is involved."

"Why don't you ask the police to investigate?" Cathy asked.

"Miss Sprengler, you don't seem to know that your father has been involved in some very serious criminal activity."

"If he has, he should be brought to justice. As far as I know, my father has only carried out his customers' orders. We are a law firm, Mr. Cavallo. I am a lawyer. You cannot scare me with the law. If you don't let us go you're in deep trouble. I'll call you before we send our final invoice. Goodbye!"

She looked at him defiantly. Cavallo's lips trembled; his hands were shaking. The butler leaned over and whispered in his master's ear: "They are the ones who liquidated Bolivar, Sir."

"So, you two were in Newport when Mr. Bolivar died?"

Mike smiled at the gangster who was making an effort to regain the initiative. Mike's smile annoyed him.

"Mr. Bolivar got what a gangster boss deserves and so did his thugs, and none of them drowned!" Mike stated.

"Now, stop behaving like a spoiled child. Do you want to stay in business or not, Mr.? I don't recall your name—Mr. Cannaille or Mr. Camillo or whatever? You know that Mr. Sprengler has not stolen anything from anybody, even from drug dealers. If you have lost your sense of perspective, let me remind you that Mr. Bolivar was at least ten times bigger than you are and his men were the best in New York...not the best in a little fishing town out in the sticks on Cape Cod. What can you expect from a fatso like that clown butler?"

Mike jerked his thumb over his shoulder, "...or the slime up there in their Borsalinos?" He pointed to the two men in light gray three-piece suits and fedoras.

"Are they trying to introduce some kind of Al Capone dress code on the Cape? I mean, get real! Arnold is a first class pilot. He has brought millions of dollars to you. He has invented new high-tech equipment making money for you. He is daring, smart and knows the law. He is ill and you are not even willing to let him have a few lousy months' rest to overcome the idea that he is responsible for his daughter's death. Have I understood you right?"

"Let me assure you, Mr. Copilot," Cavallo spit out,

"I'm not the least bit interested in your opinion."

"There's no doubt that with men like Mr. Fatpig over there and the Al Capone weirdos up there, all nodding and saying: 'Yes, Master Camillo! Of course, Master Camillo!' You believe you are the most powerful and smartest guy in town. I'll tell you the truth. I dare give you an opposing opinion. The most ruthless is not the smartest. For your own good, listen, because I'm talking sense and so is Miss Sprengler. I may be a copilot, but in case you don't know it the pilot is in the driver's seat while rats like you sit in the back seat reading the "Wall Street Journal". Now, if I decide to drive to hell, you are going to hell, too, right? But I don't drive to hell. I think you're childish and need intelligent people around to advise you. It's idiotic to threaten Arnold or me. Very stupid!"

"I'm extremely fed up listening to you."

"If you're tired you should sleep!"

"Enough! Get him the hell out of here!" Cavallo bellowed.

The butler pulled his gun. When Mike's kick hit the butler's hand a shot rang out. The gun flew in a high arc landing close to the stairs leading down to the beach. Mike's second hit landed with a thump in the fat man's solar plexus!

"See? Too slow! You really ought to replace him!"

Mike bowed politely towards Cavallo, like a Japanese karate teacher saluting his adversary, and he smiled.

***

Early that same morning Michele had called Ingrid. "I've been listening to the Sprenglers this morning. Something is cooking in Chatham! Let's rush down there and listen. It might come to some kind of a showdown."

Twenty minutes later they stopped at the parking lot near the beach below Cavallo's magnificent estate. Michele unloaded the video equipment and set up her camera aiming it at the group on

Cavallo's glassed-in veranda. The sensitive microphone clearly registered Cavallo lecturing Arnold.

She handed the extra pair of headphones to Ingrid and their eyes met when they heard Cathy's confident and insolent voice. They realized that Cavallo had two very obstinate guests. They heard Mike deliver one charge of accusations and hidden threats after another in the most explicit language. They heard Cavallo order his guards to throw the visitors out. The video got it all on tape, Mike's kick, the gun flying, and the collapsing butler.

"Darned! They should be more careful with my hypersensitive audio equipment," Michele shouted when the shot rang out.

"I think Cavallo got it," Ingrid said. "Yes, he's falling. The fat guy shot him! My God!" Ingrid tore off her headphones and ran to the lifeguard office. She rushed in and grabbed the phone, dialed zero and got the operator: "Get a police cruiser and an ambulance to the Cavallo residence on the beach here in Chatham!"

"Just a moment Ma'am, I'll give you the police."

"No, for heavens sake! They're killing each other here! You tell them yourself! Hurry! Hurry!"

"OK. Here! You're connected to the police. Give them the information they need. I'll call for an ambulance. Stand by, please!"

"Yes Ma'am, this is Sergeant Spencer," a man's voice broke in. "I'm in my cruiser near the police station. Did you say the druglord's place?"

"I said the Cavallo residence. Please hurry! Now I hear gunshots again! Several! From a machine gun! Maybe you shouldn't come here alone, Sir. They're mean people."

"Thank you, Ma'am. We'll be there! Please stand by."

Within minutes seven or eight cruisers with flashing lights blocked the road outside the villa of Mr. Cavallo, businessman, billionaire and druglord.

Mike bent over the unconscious butler and checked his breathing and heartbeat. He loosened the man's necktie and unbuttoned his shirt. "Sweet dreams," he said.

"Mike, look at Mr. Cavallo!" Cathy said.

Cavallo tried to say something, but no words came out. He slipped slowly from an upright position to half-sitting. Then, as if in slow motion, he slid down flat out on the floor. Blood oozed from his nose and mouth.

"Look out! Duck! Down on the floor for God's sake!" shouted Mike.

At that very moment a spray of bullets splintered the glass wall. Thousands of tiny glass chips glittered in the air. In a flash Mike grabbed Cathy and dragged her to shelter off the terrace. Arnold pressed his hand to a bullet wound in his shoulder. Blood trickled out between his fingers. He stared at Cavallo's dead face and smiled. "Consultation is over," he said, rising and turning toward Mike and his daughter hiding behind the upper steps of the wooden staircase leading down to the beach. He met his daughter's gaze. She looked at him in terror. He winked at her and said: "Free to go home!"

A new spray of bullets ripped the woodwork, the floor and the handrail into splinters. Arnold's body jerked in violent spasms as several bullets hit him. He fell headfirst down the stairs, landing in a grotesque position with his face buried in the sand.

Cathy rushed after her father ignoring the danger of being shot. She pulled him out of sight of the shooting madmen. She sat down and made it comfortable for him, wiping the sand off his face with her soft silk scarf. Gently she blew every little grain of sand from his closed eyes. She unbuttoned his shirt and felt his chest. He was breathing; his heart was still beating.

"Thank you, Lord! He's alive! Please let him live. I'll do something in return, I promise!"

Arnold had suffered several bullet wounds. Cathy watched helplessly as his life and his blood slowly trickled away. Tears clouded her eyes. She sat holding his head in her lap, looking down into the face of a man she had always loved.

She remembered him as a young, tanned, muscular Dad laughingly tossing her, a small girl, high in the air. She remembered him steadying the seat and running beside her on her first bike ride. She remembered him sitting on her bed telling stories. She remembered the warm summer days on the beach where they made sand castles and waded in the warm water finding pretty little shells. She remembered how they would make bracelets and necklaces, and how he would braid a wreath with flowers for her to wear like a little cap. In the winter he could give her make-believe wings to fly away to the sun, while outside a northeast wind whistled and howled shaking the whole house and thundering in the chimney. When the snowstorm blew high drifts so her school had to close, she felt safe and warm with him at home. He'd kiss her good night and leave the door to his and Mom's room open. He had always taken care of her. Now he lay here dying. He was almost dead a week ago, sitting there alone in the library with his gun in front of him, without the will to live.

She stroked his forehead gently, bent over and kissed his closed eyes whispering: "It's me, Cathy. I'm here with you, Dad. It will soon be over, this bad dream. We'll go home and Mom will be there and she'll hug you and tell you she loves you. And when the doctors say you are better, we'll walk on the beach. We'll begin a new life, free from drugs and evil people. And I'll work together with you and we'll build a new law firm on the West Coast.

"And Mom will say to you: 'It wasn't your fault that Maggie died.' And she'll be right because it was my fault, because I was with Maggie and I was the one who should have looked after her."

Cathy knew that he could hear and feel her. She didn't know what more to say to comfort him so she hummed a song her mother used to sing in the kitchen. She sat there singing softly, wishing time would stop just for a little while. But it didn't.

Arnold was completely disoriented. His mind wandered as he drifted into semi-consciousness.

He remembered looking into Cavallo's snake eyes.

"Good thing I didn't bring my gun. If I had, I would have committed murder half an hour ago. This stupid, greedy rat making a fool of himself demanding I pay him millions of dollars for tearing up our contract and letting me quit.

"I know you too well now, you skunk. You jackass, I despise you. You would kill me as soon as I handed over the money. You thought you could threaten me with the cops. You must be more stupid than I thought. I wish I had my gun. I wish this whole farce was over with. I hope I'll meet Maggie when I die. People, who say they have been dead, say they met people in a light place after walking in a long dark tunnel. I wish she could forgive me. She should have been left here on earth, not I…

"What on earth are Cathy and Mike doing here? How could they have gotten by those gorillas? Oh, am I glad they came! Her voice is like Sara's. She is so beautiful…and a good lawyer, too! I didn't know she could be that aggressive! I must try to smile, so they know I'm glad they're here. Her hands are so calm and warm and comforting. My little Cathy, she is just like Sara! She is defending me. She is finding new ways to get that jerk off my back. OK, I'll leave with her, but I'm so tired. Just let me sit a little longer.

"Thanks Mike, you are strong, but you don't need to support me I can walk out by myself, now that I'm not alone or in the hands of those goons, I feel better. You are great, Mike, I know you are a good pilot. I know you loved my Maggie, but I didn't know this polite family boy could turn into a vicious adult capable of avenging my family. Could he really have killed all three of those horrible snakes on board the *SNOWBIRD*? It was him! I asked him to do it! I am the one to blame. I'll tell him that I used his anger and sorrow to commit that crime. I used his love for Maggie and my position as employer. I'll tell him that he is not to blame and I will ask him to forgive me. After that we will never ever speak about it again.

"That Mike! I never saw a man act so fast. In one hundredth of a second he kicked and knocked that fat guy down and out. Good show, good show! I can hear a shot being fired. I can see the bullet leaving the muzzle. I can see the gun swivel around in the air. I hope that bullet hits Cavallo. I'll guide you, little bullet, so you can hit Mr. Cavallo right in his sneering mouth. Come on, little bullet, that's good. That's the right target! A little bit higher, a little bit to the left! Exactly there! Bull's eye!

"I must be sick. I actually saw the bullet. Millisecond by millisecond I guided it. I murdered Cavallo. But nobody will ever believe me! There must be a God. It must have been His will that this was the end of the rope for Joe Cavallo. Oh, Lord, was it really you, or was it Lucifer wanting to play an evil joke?

"Where did the kids go? OK, time to go home! We'll have a nice evening. I'll tell Cathy that I was tied by invisible ropes. My arms and legs weren't obeying orders. Even my logical thinking was tied down. But now I feel fine again. I am finally free! No more Cavallo. No more drug traffic! Damn! Somebody must have shot me! But why on earth did they shoot me? I haven't done anything. Now I am getting so heavy again. I can't move. Thanks, Mike! You found a spot where we can take cover. Yes, Cathy, I'll try to come over to you. Now they're shooting again! So, this is how it feels to get shot and die. Amazing, it doesn't hurt! Anyway, I don't care any more. I've had enough."

He fell headfirst and rolled down the steps hitting his head hard. Slowly he realized that he must still be alive. The sun was warm on his face.

***

The police officer stepped up on the bumper of his car and looked around in all directions. He was talking to Ingrid on his cell phone.

"Ma'am, where are you?"

"I'm here! Down by the beach! In the doorway of the bungalow office! I'm waving to you! Yes, Sir! I can see you! Tell the paramedics there's a wounded man behind the house, halfway down the stairs to the beach. Tell them to rush. A woman is sitting by him. He seems to be severely hurt! I watched them in my telephoto lens!"

***

Arnold was aware this must be the end. The damaged nerves were still in shock and didn't hurt. He felt completely at peace. He just wanted time would stop. He wanted this woman sitting beside him to stay with him and never leave. There was only one more thing. He made an effort to speak: "I wish I never got involved with these drug people. I wish you could forgive me. I wish it so much." His voice was hardly audible.

Cathy whispered back: "Yes, Dad, we forgive you. I'll stay here with you." Arnold heard her and his confused brain tried to put things in order. Memories of the past mixed with the present.

"But this couldn't be Cathy. It must be Sara. She smells like this—a clean warm body. It's the smell of life, the smell of an adoring woman. Her belly is soft and warm. Her hands are warm and friendly. I wish I were strong enough to take her hands. Or could it be you, Mom? I feel so cold. Why are my feet and legs so ice-cold? I smell the ocean. Must be the wind from the south. I hear the gulls. Somebody is talking. Someone is saying 'It's me, Cathy'. Why is Cathy here? I love her voice, but she is just a little girl sitting on the beach. It's her voice though, but a woman's voice. How strange! It's the voice of a woman I love. She kisses my eyes. How warm and loving. It could be Maggie. My women gave me the most wonderful memories of my life!"

Chapter 35

CAPE COD IN the summer is a zoo. Winter on Cape Cod is a landscape at peace. The skies are icy blue, the ocean lead gray, the beaches pale ochre with shining white snowdrifts and streaks of black, dried seaweed. It is a time for relaxation, a time for preparing for the short and hectic tourist season, a time when outside villagers are easily spotted and snake-eyed men plan the marketing of drugs for the coming summer.

Along the deserted beaches the rustling lyme grass is binding the fine beach sand, preventing it from drifting in among the thorny, gray bushes, the beach plums and the low beech pines and oak trees. The winter winds sing in the crowns of the black pines bending back and forth. Screaming sea gulls sail motionless against the wind. On drifting, big ice floes sea birds walk back and forth like old-fashioned steamboat passengers with their hands behind their backs. A couple of loons can be seen swimming so shallow only their elegant heads and long necks are visible above the water, as if they were looking for shelter between the rough waves.

This unique piece of New England has supporters defending its original purity.

A small fishing boat was headed for Barnstable Harbor with two men huddling behind the windshield. One was slapping himself with arms folded to keep warm. Two big plastic boxes with flapping, fresh, fish would bring enough money for what their women needed to bake and to buy vegetables for another week, and fuel for a few more trips out to the fishing banks. Winter, especially late winter, meant lean, tough times for many Cape Codders.

Ingrid and Ted were preparing a hearty vegetable soup in their cozy kitchen. An open fire spread warmth and light playing with shadows on the walls and the brick floor. From their table they could watch the fishing boat entering the harbor. Behind the wharf and the restaurant on stilts the setting sun painted the sky soft pink, pale orange, misty red, and the mainland a deep foggy purple.

There were several heavy, hollow knocks on the door. Ted answered. It was a beautiful young girl wearing warm ski pants, a down jacket, a red mohair scarf and a white fur hat.

"Come in!" Ingrid called from the range. "It's Miss Sprengler! Please come in."

The young woman stamped the snow from her boots and came in, closing the door behind her. She took off her boots, her woolen mittens and unwound the scarf, which had been wrapped several times around her head, leaving little showing but a red nose and two smiling eyes.

"Good afternoon," she said, "sorry to disturb you. I came an hour ago and planned to stay over the weekend to see Dad at the hospital and do some schoolwork. But, there is something wrong with our oil burner. It won't start. The house is freezing cold and I wonder if you could help me and take a quick look. I am not that familiar with technical things. Maybe there's a switch somewhere."

"I'll be right with you," said Ted, grabbing his down jacket and pulling on his fur-lined boots.

"There is plenty of soup for all of us", Ingrid said, "why don't you come back and have supper with us while your house heats up." The girl nodded 'yes' and smiled 'thanks'.

Half an hour later the two came back. It was dark by then. Ted said he couldn't fix the problem. He called the burner service and asked his friend, the owner, to come and have a look. But he couldn't come until next morning, so Ingrid invited their young neighbor to stay overnight.

"We always have a guest room ready, and you are most welcome. I called our other neighbor, Michele Renard, a few minutes ago and she'll join us for supper, too."

"Thank you! It's really very kind of you. Am I awful if I say yes? I have seen you two so many times, but I still don't know you. My name is Cathy. I guess you know my Mom and Dad. They have been your neighbors for years. I am only here during the summers. I go to school in England."

There was a noise from the garage and a light knock on the door before Michele came in. She shook the snow off her coat and hung it in the den. She put her mittens and knit hat on the radiator, embraced Ingrid and Ted and introduced herself to Cathy.

"How is your father doing? We heard he was shot and almost killed by those drug gangsters in Chatham."

"Dad was severely wounded. He's still in bad shape. I have been seeing him twice a month since October. He will survive, but he'll be an invalid for the rest of his life. He was deeply depressed, but he's better now."

They all stood around the range and were served steaming, creamy soup of cauliflower, carrots, broccoli, onions and potatoes. Out of the oven came hot toast with Swiss cheese. Everybody enjoyed the simple meal, eating heartily with little conversation. The only sounds were the wind's soughing around the house, its thunder in the chimney and the rustle from the branches of the oak tree touching and sweeping the roof. The light from the flames in the fireplace and the candles on the table flickered. It was warm and cozy.

"My sister, Maggie, was my closest friend," Cathy said. "I guess sisters often are. Our family always held together until this happened with Maggie and Dad. Mom was so shocked she refuses to come home. Dad asked me to look after our house here. I can't tell you how nice it is to be with you. I know you are Scandinavians, so Skoal, and thanks for your hospitality!"

The sherry was dry and refreshing. The fireplace opened to both the kitchen and the sitting room. The snowing had stopped and Ted helped Cathy pick up her luggage. She locked her house and car. Michele served coffee and Ingrid offered snifters of cognac. Cathy talked about her family. She had interested listeners;

"Dad is a lawyer, as you probably know. The drug czar, Cavallo in Chatham, was a customer of his, and Dad got involved and feels responsible for my sister's death. He wanted to quit but Mr. Cavallo had a hold on Dad and wouldn't let him go. We drove to Chatham and tried to talk to Mr. Cavallo when the shooting started. Cavallo's bodyguards shot at us and hit my father. The police came a few minutes later. Thank God! And the ambulance, too! Dad had lost a lot of blood and was dying in my arms when they arrived."

They sipped their coffee and brandy in silence listening to the crackling of the fire.

"That morning," said Michele, "two ladies were filming on the beach below Mr. Cavallo's house. They happened to see an armed man there and aimed their telephoto lens at you. They saw the butler pull his gun, they saw your sister's fiancé kick the gun out of the butler's hand, saw Mr. Cavallo get shot and saw you being pulled to safety by the young man. They saw your father being shot at again and again. They saw him fall headfirst down the stairs towards the beach. They saw it all."

Cathy stared at Michele.

"I didn't know there were any witnesses. I was amazed though that the ambulance was there just in time."

"Those two ladies are sitting here with you right now. Ingrid is the one who ran and called for help."

Cathy looked questioningly at Ingrid. Her eyes asked for a confirmation. When a smile and a nod said it was so, she rushed over and hugged and kissed Ingrid, smiling with her eyes filled with tears. "Thank you! Thank you! You saved Dad's life. The doctor said that one minute later would have been too late! How can I ever thank you?"

Ingrid hugged her. Then Cathy stiffened, "Oh, please forgive my behavior. I lost control. I don't even know you."

"A good hug is always right," Ted said. "By the way, I see you just got visitors!" He took Cathy to the window and pointed at her home. A big silver Lincoln was parked there. Three men carried some luggage inside.

"Who on earth are those people? Look they have keys to my house and they are walking right in! Let's go over!"

Michele stopped her. "Your father has enemies. Let's wait. Go watch from the upstairs windows. Stay in the dark so they don't see you. I don't think we should disturb them."

Minutes later the men drove off. It was snowing again. The lantern on the telephone pole squeaked as it swung back and forth in the wind. The illuminated spot below danced hither and thither. They all went out into the cutting wind. Cathy unlocked the door. Entering an empty, cold summer home on a winter night is eerie. Behind the door hung a bathrobe and a swimsuit. On the sofa in the hall was a magazine with smiling suntanned faces on the cover...in one chair a sun hat, in another a tennis racket and a sun visor.

"What are we looking for?" Cathy asked.

"Something that shouldn't be here," Ted pointed out. "Look in your father's dresser drawers, cupboards and closets, among his private things, in his bed, under it, everywhere. Maybe they left a gun with fingerprints, maybe some dope."

They searched the entire house but found nothing.

"Where would you hide something, so it wouldn't look planted?" asked Michele.

"In the attic," Ingrid suggested, "or behind the boiler, behind the oil tank, behind the fridge or stove, in the open fireplace, in the toilet water tanks, under the staircase, under heavy furniture, in a TV set, in a sofa."

Cathy held a flashlight and Michele followed her up to a frigid, pitch-black attic. Under the insulation they found something! A big heavy box wrapped in plastic.

"That's not ours," said Cathy. Michele cried out loudly so Ted and Ingrid could hear her: "We found something!" They pulled the box to the stairs and down to the garage.

"We found something, too," Ted said. "Scotch-taped under Arnold's desk - an envelope with a lot of money and cancelled checks."

Ingrid found several cocaine bags among garden tools and fertilizer sacks in the garage. They searched each room systematically. Under the carpet in the library was a second envelope with receipts and cancelled checks. That was all.

Returning to the Hallbergs' house they spread the findings out on the kitchen table.

"Let's see what we've got here," Michele said. "Approximately 50 pounds of cocaine and enough receipts, checks and money to send your father to prison for at least ten years. Here is $50,000 in bills! They are yours, Cathy. Let's hide the money and forget it till later."

They carried everything to Michele's house, leaving all the papers and the money in her vault and the bags of cocaine worth about a million dollars in her basement.

Early next morning the State Police and DEA people were there searching the Sprenglers' home. When Cathy came downstairs to join Ingrid and Ted nobody said a word. Outside the flashing blue lights on the police cruisers swept around and around. Ingrid started the coffee while Cathy helped set the table and cut the home-baked bread. She was very jittery. They could see Michele talking to a policeman with a dog. The dog was sniffing her hands and legs!

"Good thing dogs don't talk that much," Ted observed, "because this one would probably have said: 'Hey, Lady, what did you do in the Sprenglers' house last night? Your scent is all over the place.' Sometimes dogs are women's best friends!"

Chapter 36

Michael Soames jumped over the snowdrifts in the parking lot at the entrance to Boston General Hospital. The snowblowers had cleared the walkways, but the ice bark was still there and the sand was blown away by the searching wind this typical New England midwinter day. He walked up the stairs to the Neurological Rehabilitation area to see Arnold. From London Cathy had called Mike to tell him that her father finally was strong enough to have visitors and wanted to talk to him.

Arnold lay looking out the window, watching the snow-filled clouds sail by in the dark gray sky. Small snowflakes swirled down from the roof. Mike cleared his throat when he entered the room, but there was no reaction. Then he tiptoed around the bed and was glad to see that his friend was awake, smiling at him. On the bedside table was a bouquet of four big red roses. Mike handed Arnold a bunch of five small pink roses.

"I see Cathy sent you four roses," Mike said. "They are more beautiful than mine, but mine smell just as good." He held the bouquet so Arnold could inhale the fragrance. "I brought you five, because I count myself as the fifth member of your family."

Arnold nodded and whispered: "Thanks for coming. Lovely roses. Did Cathy call you?"

Slowly, with great effort his hand rose from the bedspread and reached out to Mike. Mike took it with both hands, and when he tried to loosen the grip Arnold didn't want to let go. He lowered the hands and let them rest on the bedside. Arnold whispered: "They almost got me!"

"I never should have kicked that butler," Mike said. "It's my fault. I started the whole damned shootout kicking the fat man. I am so sorry. I got so mad. If I'd kept my cool they would never have shot."

"He got what he deserved and so did Cavallo. I have to tell you something," Arnold couldn't hide the pride in his voice. "When you kicked the gun out of the fat man's hand and the shot rang out, I saw the bullet leave the muzzle as if in slow motion. And I told it to go straight into Cavallo's head. It landed exactly where I told it to! It took Cavallo a long time to realize just what had happened. He made a stupid face and slid down on the floor. Can you believe it?" Arnold breathed heavily and started to say something more but decided to wait.

"I believe you saw the bullet move because your brain was super alert. No doubt a higher force was leading that bullet exactly to the right target! Cavallo was a first-class rat!"

"The doctors say that therapy might make my hands and arms useful again, but so many nerves are damaged I'll have difficulties standing and I'll probably never walk again. But I deserve this punishment. This is the price I had to pay." He paused and sighed.

"I'll never be able to fly again, never able to run on the beach again. I'll not even be able to go to the bathroom by myself for a long time, if ever. But I guess I should be glad I'm still alive. I'll keep my Baron, and you can fly it. I want you to take me up to see the sunrise one early morning and maybe one evening to watch the sun set, sinking through the purple sky into the violet mists rolling in from the ocean. That is so beautiful."

"Do you want me to fly private taxi and develop that business? Or should I wait till we can fly together?"

"I want you to use the Baron, but you have to promise me one thing, OK? Don't fly dope! Is that clear?"

"Absolutely!"

An attractive young nurse came in. She nodded to Mike, and went up to Arnold, stroked his hair and patted his face. "You look much better now, Mr. Sprengler. You must have been talking about women or maybe about flying!"

"Nurse Molly, meet my copilot, Mike. He can take you closer to heaven than anybody else. Ask him to fly you to the Bahamas for a weekend. He's a good guy.!"

The visiting hour was over. Mike felt Arnold's grip on his hand strengthen. The two men had been holding hands during the entire visit.

"Come back next week, Mike"

"I will. Get well! Cheerio!"

He didn't know how to show his affection really. He patted Arnold's hair and his cheek. He would have bent over and kissed him if it had been his father but he thought better of it.

Empty parking spaces are scarce in Boston. Mike generally parked his car at the air club. Although Beacon Hill is the most charming part of Boston, the narrow streets offer few parking spots. By chance he found one outside his own place on Myrtle Street. At the grocery store he got Italian bread, cheese, pasta and tomatoes. Opening the door to his small apartment he sensed the fragrance of a fine perfume. The light in his tiny "living room" was switched on. Who on earth?

"Hope you don't mind us waiting for you in here," said a soft female voice. "It was so darned cold and slushy outside…and your door was open."

Jenny Greycoat and her Japanese secretary, the two young ladies he and Arnold had flown from the Bahamas, greeted him with two bewitching smiles. Mike knew his door had been locked.

"A good lie and a bad lock, but you're welcome!" Mike joked. "Hope you haven't been waiting too long. Please, accept my invitation to my pasta dinner while we talk."

He poured three glasses of a good Ruffino wine. He looked like a professional chef the way he juggled the pots, the pasta and all ingredients in his secret ragout recipe. The girls laughed at him and sipped the excellent wine.

"Vivaldi goes well with spaghetti," he said and turned on the stereo. The elegant young women looked a bit out of place, suddenly realizing that his favorite chair was worn, sagging and spotted from spilled wine, beer and all those things a bachelor uses while watching TV.

"Sorry my humble den is kind of messy and lacks the touch of a female hand."

"Then, who's that girl in the photo?" Jenny asked.

"That's Maggie, Arnold's daughter, my fiancée. She died not long ago."

"Oh, I am sorry I asked. I didn't mean to be indiscreet."

"That's alright. Drug runners killed her. You know I'm a pilot, and you know that I know that your father is involved in drug trafficking. Before you say anything I want to make one thing perfectly clear. I'll fly you wherever you want to go, but absolutely no dope on board. OK?"

"That's fine with me," Jenny agreed. "All I want is to have you fly Suzy and me on some business trips. Dad told me about the showdown at Cavallo's. I am glad you escaped unharmed."

Mike stirred the ragout and tasted it, added more red and green peppers diced into tiny cubes. He tasted again and added more diced celery. Tasted again, added Tabasco and finally seemed satisfied with the result. Grated cheese, melted garlic butter and fresh Italian bread were served. The guests were hungry. They ate in silence. The sunny weather had changed. It was dark now and snowing heavily. In less than an hour a fierce wind had blown the snow into high drifts. When Mike looked out he could hardly see his car parked only 10 feet from the window. They called for a taxi, but were told that all traffic in downtown Boston had come to a stop. Only emergency vehicles assisted by snowplows could pass through the four-foot deep snowdrifts. More snow was expected. Over the radio people were told to stay indoors. Suzy, Jenny's bodyguard-secretary, suggested he invite them to stay overnight.

"Sure! You're welcome to stay. There is a queen-size bed you can share in my bedroom and I'll sleep here on the couch. No problem. We have all we need right here."

He served coffee and Strega. Jenny talked about her plan to sell exotic seafood from the Bermudas and Bahamas to luxury restaurants in New England. "Shellfish is in great demand. It has to be delivered fresh several times a week. Therefore, your new Air Taxi business can count on a flying start!"

Both girls seemed to enjoy the consequences of the unpredictable New England weather. They showed no regrets that the night they had planned to spend in luxury at the Marriott Hotel wound up in Mike's bachelor digs. The winter storm had intensified and the apartment's heating system was not the best. Bundled up in blankets, drinking hot cocoa with Peppermint SchnappsScotch they watched the late weather forecasts on TV. When it was time to go to bed the heating system was dead. Mike pulled on another wool sweater and a second pair of heavy ski socks before he crawled under the cold sheets on the couch.

The bedroom door opened and Suzy looked out. "Your landlord must be saving heating oil, the radiators are ice cold. Jenny says that if you're freezing out here you can come and sleep in our bed. You don't even have a comforter for yourself out here."

"Thanks, but I am just fine. Good night!"

"If you change your mind, come on over, OK?"

Mike got colder and colder. The vision of sleeping between the two young women excited him. His icy toes and chattering teeth made him change his mind. With his pillow under one arm and a blanket under the other he knocked at the guests' door. Laughingly they gave him plenty of space in the middle of the bed. Nothing was said. Turning his head to the left he caught Suzy's heavy oriental fragrance; on his right he sensed Jenny's French perfume. Soon they cuddled up to him. With one beautiful girl's head on each shoulder and one hand from each girl finding its way under his jogging suit to rest on his bare chest and stomach this was a really neat place to sleep! But nonetheless he was overcome with a feeling of sadness as his thoughts drifted away from his bed companions and their soft, warm breasts pressed close to him. It was good. But when he fell asleep he dreamed about Maggie. She lay close to him holding her hand on his chest. He nestled his nose into her ruffled hair and whispered he loved her and the scent of her. It was good to be with her again. Loneliness and sorrow was gone. He dreamed he kissed her and she was his and she fell asleep on his shoulder.

A gray dawn spread a sparse light in the room when he woke up. It took a while for his drowsy self to remember what two sleeping women were doing in his bed. Their warm velvety bodies clung comfortably to him. He lay motionless so not to waken them. The clock radio buzzed and the recording of morning birds on public radio started their five minutes of singing before the news.

"I hear birds singing."

"Me, too. Where are they?"

The girls moved, stretched and yawned. It was nice and warm in the bed. His nose was cold and so was the room. The snowstorm was still raging outside and the cold draft from the window kept them under the comforter until the news came on.

"Singing birds in Boston mean breakfast," said Mike.

Suzy, still hidden under the down murmured: "I don't want sparrows nor nightingales nor any other bird for breakfast. I just want coffee and toast."

To fix coffee Mike had to climb over Jenny, but she caught him in a big hug grasping him to her with her arms and legs. "Mike, it was good to sleep with you. You lay calmly between Suzy and me all night. Not many men could have done that. And you whispered that you loved me."

"I did not!"

"No, he whispered that he loved me," said Suzy, whose ruffled hair popped up from under the down comforter.

"I must have been dreaming," he said crawling out of Jenny's embrace. He built a fire. No warm water. He went into the bathroom and took a quick cold shower. The apartment began to warm up. He fixed hot coffee and toasted English muffins.

The snow came down like never before. The weather forecasts predicted continued snowstorms until the next morning. People were cautioned to stay indoors until the streets could be cleared and plowed.

Chapter 37

FROM HER HOME Michele watched the policemen and the cruisers with flashing lights parked outside the Sprenglers' house. Crossing the yard to her Swedish friends she stopped and patted the drug-trained dog.

"Last night I noticed a silver Lincoln driving up to the Sprenglers' house." Michele told the K-9 officer, "and three men went inside. Their car had a New York license plate and I remember the number." The policeman made notes, thanked her and returned to his colleagues, who had just completed their search.

"There's no dope in that house," the policeman stated. "We've searched every inch of it, from the chimney to the sewer. Why do we take every stupid anonymous phone call seriously?" one officer asked.

"We have to," said his superior. "If one out of ten leads us to something, I'll be satisfied. You don't want our Cape Cod to be like Tacoma in Washington State, do you? There hundreds of dealers operate undisturbed and thousands of buyers from all over northwestern United States flock to get all kinds of drugs! Do you want that?"

"No, Sir! This lady said a car picked up something here last night. She gave me the New York plate number."

"They might have left Cape Cod already, but we'll alert our colleagues along Route 95 to New York" He gave orders over the radio.

Suddenly Michele got an idea. She returned to her house and picked up two big shopping bags with cocaine from the previous night's successful detective work. Keeping a safe distance from the police dog she hurried over to Ingrid's and asked her to come along for on a quick trip to Chatham.

After the repairman had fixed the burner in the Sprengler house Ingrid feared the drug traffickers might return so she asked Cathy to stay with them and use a desk in the library to do the school work she had brought with her.

Michele switched on the radar detector and was nervously looking behind her for tailgating police cruisers. She and Ingrid found, as they had expected, the silver Lincoln parked outside "The Singing Whale", the place where Bill and Bolivar had stayed during their visit on the Cape. In the breakfast room next to the front desk there were four men, dressed alike in

three-piece suits, waiting to be served. They were the ones! Michele quickly got busy with the Lincoln in the parking lot. Soon 25 small plastic bags filled with cocaine were hidden in the big trunk behind the spare tire, under the tools, under the carpet, everywhere where nobody would notice them right away. With a satisfied smile she closed the trunk and went back to their car parked a safe distance away. She and Ingrid unloaded the video equipment and aimed the telephoto lens at the entrance and waited. Half an hour later the four gangsters came out into the bright sunshine and the dazzling, snowy landscape. They seemed uncomfortable that their working day was beginning in the morning and not at dusk as usual. Michele got a close-up mug shot of each of them as well as a group photo. The men walked down the wooden stairs to the parking lot, opened the trunk of the car, threw in their bags and drove off.

Ingrid and Michelle quickly packed their equipment and followed the gangsters. They passed Joe Cavallo's former expansive estate and the trip ended at the lobster pier where Arnold's dark navy blue fishing boat lay docked. The horn from the Lincoln sounded and Jack, the skipper, came up from the cabin. Michele heard and taped everything. She heard the curses when the men slipped on the icy ground. She heard the crunching sound as they walked in the frozen snow over the gangway. Aiming at the windshield of the fishing boat, she could hear everything said in there.

The conversation revealed an interesting plan for doing business with the skipper using Arnold Sprengler's powerboat. Soon the men reappeared on unsteady legs, wobbling their way to their car. In a flash Ingrid and Michele demounted the surveillance equipment.

With spinning wheels the Lincoln climbed up the icy slope and headed towards Ryder's Cove passing Pleasant Bay and on up to the Mid-Cape expressway. The driver was surprisingly careful and drove slowly. Ingrid and Michele followed several hundred yards behind. After a few miles they noticed the flashing lights from a police cruiser stopping the New York registered Lincoln that every policeman on the Cape was looking for! From behind came one police car and from the other lane two more cruisers with flashing lights crossed the median.

The passengers in the Lincoln seemed unconcerned and relaxed when they were stopped totally unaware of the big surprise that awaited them.

***

Cathy and Ted had prepared dinner when Ingrid and Michele got home. Corned beef was served with mashed potatoes and baked leek in a white creamy sauce topped with cheese. Everybody enjoyed a good laugh when Michele related what she and Ingrid had been up to.

Cathy's house was warm and pleasant by now, but they had decided she'd better stay with Ingrid and Ted and not be alone overnight. The successful joke could call for retaliation. The men in the Lincoln must have been surprised when they realized the price for driving under the influence, illegal possession of firearms and driving with a trunk full of cocaine, the very same ones they had hidden in Sprengler's house the night before. Ingrid and Cathy sang together while one washed and the other dried the dishes.

"Don't you have a dishwasher, Ted?" Michele asked.

"Sure, but we never use it. In our house it doesn't save any time. Also, I prefer this singing rather than the noise from a dishwasher, don't you?"

"When I see Cathy doing her homework, or helping me in the kitchen it's like when our daughter was home. I love having young people around." Ingrid said and reached for her knitting basket with a half-finished cashmere sweater. The quick clicking of her needles and the sparks from the fire were the only sounds heard, except for muffled tunes of a Brandenburg concerto.

Michele knew how evenings were spent in this house. She had brought a book and was deeply involved in her favorite subject, animal behavior. Ted, too, was reading. His favorite subject, history, took him back to the Swedish king Gustavus II, the grandson of Gustav Vasa, the founder of modern Sweden.

The Cape Cod weatherman predicted icy roads, fog and a possible mix of rain and snow. Cathy had to catch a plane to London next morning, and the bad weather held off until the Hallbergs and Michele returned from taking her to the Hyannis terminal where she got the direct bus to Boston's Logan Airport.

Chapter 38

JENNY'S FATHER, HARRY Greycoat, was an officer in the Royal Air Force when he married Jeanine Dufour, one of the few female pilots in the Free French Air Forces. The slender, fragile looking, black-eyed girl with the long, thin aquiline nose was a silent, timid person everybody in the squadron loved. She flew a Hurricane fighter. This workhorse of the RAF got less recognition than the speedier Spitfires, but probably did just as great a job during the battle of Britain. Jeanine's imagination, improvisation and quick brain compensated for the set backs of her plane.

Harry was 20 then. A shy, six-foot-four Briton with a full, bushy, red mustache. He was still alive because Jeanine intervened in a fight where four of the Germans' most feared plane, the ME-109, were attacking his Spitfire. In the dogfight that followed the little French woman executed an amazing number of traps and tricks that made the Germans furious and Harry laugh out loud! She was a master! She got three Messerschmitts before the remaining one fled.

After the war Jeanine and Harry married, Baby Jenny arrived and Harry flew with British Airways. Many years later, quite by chance, he found a book in his library on aerobatics written by his wife. It was then he learned that she, without his knowing it, had taught aerobatics for years and that her lessons were considered to be the finest in the business. When he asked her about it she replied that she never told him because she did not want to make him nervous. Her flying was not any riskier than his. Also she, like him, could not live without flying.

Jenny was given a fine education and after Harry retired her parents moved to Bermuda. They had lived there less than a year when the tragedy hit the family. Jeanine was flying a wealthy British businessman from Nassau to Colombia. Her Cessna was reported missing and was never found. Harry visited every spot along its route and finally he learned that some people had seen a small aircraft explode in midair over the Colombian coast. A witness said it looked like it had been shot down with a ground-to-air missile. He also learned that Jeanine's passenger was a drug carrier with few friends and a great many enemies.

That's how Harry's private drug war started. He began to rob drug dealers. He made more money than he could ever use. He had bank accounts and trust funds in England, Switzerland, Colombia, Mexico and the United States. To get the right connections he involved himself with the big sharks and shipped drugs himself. He became acquainted with Bertie Brown, a former officer in the Royal Navy, who knew every island, every little beach and hidden bay in the Caribbean. Bertie and Harry were behind most lost transports of drugs and drug money in the area. The more money they made the more they stole.

Jenny loved to fly, but she preferred gliding and the quiet sound of the air sweeping around the sleek fuselage, and being carried by upward winds. Hovering like a bird she felt free. It was when she was learning skydiving that she met Suzy. This sweet and innocent-looking, totally fearless Japanese was not only teaching casting but was also a black belt Karate expert teaching self defense at a well-known school for martial arts in London. The two young women became close friends. When Jenny introduced Suzy to her father he fell completely for her charm and brilliant intellect. He hired her at a very generous salary to be his daughter's bodyguard, which he had a strong feeling could be necessary, and her secretary. He adored the two, smart, pretty young women and he always treated Suzy as Jenny's sister.

Now the two girlfriends had a plan in which Mike could play an important role. Harry was a sly old fox in the game of judging people. Mike, he knew, was not only a terrific pilot but also a gentleman and a smart one. The main reason for the two girls' trip to New England was to find new channels for drug distribution. What they found out was that a certain Mr. Bolivar in New York, the most aggressive dealer, had started to work in company with Joe Cavallo in Chatham. They also found out that both these men had been killed recently and that a former right hand of Bolivar's was pushing to take over Bolivar's empire and also to grab a chunk of the market held by a powerful Providence group.

Mike's insistence at not flying coke did not stop the two ladies from including him in their plans. They had found Mike very attractive and now, snowed in his little apartment, they appreciated his hospitality. That first night Jenny was thrilled when she heard Mike whisper, "I love you." When she was sure he was asleep she could not resist stroking his broad chest. It gave her a feeling he was hers. She never guessed that Suzy at that very moment had the same feelings and was caressing Mike's warm, hairy stomach in response to his kiss on her forehead, unaware of the fact that he was dreaming of Maggie!

The second day of the snowstorm was spent in front of Mike's open fireplace, consuming pot after pot of tea. They talked about flying and gliding and Mike admitted he had never practiced skydiving but his two guests had extensive experience and invited him to dive with them.

The snowstorm had tapered off. The heavy snowfall had clogged all streets in the area and it was sensational to open a window to the silent, white cotton-clothed Boston. The customary murmuring sounds of the big city were gone. Mother Nature had taken charge. There was a healing peace. From the Government Center only a few blocks away they could hear the big snowplows and Army trucks removing snow masses. A five-foot snowdrift blocked their outer door and the narrow street was impassable. It was still bitter cold outside when it was time to go to bed. They let the open fire die. The rooms turned bitter cold quickly. Jenny and Suzy told Mike that he might as well come in with them right away so they could keep warm together. All three of them snuggled into the big bed. At first it was ice cold but it soon became warm and comfortable.

They talked late in the dark. In the pale light filtering in from moonlit sky they could see steam rising as they spoke. Mike was thinking of Maggie; he missed her terribly. When he dozed off she became alive. His mind did not want to accept the fact that she was dead and that their dreams were never to be realized. He forgot the two women beside him.

He was deeply asleep and totally unconscious when Jenny decided to find out if her charm and femininity really had failed to make any impression on him—if, at least, he was erected. But her hand found the place already occupied by Suzy's hand. Jenny sat up in the dark and tried to look angrily at Suzy. She bent forwards telling her friend to "Let go! He's mine!" In the dark their foreheads collided and Suzy whispered back "No, he is mine! He loves me!" Jenny protested.

The operetta scene froze when they heard his sleepy voice murmuring: "Oh Maggie, I love you, but you're crazy."

Suzy sounded like a teasing schoolgirl when she whispered: "He loves Maggie, not you. I feel him growing. Want to feel it? But I want him back. I found it! Finder's keepers!"

Jenny's soft and firm hand felt Mike's strong pulsing erection. It excited her. "I want to ride on him!" she said.

"You are crazy!" Suzy whispered. "Should we wake him up?"

"Heavens no! I think he is so adorable when he's asleep! I'm going to sit on him. I'll just sit still." Jenny pulled off her panties and climbed on Mike, sitting on him quietly to start with but soon having to move slowly. Mike still seemed unconscious.

"It's my turn now," whispered her friend. "Is he still good?"

"I need a few more minutes. He is super! Oh! he is so good to me! Oh! I'm exploding," she moaned.

They changed places slowly and cautiously. Mike moved and stretched with pleasure when the supple Suzy slid down over him. She was quivering with desire but didn't want to awaken him so she sat silently and motionless gazing out in the moon blue darkness. She felt the pulsing manhood inside her and she knew Jenny was satisfied and asleep. This was crazy! A crazy pleasure. She could not believe that he kept sleeping. She leaned forward and kissed him softly.

"Are you asleep, Mike?" she whispered.

No answer. But he had hold of her hips. After almost an hour she could not resist moving slowly and rhythmically. He still seemed to sleep undisturbed, unaware of the ecstatic rider with her eyes tightly shut, concentrating on holding back her wild desire of screaming out her pleasure. Finally, satisfied, tired and full of tenderness she lay down beside him kissing him good night.

In the morning the pink light from the pale New England winter sun woke him up. He lay completely still, pleased to have a girl with a happy expression of peaceful beauty on each shoulder. The birds announcing the morning program on the public radio woke up his bed companions. They crawled up closer to him and suddenly he got a shower of kisses all over his face from both women.

"Oops! Aren't you the sweetest bed companions!"

"Did you have sweet dreams, Mike?"

"You bet!"

"What did you dream?"

"I dreamed about Maggie."

"Was she nice to you?"

He did not answer the question. Their expressions of playfulness disappeared. Was he toying with them or had they used his longing, his feeling of loneliness, in a way they never thought of or had wanted? This feeling of guilt contrasted radically with the fun of the practical joke of the night before. In a way they had raped him. They felt like intruders.

"I have met many girls, but there was never one like Maggie. She was so…pure. She was with me here tonight."

"You are sweet, Mike. You will soon find a new woman. And she will say 'Here I am, the one you waited for'."

He smiled at Jenny's efforts to comfort him. He slipped out from under the comforter and jumped with big steps over to the bathroom. "The hot water is back!" he shouted. They heard him shower and shave.

The weatherman promised sunshine. Heavy snowplows and street sweepers moving outside made the whole building tremble. People opened their windows and looked out as if to convince themselves that it was a perfect sunny Sunday morning. The blinding, clean, white snow sprinkled with myriads of sparkling crystals made the narrow street look like an English Christmas card. There were the gas lamps, the old brick buildings with artistically sculptured entrance doors, thick, sculptured, gilded or painted wooden signs hanging from ornamented wrought iron brackets outside the small stores. Only the old English post coach was missing.

***

Mike visited Arnold almost every day. Cathy had written from London and told her father that unknown men had been entering the home in Barnstable. Maybe she needed protection, Arnold thought. Maybe Mike could look after the house since Cathy was only there every two weeks during the winter. Mike told about the flying he was going to do for Jenny. Arnold was glad the Baron could be used, but repeated that he did not approve of any drug transports.

"I'll donate the coke-mine to a museum so the police can learn about new techniques," he said. "The apparatus is after all a pretty simple, uncomplicated thing. It's undetectable by sonar and could be used to transport illegal material across borders. Evil powers could use it for smuggling nuclear devises, explosives, bacterial weapons or containers with war gases and nervgases…"

That evening Jenny, Suzy and Mike had a delicious dinner together at the Marriott. Jenny told Mike that she had been informed that one representative from each of the two drug traffic organizations in New York and on Cape Cod had met and created one import and distribution company of Bolivar's and Cavallo's two drug empires.

That night Mike fell asleep alone in his big bed, where the pillows still carried the fragrances of his two recent bedmates. He dreamed sweet dreams. But not as intensely as the night before.

Chapter 39

MICHELE STARTED THE video. Ingrid and Ted watched. The monitor showed the four New York gangsters coming out of "The Singing Whale", their eyes more used to moonlight than to the bright sunlight intensified by the snow. The next sequence showed the Chatham Lobster Pier, Sprengler's boat and the men walking on board. Every sound and every word from the cabin was clearly registered. The clinking glasses, bottles being opened, drinks poured, cheers and gulps and "ahhhs" constantly repeated. In spite of the considerable alcohol consumption the men had no difficulty in planning their objective. They were going to "borrow" Arnold's coke-mine and drop it from a boat instead of a plane. Using Arnold's boat, Captain Jack would pick up and store the coke.

Ingrid shook her head and jotted down some notes. The distribution in the Boston area and on Cape Cod would be managed by a man named Benny Mikellis. Their sale of cocaine the coming summer was estimated to be between 50 and 100 million dollars. A test shipment was to be arranged as soon as possible. A Panamanian freighter would drop the container 50 miles east of Chatham on its way to Portland, Maine. Jack, the skipper, was prepared to cooperate and make fifty grand on this trial delivery.

"No problem, I know the equipment, but there is a great risk of being stopped and checked by the Coast Guard or the local police this time of the year."

"You're allowed to trap lobster year round, right?"

"Yes, but the demand is not like it is in the summer; nobody needs an awful lot of lobster now."

"So?"

"So I'll need seventy-five grand for any shipment I get involved in. Also, the container belongs to this boat and to Mr. Sprengler. You better not try to steal it. You know what happened to Mr. Bolivar and Mr. Cavallo…and to your friends in the Bahamas."

There was some mumbling and then somebody said: "OK, have that container ready to be picked up at sea by a passing Panamanian freighter heading south next week. You'll get specifics about time and place later.

"I also need a deposit for the container; $75,000 in a money order marked 'Down payment for summer house on Little Beach Road'. You will get it back signed as soon as I have the container back," Captain Jack stated decisively.

Now there was more mumbling. "Twenty-five thousand and we are in business!"

"Forget it! I'm not bargaining. I know the value of this equipment and I don't know you well enough to trust you— seventy-five or I have to ask Mr. Sprengler."

"We are honest people!"

"Seventy-five or no deal this week. You'll find that I'm good to work with. I know the game. You don't."

"OK, Jack! You're a ripper but you serve a good whiskey on board this ship, so we'll be reasonable. It's a deal. We have to trust each other. I am Benny Mikellis and I live here on the Cape. We'll see each other frequently, so I'll get you the check by tomorrow. You'll get your payment along with your final instructions."

Michele, Ingrid and Ted heard the men leaving and saw them walking on unsteady legs back to their car. Their whole appearance was alien to any Cape Codder because of the Italian kid shoes, tailored overcoats, three-piece suits and soft Italian hats. In the icy, bone-chilling wind from the ocean Cape Codders wear the only sensible choice of clothing: Heavy boots, casual warm sports pants and wool sweaters, thermal vests, leather jackets and knit or fur hats. The video film tuned out in black.

"You are a good camera crew," Ted complimented Michele and Ingrid. "The shots are sharp and we couldn't ask for better sound effects. One thing puzzles me though: Is Mr. Sprengler really aware of this? Cathy said he would never again be involved with drugs. Apparently they want Arnold Sprengler behind bars so they can use his boat and his coke-mine. We need to know where and when the goods will be landed. Then we will intervene."

Chapter 40

MICHELE WAS ENJOYING her stay in London. The zoologists' conference turned out to be a success. Three thousand zoologists, psychologists and researchers working on the protection of endangered species and wildlife environment met for six consecutive days. More than 60 lectures had been held. On the first day she came by chance to be seated in the first row near a tall, lanky Briton with a prominent aquiline nose. A monocle swung on a black, braided silk cord from the buttonhole of his tweed jacket and he used it every now and then for a closer look in his program or notebooks. He sat quietly, absorbing the speaker's every word. Michele made notes throughout the lecture.

The next lecture, an hour later, was about Bengal, Siberian and Malayan tigers. Once again Michele had an excellent place in the front row. Before the lecture the man with the monocle took the seat next to her. He was in his early 60s wearing an off-white tweed suit with golf plus four trousers and a yellow vest. Michele opened her old briefcase. There, in a plastic pocket was her old yellowed photo of Richard and herself taken years ago. Looking at it she experienced an intense feeling of solitude. She felt the monocle man lightly laying his hand on hers and when she looked at him she met a sharp, inquisitive gaze from friendly eyes in a smiling face. He bent closer to her and whispered: "Excuse me, Madame. You couldn't possibly be Mrs. Michele Renard, could you?"

Michele was so surprised she didn't know what to say. She did not want to miss a single word of the lecture, so she just nodded, put a finger to her lips and whispered: "Shush!"

It was an excellent, fascinating, and informative lecture, touched with amusing anecdotes by a French professor. The applause was enthusiastic and long. The man with the monocle went up to the speaker, took the microphone and on behalf of the organizers thanked the lecturer for the inspiring and interesting speech. More applause. People in the audience came up to ask questions, but the French professor was brought over to Michele by the man with the monocle as she was just about to leave. She and introduced to Professor Jean Simon de Pret as "Mrs. Michele Renard, Richard's wife!"

The face of the Frenchman lit up in a big smile. He put both hands on her shoulders looked at her as if she were an old family friend! "Madame Renard! *Enchanté, enchanté*! I'm so glad to meet you and..." He became solicitous saying, "I'm so sorry Rich is no longer with us. Please accept our condolences. With him gone we lost one of our most skilled scientists. Nobody knew more than he did...but he always said there was one he could not beat and that was his wife. I'm so glad you are here! Where did Alec find you?"

This was really a crazy coincidence. Here she was among Richard's old friends, devoted scientists in her own field...friends he had often spoken of but she had not met because she never went to the conferences. She had always stayed home with their daughter, organizing notes, photos and films from their expeditions. That was her joy. She loved to put things in order and she was an expert at it. Rich was the one who kept in contact with colleagues and old university friends. He was the outgoing one who lectured and gave the speeches. She just wrote them.

"Isn't this funny?" said the man with the monocle. "This lady sitting next to me suddenly takes up an old briefcase I recognize as belonging to my best friend, and when she opens it I cannot help looking for a photo I knew he always kept there—of himself and his wife. And there it was. I look at the lady beside me and she is the one on the photo. Yes, indeed! We must celebrate this tonight! But first I have one more lecture to attend…about the panthers in Trafalgar Hall! I guess we all planned to go."

"Yes, I have," Michele nodded.

"Of course," said the Frenchman. "Let's go. I'll just find Rosinne. She's here somewhere in the audience. She'll be happy to meet you, Madame Renard, Rich was one of our favorite friends!"

The French professor had to answer questions from colleagues, talking, congratulating, and shaking hands. A tiny, blond woman in a dress that could only have been tailored in Paris appeared behind him. She embraced the man with the monocle, who introduced her to Michele. The French lady was Rosinne, the professor's wife.

She embraced Michele kissing her cheeks. "I am so glad to finally meet you, Madame Renard," she said. "It was always Alec and his wife, Elly, Jean and me and Rich with no lady. Women often have a different approach to things than men, so Elly and I stuck together defending our viewpoints. I miss Elly. We were shocked to hear about Rich. We tried but we could not trace you. We miss Rich so much. I feel very sorry for you. He really was the best." She had tears in her eyes when she looked at Michele. "My condolences," she said in a choked voice and blew her nose using a small, lace-edged hanky. "Mais oui! He was the best."

"Maybe I should introduce myself," said the man with the monocle. "I'm David Caesar Alexander, the eleventh Earl of Kennedale. Please call me Alec. Your husband, Richard, and I became close friends when we were teenagers. For years we shared a room at Oxford. We kept in contact ever since. I am very pleased to meet you. Now the four of us will have a splendid time together. Rich told me that you had uncovered a lot of new information and that you had it all documented. We are very curious about it. I'll be happy to help you publish your findings."

His card, she noticed, had a coat of arms, one address in Dorset and one to his club in the City.

At the panther lecture Michele sat with her new friends listening and taking notes. It was about comparative studies of panthers at zoos, in circuses, in national park vet clinics and in full freedom. The speaker was a young doctor, veterinarian and psychologist from Switzerland. After his lecture Alec introduced him to Michele who was truly amazed when he told her Rich had been his professor.

On her way to London she had felt like the loneliest person in the world. After Richard and Marianne died she didn't want to see people. Her face had changed so. Her expression was sad and she was sort of oldish looking, she thought. She always seemed too tired to do much of anything. And now here she was in a group of new friends. They all felt they knew her well. She understood Rich had had an important position among his colleagues, but this was much more than she had ever expected. She felt a wave of enthusiasm and self-confidence. Her work could really get a push forward by the influx and stimulation of these top scientists.

"Finally, I'm back in business!" a jubilant voice sang inside her.

Alec, the eleventh Earl of Kennedale, reached out his long arms embracing his three friends. "Tonight I want you all to be my guests and we will celebrate our reunion and the reinforcement of our brain trust. I'll make reservations for dinner at 8 at the Greenhouse."

Everybody gladly accepted the invitation and they separated going to their own quarters to rest, freshen up and dress for dinner.

"Michele, where are you staying? May I give you a ride?"

"At the Congress Center's hotel," she said

"Can I pick you up at 7:30?"

Alec accompanied her through a shopping mall and to the hotel lounge. He convinced her to sit down and have a quiet drink with him. He was an utterly forthcoming and polite man. She loved the way he spoke this beautiful language with a charming British accent. Maybe she also had a weakness for the Oxford accent her husband had adopted. She said yes to a martini mixed the British way with a fine gin and Italian white dry vermouth, not too strong, but very dry, and not diluted with ice cubes.

He lifted his glass of Irish whiskey saying: "Cheers. Welcome to us! Originally we were three. It was Rich, Elly and I. We studied zoology at Oxford at the same time. Then Jean joined us with his Rosinne. They are both very skilled. He is from Bordeaux. She is a Parisian. She is a professor, too, and a veterinarian and a psychologist. She's a darling! For years we were five. Your Rich never seemed to have the time for girls! Then he married you and we expected you to join the club. But you never showed up. We were very eager to meet you because he told us that you, too, worked in this field. He said you wrote all his speeches! So you must know a lot. Also we realized that when Rich had finally chosen his woman she had to be a very, very special girl." He smiled at her and she laughed.

Alec went on and talked about his wife. "She was originally a New Englander from Boston. Her father was a physician and her mother came from Cape Cod. Elly was the most charming and beautiful girl in Oxford. All young men tried to date her. Heaven only knows how she came to choose me. Maybe because I did not become romantic and flirtatious each time we met. We always were best pals; we always had the best time when we were together.

"Elly had a beautiful contralto voice and when she sang spirituals and blues everybody got goose bumps. And could she tap dance! We wrote student farces together and Rich, who was a great joker, joined the team. After knowing each other for a considerably long time Elly and I fell in love like crazy! We married and Rich was my best man. Elly and I worked together for years. We have a son, Henry. In my family boys are either Henry or Alexander. My name is Alexander, so my son's name is Henry. His son's name will be Alexander. That's how it is when you are an Earl of Kennedale. Anyway, Rich and I kept in touch through the years. We discussed things and exchanged views and research findings. So, I know that the research you have been working on is quite exciting. Elly died five years ago of cancer. About the same time we lost Rich. Now I am working with Jean and Rosinne. We select the best among young zoologists and sponsor their research in our field. It has resulted in some really great steps forward."

Michele enjoyed listening to him and was pleased every time he mentioned Richard. "You said your mother-in-law came from Cape Cod."

"Oh, yes! She was born in Osterville, a nice little town, very much Old New England."

"I live on the Cape, about a 15-minute drive from there, in Barnstable Harbor! Next time you visit the States, you must drop by."

"Sink me if I don't! Of course I will! I still keep the place in Osterville. I'm seldom there, but Henry spends every summer there looking after it. Last time I was there was the year you lost the America's Cup to the Aussies."

He left and promised to pick her up an hour later. When she entered her room there was an enormous arrangement of red roses in a tall silver cup. There must have been at least 50, and a card with the Earl of Kennedale's coat of arms and she couldn't help thinking: "Oh, these eternal Don Juans!" The writing in a forceful, running hand read:

Dear Michele,

You are like an incarnation of our very dearest friend, Rich. May you always feel welcome among us and listen to and talk about theories and experiences the way we have always done. We will tell you everything we know and you can discuss your findings and ideas with us without risking leakage or improper use of your discoveries. We will support you in your research for the best of our science, the survival of our cat friends and for our own fun.

Rosinne, Jean, Alec."

There was a knock on the door. A uniformed maid wearing a Tudor outfit and a starched bonnet entered. "I'm Mary, Madame. Is there anything you want? Would you like some refreshments, a nice cup of tea or coffee, or do you want me to light the open fire? Or maybe a relaxing bath?"

After reciting this flawlessly by heart, she took a deep breath and said: "Oh, dear! Mrs. Renard! Those roses—they are truly magnificent!"

"Thank you, they really are beautiful. Smell them! They are from three cat lovers!"

"I love cats and I, too, have friends who do! But I never get roses because of that!"

"Maybe you will, if you love the right kind of cats. I think your idea of a bath and a cup of coffee is wonderful."

The girl went into the bathroom and ran the water in the Jacuzzi. She sang while she worked and returned a couple of minutes later serving the coffee so Michele could reach it while sitting in the tub. She brought Michele a bathrobe and a big bath towel, curtsied and left. Michele sank into the steaming, rippling water and enjoyed the feeling when goose bumps indicate a sense of well-being.

Chapter 41

ALEC PICKED HER up at a quarter of eight. They drove in his dark gray Rolls to Chesterfield Hills and walked around the corner to the Greenhouse. Michele wore a dark wine red dress and her silver fox fur. Alec, with his monocle in place, was dressed in a black tux with a no-frills shirt and a small black butterfly tie with thin silver threads running through it. He was the most British gentleman a British gentleman could ever be. She felt a bit of a thrill walking by his side into the bar where a waiter with slicked-down black hair, wearing a white mess jacket took their order. She had a Dubonnet and he, as always he said, his Jameson's whiskey, with iced soda water in a separate glass.

He talked about Rich and old times. She told him about safaris Richard and she had led, and about their research in Kenya. After a little while Rosinne and Jean joined them. Rosinne was stunning in a simple body-clinging black crepe dress cut in the diagonal lines created by the top Paris couturier designers. With it she chose a small black mujahedin-style hat with a veil. She looked very chic, very French and not the way people would expect a scientist and professor to look! Michele was fascinated by the way she sipped her Tequila through the veil.

"That's why I never drink martinis! What would it look like having olives, cherries or lemon twists dangling in the net here under my nose!" she explained.

"How do you manage to eat the dinner through the veil? What about French fries dangling from it!" Michele teased.

"But, of course. I turn the hat with the front in back!" was Rosinne's answer.

The conversation was animated and stimulating, the words flying back and forth easily, quickly with esprit and humor. Alec was a true gourmet. They were served cantaloupe with caviar, turtle soup with small fragile cheese sticks, trout simmered in champagne, succulent bite-size lamb fillets, poulard with chicken and quail in small pirogues together with vegetables, a cheese soufflé and finally a peach and raspberry Melba! Everything was in small delicious servings, so nobody felt stuffed. The wine was white, fresh and French.

"This was a meal worthy of a king," Jean said. "If I remember correctly, this menu is very French, and was created by Monsieur Escoffier for a king visiting Paris. It was back in the late 1800s at the crazy time of the "cancan" at the Moulin Rouge and the 'Phantom of the Opera.'"

He turned to Alec. "I hope I haven't hurt your British feelings?"

"No, no, my friend. The British kitchen went out of fashion when French noblemen fled the revolution and brought their cooks with them here. The French took the lead when it came to elegant and sophisticated cooking! There is an old English gourmet tradition, though. You find it in the countryside, often carried on by women cooks, not by male chefs. Right now there is a place here in London called the River Café where British women chefs prove they are among the best or even the best in the world. In the British Isles you can be served trout like nowhere else in the world, lamb steaks so delicious that M. Escoffier would have said: 'This is what an agneau should taste like.' And about a fine British roast beef, he would say: 'Mes amis, I have to confess this is the ultimate.'

"The British kitchen today usually means heavy food like rich puddings and stews for hungry people shivering from the cold. Good, simple everyday food demanded high quality, fresh ingredients. But such products became scarce in the densely populated industrialized areas of England. So, people added breadcrumbs or vegetables or potatoes to make expensive ingredients go further. Adding spices from our colonies made a low cost, simple meal taste mighty good."

After dinner and hours of good conversation they separated. Alec took Michele for a walk to catch some fresh air. They ended up at a small pub where they had a nightcap and discussed the program for the coming week. Alec knew all the lecturers. He knew which were worth listening to. He also suggested entertainment such as concerts by the Academy of Saint Martin-in-the-Fields and the London Symphony. He invited her to an opera at Covent Garden and a ballet at the Royal Opera House as they walked to her hotel. When he said good night he hugged her and then kissed her hand.

"That was a funny combination," she said.

"So are we," he replied. "Good night, my dear!"

When Michele entered her room she kicked off her shoes, poured herself a glass of club soda and stretched out in front of the open fire. She realized she would be completely exhausted when her stay was over. But being in London and not taking advantage of what it offered would be insane

The next morning she was up early. The lecture schedule started at 9. She obtained written transcripts of all the lectures so she could study them in detail after she returned home.

During the "free time" between and after lectures, Michel found Rosinne a pleasant companion, and they enjoyed each other's company. She told Michele about Alec.

"He has a place in Devon. A castle with 300 rooms and an enormous park. He has so much money he doesn't even know how much. Merrill Lynch and an English investment company take care of it at a growth rate of 10 to 15 percent a year. He is constantly short of cash. He only pays with credit cards. When he lost Elly he almost went nuts especially because she had always handled everything. He had never bothered with his finances."

Rosinne spoke rapidly like most French do. Her accent was remarkably discreet, but her gestures were extremely expressive.

"The first time I met him, Jean had invited him to our place in Lainville outside Versaille. He took the train from Paris and I was supposed to meet him at the station. My Renault did not start so I called some friends for help. But no one was home. The closest taxi was 20 miles away. Finally I asked our neighbor, a farmer. He had a Volvo station wagon and told me I could come and take it anytime. The keys were always in it, he said. I was late, so I rushed over the meadow with the grazing cows, jumped into the car and was on my way. I drove like mad. Not until I was on the expressway halfway to the railway station did I realize I had company. A big, and I mean BIG, pig sat behind me in the back seat enjoying the ride and the passing landscape. Every now and then he commented on something he saw with happy gruntings. I began to cry and the sympathetic pig snuffed and blew in my hair to comfort me. You know, like pigs do!"

"No, not really! So, he was a nice pig?"

"Sure, he was really gentlemanly. But what was I to do? I was so late. I stopped outside the train station and noticed a tall foreign-looking man with a red mustache. That was the only distinctive feature Jean had mentioned to me. That was the only red mustache around, so I approached him, said hello, introduced myself and tried to explain my dilemma.

"'Well! Well!' was his only comment. He opened the front door of the car, scratched the pig behind the ears and got in. And that was it! The pig was clearly happy to have the company of someone who wasn't crying. Alec and I talked about animal psychology all the way home and had a fabulous time—all three of us!

"Later the farmer said he was happy for the pig. 'This piggy, he likes nice company,' he said. 'He is a very sociable pig. A real thoroughbred! His trip with you will give me better bacon because the taste of the meat is influenced by the animal's mood. He will tell all his piggy friends about this wonderful trip and they will all be looking forward to travelling. They will be happy all the way to the slaughterhouse. And it is a fact that a scared pig means bitter bacon. A happy pig means better bacon!'"

***

When it was time for Michele to leave London her three new friends accompanied her to Heathrow to say goodbye. They hugged her, kissed her and promised to see her at the convention the following spring in Boston. Alec seemed sad when Michele boarded the plane. She blew him a kiss and he smiled back and waved. She had a considerable collection of transcripts to read and was busy all the way to Boston were Ingrid and Ted met her at Logan. They had exciting news to tell about the drug traffickers.

Chapter 42

MIKE CARRIED JENNY and Suzy's luggage on board the plane and took the yoke, started the engines and read the check list and taxied out. He had permission from the tower to make a turn over central Boston. When he was sure he could be seen from Arnold's bed at the hospital he dipped his wings repeatedly. He knew Arnold would recognize his plane and appreciate the greeting.

He headed straight for the Bermudas, out there somewhere, where the gray-blue ocean became the light blue sky. Cape Cod lay in a sun-sparkling ocean and a minute later they were high enough to see Narragansett Bay and Newport. Mike tried to clear his mind of the memories of Maggie's body on the stretcher and how he had killed Bolivar and the two bodyguards. However, he could still see the grotesque positions of their heads after he had hit their necks, and their glassy dead eyes. The men had seemed paralyzed.

At the moment he committed the murders he had believed his act to be justified. But as time passed by he became more and more horrified by what he had done. He did not want to be a murderer. He did not want to be a hangman. His need for revenge had disappeared only moments after the killings and given way to an all-consuming feeling of guilt. The police must have understood that he was the killer and had committed the crimes in a rash of uncontrollable anger. He was sure they had let him go because they needed more evidence against him. He would never be free from the knowledge that they would keep an eye on him waiting for the right moment to get him. One day the cops would knock on his door.

It would have been comforting to talk to somebody about it. His thoughts and nightmare dreams had become more frequent and an increasingly heavy burden. He wished he were a Catholic. Then, he thought, he could talk to his confessor and get rid of it. It seemed so simple and easy. But he would never, ever, be able to talk to anybody but Arnold about the killing. Arnold would understand, but it would mean loading the burden onto him.

"There is but one way to restore peace and self-respect," he told himself, "to confess, to ask for forgiveness, accept the consequences of breaking the rules of society and then take the punishment."

When Cathy had asked him straight out if he was the killer, he had been unable to tell her. She might have felt disgust. Any woman would be afraid of him and avoid him if she knew he were a killer. Praying to his own Lutheran God for forgiveness had not helped much so far.

Over and over again his conscience nagged at him. Killing three human beings is not like stepping on three ants. Would he ever, ever overcome it? Would he ever, ever again meet someone like Maggie? Would anyone ever understand that he had been under great emotional distress, blinded by grief and anger?

"Maybe I should sneak into a Catholic church and talk to a confession father...just to get his opinion." Mike said to himself and his mumbling monologue went on: "What advice would I give to a friend who came to me with such a secret? A year ago I would have replied that they deserved it, an eye for an eye, and they knew the rules in the trade. Now I wouldn't say so. Now it doesn't make any difference if the victim is evil. It's a matter of respect for life itself.

"I would have asked a murderer: 'What can you do to make up for it?' I think my father would have said—first make good, then be judged, then punished and finally forgiven. I am not afraid of the punishment, but I see it as an obstacle for making good, which has to come first. I have to live with my guilt. In my nightmares I kill friends and their little children against my will. I see my mother and father crying for me...and I wake up in horror. This is slowly driving me insane. That is probably my Lord's way of punishing me."

Mike sat silent at the yoke. He always felt at ease and happy when he was flying. He liked the humming of the engines, the blue sky and the clouds above. He heard the voices of the two women mixing with the sound in the aircraft. They had juice and snacks and had read some European fashion magazines. Jenny seemed to be napping and Suzy came up to the cockpit asking if there was anything he wanted, juice or a snack?

"Yes, sit down in the copilot's seat, I'd like your company for a little while if you don't mind."

"I am not a pilot. I do like to fly though, like a bird. If you teach me to fly this plane I'll teach you skydiving," Suzy said. "I have made about 200 jumps. It's very, very beautiful and very, very pleasurable to skydive together with friends holding hands and forming a ring. Landing these days is not difficult at all. Using a canopy parachute you steer it and glide in for a nicely controlled landing. No trauma! Not as in the old days when it was like jumping from the third story porch and you needed high, sturdy boots to protect your ankles."

"Still it seems wild to me, but I'll go with you and watch you dive. OK? If that convinces me I'll try it!"

Mike explained basic aerodynamics to her; how the air on the top of the wing, because of the wing's profile, has a longer distance to go than the air under it, and how that creates a vacuum lifting the wing. He explained the rudders and demonstrated how they worked. Suzy tried a loop. The well-trimmed Baron dove, caught speed and swung playfully over on its back and looped around. They laughed while Jenny with her safety belt on was still snoozing. Approaching the Bahamas they phoned Harry. He welcomed them back and met them at the airport.

At dinner Mike told Harry that Arnold was badly hurt and would probably never be able to walk again. Harry knew Maggie had been killed by the New York gang. "I understand you were in Newport when they met their well-deserved fate," he said.

"Yes," Mike answered.

Jenny and Suzy told them they had learned that men from Bolivar's organization had joined forces with some of Cavallo's gang and were now planning to import cocaine using Arnold's equipment.

"Arnold has given me strict instructions not to use his aircraft for flying drugs and I'll obey his orders," Mike stated emphatically.

Harry's disappointment was in his voice: "But, Mike, I have plans for the New Yorkers..."

"Look, Harry, I don't want to know anything about any plans involving drugs. I don't want to be part of it. I want to quit this drug business. I have earned enough money to live well on an honest job. All I want to do is to fly. Please, don't ask me. Don't try to tempt me to break my promise to Arnold. Maggie was killed with cocaine we had supplied. Arnold and I have had it with drugs. Can't you understand that?"

"OK, my friend. But my plan is to stop the traffic."

Mike didn't believe his ears, but said nothing.

"First we gain their confidence," Harry went on. "You need not be involved. Your only responsibility would be to fly. Nothing else. Think it over. I'll pay you well. You could have your own Baron in a few months."

Mike had already made up his mind, but Harry didn't give up easily. "My girls will take care of everything and you will not be responsible for a thing. They might need your protection and I'm sure you can get rid of their offenders the same way Bolivar went."

"Sorry, Harry. I am not a killer for hire. OK?"

"But who killed those men on board Bolivar's boat?"

The open fire burned peacefully and threw lights and shadows across the room. Mike did not answer Harry's question. Jenny and Suzy were silent. The conversation had not taken the turn they expected.

"Mike, there is a war going on," Jenny finally said.

"It's not my war, Jenny."

"Yes, Mike, it is! It's everybody's war against drugs and we all have to pitch in," Harry asserted.

"Arnold and I decided to stay out of it and I intend to stay out of it!"

Mike and Harry had a game of backgammon. The older man studied Mike over his gold-rimmed reading glasses. He knew this was the right man to enroll for his plan. He didn't take Mike's resistance too seriously. He held great trumps in hand—heaps of money and one terrific young daughter.

"I have to talk to the girls. I want this man. I want my daughter to have him," he said to himself. "Dammit! He's a good backgammon player! Did I have too much to drink? Why didn't I see his trap? Oh, yes! I could make this cool, self-controlled pilot a millionaire in a less than a year."

He had to come up with some convincing arguments that would encourage Mike to change his mind. He leaned his right elbow on the table and rested his head in his hand, scratching his chin, studying the backgammon pieces. "I'll pay you five thousand in cash and ninety-five thousand to a Swiss bank account for each trip you make for my daughter."

Mike rolled the dice. "It's a generous offer, but money's not the issue. I'll discuss it with Arnold, though."

"We can make drug sharks bite their nails in despair and pull their hair asking themselves why they ever went into the cocaine business."

Mike laughed.

"I think I pulled him an inch or even more over to my side," Harry thought. "The girls will have to do the rest."

He took his glass with crushed ice and Perrier and sat down at his Steinway. He turned the pages in a Bach book, then found a Beethoven book and began to play. The melody came out softly and hesitantly almost as if it was trying to find its way. Harry was a good pianist and the Beethoven Sonata made him dream about a happy time, when he was young living with a darling wife with a French accent and when Jenny was a hop scotching pony-tailed kid.

Mike's eyes met Suzy's. She smiled at him. Mike liked her— everything about her. Her face, with her secretive and innocent black eyes, was the loveliest he had ever seen. She raised her glass slowly and drank to him. He nodded back and sipped his whiskey. He felt she wanted to support his efforts to stay out of the drug trade.

When the sonata finally died out, Harry's dream had come to an end. He opened his eyes when he felt Jenny's kiss on his forehead and her fingers combing through his hair. "You know, Dad, nobody can play like you and make problems fly away and put every listener in a harmonious mood. It was beautiful. Thank you."

Harry patted her cheek. "Why don't you young people stay here in front of the fire? It's time for Methuselah to go to bed. Good night everybody."

He went upstairs and closed the bedroom door behind him. Mike looked at Suzy. The music had made her thoughts fly far away. She smiled absent-mindedly, her lips moved as if singing. He was fascinated by her beautiful lips. There was a book in her lap.

"What are you reading, Suzy?"

"Oh, just a poem. A Japanese poem."

Jenny joined her father upstairs and sat down on his bed. They talked quietly for half an hour before kissing good night. She tucked the covers over him and went downstairs.

Suzy had decided to sneak over to Mike's room to tell him in private that she approved of his refusal to Harry's invitations. She put on her best nightgown—a wide, full-length, white silk gown with long wide puff sleeves and small, embroidered golden butterflies flying over her small, round breasts. She knew she was sexy in that outfit. She had let her hair grow to her shoulders, but she did not dare to let it hang free. That would be too inviting, she thought. Quietly she went out into the hall, but who came along heading for the same door? Jenny! The two young women half-glared at one another. Jenny was wearing a short, black nightgown with deep décolletage, the sexiest she owned. She smiled a malicious smile whispering "shush" and pointing at Harry's door at the far end of the corridor. Without knocking they went into Mike's room. He was coming out of the bathroom whistling softly and wearing nothing more than his pajama bottoms.

"Welcome to my pajama party!" he said. "Make yourselves comfortable. Lie down or sit down somewhere!"

Both girls made the same choice and jumped onto his bed. Mike sat down in a chair and reached for a bottle of iced soda water.

"Wait! I'll get something better," Jenny said and went out of the room returning a few minutes later with three glasses and two bottles of champagne. Mike opened one, popping the cork properly, poured and served. Jenny tried to talk him into flying cocaine to Cape Cod with her. But he just shook his head and said "No way!"

He filled the glasses with more champagne. Jenny thanked him with a big kiss. She looked gorgeous and she knew it. The transparent gown did nothing to conceal her full, beautiful breasts, so appealing Mike couldn't resist staring. He opened the second bottle. They talked skydiving and enjoyed the bubbly. Jenny succeeded in leading the discussion into ways to set traps for the drug dealers, luring them into it and then robbing them.

"Present me with a foolproof plan and I might consider flying for you." Mike said, convinced the whole idea was impossible.

Suzy suggested a solution: "I know! Jenny and I jump out of the plane. Each of us with a good-size container. We hide them and then you pick us up. Simple!"

"There are Air Force and Coast Guard bases with radar at Otis and Wellfleet. The radar station at Otis watches the coastline from Newfoundland to Washington, DC. They see everything, day and night, foggy or clear. The Cape is full of tourists from June to September and every beach is packed with people 24 hours a day," Mike pointed out.

"How about Sandy Neck," Jenny suggested. "Nobody is there at night. We could escape by boat or by car, or jog away. We could hide the containers with the dope and the canopy parachutes in the water so the K-9 police wouldn't be able to find anything. The element of surprise will do the trick! The whole operation could be over in one hour. Dad said the police will still be rubbing their sleepy eyes when we are out of there." Jenny talked slowly. She could not hide her excitement, nor could she hide the fact she'd had too much champagne. She watched Mike through half-closed eyes.

"I knew you would like to help me," she said. "Now we have to go to bed. Come here! Be a good boy and lie between us."

"I think I'll take the two of you to your own beds first so we can sleep without any hanky panky. Tomorrow we will refine our plan and do some skydiving."

"Suzy is already asleep, so why don't you take her first," Jenny suggested.

Mike carried Suzy to her room, tucked her in and returned to Jenny. She slipped her panties off and said: "I'm too hot to wear these!"

"Jenny, you are a naughty girl. You are too drunk and I don't want to."

"Mike, I'll hate you forever if you don't."

"No, Jenny. I simply cannot."

"You miss Maggie. Come, I'll comfort you."

He sat at the bedside and hid his face in his hands. She gave up. He carried her into her room and put her in bed. She kissed him good night. Returning to his bed he stopped. Somebody was in it. He pulled the sheet aside. Suzy looked at him, smiling.

"Don't touch me," she whispered, "or I'll scream like mad that you're trying to rape me!"

Mike didn't argue and slid in under the comforter.

"At least I can tell Jenny that I slept with you!"

"Please don't! Good night."

"You have to kiss me good night!"

"I did when you were asleep."

"That doesn't count and it was in the wrong room."

"OK. Good night, Suzy, sleep well." He kissed her mouth…a long satisfying kiss.

"OK now?"

"OK." Her hand traveled from his chest down and touched him lightly.

"You are big." she said.

"Boys grow."

"You don't love me?"

"No. You are a great girl and I like you very much."

"Do you love Jenny?"

"No, how could I? I hardly know either of you."

"That's good. Do you think you could love me."

"Why do you ask?"

"Because I am Japanese and because I love you."

"Be proud of your origin and your culture. When I choose a woman and fall in love it is because of her personality, how she is, what she wishes, what we dream of together and the spirit she will add to our common future. That's what counts. I can hardly believe you are in love with me. You just want to compete with Jenny and show you're better."

"So, you don't love Jenny and you could think of loving me. Yes?"

He nodded and added: "May I sleep now?"

"Yes, Mike, good night!"

She crawled up on him and hugged him and held his head in her hands and kissed him several times. She was light and slim and soft and warm and silky. He suddenly was overwhelmed by a feeling of harmony and indescribable happiness. He held his arms around her and fondled every part of her body and she touched every part of him. They lay still for a long while.

"Mike, I'm so happy," Suzy murmured. "You make me happy. I want to be yours and you will be mine. You will be my husband. And you will be a very contented man with a very good wife. You will see!"

She turned over and they fell asleep back-to-back.

Chapter 43

SHE WAS GONE when he woke up. The fragrance of her perfume still lingered from her pillow. He bent over and inhaled it giving him sensual pleasure. He liked Suzy a lot. He sang in the shower, as always that stupid song about the Danish farmer who went out for beer.

He went downstairs and joined Harry who was sitting near a window with a splendid view over the beach and the ocean, reading the Wall Street Journal. He looked at Mike over his gold-rimmed glasses and smiled a greeting. Jenny came in and kissed Harry good morning and Suzy danced down the stairs dressed in skydiving gear.

Bacon and eggs, tea and toast were served and after breakfast. He and Suzy drove out to the airport and boarded the Baron. Suzy prepared her gear while Mike took the plane up to the right altitude. He continuously informed her on altitude, heading, wind, etc. With a map in her hand she told him where to fly and gave him a basic lesson in skydiving. Then she went over to the door with her big, blue backpack and the small emergency parachute buckled onto her chest. Opening the door she looked at her watch and altitude meter. She confirmed heading, speed, wind speed, wind direction and altitude. Then she pulled her goggles down from her helmet, turned around, smiled goodbye and dove out into the icy emptiness and the howling wind. Mike switched to autopilot, closed the door and reset the locks.

He was intensely uneasy. He didn't like having this girl play with her life. To him parachuting was an emergency action. During his Air Force training he had made 10 jumps and it was no fun. The falling was great in itself, floating around in the air with the wind howling, the ground zooming in was fine, but he never overcame the fear that grabbed him the closer he came to the ground. He remembered landing with bent knees and feet firmly pressed together like in downhill skiing. Sturdy, high boots protected his feet and ankles. There was a merciless, hard jolt as he hit the ground, then a rapid bounce forward, a twisting, and a landing on his right shoulder to make a full somersault. His feet would "sing" for hours.

Suzy wore regular sneakers only. He hated to think of her landing in sneakers taking the risk of breaking her graceful ankles. "Why on earth should this girl be this mad? I seem to attract only crazy girls," he said to himself making a turn, diving, watching her. She floated with hands and feet spread out, her parachute still not open. She smiled and waved at him! After waiting a long time, too long he thought, he saw the beautiful rectangular parachute coming out. From the terrace door Harry watched thoughtfully when she landed on the lawn in front of him. She didn't even kneel and moments later she was pulling in the big orange-yellow-blue striped nylon canopy. The business section of his brain went to work. He had found a new use for this easy way of landing almost anywhere.

Jenny and Suzy convinced Mike to try a jump. The local casting club provided parachutes and a young pilot was glad to take them up. Mike's first jump was made with a large canopy and a special two-person harness buckled up together with Suzy.

Standing in the cabin door ready to jump she made a last check of the equipment and then, "OK! Let's go!"

Out they flew! His first sensation was the whistling, icy wind. The feeling of falling was like flying. Sue's warm body tied close to him transmitted her confidence, complete control and pleasure. The earth tipped over a bit, began to spin slowly, was over them! He recognized the illusions. He made the same movements as she did. Their outstretched hands and legs stabilized their movements. The earth came back under them. It was like swimming. They turned so their heads pointed to the north, to the east and all around. She showed him her wrist altimeter. It indicated 4500 feet. The world turned slowly. The ground became larger. Her soft, confident voice came from the microphone inside his helmet:

"Isn't this great? We are now at 1500 feet! Here comes the canopy!" He heard the nylon rattle out over them. A strong force stopped the fall when the parachute unfolded. Firmly pressed together they hung comfortably, floating in the air. It was a fantastic feeling. She embraced him from behind. She pointed at the lawn near the air club where they were going to land. She told him how to steer. His hands followed hers when she maneuvered the canopy by pulling the lines. They floated over the big elm trees almost touching the tops and landed perfectly. No trauma, no somersaulting forward on the right shoulder, no broken legs, no singing feet, no fear. She untied him and collected the big colorful piece of nylon. Then she showed him how to fold it. They made two more jumps in the same harness enjoying falling tied together. That same day Mike made his first jump alone landing as if sailing in over the lawn and intoxicated with the feeling of being alive.

Chapter 44

FROM THE BAHAMAS Mike flew Harry, Jenny and Suzy to Boston. It was February and cold. The women went shopping while Harry and Mike visited Arnold at the hospital. He was feeling much better but was not particularly excited about their plan to steal drug money or a shipment of cocaine or heroine. Cathy had told him about the men who planted cocaine in their home and how the police had been there searching. He had no doubt it must have been Bolivar's or Cavallo's successors, so he thought it was OK to teach them a lesson.

"I do not want you to use my plane for smuggling, and I do not want you to store cocaine or money in my house," Arnold told them.

After leaving the hospital they had dinner and Harry brought up a rough plan for landing cocaine on Sandy Neck with a parachutist. Mike protested and reminded Harry what Arnold had said, but he was intrigued with the idea of cheating Cavallo's and Bolivar's new gangs.

"The buyers will find out. They'll go after Arnold's daughter and me until they get us." Mike said.

"I'll figure out a safe plan. You will just do the flying and look after Jenny's security."

Mike shook his head. "Harry! For God's sake be sensible! Don't involve Jenny in this business like this. She's a sitting duck"

"Not with you around!"

"Arnold does not want me to do this, but I'll fly in one shipment for. After that I do not want to be involved."

Harry looked at Jenny. She nodded approvingly.

"Alright, my friend! It's a deal," Harry smiled knowing he had won the first round, meaning at least two million dollars in his pocket.

The following day Mike flew Harry, Jenny and Suzy to Cape Cod to look for places for skydivers to land on Sandy Neck. It was a beautiful sunny late winter day. They walked over the sand dunes and discussed plans for dropping and hiding the goods, and pinpointing alternative escape routes. They stopped by Arnold's place to drop off some supplies they would need after the cocaine was parachuted. From her studio Michele kept a close eye on the visitors. She overheard their conversation and taped it.

***

The weeks passed quickly. Mike bought a 20-foot speedboat and docked it on the south shore of Sandy Neck. A four-wheel drive Jeep was parked in Arnold's garage. Harry was convinced that neither the Massachusetts Coast Guard nor the DEA expected drug smuggling in their area at that time of year and a surprise move like this would work well. According to his sources neither the girls nor their parachutes would show up on the radar.

Sandy Neck was an ideal location with only two weak points. Otis Air Base was only a few miles away and would be monitoring everything in the air. No bribes in the world could close those electronic eyes. Personnel could be in place on short notice. Also, residents in several homes on the north shore of Cape Cod might observe the parachutists. But, Mike and the girls would have gone leaving no traces while the Coast Guard or police were still trying to find out what had happened.

Mike astonished himself at not being afraid or even caring about the consequences of a failure. This was going to be his last drug flight. He had to take a chance on it.

Two big waterproof aluminum trunks, used by personnel on duty in the tropics, had been provided with a thick foam skin to absorb radar waves. Two parachute harnesses for twin jumps had been modified to carry a trunk instead of a second person. The sun was setting when they left the Bahamas, and from the plane they could watch freighters and tankers struggling against the rough, dark blue-gray sea. Sometimes the big ships were completely covered with cascades of greenish white, icy foam. Closer to the coast trawlers were seen fighting the storm in a dramatic contest to protect their own safety. Night fell and the lights from the coastline became visible.

Mike had been flying out at sea following the east coastline of the United States. When he was within a few hundred miles from Boston he turned towards the mainland. "OK, girls, be ready. We'll soon be there," Mike shouted. He gave them altitude, wind and heading as they flew in over Cape Cod.

"OK!" Suzy said and opened the door. The wind hurled. Jenny jumped first. Before Suzy jumped out she turned to Mike and blew him a kiss. He rushed over and closed the door after her. Then he called Hyannis airport to ask for permission to land immediately. He said he was having problems with an engine and did not want to take the chance of continuing to Boston. He was granted permission. Minutes later he landed and taxied to the hangar. He shut off the engines and ran over to his VW Golf, which he had left parked there. Stopping at a pay phone he dialed the local number Harry had given him. He was exactly on time. His phone call was expected. A New Yorker's voice answered. A few confirming words were exchanged and he hung up.

With tires screaming he braked outside the Sprengler house. He opened the garage door, drove the Jeep out, put his VWGolf in the garage and sped off.

Chapter 45

DRIVING THE JEEP Mike passed the gates to the protected area of Sandy Neck and drove along the north beach maintaining a good speed. He found the path leading south to the place where Jenny and Suzy were waiting for him and where he had anchored the speedboat the week before. He found them bundled up in their parachutes jumping up and down to keep warm. He hauled in the boat and carried the two heavy trunks with the cocaine on board.

"There is at least 100 pounds in each," he said. "It was supposed to be only 50!"

"We saw the boat and steered this way. We landed right here! So we didn't need to carry them!"

"The DEA guys will check our plane in Hyannis. I am sure the Otis radar tracked us. They'll soon be here with a Coast Guard helicopter. Let's call the New Yorkers to postpone the exchange."

Jenny agreed. They put the parachutes in a net bag with a big, heavy rock and tied it together with the trunks and the speedboat's anchor. Three hundred yards from the beach he let it sink. "The water is about 20 feet deep there," Mike said. "The buoy is the marker. We'll come back tomorrow and haul it up. Let's get out of here". He stiffened. "I hear a chopper! Quick, jump in the Jeep!"

They sped over to the north side with no headlights on. Mike stopped, switched off the engine and listened. The chopper was approaching, but they couldn't see it. "If we take off in the speedboat they'll see us right away," he told the girls. "We must hide. It's too dark for them to see us right now. They're coming closer!"

He started the engine and drove eastwards towards a group of empty summer buildings and stopped under a roof to a carport. The air was cold and raw. The moon was gone. Mist rolled in from the bay. They heard the helicopter land. Across the water on the mainland they could see police cruisers speeding along Route 6A with their flashing lights on, but no sirens. Mike knew he was trapped.

***

Hidden in a dense growth of evergreens behind some stores and a small restaurant on Route 6A at Sandy Neck Road, two men sat in a silver Lincoln. The big car was warm and comfortable and they had a generous supply of snacks, sandwiches and beer. They did not see nor hear the helicopter but were shaken when several police cruisers passed them at high speed. Farther down the road their boss was waiting to meet the parachutist with the cocaine. The police cars switched off their headlights. The man in the Lincoln's passenger seat grabbed the telephone and called his boss. No answer. He dialed again. Still no response. The two men stared at each other. "We were told to wait, so we'll wait," said the man at the wheel.

***

Mike listened, then said: "The police have to stop at the parking lot because the cruisers don't have four-wheel drive. If I were in charge of the search I would fine comb the entire peninsula, waking up every living soul asking for their IDs. We have to get out of here fast. They know me. They know I have been flying for Arnold. They know that I was the one who flew the Baron over here an hour ago."

"You must try to reach the speedboat and…either come here and pick us up or take it across to Barnstable Harbor," Suzy said. "Jenny and I can hide here and drive the Jeep to Arnold's house when the sun rises."

"They'll be here pretty soon. If they find two women from Bermuda, where the suspicious airplane also happened to come from, they would never stop searching. And they would find what they were looking for." Jenny filled in.

"Mike, you must try to get out of here."

"I'll run back to get the boat, wait here for me," Mike said jumping down from the Jeep. He started running along the beach. It made him warm again. When he saw the boat some 300 yards away he ran faster. He heard the chain of policemen searching through the bushes advancing toward him. He heard them swearing and falling and branches snapping under heavy boots on the other side of the dune only about 200 yards away. He held his breath and listened. A small boat, a skiff, was anchored nearby. He had but one way to go. The icy water filled his boots when he walked slowly out onto the smooth sandy bottom.

The cold water on Cape Cod's north shore is cold even in the summer. It comes straight from the North Pole—or rather from the Arctic Ocean and Greenland. This water is so cold one forgets to breathe once into it even on a hot summer day!

Mike bent his knees and crouched down behind the protecting foot-high boat hull. Only his head was above the surface. He heard the policemen talking, encouraging their dogs to go on searching. Had he left any traces? Could they see his footprints leading into the water? He was so cold his teeth clattered. He clamped his mouth firmly together so as not to sound like a woodpecker. That sound would have made the dogs really curious, he thought, laughing at himself. The icy water in his clothes was being warmed by his body. He needed to sneeze. A nasty cold was on its way! The policemen continued their search with dogs and flashlights, 20 men in a line, 50 feet apart. Several chains of searching policemen were stretched over the dunes. They advanced, fine combing every interesting spot—bushes and obvious hiding places. The empty beach where Mike had been running couldn't hide anybody, so they didn't need to search near the water.

The mist got thicker and thicker. Mike could not see the beach when he, half-swimming, half-walking, reached his speedboat. He heaved himself on board, lay flat and listened. The fog was getting really dense. He untied the boat, leaving the buoy and the anchor with its illegal, valuable load. The tide carried him along the shoreline slowly without a sound. The shed where Jenny and Suzy were waiting became visible in the mist. They wanted to drive back and let him take the boat. He hesitated. Harry had told him and Suzy to protect Jenny. He could not leave her here.

"Jenny, you have to come with me," he insisted. After some arguing Jenny waded out and climbed on board.

"I'll find my way," said Suzy and waved them off. Mike let the boat drift with the streaming tide into the thickening, protecting mist. Fifteen long minutes passed. The engine started, its sound muffled by the mist. Jenny was soaked up to her crotch and Mike was wet all over. He raised the speed a little and headed southward. He found the markings of the dredged channel into the little Barnstable Harbor and landed at the Sprenglers' dock.

He was so frozen he could hardly walk the short distance up to Arnold's house. His clothes were like sheet metal. He found the key and entered. Jenny looked around. She drew him a hot bath and put his wet clothes in the washing machine and hers in the dryer.

He sank into the warm water. After a long time in the hot shower Jenny walked in to him. He was half asleep and he gave her a tired smile. She sat down on the bathtub edge and studied his muscular, suntanned body. She let her bathrobe fall from her shoulders and was as God created her. He opened his eyes a little and smiled. She held his hand to her breast...a broad hand with long muscular fingers like a musician's. He fondled her nipples tenderly, feeling them stiffen. Her vagina was moist and ready. Her heartbeat pounded in his hand. Her eyes watched his erection rising out of the water. She blushed and kissed him.

Chapter 46

MICHELE BECAME WIDE awake when she heard Mike's car swish into the square and brake in front of the Sprengler house. She looked out the window. It was dark but she could see the man in the car open Sprengler's garage and drive out in a Jeep she didn't know was there. She was certain that something was about to happen. She had already become suspicious when, a half-hour before, she heard the airplane make a turn over Sandy Neck. A maneuver like that in the middle of the night followed by a visit of the young pilot at Sprenglers' could mean but one thing—this was the night for the business the visitors had been talking about that sunny winter day a few weeks earlier.

She quickly pulled a black jogging suit over her pajamas and put on warm, heavy boots. Running into the garage she picked up a woolen hat and a fur coat. She threw the clothes in the back seat together with her video equipment. For safety's sake she grabbed her hunting bag and a rifle. She didn't like to go alone on a mission like this, but there was no time to call Ingrid and Ted. Anyway, to call Ingrid would mean she could loose track of the Jeep so she decided to go on her own.

She followed the red taillights of the Jeep through Barnstable Village and headed west on Route 6A. The moon was almost full and in its bright light she could see large patches of snow-free bare ground with crocus buds peeping up. Spring was late this year. When she crossed the line into East Sandwich she entered an open, snow-covered landscape with meadows on the south side and moors with salt marshes on the north. Far ahead she saw the red taillights of Mike's Jeep turning right into Sandy Neck Road. She switched off her headlights. She had figured the situation correctly—Mike was going to pick up a parachutist with a drug shipment and shortly after meet with the "Gotham people" at Shaw Road. The New Yorkers could, of course, already be there and she might even bump right into them. But she thought it made more sense for Mike to pick the goods up first.

Michele was alone on the road, but as she turned right heading out to the sandy peninsula she noticed the headlights of two cars approaching from the Sandwich area. The road took her to a hill and from there she could see the Jeep speeding along the north beach. She turned left at Shaw Road and parked outside a deserted summer home several hundred yards ahead. She tried the garage door. It was locked. She took her video camera with the "super microphone" and hung the shotgun over one shoulder and the bag with ammo over the other. The tripod with the video camera was heavy. Sweat pearled down her forehead. "I'll only watch and tape, not intervene at all," she said to herself. The tranquilizer gun swung back and forth and hit the video tripod with a "dong" that she thought must have been heard miles away. At the crossing she hid behind some juniper bushes under the dark, protecting branches of a high spruce. She set up the tripod and loaded the double-barreled tranquilizer gun.

A car was approaching slowly. It stopped. She could not see it, but she heard it backing into a parking lot behind a summer home on the other side of the road. There were footsteps in the gravel on the roadside. Two men stopped in the moonlight 50 yards from her. Each was carrying a big tennis bag. It was chilly. Her nose began to run but she didn't dare blow it. She heard the clapping noise of a helicopter become more and more distinct. The parachutists must have been scanned by the Otis radar and the Coast Guard was on alert! The DEA had not been asleep! She knew their radar had the capacity to observe everything in the air much farther away than Bermuda. Knowing the pilot and knowing he was heading for Boston the DEA had good reason to be suspicious and keep track of him.

Michele put on the earphones in order to hear if the two men had anything interesting to say. They were only 15 or 20 yards away from her hiding place. Her infra-camera watched them through the darkness. On the small screen the men looked like green monsters. Her nose tickled and ran but she sat in the darkness, quiet as a mouse.

"Damned cold tonight! I feel kind of bad giving away four million in cash like this, but it's still good business. These people always deliver clean, pure cocaine…no Inositol, no baking powder, no nothing, so we can double the quantity, probably triple it, without problems," one man said and lit a cigarette. He walked back and forth in silence. The sound from the chopper came closer.

Michele got an idea. She took aim with the infrascope on the tranquilizing gun.

"Pooff!" The muffled sound was swallowed by the noise from the approaching helicopter. Michele's shot hit the man with the cigarette in the back. He turned around and looked angrily at his companion. "What the hell are you doing? Is this some kind of game or what?" Slowly, without a word he slumped to the ground.

Michele aimed at gangster Number Two. "Hope he didn't break my syringe," she said to herself and started counting. The man bent down over his friend, who had passed out. "Damn it! What the hell is wrong with you?" he said. "Did you have a stroke? Hell, and here come the cops in their chopper. Great timing!" His monologue was interrupted by Michele's second shot, "Pooff"!

He stood wobbling on his feet. He couldn't understand what had happened to his sense of balance, and then he pitched forward. He was still rolling over his friend when Michele dashed out from under the trees and quickly grabbed the two heavy tennis bags. Because of their weight she had to make two trips. She ran with the bags, placed them in her car and huffing and puffing went back to collect the rest of her equipment. Halfway back to her car she remembered the syringes. She left her bags and ran back. The helicopter was straight above her now. The noise was incredible. Its strong floodlights cut through the darkness. She hid under a dense pine tree. For a second she stood frozen and held her breath. Cones of light from the chopper searched the road towards the beach. She found one of the projectiles right away but had to turn the two heavy men over and feel their backs before she finally located the second syringe.

She dragged the men under a big dense spruce so they could not be seen from the air or the road. "This will keep you asleep for 15 minutes," she whispered to them. She was on her way out of hiding when a police cruiser passed less than 10 yards from her! She froze. She had been too busy to notice it! The car moved slowly down the hill without a sound, no lights on. It was a

K-9 car. She hurried back towards her car. Sweat poured down her forehead and down her spine. This was crazy! She hadn't counted on the police coming this early with dogs and a complete show! She tried to run, but the straps of the gun and the bag cut into her shoulders and hurt. The helicopter was landing, probably in the parking lot close to the beach. She heard the clapping from the rotors changing to a whizzing sound, which meant it had landed.

She stopped in front of her car and looked at it, thinking: "This disintegrating old car is mine! Here I stand with four million bucks in cash and I don't even dare to think of replacing this ugly duckling!"

She noticed that one of the screws holding the registration plate had fallen off and the one left was loose, so she took the plate off and threw it in the back seat. She knew the police dogs would not need much time to track her. She had to hide. There was a door around the garage corner held shut by a simple lock. With the knife in her hunter's bag she forced the deadbolt aside. From inside she opened the electric garage door. It made a terrible noise. She drove her car into the garage, hid the money stuffed tennis bags, the gun and the video camera on a shelf high up near the roof. Then she closed and locked the garage door.

As soon as the dogs found the men, it would not take long until the police would start looking for the bags with the cash. She had to stop those dogs! She seized her spare tank of gasoline and ran back along the road. She stopped, held her breath and listened. She heard policemen giving orders to their search teams down the hill no more than 150 yards away.

"Hope they start searching along the beach and not up here close to the road," she muttered to herself as she tiptoed forwards. Her heart bolted. Her whole body trembled with exhaustion and nervousness. The two men were still peacefully asleep under the tree.

"Good thing they don't snore!" she thought watching the policemen downhill form a search line across the dunes. Amazingly enough the police dogs didn't bark. More police cruisers had arrived. She poured gasoline under the tree where she had been hiding and in a wide line on the gravel across the road. The cold weather would make the gasoline stay for quite a while and the fumes from the liquid would dull the dogs' sense of smell long enough to lead them off her path. Then she hurried back to the garage and locked the doors from inside.

"Fortunately there is no snow to disclose marks from tires or foot prints," she said to herself. It was cold in her car. She pulled her knit hat down over her ears and wrapped herself in her fur coat. She was completely exhausted, her heart was still pounding and the veins in her temples and neck were throbbing heavily. "This is too much!" she thought. "A woman my age shouldn't be running around like this. Without my daily jogging I never would have had the strength to pull this off!"

There was total silence and she fell asleep. About two hours later the voices from two police officers walking around the garage awakened her. She realized someone was looking in through the garage door window.

"This house is a summer home boarded up for the winter. Let's go search down the road!"

"But look! There's a car in this garage!"

Michele's heart almost stopped. She held her breath so the smoke from it would not reveal she was hiding there.

"Are you kidding? Do you think drug runners use cars like that? That thing is an antique for Christ's sake! Must be from the 60s and it's not even registered. See! No license plate. Nobody would be crazy enough to drive a thing like that in the middle of the winter!"

She heard them walking away before she fell asleep again.

Chapter 47

THIS KIND OF manhunt operation had been so well organized and trained it could be put into operation in a flash. A Coast Guard helicopter took off from Otis and minutes later its strong floodlights swept over the dunes crisscrossing the peninsula. The moonlight helped the crew observe what was going on. K-9 teams were flown out to the tip of the peninsula and men with night vision binoculars scrutinized the land below. But the only living creatures to be found were some foxes and cayotes disturbed by the unfamiliar noises. After the mist set in, the crew had to land. The police and the DEA had set up temporary headquarters at the parking lot.

The military radar had followed the Baron since east of Norfolk. It had recorded Mike's unnecessary turn over Sandy Neck before landing, and a patrolling police crew had called in to report that they had seen something they considered suspicious. They described it as two big kites over Sandy Neck. That information made the Coast Guard take a closer look at the radar pictures. The radar showed that two objects could have fallen from the plane. The plane was identified; the owner and the pilot were known. The men in the search teams were sure they would make a catch. Warm and sweating from running after the dogs through the bushes the men searched along the south shore. Their dogs gave several indications, but it might have been fox scent. Some small boats had been spotted at anchor off the shore, but it was obvious that nobody was in them.

Suzy saw the speedboat with her two friends drifting away, disappearing in the mist. She was an experienced caster and was dressed to stay warm. She wore thermal underwear and a thin, llama wool set under her pink, weatherproof jogging suit. She was not going to let the searching police catch her. She saw the helicopter flying back and forth until the mist forced them to abandon the mission for the time being.

"The obvious place to hide is in a house or a shed so that is what I will not do," she thought.

With no headlights on she drove eastwards following the shoreline. She had covered her brake lights with Mike's gloves. Lights were on in one of the houses and a big four-wheel drive van was parked outside. The tracks from the van led northwards. She followed them. Studying her reflection in the rearview mirror she thought: "I'm not really that homely. Jenny is more beautiful and Mike might fall for her charm and Harry's money. I'm probably too foreign for him. Look at my silly, almost Mongolian eyes! I wish I had Jenny's beautiful green eyes. My face is too flat and my nose too small. And this thin, small mouth with the high Cupid's bow almost right under my nose! Oh, I wish I had her round pouty, sexy mouth, and her big, full bust, not these small breasts. I wish I had her round hips and her round behind not my flat one. Jenny has beautiful brown, long hair. I hate my straight, blue-black hair. But Mike cannot hide the fact he is attracted to me. I feel there is magnetism. Jenny wants him, but I'll get him because I truly love him!

"I am not unattractive. A Japanese girl looks like this, damn it! I am happy to be Japanese! Why should I pity myself because I am not a white European when I am an American! And I want—I really want—to get out of this stupid game, played by moneymad people. They have completely lost their sense of morals and their respect for ethical values. The only good thing about this dirty business is that I have met Mike."

She was talking to the girl in the mirror. She felt miserable. "Hope the police won't get him. This was a stupid plan. I cannot believe Harry is risking the three of us for the almighty dollar. He has changed a lot since the first time I met him. Now Harry is ready to sacrifice his own daughter for money. He is obsessed with the power of money. He dares to risk her because he knows that if things go wrong he can buy her freedom. Just wonder if he would buy freedom for Mike or me, too. I doubt it!"

Suzy drove along the dark beach. She heard the waves break rhythmically. Every now and then the Jeep splashed through the shallow water. The sand was wet, firm and flat. She had to hurry to Arnold's house and brew fresh coffee for them and run a hot bath for Mike. Thinking of being with him cheered her up. She switched on the headlights. She expected to be stopped. Several policemen became visible in the mist. Throwing a last look in the mirror she noticed the emblem of her British casting club on the lapel of her jacket!

"Gosh, that was close!" she said, putting the pin with a small, golden parachute in her breast pocket. Uniformed men at the gate signaled her to stop.

"What's up?" she asked with a smile she knew was irresistible in its innocence.

"We are looking for some parachutists, probably drug smugglers. Maybe one or two men. Your ID please."

She took her false press card from Time-Life and said: "I am with the press. TIME magazine. Where can I park my Jeep? I'd like to ask some questions. Who's your officer in charge?"

"That man over there with gold all over his hat. Just a moment, please! What are you doing here at 3:30 in the morning?"

"I was seeing someone."

"Who and why?"

"That's personal. I was with someone I love"

"Who? We need to know."

"Please don't ask me, or at least please don't report his name. I slept with a married man. If I tell you who, his marriage would be ruined. Do I look like a paratrooper? Please be reasonable."

"OK! Park over there," said the policeman.

Unexpectedly she bent forward and kissed him. Surprised but quick to react to his laughing colleagues he said: "She knew the password!"

Suzy parked and showed her press card, an excellent reproduction made by an artisan in Chinatown. She did a quick interview with the search leader, a police woman and some K-9 men. Wishing them good luck she drove off.

Mike was enjoying the hot bath. With his eyes half closed he watched Jenny standing over him, one foot on each side of him. His erection rose out of the water. She crouched down holding him so he could penetrate her and smiling she looked straight into his eyes. Their sexes just met when Suzy's Jeep was heard stopping outside.

"Damn it!" she said. She rose, stepped out of the water, and gesturing irritably wrapped herself in a terry robe and left. He was aware she was wearing Maggie's bathrobe and felt disgusted with himself that he hadn't resisted her sexual invitation.

Jenny was halfway down the stairs when Suzy rushed in cheering. "Hello, here I am. I made it!"

"Thank God! And you aren't even wet!"

"No, but a bit frozen. Where's Mike?"

"Upstairs, thawing in the tub!"

"You seem to have defrosted. How is he?"

"Still cold. He seems clear of pneumonia."

"Good! Did you have time to seduce him?" Suzy asked going into the kitchen. She started the coffeemaker and went upstairs. The bathroom door was not closed and she heard Mike moving in the water. She knocked.

"Is that you, Suzy? Peep in; I want to see you smile. I'll just rest a little longer, then you can have the tub! How did you get by them?"

"I'll tell you everything. I have made some coffee."

"Suzy, please come here."

He closed his eyes and turned up his mouth to be kissed. Their lips met and she whispered: "Mike, what we did today was very, very stupid. I'm so relieved you made it back here."

Chapter 48

THE TWO MEN under the spruce slowly returned to consciousness realizing they were sitting out in the cold. They tried to speak, but only some blurry babbling came out. Their tongues were thick like after a dentist's anesthesia! Some police cruisers passed by. The two men looked at each other and realized where they were.

"They got us!" one of them spit out. "Somebody robbed us, and here we are sitting like 'in the shade of an old apple tree' watching some stupid Christmas show. The cops will take the thieves and our money, and the coke as well. Why on earth are people so dishonest? Why can't they do business an old-fashioned, honest way?" He talked with his tongue hanging out and his words sounded so funny his companion had to laugh.

But the laughing soon turned to wailing. They helped each other get up on their feet and leaning on each other they staggered over to their car parked outside a nearby garage, not visible from the road. The policemen had paid no attention to it. "We don't have Massachusetts licenses for our Uzis," the man went on. "We better hide them somewhere." He wrapped the two Uzi guns in a plastic bag and hid them under a basement window dome.

"You know, when Boss Bolivar wanted to take over this market he got killed along with two of his toughest guys—not strangled, not cut up, not shot—simply dead with broken necks on board their own boat. This Cape Cod organization means business. I have to get the goods or the money back. I'll arrange a meeting with these damned paratroopers. Now let's go home and get some sleep," he said and let the car roll out on the road.

After half a mile, they were stopped by the police. They had to show IDs and registration. Names and license plates were noted and their car was searched. The men had difficulty explaining why they were there and what they had been doing earlier that night. Finally they were let go. Followed by the two waiting colleagues in the Lincoln they drove to their motel in Sandwich and downed quantities of bourbon. The two gangster bosses couldn't explain to their colleagues what had happened or how things could go so wrong.

"Only the pilot, the paratrooper, the supplier, you and me knew of this and it's not me!"

"It's not me. I was with you all the time."

"You and I had some drinks before we left. Out there we didn't meet anybody. Who the hell is walking around here at this time of nightanyway, except the paratroopers."

"Let's get some rest and start fresh tomorrow. OK, boys! Dismissed!"

They returned to their rooms and soon everybody slept except Tom, the New Yorker, who was in charge of the missing four millions. This Benny guy from Cape Cod made him nervous. Why had he ever trusted him? Some of the lost money was Benny's and some was his own, but most came from lenders. Tom tried to think of ways to pay it back. He saw but one way—he clasped his hands and prayed, "OK, Lord, forgive my sins. Please return that money to me. My financiers in New York will kill me if you don't return it or help me get the cocaine back. At least some of it, so I can dilute it and get paid at least enough to cover the money the others have given to me. I promise you I'll give 25 percent, no 40 percent, of my profit to my church first thing once the deal is through…For Thine is the kingdom and the glory for ever, Amen."

It made him feel better. Returning without money or coke, he would be interrogated and tortured and his body would be found in a dumpster somewhere. Such are the rules.

***

Michele woke up shaking from the cold. It was morning, almost 7 am, still not full daylight. She was longing for a hot shower, a hot cup of coffee and a chat with Ingrid and Ted about this new and exciting turn of events. She got out of the car, stretched her aching limbs and peeked out the window of the garage door. It was crisp and cold outside. The morning mists were blowing away and some rose finches were trying to cheer each other up. It was going to be a nice, late winter day or early, spring day. She decided to make a jogging recognizance tour, and started dashing along the small road. The gangsters and their car were gone; the police were gone, too, except for one single cruiser near the beach. She jogged back to the garage. Prepared to be stopped by the police, she headed home leaving the bags with money, tranquilizer gun and ammo to be picked up later. She brought only the video and listening gear with her.

A police cruiser was parked at the Route 6A intersection. She recognized the two tired policemen, waved and smiled at them. They nodded back. She stopped by the bakery and picked up some oven fresh bagels. She noticed the Jeep hidden in the reeds behind the Sprenglers' house.

She undressed to take a hot shower but decided instead to listen in on the Sprenglers' house. In her studio she aimed her parabolic microphone at their kitchen window. A woman was singing. It wasn't Cathy. A second woman's voice shouted, "You stay away from him, Suzy!"

"He is not yours until he says so himself," responded a very self-confident, happy voice.

Michele heard the pilot coming down the stairs.

"Good morning, everybody! What a night!" He started telling how he had escaped the police and their dogs by walking into the freezing water, hiding behind a small skiff, only his nose above the water. He had stayed there for more than 20 minutes. The woman who had been singing told how she had managed to sneak through the policemen's net.

"We have to call the New Yorkers" the pilot said, "to explain what happened yesterday and why we couldn't come. I'll call them, but not from Arnold's phone. That would help the police trace the call."

Michele heard them eating and talking. Soon after she saw Mike driving away in the Jeep. He returned in half an hour. Again Michele switched on the tape recorder. She heard him entering the kitchen, saying: "The New Yorkers want the goods today. "

There was silence.

Michele heard Mike's voice again: "OK, girls! I'll meet them at 11 at Santo Gringo. To prevent an ambush we decided to let the dice choose one of six meeting places. Then we will go there right away."

"Suzy and I will be there. We can handle a few pranksters. Can't we, Suzy?"

"Sorry, Jenny, I am not going with you! That's not what I was hired for. I'll protect you from these people. But, I prefer to stay at a distance to see that everything works out all right. If Mike is crazy enough to go with you that's his business. I won't intervene unless things become so complicated you can't get out of the mess on your own."

"That's all I need to know," said Michele, switched off the tape recorder, took off her earphones and went to take the hot shower she'd been looking forward to.

Chapter 49

MIKE EXPECTED THE police to look for him at the Sprenglers' house. So he had taken all their luggage over to the Sheraton. He parked the rented red sports car outside the Santo Gringo, walked in and ordered a bourbon. With his back against the brass rail he noticed two men entering the bar. He recognized the snake-eyed Benny, one of Cavallo's men who shot at Arnold. The other one was Tom, a New Yorker, who really looked out of place in his Italian cut, full-length coat reaching almost to his feet. Benny blew into his frozen hands and stretched out one thin, feminine-looking hand. Mike shook it:

"So, you are Gotham?"

"Yeah, and you must be Bermuda."

"That's me. Sorry we could not make it yesterday," Mike stated. "The Coast Guard radar must have seen us. Soon after I picked up the trunks, a chopper came and we had to lay low until the search was over. I have two heavy trunks ready for you, let's make the switch."

"Yes, why don't we roll the dice and go ahead.

"OK, here it is. Be my guest."

Benny rolled the dice.

"Meeting place number four. That is in front of the Citizen's Bank at Hyannis Airport. OK, let's meet there at ten tonight."

"OK, but no shooting this time," Mike said with a smile. The snake eyes did not smile back.

Jenny was a bit shaky when Suzy helped her load the trunks in the Jeep. This was really the first time she was going to meet a gangster, as a gangster, face to face.

"You don't think I am letting you go all alone into the lion's den, do you?" Suzy asked. "Open your blouse and let me fasten this little bug to your bra. Let's wind the antenna around the strap. You won't need to hear from me so this one-way device will do just fine." Suzy held a small radio receiver in one hand and with the other she tapped on Jenny's breast and listened.

"OK, it works fine. I'll drive behind you in Mike's Volkswagen. I will only jump in if anything goes wrong, and if I really have to do something. Remember that you don't know me. You don't carry a gun, do you? Please don't. Guns mean trouble. OK?"

"Alright!"

"Jenny, you have to change clothes. Take those golf shoes over there and Mr. Sprengler's golf hat and the trench coat and Mike's sunglasses and those gloves. Perfect! You look just like a man. Now, let's go. Stay cool and don't say a thing. Give them orders with your hands and head! Yes! Exactly like that!"

Jenny definitely looked like a vacationing New Englander when she parked the Jeep, jumped out and stood waiting. The big Lincoln came gliding in and parked 10 yards away from her. Benny got out. He looked like a real Al Capone bodyguard. Jenny felt uncomfortable. Where was Mike? She couldn't see Suzy either. Why did they leave her alone like this?

Benny walked halfway over to her and hissed: "Where's the goods?"

Jenny pointed at the Jeep. Then she pointed at the Lincoln and signaled for them to unload the money. Benny shook his head. "Put the goods here first!"

Jenny opened the back door and took out one of the trunks. It was really much too heavy for her, but she made an effort and swung it to the ground close to the Jeep. A man got out the Lincoln. He carried a big tennis bag.

Mike in the red sports car pulled into the parking lot and stopped behind the Lincoln, blocking its way out. He jumped out and walked straight up to Tom.

"Hi, let me have a look at your money." Mike bent down to open the tennis bag. He was hit in his back head and pitched forward unconscious.

"Mike's just been knocked out", said Jenny in a low voice so Suzy could hear it on her radio, "and now the man aims a gun at me!"

"Stop mumbling and stick them up, kid!" Tom hissed.

A Volkswagen Rabbit with no headlights on drove into the parking lot and braked right behind Jenny's Jeep. Out came Suzy. She wore small eyeglasses and looked like an old-fashioned schoolmarm with her hair piled in a bun on her head. She looked at Benny with narrowed eyes and said in a piercing voice: "Could you boys please help me? I can hardly see anything and my headlights went dead. It must be a fuse or something. It usually is. You there, with that tool in your hand, come here and help me. I'll give you a dollar if you fix it!"

"Get out of here or you'll be sorry, lady!"

"What do you mean? Now then, young man, get going!" She held up her umbrella and shook it vigorously under his nose. "Please, young man, show some manners and do as I asked you to. OK, I'll give you two dollars. You don't look familiar", she said moving closer to him. "You didn't go to Hyannis High, did you?"

Her sharp knee hit his crotch so hard he jumped two feet in the air. Unwisely he bent forward and on his way down he was met with a kick so terrifically hard it flattened his nose. Suzy was already holding the gangster's gun in her hand when the other gangster realized what had happened.

"Open up that bag!" Suzy said with the voice of a drill sergeant. He obeyed. Tom attempted to rise. Blood streamed from his nose. Jenny turned to the man with the tennis bag, took a hanky from his breast pocket and gave it to his bleeding companion.

"You brought the wrong bag, pal," Suzy snarled pointing at the bunch of newspapers in it.

"You there," she ordered Tom, "sit on the sidewalk and don't move, or I'll shoot little holes in your nice Italian coat. Let's put our merchandise back and negotiate a new meeting. Have you filed for Chapter 11 or why the heck haven't you got that money!"

Jenny bent down to lift up the trunk. That's when she saw Benny's feet, the man Mike had met at the bar a little earlier. He had sneaked up behind the Jeep with his favorite toy, the Uzi. Jenny flung open the back door of the Jeep. It hit him hard enough to make him totter backward. She was quick, and a strong kick-off kick with Arnold's golf shoes sent Benny flat on the lawn behind them. She collected the Uzi and threw it into the Jeep.

Suzy turned to the only man still unhurt and asked him in a friendly voice: "Why on earth did you invite us to this circus? Don't you know that you have to be legit in order to deal with us? The moment I give the order, you are no more. Understood?"

The man looked more amused than terrified. He shook his head and said slowly, "Why did you steal all our money last night?"

"What?" Suzy spit out. "We haven't stolen any money. We ran into trouble last night. We were never even near you. We had to go way out on the peninsula and had a tough time avoiding all those cops. Besides, we don't steal money from our customers. For

God's sake! I swear. Now, let's help your kayoed friends." She went over to Tom who was still bleeding heavily.

"Sorry I had to be rough," said Suzy. "You drew first, remember. Now, help your pal on the lawn. He seems to have passed out. Take him to your car, and let the artillery under the seats stay there. There will be no shooting tonight, OK? I cannot believe you let yourselves get ripped off! Amateurs! Damned amateurs! You have to improve your technique if you're going to do business with us. We are big and very strong. You are still new and so small I don't understand how you could even think of something so stupid as trying to cheat us. I'll call our office for instructions. We'll contact you tomorrow."

Suzy followed him over to Benny who had just come to. He shook his head. Tom and Benny finally realized that the game was over.

"What's your name?" Suzy asked.

"Tom. Who are you?"

"Call me Miss. Who's he?"

"He's Benny. He's from Cape Cod, Miss."

"Now listen, Tommy and Benny, don't shoot at me. It would only complicate things for you. You see, if you do, all of you would be wiped out in a matter of hours. Our top man is a good guy. He prefers not to use violence and he might be able to help you out of this nasty money situation if it's good for business and if you're telling the truth. But we need a report on the theft. We'll talk tomorrow! Now, drive home! Sorry for my bronco kick! Good night."

"Good night, Miss!"

Jenny had helped Mike into the sports car. He was now alert enough to drive the half-mile to the Sheraton. From across the rotary the whole show had been followed by a little lady with a powerful bird watcher's microphone and a tape recorder.

Tom was driving with one hand on the wheel the other pressing the handkerchief to his bleeding nose. In the passenger's seat Benny sat holding his head in both hands saying "I sure got a kick out of that lady. It's still ringing and pounding in my head. How could anybody steal our money just like that? Can you believe the way these people just knocked us out? I've never heard of anything like it. We both got whacked silly by little girls for Christ's sake! Unbelievable!"

"You think the one with the Jeep was a girl too?"

"Sure, I heard her talk to the pilot. These people are real pros. The man in the sports car is the one who kissed Bolivar and his two men goodbye. He was the one who started the fight in Chatham that ended up with Cavallo dead. He's very dangerous. Wise to stay away from him."

"Do you think they are so dumb they think they can first steal our money and then sell us the stuff? It doesn't make sense! What do you think she meant when she said they might help us? Do you think they'll give us the goods and let us pay in 30 days? Do you believe in Santa?"

"If they were the ones who stole the money, they would have known we had no money and they would not have behaved the way they did. They would have expected some sort of trap and would never have walked right into it. Also, if they wanted it to be a one-time deal they would just have taken off instead of staying and making out like some kind of nurses. I don't have a clue as to what's going on. I think they are clean! I think a Cape Codder stole it."

"There is nobody here on the Cape who would dare!"

"But you!"

"Are you completely nuts?"

"Can you prove it's not you!"

"How about you doing it? How about you hiding the money after you doped me! You don't hear me accusing you, do you? No, because I think before I speak! Bolivar, your old boss, was a clever man, a thinking man. That's what you have to be if you want to build an empire like he did. Keep your suspicions under control. I didn't set up that robbery and you better believe me. What about this Arnold guy?"

They kept quiet. The tensions between them rose. When they got to Tom's motel Tom went in but Benny drove off in his BMW without a word.

There was a small party going on at Benny's place in Centerville. The usual people, three girls and two of his men were sprawled out half-naked in the Jacuzzi.

"We've been waiting for you, why did a simple pickup take so long?" one man asked.

"Because there was a problem. And it was not a simple pickup."

The girls, all under 20, wore scanty bikini panties and no bras. The men had on some obscene-looking gadgets they found tremendously amusing; one was shaped like an elephant's head with a thick trunk and the other like a snake's head. A girl undressed Benny, folded his clothes neatly and carried them into his bedroom. She sat in front of him in the warm bath and aroused him until she could sit in his lap, facing him with her legs spread apart and do what he paid her to do…perform sex games. He liked that girl, especially her pointed, pear-shaped breasts touching his hairy chest. This was his idea of an earthly paradise. Beautiful, willing young women without inhibitions, doing things they knew he liked, and doing them without asking, and not minding doing them in front of all the others.

He found the scene with copulating friends exciting. With lots of money and cocaine he could have all these wonderful things! His girl's eyes with their pinpoint pupils showed she was on cocaine. He owned her fully. He considered these beautiful obedient women his well-paid slaves! Thoughts of decadence and lost feelings were long gone and so were objections to making love without love, loss of dignity and charm, or lack of finesse, caress and friendship. His face was as devoid of expression as was that of the pretty little junkie on his lap, her eyes blurry and saliva dribbling from her half-open mouth.

***

Tom could not sleep. His men had asked him if he wanted a girl. Would that help? No thanks. Just mentioning the word "girl" made him think of the ones who had done that number on Benny and himself a few hours earlier. His face was still red with embarrassment and fury. The scary thing was that his simple plan had not worked out. He was now four million bucks in the red. He tried to think of different ways of making the whole puzzle fit. He was in a cold sweat thinking of how his colleagues in New York would react when they found out. If he was lucky they would give him one week, maybe two, to come up with the money. If he wasn't that lucky—Adios. That's how things work in their business.

When capital punishment is accepted, killing innocent ones is also accepted. The good thing was that his prayer had been heard. Otherwise, why should that "Miss" have been talking about a possibility of helping him out of his bad money situation? God is good. He is the greatest!

The religious gangster had a few more bourbons and took solace in the thought that in the civilized world's legal philosophy an innocent person will not be punished. That, finally, made his fears subside and he dozed off.

Chapter 50

MICHELE ENTERED INGRID'S kitchen announcing: "I brought you a cake. Can we sit down and talk?"

"Sure! What's up? Dinner's about ready. There is enough hash for the three of us. Let's save the cake for the coffee. Will you please tell Ted dinner is ready."

"It smells great, I can't resist."

They sat in the deep comfortable chairs in front of the open fireplace. Ingrid broke the silence: "No problems I hope, Michele?"

"No, but I have quite a bit to tell you!"

She started by reporting that it was some time ago Mr. Sprengler's copilot had visited the house together with two women and an older man. The pilot had mentioned a parachute landing with cocaine on Sandy Neck at night. The other night she had heard a small private plane make a turn over Sandy Neck and soon after the pilot came to the Sprenglers' house changing cars. She told how she had a hunch that a shipment was on its way and that the transaction would take place that night. But it had not. Michele told how she had followed Mike's Jeep, tranquilized the drug dealers and stolen their bags

"I counted it roughly. It's about $4,000,000 now safely stored in my basement. But that's not the end of the story."

"You know, Michele," Ingrid interrupted, "you shouldn't do things like that alone. I hate to see you risk your life playing games with professional criminals without any kind of help or back up. I am glad you made it. You are our closest friend and…"

Ted looked at his wife. Her lower lip trembled. She continued in a low voice: "I love you, Mich. You are a danger to yourself. You have to stop risking your life for this stupid money and your desire for revenge. We sleep lightly and would have been ready to go as fast as you were. Their drug business is not your business! And not ours either. You are still alive simply because you had unbelievable luck!"

"But Ingrid…"

"Michele, please call us next time. You're much too wild when you are alone!"

"I have kept an eye on them,"

Michele said that she witnessed the fight that ended in victory for the two young women. Ted and Ingrid sat silent.

"I have been thinking of Arnold Sprengler," Ted said after a while. "He is an intelligent man. Cathy will tell him that the two of you witnessed the meeting and shoot-out at Cavallo's. He knows what special equipment is needed to see and hear what you saw and heard. He will understand you were there not by chance but because you were tailing him. Arnold might tell Mike about us."

The cozy atmosphere was gone. Michele was nervous and shifted restlessly in her chair before she spoke: "I didn't think Mike would be involved in any more drug shipments. Arnold doesn't want his plane used for smuggling. We heard him say that he wanted to quit the business. There is a chance they might take revenge on us."

"We have to keep ourselves informed of their plans," Ted said sipping his coffee, "so we can hit first if they target us. Cavallo and Bolivar are gone. Arnold has resigned. This is a totally new war."

Ingrid was knitting. Her quick fingers working the needles and yarn without interruption, She had been listening intently and finally she spoke: "I like the idea of chasing them away from our area. But this is a job for professionals, we should not be involved much longer."

Michele agreed and nodded. Ingrid went on: "Why should we risk our lives when sloppy authorities let drugs flow freely in our streets, in the schools and in most prisons where inmates are made addicts. Is that included in the sentence? Where is America's social conscience? Where is the good will to help the unlucky and unfortunate? America has returned to a pre-Christian state where egotism, fear, punishment and retaliation rule, not humanism, forgiveness or trust, no helping hand...don't love thy neighbor as yourself, don't turn the other cheek.

"The three of us should not resign to injustice as do millions who never vote simply because there is not one single, honest, trustworthy person to represent them; not one darned single human is on the side of 'Les Miserables'. Not one single congressman or senator dares admit that contributions are bribes tied to conditions to vote for what's in the interest of the donor. It might be building warships or bombers we don't need, or bombing countries fighting our interests, or supporting a religious war or private American oil interests in the Middle East. Not one darned single so-called representative of the people dares speak up against idiotic politicians who say we cannot afford to help the hungry or sick or the uneducated poor because it's not good business!

"We must realize that this drug-crime problem should be solved the political way by collecting facts, raising peoples' interest, talking to our senator, talking to the DEA, informing the Coast Guard and the police so they can stop the crooks. We must tell our local FBI or CIA representatives. It's against my principles to take the law into my own hands. It means accepting America as a society where justice does not prevail because lawmakers are mostly lawyers unable to express the profound meaning of their laws. Their knowledge of their language is so bad that their wording can always be twisted. A law must consist of two parts: (A) the best possible wording, and (B) the meaning of the law. If I am still alive after knocking these gangsters out of business I will write a book about it!

"Where in our Constitution does it state that companies, interest groups or others with no voting privileges have any right to get involved in the voting process supporting their private economic or religious interest? Nowhere! Nowhere! Quibbling lawyers tell us that they have the right to free speech. Not true. No voting right—no right to interfere in the voting process. That is common sense. Crooks! That is what they are. Moneymad, unchristian despicable crooks!

"This is not how our American society should be according to our Constitution. Attorneys quibbling about 'free speech' have succeeded in killing our democracy because today all candidates need contributions from 'Big Money' to have a chance to win a campaign. The Constitution does not say that every form of activity must be run with private profit in mind."

Ingrid paused and then went on. "It does not say that rich people should have more to say than poor people. These rich people and big companies cannot afford to pay taxes but they can afford to give political contributions! And they do not give anything without getting something. They write the laws! That's the truth! Today you have the right to vote, but you have no right to demand that your vote is counted! What a sick law! The money mongers have taken over. A very humane and clear thinking journalist, Barbara Ehrenreich, has a very Christian way of analyzing what has happened to America. She says 'Finally the money mongers have driven Jesus out of the temple.'"

Ted and Michele smiled at Ingrid's high-spirited wrapping up of her viewpoints. They knew her strong desire to work for a humane society where people care for each other and where every person is treated as an asset to society. She expected a civilized society to invest in infrastructure and housing, in care, education and jobs where the private sector cannot or does not make enough profit. It struck Michele that she had heard the same thing said somewhere before. Bill had expressed exactly the same thing about big money ruling congressmen and senators, democrats as well as republicans, taking the peoples' democratic rights away.

***

It was a Friday afternoon. Ingrid met Cathy at the bus station in Hyannis. During the few times they had met they had developed a mutual feeling of trust and affection. The quiet Swedish woman liked the high-spirited young American in her last year at law school. Ingrid was pleased that she was treated both as a mother and as a friend. She understood that Cathy and her mother had a wonderful relationship. Stepping down from the bus Cathy looked around and when she saw Ingrid rushed to greet her with a big hug.

"It's really good of you to come and pick me up."

"Nice to see you again. How is London?"

"Foggy and gray, but spring is there. Spring is spring and London is London. I love both! You look so good! Is everything OK here?"

"Yes, sure. How about your mother and father?"

"Dad is still very weak and Mom is still deeply depressed. She is difficult to talk to. She is staying with her cousin in New Jersey. I'll call her tomorrow. I would have liked to see her, but I won't have the time to go to Bethesda in Maryland and still be back in London on schedule."

"Why don't you ask your father to have the young pilot, Mike, fly you?" Ingrid suggested. "He could probably take you back and forth the same day. I think you need to talk to your mother and let it take the time it takes. Ted and I are going to an art show in Boston on Sunday. Why don't you come with us? We could drop you at the hospital. Afterwards we could meet and have a bite before returning to the Cape."

"Great idea", Cathy agreed. "Maybe Mike could fly me to Bethesda on Monday and back on Tuesday."

Next morning when Ted and Ingrid started their daily walk they noticed a dark blue Rolls Royce parked outside Michele's house. Maybe, they thought, she became fed up with her rusty old Toyota and she had finally bought herself a Rolls. They didn't want to believe it, but there it was. They returned after walking two miles in silence. Passing Michele's house she opened the door and called to them. "I have a surprise for you."

"Thanks, we've already seen it," said Ted.

"No you haven't. Come on in," she held the door open for them.

When they went inside she said: "This is Sir Alec Kennedale. Alec, these are my closest friends, Ingrid and Ted Hallberg."

They shook hands.

"I guess you find it strange that my car has been parked here all night," he winked and grinned. Ingrid rushed over and hugged Michele saying, "I am so glad it's not your car, Michele."

"That's the first time I've ever heard somebody comment on my Rolls that way," said the Briton.

"Oh, I meant there must be a lot of problems in having that kind of prestigious car. Of course I wish Michele could afford a Rolls." Ingrid whispered apologetically.

Ted was curious about the overnight stay but knew full well he'd find out everything sooner or later.

"Nice to meet you, Alec," he said, "I guess all of us like your car. I didn't notice it was parked here all night, but I can see at least one good reason!"

"Alec dropped by last night," Michele interrupted, "and I was so glad to see him. I had to show him the work you two have helped me with, editing my script and arranging all the pictures and notes Rich and I collected. This is his field, too, as you already know. I did tell you Alec was my husband's best friend. Anyway, Alec began to look through Rich's notes and he added things here and there - things we had been talking about; facts I had forgotten. We had such fun working together that we have been sitting here working on my book all night. I should be tired and I know I look awful but, boy, do I feel great!"

"Ted and Ingrid you have done a great job. The way you work with pictures is terrific! I wish you could help me with my presentations." Alec said.

"Pancakes for everybody! Breakfast is served! My blueberry jam is to die for!" Michele called from the kitchen.

"It must be 20 years since I worked around the clock," Alec said, "but this was such fun. We forgot about time. Great pancakes by the way. Simply delicious, with that jam. And, my dear, after breakfast I'll go over to my house in Osterville and take a nap. You need one too, you know. We can meet here later and continue our work."

Michele was filled with excitement and nodded. Then she said: "Alec is flying to New York tomorrow. He'll be back next weekend and I think we should talk to him about drug money. What do you say, Ted?"

Chapter 51

CATHY WAS BOTH surprised and pleased to see the recovery Arnold had made since her last visit. He had been waiting for her, like only a lonely person in a hospital bed can do...longing, imagining her standing there in the door. He had made a list of subjects he needed to discuss with her and questions he must not forget to ask.

He had never felt this close to his elder daughter. She had always been his wife's favorite and he never expected Cathy to give him such strong support. But, from the moment she and Mike had entered Cavallo's office to help him, Cathy had become a completely new person compared to the girlish college student he had known earlier. He was not only proud of her, he looked up to her. She had proven to be daring, fast thinking and able to tangle with a tough and ruthless person like Cavallo and make a fool of him. She really was her mother's child. Like Sara, she seemed timid and shy. But, they were the two individuals in his acquaintanceship with the strongest stamina, the quickest, most razor-sharp replies and an amazing supply of knowledge and fighting spirit, besides which Cathy was charming and soft-spoken.

Arnold had misjudged Sara on one point. He had assumed she was his. But she belonged first of all to her children. He had stepped on some of her most sacred ideals. He believed that money would make her forgive his lack of respect for the law. He had provided the drugs that killed their daughter. That was the ultimate, unforgivable crime against her and her family. He pushed his somber thoughts aside when Cathy entered the room.

"I'm so glad to see you, Dad. I'm glad you look so much better. I brought you some flowers." She kissed him on his cheeks, his hands and on his eyes. A wave of affection surged through him. His eyes filled with tears and he had to swallow hard to get rid of the lump in his throat. "I also got you a little IPod with music, some Mozart, some Beethoven, and also some readings of Hemmingway and Steinbeck, and the latest issue of TIME magazine. How are your hands coming along?"

"Thank you, sweetheart. You are wonderful. I know I'll enjoy the music. I've never listened to taped books but I like the authors you chose." Arnold paused. Starting again he spoke slowly in a low voice, making an effort to talk distinctly and decisively: "My arms are still very weak and slow. My hands are coming along and my fingers are now quite flexible, so it would seem my recuperation is heading in the right direction. I have been working on my computer and I am beginning to understand it. It's fun."

They talked for over an hour. When she noticed he was becoming tired she asked him to take a short nap while she read a little. He snoozed for a while, and then they talked. He snoozed again and they talked some more. From his bed Arnold called Mike, who said he was more than happy to fly Cathy to see her mother. Visiting hours passed quickly and the sun was sinking like an orange in a purple cloud when Cathy said goodbye. As she started to walk towards the museum she heard a car honking from the other side of the street. It was Ingrid and Ted waiting for her.

Before driving home to Cape Cod they had dinner at the Panhandler's in Faneuil Hall.

Early on Monday morning Mike came to pick up Cathy. They had breakfast together but hardly talked at all while they ate.

"I was up at five, still dusk when I flew from Boston to Hyannis. The sunrise was beautiful. We'll have nice weather all the way to Bethesda," Mike finally said.

Her pensive expression indicated to him that she was perhaps thinking about what to say to her mother. Arnold had told him about the situation. Mike studied Cathy as soon as he thought she wasn't looking his way. He liked her appearance, the way she dressed and the way she moved. Now he was more than ever aware of the distance between them. Somehow he felt she was several steps above him.

"I saw Dad yesterday," she said, "In a few months he should be well enough to come home. But, he needs somebody to be with him 24 hours a day. I'll try to talk Mom into it."

"You'll make it."

"I am not that sure. She is very bitter."

Mike didn't like this conversation. Why couldn't they talk about flying instead?

"Have you packed everything you need?"

"Yes, I'm ready."

She carried a small travel case and a basket with sandwiches and a thermos of coffee.

"I enjoy flying," she said, "especially sitting in the cockpit. I understand Dad's fascination with it."

Violet veils of morning mist blew away over the airstrip when they taxied out. The voice from the tower sounded crusty and formal when it said "Wheels up at seven hundred." Then, suddenly, the voice became soft and friendly adding: "We wish you a pleasant trip, Miss Sprengler, and welcome back."

Mike had come to accept the fact that he no longer had the respect of some of his associates. Everybody must have known he had outsmarted the police in the "Sandy Neck parachute mystery", as the local press called it. His involvement in drug smuggling prompted the traffic controller in the tower to wish him behind bars rather than welcoming him back to Cape Cod.

Everybody around knew what had happened to the Sprengler family. One newspaper had run a long article about drug smuggling and the shoot-out at Cavallo's house. Cathy and her mother had everybody's sympathy. The story had been twisted so as to imply that Arnold, because of his daughter's death, was seeing the Chatham drug lord to warn him and advising him to leave the Cape.

When they were over Connecticut, Cathy served the coffee and sandwiches. She pointed at the transparent light green veil over the woods. Spring was on its way. When they landed in Bethesda spring was already there.

Sara had been waiting all morning. She stood in the doorway when Cathy paid the taxi, opened the wrought iron gate and started up the brick walk. They met halfway in a big hug.

Sara's cousin, Aunt Louisa, called Loulou, was a six-foot, 200-pound lady with most of those pounds placed above her amazingly small waist. As usual Loulou was wearing a cocktail dress, this time a black, very close-fitting creation with sequins in silver, black and blue-black, emphasizing her slim hips and big bosom. Her dyed silver-blue hair was styled in a pageboy cut with a mop of hair combed over to one side and almost smoothly shingled on the other. She nearly suffocated Cathy in a generous embrace, took her bag and carried it into the big open hall. In the living room nearby she invited Cathy and Sara to sit down and have a glass of sherry.

"It's a fine sherry as you will agree. Unfortunately, my stomach revolts vigorously whenever I drink sherry, so I have to stay with my usual." She poured herself a double bourbon.

Her husband, Uncle Maxi, was a tall wiry, silver-haired gentleman who wore a monocle. He was rarely ever at home, but knowing that the young attractive Cathy was coming he was there greeting her with a kiss on her hand. He was a retired cavalry general, who, after some lucrative transactions on Wall Street, could afford to indulge his every whim. He was still consulted by the Pentagon on questions regarding his specialty—chemical and bacteriological warfare.

An excellent dinner of roasted lamb cutlets, glazed beans, mushrooms, raw-fried hazelnut potatoes and mint gravy was served and halfway through the meal the general excused himself and disappeared.

"This is his bridge night", Aunt Loulou explained. "He usually comes home late from bridge. He always wins. In the morning his pockets are full of money. I can take it, he says. He doesn't care. He doesn't even know how much is there."

After dinner Loulou left Cathy and Sara alone in the big, luxurious house looked after by Gabriella, the Hispanic maid, who regularly checked to see if the two guests needed anything—snacks, drinks, coffee or fruit.

Cathy looked at her mother. Sara's eyes didn't sparkle the way they used to. She had lost a lot of weight and her elegantly tailored suit hung awkwardly on her thin body. Her beautiful black hair had turned gray with only a few strands of black remaining and had lost its luster. She looked tired, unhappy and depressed.

"Have you seen a doctor, Mom?"

"No! No doctor can bring my Maggie back."

"Mom, long ago you lived without Maggie. You have to accept the fact that all of us live just for a while and that life has to go on."

"Phrases, my dear Cathy. Phrases. If Arnold had not..." she interrupted herself, feeling that her daughter didn't like hearing her father being criticized.

"Mother, I want you to come back and take care of Dad."

"I knew you'd ask me that. I have already thought this over very carefully and my answer is: No way! We were very happy once, but your father's greed and willingness to do business with drugs ruined our lives. He has millions he could spend on doctors and nurses to look after himself day and night. He doesn't need me and I don't need him."

"But Mom, it will be like burying him alive."

"So what? His appetite for luxury and money had no limits. I told him over and over again that I could not go along with it. He ignored me when it was still possible for him to quit the drug trade. He always found new reasons for making one more flight and a few more millions. Long ago he accepted the fact that his activity was killing thousands of young Americans. Weren't they buried alive, too?

"Arnold is an intelligent man and he knew darned well about all the grief and misery he was creating. He took the risks and now he has to pay. He should be grateful the police didn't lock him up for 30 or 40 years, which they would have done had he been black or poor. And he should be glad I did not talk to the DEA, which was my social duty. He got what he deserved!"

"Mom, he is your husband. He is my father. I will not admit that our family is falling apart. I will not accept the idea that a man I have always loved be left out in the cold. It's our duty to help each other...it's our duty as Christians to forgive."

Her voice broke and her eyes filled with tears. "I am not a very good Christian", she continued, "but I do believe in what you once told me that we have to be prepared to forgive and accept a person's request for forgiveness. If your principles of crime and punishment stop you from coming back to us, you are not the Mom who brought up Maggie and me. Your sorrow and bitterness has stopped you from thinking constructively."

Cathy found a hanky in her purse and blew her nose. "You are having a serious depression, Mom. Your thoughts are probably not leading anywhere, just returning, repeating themselves, eating at you. But, there is a future where love persists; a future without bitterness and self-pity." Cathy's eyes sought contact with Sara's in vain. "If your principles stop you from forgiving a member of our family I feel sorry for you. You don't need Dad! You are a good teacher. You will easily find a position, and you have enough money to be on your own and start a new life. But I don't think that you can cut ties with Dad and me without suffering. Your new life will be nothing but bitterness."

Sara was silent, too tired to carry on the arguing. "Leave me alone. I wish I were dead," she said with a deep sigh.

Cathy opened her purse and took out a business card. "A healthy person doesn't want to die. You are ill and need help. This is a very nice and skilled doctor. I know her. She is your age and I have already talked to her. Not about you, but to help me. She will help you, too. Please, Mom, killing yourself does not solve any problems. I want you to live. I want you to fight your destructive thoughts.

"I am old and tired."

"Mom, I came to tell you that I have met a young man and I love him. He has proposed and I want to marry him." Her words came much faster than she had intended. "He is a fine man and I want you to be at my wedding." Cathy paused and breathed deeply. She was crying and tears streamed down her cheeks. "I want you to see and hold my children. Don't you understand?" She blew her nose again. "I need your friendship. I need you to talk to and to turn to. I would be very lonely without you. You are part of my future, and so is Dad."

Sara smiled. "Of course you should marry him if you love him. You have always been clever and able to make good decisions. I am so happy for you, my dear girl. When will the wedding be?"

"There might not be one. I am going to say 'no' and take care of Dad if you won't."

"But, Cathy! That is completely insane. Why should you sacrifice your life for a greedy old man?"

Sara recognized the fighting spirit in her daughter's eyes, when her reply came: "Because my Dad is not a greedy old man! I remember the hardship that forced him to be a taxi driver and work around the clock. I remember why he fell for the temptation to work for Mr. Cavallo. I was there when he wanted to quit, but Cavallo wouldn't let him. I remember times when we were happy. I have always loved him. He has always cared for me and it's my duty to take care of him.

I am not going to let him live the rest of his life in some institution. No way! He can count on me. Thanks to your way of bringing me up! I told Henry that I was not going to let Dad down."

"Cathy this is blackmail! How can you do this?"

"Dad is not a criminal, maybe merely borderline. He has told me a lot. He is a good man. He has asked for forgiveness. He will pay for what he did. If you go back to him you will have a rich life together with a man punished by his owns deeds...the gentle, humble man you once loved. I'll help you anytime you ask me to. You will have the resources to get all the helping hands you need. Please, Mom. It was not Dad's fault that Maggie died. It was my fault more than his. I was there. I knew her weakness, but I didn't look after her the way I should have. My guilt will be less of a burden if I can make up for my negligence. I think that you can be happy again with my father. Please, Mom, try!"

Sara sat silent, her eyes staring far away. She knew her daughter. She knew Cathy meant what she said. Cathy had inherited her own penchant for solidarity and fairness. Sara tried to look at herself from outside, thinking: "I can't let Cathy down. I can't allow this wonderful young woman to spend the rest of her life taking care of Arnold. Smart girl, smart ploy. But, why couldn't Arnold himself have asked? Or had he?"

She didn't remember. She was too tired to remember or try to remember. Cathy was right when she said a healthy person doesn't want to die.

"Cathy, you are my only joy. I want you to be happy and I want to help you. I don't think I will ever love Arnold again. I doubt that he wants to have me around. And really, I cannot even think of seeing him every day. I am too tired to make a decision now. However, I will take your advice to see this doctor. Maybe she could prescribe something so I won't feel so darned tired."

"Mom, I'll be there when you need me. Henry's dad has a house in Osterville. We are going to live there to start with. You will love Henry and his dad. You and I will see each other every day. Oh! Mom, we'll have such a good time together; walking on the beach, talking, doing things, shopping. We'll even go to New York to the Met and Carnegie Hall. I can't wait! You are my best and dearest friend and I have so much I want to talk to you about!"

Sara cried softly, smiling and nodding again and again.

The housemaid with the Spanish accent came in and suggested a nightcap. "Senora and Senorita, I make the greatest egg royale with a mushroom stew and small fried saucisson. Senora, you look like a new woman! Should I bring you another glass of sherry?"

"Finally something positive in this darned, depressing world," Sara thought. She took her daughter's hands, lifted them to her lips and kissed them. She remembered those hands when they were tiny, tiny ones - just big enough to grab one of her fingers. Now they were the hands helping her. It had been a long, long time since she felt such an intense sense of joy. She really loved to be with Cathy.

Cathy bent over and hugged her. "Mom, you're finally smiling. You taught me to love life. All you need is rest and sleep and peace to regain strength."

"When will the wedding be and where?"

Cathy patted her mother's cheeks and gently touched her eyes—happy, tired eyes with hundreds of fine wrinkles, which had not been there last year.

"We plan the wedding for midsummer in Osterville or Barnstable. You won't be fully recuperated then, but you'll be well enough to dance with Henry!"

"I'll be there, but I cannot even think of dancing!"

"No, not now, but then!"

The housemaid had followed the conversation: "Senora Sara, may I say that little babies need grandmothers."

They smiled. Cathy told Gabriella they'd like to try her specialty and they would also like a glass of a chilled white wine...nothing fancy.

"Ah, Senorita! Senora Sara's smiling must be celebrated".

Chapter 52

MICHELE HAD INVITED Ingrid and Ted to dinner. Alec's Rolls was parked in her driveway but nobody answered the doorbell. The hostess wasn't there when they entered her kitchen—no pots on the range and nothing in the oven.

"They have forgotten about the dinner, hope we don't embarrass them."

"Hey, you down there, come on up!" came Michele's voice from upstairs

"Hello! You said dinner, so we brought some bread I just baked, some cheese and a bottle of wine," said Ingrid entering Michele's studio.

"Hello. We've been so busy we forgot about time," said Alec, pointing at piles of scripts and layout sketches scattered all over the floor, the chairs, the table and the sofa. "Michele's book is slowly taking shape."

"If you forgot about the dinner, I'll fix one in a flash," Ingrid said. "Ted, why don't you open the wine…?"

"Wait, wait!" Alec broke in. "Dinner will be ready in a little while at my place in Osterville. I am sure you'll enjoy it."

Michele shut off the computer. "Sorry, it took me so long to do all the corrections. I'll hurry and change into a nicer dress."

Alec and Ted went downstairs together.

"Bring that bottle with you and your wife's home-baked bread. I'd appreciate that. I haven't tasted real home-baked bread for years," Alec said. "I must say you have chosen a nice life style and a nice corner of the world to live in. Also, I must compliment you on your choice of female companions. Your wife and Michele are delightful ladies..."

"Michele told us you were a longtime friend of her late husband. Did you do the same kind or research?"

"To start with, yes. After we left Oxford we led safaris together. We were both interested in the big cats. My wife, Elly, and I studied their pathological problems. Mich and Rich worked with cats' behavior."

"Michele and Rich collected lots of material", Ted said. "It will take her a long time to go through it all. We've tried to help with copy and picture editing, but she needs someone who can properly evaluate the discoveries and give her advice."

"Right. Rich and I talked about what he and Michele were working on, so I might actually add some helpful facts."

Minutes later Michele sat in front with Alex and with Ingrid and Ted in the back seat of the Rolls Royce as it glided soundlessly through Barnstable, southwards to Osterville. They pulled up in front of a white mansion.

Alec led his guests through a hall into a cozy library. An open fire was burning briskly and a gentleman in medieval attire looked down at them from a painting over the mantel. Across the hall they could see an impressive dinner table laid with shining silverware and sparkling crystal. A lady whom Ingrid recognized as a French speaking villager nodded and welcome them saying dinner would be served shortly. Alec opened a panel in the wall and asked "Scotch or champagne?" They had champagne.

"I hear Henry, my son, coming in," he told his guests. "Actually this is his party. We are going to celebrate his engagement to a wonderful girl."

A young man entered the room with a young girl announcing that she was his fiancée, Catherine Sprengler, whom he had met in London two years before and that "we just got engaged."

"Congratulations! You have chosen one of the finest girls there is. We all know Cathy. She's our neighbor," Ted said.

Alec smiled, tapped the young man's shoulder and introduced the young couple. Michele was nervous. This was a scary situation. Young Henry could have learned about her scientific work and her equipment

"Michele, aren't you feeling well? Somehow you don't seem like your usual cheerful self tonight. What's bothering you?" Alec looked concerned. "Maybe you've been working a bit too hard on this project lately. We're not 40 any longer, you know, and you have to stop working around the clock!"

"I feel fine," Michele replied, "and the champagne is great! I just happened to think of something."

"Relax, Michele," Ingrid whispered." We won't talk about tranquilizers now. We just have to talk to Cathy, that's all!"

Ted and Alec were discussing wines for dinner.

"With pheasant I think the burgundy I brought will be just right. We'll open it and let it sit for half an hour or so. It's a Geissweiler of decent vintage. You'll like it. I always choose it for our annual goose dinner on the 11th of November, the day for celebrating Marten Goose or it may be Martin Luther, I am not sure which!"

Whispering, Alec asked Ingrid what was wrong with Michele.

"She's just tired. She doesn't want to talk business tonight, she said. Also she's been very lonely for years now. She never took any initiative to make new friends until she decided to go and see her 'cat friends' in London, and she met you. She's actually become a new person since that trip. She needs somebody who can stimulate her in her work. You really mean a lot to her. She knows of the difficult time Cathy had to go through. Maybe she is a bit sad thinking of Cathy's happiness and her own loneliness."

"A beautiful, intelligent woman like Mich? How come men are not standing in line courting her?"

"She tried to ignore her loneliness by burying herself in hard work, doing what she and her husband planned to do together. What she really needs is the input from a fellow scientist."

The gilded clock on the wall chimed 8 melodious strikes.

Ingrid talked to Alec while he served more champagne: "There was a man who was seriously in love with her and wanted to marry her. He was fun and utterly charming. We met him. He had all the money in the world and wanted to give her everything. But, he was not a 'cat' man. She may seem tough, calculating and crazy, but the real Michele is a darling, shy and lonely person…the best friend I've ever had. We must cheer her up!"

Ingrid was afraid her pushing them together might have been too obvious, but Alec was a shy person and a little shove wouldn't hurt, she thought.

Cathy told Ingrid about seeing her mother and talking her into coming back home. Her father was doing very well. He had started an air taxi with Mike. Also, Cathy said she had noticed that somebody had been in her house.

"Yes, Mike, the pilot, and two women were there one night," Ingrid said. "Maybe I shouldn't say this, but I think he might be involved with drug smuggling."

"That's bad news. Dad will be very upset if his plane is being used for flying drugs." Cathy looked puzzled. "Anyway, I would like you to meet my mom. She is great. The three of us could have some good times together."

Ted and Alec talked about money and drug money's way to Wall Street, and Ted took advantage of the conversation to ask Alec what he would do if he had $15,000,000 in cash.

"There are hundreds of options. Funny thing, though", Alec laughed. "Michele asked me exactly the same question just the other day. You Americans spend hundreds of millions of dollars every week for the privilege of dreaming of money, dreaming you win Megabucks, Big Game, PowerBall and other lotteries! And did you know that while the State of Massachusetts pays out millions and millions every week that represents only 2 cents of every dollar the public pays for lottery tickets. So dreams are big business with big profits."

The lady in the dining room doorway clapped her hands and announced that dinner was served and said: "Will Mrs. Renard please take the seat beside our host here, Mrs. and Mr. Hallberg over here, and Miss Sprengler and Master Henry here. Please, be seated."

This Osterville woman was famous for her superb cooking. She had hosted dinners for senators and presidents. The menu proved it: First, lobster bisque with cheese croquettes; followed by broiled pheasant with baby carrots, snow peas and corn, a small casserole of cauliflower and broccoli in a cheese gratin accompanied by wild rice and a chanterelle gravy. The condiments were simply two different kinds of clear jelly, black currant and cranberry. After the main course, in the European custom, came Camembert cheese and an endive salad with mandarin slices. The dessert was a refreshing, light Charlotte Russe—slices of homemade jelly roll in a jellied lemon mousse served in a beautiful crystal bowl.

"Michele," Henry said, "my father told me about the videos and films you made in Kenya. I'd like to see them some time. I'm also interested in learning more about your sophisticated equipment." He was sitting next to Michele, but everyone at the table heard what he had said. She moved uneasily and wished somebody would change the subject. But Henry cheerfully continued, happy to have found a fascinating subject he knew Michele could talk about.

"The shots you used to tranquilize a lioness without hurting her would have to be exactly the right dose. How could you be sure you had the correct dose?"

"I explain that in my book. We had ampoules of different sizes and tranquilizers of different strength and different effects."

"Just as I guessed! But how could you aim right and shoot in the dark when night hunting beasts of pry could see you but human eyes could not see much?"

"With an infra-scope, nothing very complicated, but it was new at that time." She spoke softly to escape everybody's attention.

"Also, those sound segments of lionesses playing with their cubs. You used a parabolic microphone, didn't you?"

Avoiding the questions would only have seemed strange, since she was the expert, so she answered them.

The young man didn't understand her dilemma and went on: "With that equipment a creative criminal could easily make a million bucks a week!"

Michele wished Cathy had not been there listening. Would she tell Arnold? Of course! Michele's nervous eyes met Ingrid's calm gaze.

"I am sure dishonest people don't need electronic devices to smell dollar bills. But this equipment could also be used against crime, so it all depends on who's the smartest the bad boys or the good boys?"

"Or girls!" Cathy threw in. She had followed the conversation with interest.

Chapter 53

WHEN CATHY ENTERED Arnold's hospital room, she found him leaning back, asleep with his mouth half open. His lap top computer lay humming in his lap. His skin was pale and pinkish and Cathy noticed some big brown spots she had never seen before on his temples - a pigment change occurring only in older people. It saddened her to accept the fact that this tired-looking old man was actually her own Dad. She sat at his bedside, silent, looking at him, taking his hand. He looked up, squeezed her hand. Suddenly his face changed and in just a moment's time he looked happy and 10 years younger.

"Am I glad to see you, Cathy! I am trying to work myself out of this. I am not going to be a vegetable! I have to learn Windows, word processing and working with a database. It's fun! My hands obey orders much better now, but my legs are so stubborn they refuse to do what I tell them to. Heck! If I could only manipulate the remaining nerves. I have to be a patient patient! However, you look happy. What's new?"

"I saw Mom. She is depressed and very bitter, but she is seeing a doctor now and I think she might be all right in six months or so.

A deep depression takes at least a year. She's in bad shape but she has a strong will. I cheered her up by telling her a secret."

"What on earth did you say to her?"

"I invited her and you to my wedding!"

"You did what?"

"I'm getting married and I want you and Mom to come to my wedding. It's going to be on Cape Cod and I am going to take you there."

"That man had better be a darned good guy because he is marrying a darned good girl. What did Sara say?"

"She got a kick out of it!"

"I might have guessed that. She loves you an awful lot. I'm thinking day and night about how I could make up for... We never had any problems until this drug business. I am so sorry I got involved in it. I am sorry she had good reason to leave me. I never thought things could go this wrong. I feel so damned rotten and I miss her so. I miss her friendship, her confidence and her support. I'll never, ever forgive myself."

"When she comes out of her depression I think there is a good chance you two can get together and talk."

"I doubt it. She said she would never see me again. By the way, who is this young man?

Can he support you?"

"Yes, we can support ourselves. His dad is a scientist. We had dinner together last night. There were other guests, too. Guess who? Our neighbors in Barnstable, the Swedes and the widow living across from our house, Mrs. Renard. She is a colleague of Henry's dad, a wildlife photographer and scientist. She's writing a book."

"So, she is a scientist. She does look like a scientist. Is she still driving that ugly old car? Did you say her name was Mrs. Renard?"

"Yes, Michele Renard. She's very nice."

"You know what 'RENARD' means in French, don't you?"

"You mean 'FOX'?"

"Yes. There was a Dr. Richard Renard, a professor and zoologist I admired. He was very smart and would only marry a very smart woman. He wrote about wildlife and big game hunting with a camera, but he died some years ago. She might be Mrs. Richard Renard."

"Dad, somebody has been in our house. I noticed it last time. Our neighbors said it was Mike. Is he still flying cocaine? If he is I am going to get really mad! And you better put an end to it immediately!"

"He promised me not to use my Baron for smuggling. I will tell you everything, so we can discuss getting things back to normal."

He talked slowly in a low voice and told Cathy the whole story; how he was flying cocaine first with the old Cessna then with the Baron, how he and Mike had dropped the cocaine containers in the ocean, how Captain Jack had picked it up and how the routine had worked. He told her that some mysterious robberies had taken place and that buyers in New York had lost many millions right in Barnstable.

"I did not do it", Arnold said. "I did not know anything about those robberies, but I was blamed for the losses. However, the men who lost the money are dead now, so nobody cares any more. They got killed on board the *SNOWBIRD* in Newport along with the one who killed Maggie."

Cathy did not interrupt his long, detailed "confession".

"How involved was Mike?" she asked.

"He was with me and met the suppliers. Together we flew and dropped the goods. He had nothing to do with the deals and he cannot have been involved in the robberies. But, he did ask me for permission to make some flights for our supplier. His name is Harry Greycoat and he has a beautiful daughter. Harry wants me to join him in some business that I could do on my computer. He is two faced and his notions of what's legal and illegal are very personal and diffuse. His wife was killed by drug crooks and he got revenge by robbing those crooks - millions and millions of dollars. And, you know, making money is addictive, so now he's a drug dealer as well. He is very personable and persuasive and he just might try to talk Mike into working with him."

"Dad, what would you do if you found out who robbed those New Yorkers?"

"Nothing. They didn't steal any money from me. They stole some cocaine I don't want any longer. I don't owe them anything. I would feel a bit wary though because they could blackmail me or go to the police. They might have evidence...but, I would never start anything."

"What are you going to do with the drug bombs?"

"One should be on board my fishing boat and the other is in Bermuda with Harry. He will probably steal it and later send me a fat check as compensation for 'lost goods'. Mike said the one on board my fishing boat seems to be missing. What do you suggest I do?"

"Nothing right now! Just get well!" She kissed him goodbye.

"You should have told Sara that I love her and that I want her to try to forgive me."

"I did!"

"Bye, sweetheart. I'm glad you found a good man to marry. I hope you'll be happy together."

On her way out Cathy ran into Mike in the doorway. They greeted each other with just a casual "Hi" and Cathy rushed to get a taxi.

"Harry planned to rob some drug buyers." Mike told Arnold. "He wanted me to fly in the stuff. I said no. Then he offered me a quarter of a million dollars if I flew his daughter and Suzy, her secretary, and parachuted them over Sandy Neck".

"Are you totally insane, Mike?"

"I assumed everything would be pretty clean since his own daughter would be involved. I'm sorry Arnold; I broke my promise. I really am sorry. I said yes."

"You dropped them on Sandy Neck? A few miles away from the strongest radar station on this hemisphere! They must have seen you take off from Bermuda! The DEA could have been there before the girls even landed!"

"Yes, Harry's plan didn't work out."

"He never had any plan! He is blinded by money."

Mike looked miserable. "Arnold, please forgive me. If you still want me to fly the Baron I promise never to let this happen again."

"That was really a stupid thing to do, but let's not talk about it any more. It was the last time, promise?"

"Yes, Arnold. But that was not the end of it. Somebody robbed the buyer waiting for us on Sandy Neck with four million dollars in cash and they believe we did it!"

Chapter 54

CATHY WAS JOGGING along the north beach. Her regular round would take her over the sandbanks, through the woods and after a short brake back again over the meadows, through the juniper-, wild rose- and sloe vegetation along the old country road, back home to take a shower and have breakfast.

She was a fast runner and kept good speed to keep warm this chilly morning. She stopped to relax and let her heartbeat return to normal and to do some aerobics and pushups at her usual place in a sunny glade. She lay flat on the sun-warmed ground covered with a soft, thick layer of pine needles. She watched the clear blue sky and the white cotton clouds lazily sailing by. What a wonderful feeling. She closed her eyes and inhaled the oxygen rich, pine perfumed air with breathing…

The man came out of nowhere. Suddenly he sat on her and seconds later he held a firm grip around her throat with one hand, pressing her down. With the other hand, in a matter of seconds he had torn down her jogging pants locking her feet, so she could not kick him. He tore her panties apart and forced his hand in between her legs.

His attack came suddenly. She had been totally unaware of any danger in this peaceful, silent glade. So there was not a chance that anybody could come to help her.

Many times she had been thinking of rape victims and what they should do to protect themselves and fight back. And now, all of a sudden, she herself was in this hysterical situation of being raped. She was simply in a state of chock, unable to mobilize any rational defense.

His strong grip around her throat made her pulse pound heavily in her head. She crossed her legs and bent slightly. He tried to pull her jacket up over her face, but she kept her arms straight down preventing it. She looked into his face. Never ever will she forget it. He was bloodshot red, his forehead all wet by sweat and his red hair hanging in wet wisps. His mouth was wide open and saliva flowed down on her face. He had a big aquiline nose and he bent down to kiss her. She felt his penis on her belly. Strange it was not as hard as she had expected. He was obviously so nervous that his potency was disappearing. She felt how he pulled his penis over and over again and tried to force her to separate her legs. He bent down to reach her breasts with his mouth.

Only now did she scream "h-e-e-e-l-p!" The sound was distorted by his strangling grip. Out of her mouth came a long, terrified haul sounding like from a wounded dog. It drowned in the bushes and faded among the trees. He moved his hand from her throat to cover her mouth. With his other hand he had forced his fingers in between her legs and into her. Her feeling of intrusion and violation of her privacy, his disrespect of her dignity suddenly made her furious. Her hands were free now and a passage in a little handbook by her Swedish friend and neighbor Ted Hallgren came to her mind, "Don't fight a man the way men fight. Save your energy. Make sudden attacks. Not to get free, not to stop him from doing what he's doing, but to hurt him…"

"You wonderful little bitch…" His saliva dripping lips slurred. "I have seen you pass by here several times. I've been waiting for you and I want you to be mine. Just relax and I will give you one hell of a wonderful ride."

"OK," she nodded and now with both her hands free she formed the classical V-sign for victory with her index and long fingers. In one millisecond both her hands flew up against his face. With his hand that had covered her mouth he grabbed her left hand, but her right hand fingers were already on their way… With all the force she could mobilize, she bored them into his eyes. She felt a bitter taste of disgust in her mouth, when her fingers found their way in under his eyeballs. She felt as if her hand was stuck into his head. She fulfilled the attack. She bent her fingers so her long, strong nails became like animal claws…and with her full power she scratched his eyes, the lower eye lids and down his cheeks.

He screamed uncontrolled and blood gushed out of his eye sockets and from the long, deep scratches down his cheeks… Too late his hands flew up to protect his eyes. She rolled away from him. In a flash she was on her feet, pulled up her pants and threw some handfuls of dirt into his face.

"Willy, Willy, help! Help! Help!" He hauled. "I'm blind! I'm blind! I cannot see! She scratched out my eyes! Oh, Willy help me!

Cathy heard somebody approaching through the dense bushes and before she ran away, she caught a glimpse of a big, chunky man in black hair and oversized light blue shorts walking up to the rapist and bending over him. Disgusted he looked at his bleeding friend.

"You goddamned idiot, why can't you chose your own kind of men and whores who'll accept your sick sexuality. Now you are marked, so no jury or police or even a doctor will believe any story that could free you. I saw her running away. She disappeared fast like a deer between the trees and I am sure we can expect the cops to be here in a few minutes."

The blood flow from the wounded face was simply terrible. It pulsed down his cheeks. His eyes looked like red rolling balls. When he tried to see everything was just red.

"Man, you need a doctor to help you right away. This looks bad., really bad," said the big guy helping his bleeding friend to stand up. With blood soiled hands the rapist got his slouching manhood back where it belonged and pulled up his fly zipper.

"I'm blind! The damned bitch scratched my eyes out! Damn it! How can anybody do such a thing! Hell and devils, it hurts. All I see is red! Oh, I'm blind," he sobbed. "Damned cat-woman! Why did God give me this appetite for sex and beautiful women?"

"Don't you blame the lord for this! You are an idiot and your desire to force people to do what you want, is simply sick. Power alone can't suppress a smart and decisive woman. Come now. Let's get out of here! Hold my hand and let's take the car to Hyannis Hospital."

"No, no, for God's sake. You have to take me to the hotel, so we can wash these wounds clean and see if there is something we can do to stop the bleeding. The hospital would call the cops right away! No Willy, you have to drive me to a hospital far away from here. Maybe we don't even need to go to a hospital. I think I begin to see now. It's blurry. Everything is still red and it itches like hell, but I am not blind…"

"Cathy dear, what's happened?" Michele tried to stop her running friend. "You've been crying, dear."

Cathy slowed down. She covered her face with both her hands and sat down on the stairs at the porch. She sat quiet while her breathing returned to normal. Michele sat down beside her.

"Those men, the ones we saw placing dope in our house that winter night… They tried to rape me. Gosh, that was close! I was laying resting after a long, fast jogging stretch, when suddenly he was over me, strangling me. He tore down my jogging pants and ripped my panties apart and tried to force me. I felt completely helpless... Then I came to think of the French police recommendations I read about in Ted's book: 'Don't fight a man the way men fight...' so I made the classic Victory sigh with my fingers and with all my strength I stuck them into his eyes and scratched down the hardest I could! There was blood all over the place! And he screamed like an animal. It was horrible. He let go his grip... and I got up and ran away like I never ran before... Jeepers, that was close!"

"Where did this happen?" Michele asked. "Lets go there right away and stop by the police station and file a report."

They took Cathy's car and followed the Kings Highway turning down the Indian trail and stopped at the beach. On the narrow plank bridge over the Indian Creek they met a woman with a dog. Michele asked if she had seen two men. Yes she had.

"One had fallen and hit his eyes. Poor guy. They drove off in a nice new car, maybe 5 or 10 minutes ago," she said and patted her dog.

"What did the car look like I think it was a Lincoln, a big white limousine. They were driving to the hospital, I guess..."

"Thank you, Mam," said Cathy.

"Come on Mich, I'll show you the glade where I always rest and do a little aerobics before running back home. Never again will I go there. How stupid of me. I even closed my eyes and dozed off for a few minutes. I never thought of any danger..."

"Nor did he, I guess!"

"I feel sorry for the creep!"

"For heavens sake don't. I hope this taught him a lesson. Now, let's go to the police station and tell the whole story."

"No, I don't want to tell the police!"

"But why? These scums must be brought to justice and punished!"

"No, you see, if Dad got to know it, his feelings of guilt would get even stronger and he would blame himself even more for getting involved with these rotten people. He has problem enough, as is. Making the rapist blind, I think, is punishment enough!"

"You know, Mich. He was so close of raping me it's a wonder I got away. He was so strong and heavy. First I thought I didn't have a chance to stop him. Isn't it strange that it was Ted's advise that saved me. This peaceful, gentle man, who rarely rises his voice, he was the one who recommended me to use ultimate cruelty, fast and unexpected, to stop an offender and give me, the victim, a chance to run away. He is the last I would expect to write a textbook about preventing rapes with utmost cruelty.

Chapter 55

JENNY CALLED HER father for instructions. He could not understand how this absolutely reliable New York connection could have flunked. A mole must have told the police. For his daughter's safety he decided to help Benny out by granting 30 days' credit. Suzy volunteered to deliver the two parachuted trunks of cocaine to Benny and she parked the sports car outside the big, ugly villa with the wonderful ocean view. A young girl dressed in a bikini opened the door and asked Suzy to come in.

"Are you gonna work here?" she asked.

"Work? Doing what?"

"You know, whenever they like it. Three thousand a month and everything free including all the dope you need."

"I would like to talk to Benny."

The girl shouted: "Benny, you got a visitor!"

From upstairs came a loud order: "Ask him to come up."

Suzy and the girl went upstairs. The sun shone in through the windows and the reflections from the glittering ocean played on the ceiling. Benny met Suzy and was wearing nothing more than a towel around his waist. Suzy looked at the well-built, muscular, evenly tanned body, a copy of Michelangelo's David exept for those cold snake eyes.

"Oh, it's you, Miss. Come in, join our party."

She followed him into a big room with a spacious Jacuzzi. Two very beautiful and very young girls wearing only mini bikini bottomspanties were massaging a man, paying special attention to his private parts. Watching the performance were two other men sitting in the foaming water holding icy glasses. She recognized them. They were the ones she and Jenny had given a brief lesson in kickboxing. They nodded to her.

The girl offered to take Suzy's jacket. "Come on, you're gorgeous! You could ask for five thousand. Don't go under five!" she whispered.

"Get lost, Patti!" Benny said, and asked Suzy if he could pour her a glass of champagne, a Bloody Mary or…

"No thanks. I've got the goods we promised. Come!"

She turned and went down the stairs, out the door and to the car. A chilly wind blew in from northeast. Benny had obeyed instinctively. He was still wearing only the terry towel when he followed her. She opened the trunk and pointed at the containers with cocaine.

"You will have to pay for it in 30 days. Also, I don't like sloppiness. Next time we meet I want you to be dressed - like a gentleman, OK?"

"Yes, Miss."

He grabbed the first trunk and had to run back and forth twice to get them both indoors. Suzy was amazed that Harry had been in contact with people like this. She drove off leaving the embarrassed Benny to return to his party.

"She was really something! Boy, why didn't she stay?" one of the men asked.

"Because," replied Benny, "she didn't like me running around dressed in a towel!"

"You mean she wanted you to take it off?"

They laughed.

"You don't understand anything about leaders," Benny replied. "She's a top manager and she saved our lives. She gave me the goods, to be paid for in 30 days. She saw I had class. She saw she could trust me. She saved your lives!"

***

Suzy parked the sports car near the hangar. The mechanic could not help giving Mike a knowing glance and wink when he saw Jenny's and Suzy's well-shaped legs disappear in the interior of the Baron. The man on the tarmac removed the blocks from the wheels and waved them off.

In spite of the great weather and the excellent forecasts Mike was in a melancholy mood. This trip had not worked out the way he had hoped. He could not understand why he had agreed to this operation, neglecting risk evaluations and security exits. Together with Jenny he had come up with the idea, but had found it too risky. Harry, however, believed strongly in the "surprise effect" and he had convinced them to come along.

Mike had nobody but himself to blame. Why had he not objected to a plan so full of weak spots? Had the loss of Maggie made him indifferent? Had his desire to impress Jenny and Suzy made him take stupid chances? Good thing it was all over. Or was it? The police and the buyers as well suspected him of the robbery.

The engines hummed. Suzy and Jenny were talking about the gifts they had bought in Boston—music CDs for Harry, some books, a Swiss Army knife for the butler, a beautiful blouse for Nanny, the butler's wife.

Suzy was looking at a book with Japanese paintings, at another with poetry from Japan and at a third, a Japanese cookbook. Many of the dishes were familiar to her but she had never learned to cook. Now she was caught by a desire to revive tastes from her childhood. Mike had said she should be proud of her heritage. No Anglo-American had ever said that to her before. She realized her roots could give strength and character. From her work with Jenny she had developed disgust for a lifestyle that stimulates egotism and money-mad people.

She longed for her parents. She wanted to know more about the culture that had given them their moral stability. Her father was a hard working, honest man. He went to work dressed in striped pants, a redingote and a bowler hat. After work he changed to a soft black silk gown. He loved poetry, especially Japanese poems. When she was a little girl she liked his lifestyle. As a teenager she had found the traditional customs ridiculous and un-American. Now she understood they gave him the strength to be himself. Suzy's fragile, soft-spoken mother had taught her to be humble and proud. There was an atmosphere of order and neatness, calm and harmony around her. Now Suzy wanted to go and see them. She wanted them to meet her choice of man. It was still too early but she sensed Mike was hers.

This trip had completely changed her opinion of her employer. She had always looked up to Harry but he had ignored Mike's skepticism. He had asked them to jump a few miles away from a radar station and a Coast Guard base. He had no backup plans. Jenny, Mike and she had been exposed to the buyers. Mike was reliable and good in this crazy business. He would be a good leader in any business. This trip must have made him decide it was to be the last one. She had already made up her mind.

Jenny was asleep. Suzy moved up and took the copilot's place. She looked at Mike and wanted him to look back at her with approval. But he was gloomy, concentrating on the instruments. Then she felt his hand taking hers. She let it happen and waited. She lifted and kissed his hand. His grip tightened and he leaned over and kissed hers.

"Gotcha," she said to herself and smiled.

"I love you, Suzy," he whispered.

"I am yours," she whispered back.

She stayed in the seat near to him. They didn't talk. Now and then he stroked her blue-black hair. When they approached Nassau she moved back and sat beside Jenny.

Harry was waiting for them at the airport. He was obviously relieved to see Jenny again.

"I am sorry, Dad. It didn't work out."

"I am really very happy you are back."

"Dad, please don't ask me to do this again."

He realized that his own greed and weakness for taking chances had put Jenny in great danger. She was now known and recognized by some very dangerous people. The least he could have done was to let the buyers have the goods. But who had snatched the money? He had found out the same thing as Bolivar and Cavallo; That Cape Cod was not a good place for drug runners!

Harry and Mike had drinks on the veranda, watching the ocean. A four-masted cruise ship with impressive sets of sails passed by in the brisk wind.

"Oh, isn't she a beauty!" Harry said, "I remember, when I was a boy in Margate, England. I saw schooners and barges, trawlers and barks pass by. Most of them had engines for easier docking. When the wind died, you could hear their slow donk, donk, donk from miles away. Ever so often we saw full riggers or clipper ships. Did you know a clipper could make an average speed of almost 20 knots during a passage from Hong-Kong to London? Amazing, isn't it!"

Mike didn't interrupt.

"Mike, I am truly sorry. I really am!"

"We should have let Arnold plan the whole operation."

"Arnold told me to stay away from it. He has made his last drug run. He's had enough," said Harry.

"Haven't you?"

"Yes, I think so. I have a question for you."

"Yes."

"I like you a lot, Mike. I have a lovely daughter who is very fond of you. She even says she would like to marry you. That would please me greatly. It would make you a very wealthy man, with a personal fortune of many million American dollars and a few million British pounds. May I suggest that you propose to her and make her a happy wife?"

Before Harry finished the sentence, he knew the answer would not be what he had hoped for. "Talk to Jenny tonight and make up your mind."

Mike had his answer ready but didn't want to ruin the atmosphere of friendship and trust. "Yes, why don't we talk about it tomorrow," he said.

After dinner they had coffee, watching the sunset and the blue hour turn into dark night.

Harry played something moody on the piano before he said good night and retired. Jenny went upstairs to tuck him in and they had their little talk at his bedside—something they had done for years.

Mike wanted to be alone and went for a walk. He found a gate and walked along a stretch of beach under high palm trees. Jenny was one heck of a girl and Harry would be a great father-in-law, sure! And all the money and the posh lifestyle they offered were tempting. But he simply couldn't ignore his own private emotions. He didn't want to hurt Jenny and he knew Harry would be disappointed and upset if he said "no"—so the smartest thing would simply be to say "yes".

Suzy was left alone reading her new poetry book.

"So, you are sitting here in your solitude?" Jenny said coming back downstairs. "Where is Mike?"

"He went for a walk. I got the feeling he wanted to be alone and I didn't want to intrude."

"I admire your composure. I thought you wanted him and all set to fight for him."

"Jenny, you and I are best friends. I truly love you. I know how to fight but I will not fight with you. You should know that. I don't have your beauty. I don't have a father as wealthy as Harry and I want Mike to have his freedom. I believe that one day the man I love will choose me because I offer him harmony and support, strength and inner peace, with no need for financial backing."

"I am sorry, Sue, you are a great friend. But you are a dreamer and idealist. I'll get him, because I want him."

"Good night, Jenny." Suzy went upstairs to her room and closed the door behind her. Never before had she felt that the cultures they represented made any difference. She loved America and the spirit of America and the respect for money, as long as money represented the result of work and sacrifice. But she disliked the weakness for money, the servile crawling for financial power, and the false image of culture that money usually created. Too often money was serving and fertilizing selfishness and greed. Self-interest and money madness was killing democracy in America.

Wearing the white nightgown with the golden butterflies she combed her shoulder-length hair, which she let hang free held loosely in back with a small red bow. She lit a candle in front of a small picture of her mother and father and sat on the floor with her legs crossed and looking into the flame. She breathed slowly. Her hands rested on her knees. She was in total harmony with herself. There was a soft knock on her door. She didn't care. The door opened slowly. Mike did not enter. He stopped respectfully, fascinated by the peace in the room and the beautiful woman sitting relaxed and motionless with her eyes looking into the candle's flame. He did not want to disturb her. He closed the door quietly and returned downstairs.

Jenny served him a snifter of cognac. She sat up in his lap and embraced him. She wanted to be kissed. Her fingers combed through his curly hair.

"Mike, I love you, I want you. Did you talk to Dad?"

"Yes, he's really generous. He is offering us all the money we would ever need."

"You said yes, didn't you?"

"He suggested that we talk about it tomorrow."

"Mike, I'll be very happy with you."

She kneeled in front of him and kissed him over and over again on his mouth, cheeks and eyes. He didn't have the strength to say "no" right away.

"Please come to me tonight," she said. "I want you. I want you to kiss me all over. I'll make you feel good—very good!"

Halfway up the stairs she stopped. "I'll be waiting for you," she whispered.

"No, Jenny. No hanky panky tonight. Good night."

"Stupid boy!" He heard her closing her door.

The thick carpets made his steps completely silent. He turned the knob to Suzy's room, opened the door and closed it behind him. She was still sitting in the same position. He remained standing motionless.

She did not turn towards him but said, "I knew you would come."

"I'm here to ask you to come to Boston with me."

"Please, sit here with me."

He sat down beside her. He looked at the little photo with the Oriental couple posing in their traditional clothes. They appeared innocent, honest and kind-hearted.

"I was lonely. I am longing for them. They are good, wonderful people. They live in San Francisco. I would like you to go there with me and see them. You will love them."

"I am sure I will. I have to talk to Harry tomorrow."

"He offered you a fortune and Jenny, didn't he?"

"Yes, I would become a multimillionaire."

"Why don't you take her? She is a clever girl."

"It feels very wrong."

"Nonsense! Money is worth a little sacrifice!"

"A little, yes, not everything. I want someone I can look up to, someone better then I. I want it to be you."

"I'll come with you. I'll be yours and you'll be happy with me. When do you want us to leave?"

The following morning at the breakfast table Mike gave Harry the disappointing decision. Jenny looked down at her plate during the entire meal. Neither of them could comprehend how Mike could possibly say no to such a generous offer.

Because of their respect and close ties to Suzy they both went to the airport to say a final goodbye to her.

Mike felt free. The joy of flying was back. Suzy was in the copilot's seat. She had something on her mind, but she did not quite know how to start. Suddenly she said: "I have been fully aware for a long time that it was you who killed the three men on board the *SNOWBIRD*."

"Do we have to talk about that? It's a closed chapter. It's forgotten. It's in the hands of the police."

"No, Mike. It will never be forgotten. I want you to talk about it. I want you to tell me the truth!"

"I have nothing to say." Watching the instruments he switched to autopilot, leaned back and took a deep breath.

"Yes you do," she said. "Tell me now."

"I can't. You'll be afraid of me and hate me if I tell you I did it. You really want me to say I am innocent, and you will not believe me if I say I am."

"I want you to talk to me about it. I want you to confess to me. You loved Maggie an awful lot didn't you?"

"Yes."

"You got mad and you demanded revenge?"

He hesitated but a force inside him pushed for the true answer: "Yes."

"So you went on board and you killed them!"

His eyes filled with tears. This was what he had feared most. Harry and Jenny would never have started an interrogation like this. To them that killing was OK. Not so with Suzy—because he was a murderer. Nobody he really respected and wanted would ever want him.

"Yes," he whispered. "I killed them. At that time I thought it was right. I don't think so any more. I wish I never did it. Every night I dream I kill people, innocent people, people I love. In my dreams my Mom and Dad are there watching me, crying for me."

He couldn't hold back his emotions. Big tears ran down his cheeks and he sobbed uncontrollably and unashamedly with his head down and both hands covering his face.

"No, you should not have killed them. Your guilt will haunt you until you are forgiven."

His sobbing made it almost impossible to hear what he whispered. His voice was thick. Finally he managed a couple of deep breaths and repeated what he had just tried to say: "Nobody can forgive me. Nobody I love can love a man who has murdered three people in cold blood."

"You are wrong. I love you. And where there is love, there is forgiveness. The evil you did will be forgiven if you regret it with all your heart and truly ask to be forgiven. For the rest of our lives we will have to do what's good in order to compensate for the evil we did."

With the back of his hand he wiped his eyes. Slowly shaking his head his gaze met hers. She smiled back and with both hands stroked his hair and cheeks. Pressing her cheek to his she whispered in his ear: "Yes, Mike. You and I will never again have anything to do with drugs or crime. I want to live with you. In me you will find peace. I want you to live on in me—in good, new little Mikes or Suzys."

Chapter 56

INGRID WAS HIDING in the bushes behind a stonewall on the highest point of Dowses Beach, close to the lifeguard's shed. She scrutinized the shoreline; the dark waters and the fishing boat heaving up and down in the rough sea near the inlet to East Bay. With her sensitive night vision binoculars she could see men working on board. They let something plunge into the water. After that the boat headed out to sea. Wasn't somebody swimming there? Yes, a couple of scuba divers in black wet suits.

Ingrid was the brain behind this operation. She had planned it carefully with wide safety margins. Ted, Michele and she had taken turns following the activity on board Arnold's fishing boat. For days they had not let the skipper out of sight from early morning until late night. This was the first shipment that Jack, the skipper, was going to pick up at sea and deliver to the new coalition of drug runners from New York and Cape Cod. A few days earlier there had been a conversation between Jack and his two crewmembers that had hinted about a shipment being on its way. A Panamanian freighter had dropped the coke-mine east of Cape Cod and Jack had just picked it up.

Ted had borrowed an old Jeep for following the smugglers. He had left it in the beach parking lot loaded with old ropes, fishnets and clamming gear so it looked like it belonged to a fisherman. Dowses Beach, a favorite with Osterville folks in the summer, was always totally deserted on a winter night.

Some 50 yards away from the Jeep, hidden in the dense juniper bushes and wild roses, Michele lay flat on an insulated camping mattress. She had followed the activity on the boat but did not dare use her night vision infra-scope because it might be picked up on the radar screen on board. It was too dark to make out any details with the naked eye. She was munching on slices of raw carrots.

"It will improve your night vision." Ted had said. He had thousands of funny ideas like that, but she had accepted his little bag of homemade vegetable snacks, and now she liked them.

Suddenly she heard voices close by. The soughing wind and the roar of the sea made it impossible to hear what they said. Only 25 yards away from her a man in a dark wet suit rose slowly from the black rocks. Michele's heart almost stopped. She lay quietly, her eyes almost closed. A second diver came up beside the first one. Bright lights from a car swept across the parking lot and stopped near the truck. The divers disappeared, hidden from view. She heard their excited, jittery voices:

"It's a police cruiser for Pete's sake!"

"Who the hell squealed?"

The police cruiser stopped. A female officer walked around the Jeep and peeked under the tarp. She yawned.

"Good thing it's not a K-9 cruiser!" Michele thought. "A dog would have walked straight up to me."

The policewoman talked to a colleague in the cruiser, she inhaled some crisp ocean air and got back into the car. The cruiser drove away slowly on the bumpy beach road. Ted had hidden the motorcycle behind the fence and cedar bushes at the entrance to the beach. It was cold. He stamped his feet and blew into his fists. He expected the drug dealers to come in a car, pass him and drive out to the tip of the sand reef. Instead a police cruiser showed up. He couldn't believe his eyes! Seconds later a big silver Lincoln appeared almost beside him, without any lights on. It moved soundlessly, stopped at the entrance but did not turn to follow the cruiser. Instead it continued straight ahead and moments later it was lost in the dark shadows of tall pines and spruces along the road.

Ted could hardly have been detected, but it scared him that he had not been alert enough to see the car coming. He remained motionless in his hideout. After a while the cruiser left the beach area. Minutes later the silver Lincoln reappeared passing through the gates out to the beach. Ted heard a tapping sound in his earphones, two taps twice. That was Ingrid. She whispered: "Lie dead still, Mich. They are coming behind you. Their car is absolutely soundless. Now they are leaving their car. They are walking towards you. Don't run the tape recorder. They could hear it. Oh, my God!"

In their earphones Michele's pounding heart could be heard along with the sound of heavy boots tramping through the lyme grass only yards from Michele's hiding place. Minutes went by at a snail's pace Then Michele's whispering voice came through: "I see two divers carrying big boxes from the water to the car. Nobody is closer to me than 50 yards right now. Here come two more boxes, and another two! The divers disappeared into the water. I can see them swimming across the sound to Long Beach. Look out now, Ted! The car is on its way. Don't lose it. Ingrid and I will follow."

The Lincoln passed Ted's hideout. Its headlights were switched on. Ted started the Yamaha. He was grateful for its quiet engine. He had no lights on and stayed 200 yards behind the Lincoln.

"Stay put, Michele! In a moment the divers will disappear behind the pines on Long Beach. OK! Now, GO!"

Michele ran over to the old Jeep. She started the engine and drove slowly without headlights and picked up Ingrid.

"We're heading for Exit 5", Ted's voice came over the radio. "Are you coming?"

The Jeep jounced through the sleeping Osterville Village. Ted still had his walkie-talkie on and Ingrid heard him say: "I am now on the Mid-Cape highway heading west."

Several minutes later the Jeep swung into the fast lane of the expressway.

Michele was all keyed up with excitement when she told Ingrid how she had watched the smugglers landing the goods. One of the divers was Benny, she said.

"They were just a few yards away and I noticed a funny thing," she went on. "At first, when they came out of the water, I was scared and convinced they would see me. Then I calmed down and I was really longing to plant a tranquilizer in their butts. I really wanted to give them a lesson. It would have ruined our plans. But next time…"

"There will be no next time, Michele. This is it. No more crazy robberies. You have promised me that!"

"OK, you're right. This is it. There's no more need for revenge. I've got my bitterness and loneliness out of my system. I'm happy again. I have a great job, I have a wonderful man who shares my interests and I have you, a true friend. I will find peace again and I will be strong and sound enough to control the crazy me!"

At the Sagamore Bridge Michele stopped and called the DEA. An alert voice answered. Michele knew the moment her call went through they would start tracing her and try to get her. She talked fast. "A big shipment of cocaine is on its way from Cape Cod right now. They are driving a silver Lincoln and passed Sagamore Bridge a few minutes ago, probably on their way to Providence or New York. They're at least two armed men with six big cases of cocaine. Get them!"

"Just a sec, I'll switch you to the man in charge."

Knowing this was just a way to keep her on the phone long enough to trace her call, she hung up. With Ingrid at the wheel they were driving fast along the Cape Cod Canal. Near the Bourne Rotary they were passed by three police cruisers driving at a furious speed without sirens or flashing lights.

"Hi, Ted, are you there?"

"Sure. We passed the tugboat landmark at the Bourne Rotary a while ago. They are driving fast now. I can see their taillights. It's damned cold; I forgot my gloves!"

Ted's voice was close and clear: "Whoops, something is happening half a mile ahead. A lot of flashing red lights! The road has been blocked by a big trailer. There are cops and red flashers all over the place. The Lincoln is crossing the median to reach the northbound lane, but a couple of cruisers behind me have crossed over, too. My God! They are shooting like crazy! I can see the live tracer ammo. I guess that's the end of it."

Ingrid pulled up behind Ted. He was sitting on the motorcycle, red eyed as if he had been weeping. In the opposite lane the police were in charge. Three men got out of the Lincoln and were handcuffed.

"Let's drive home," said Ingrid. "I have an idea."

They stopped in the rear of Ingrid's store in Osterville and carried all the cocaine from the basement out to the Jeep. Then they drove the few miles to Benny's house and stopped near his driveway. Running back and forth they loaded all the cocaine into Benny's BMW. Breathing hard they got back into the Jeep and drove off.

Michele found her cell phone called DEA for the second time: "Hurry, hurry to Centerville, White Beach Lane, number 750, and get the supplier who landed the cocaine you seized an hour ago on the Mid-Cape near Wareham. You will find their scuba gear and wet suits there and more cocaine in their BMW. Hurry! Get them!"

"Ma'am, please stand by. We need to talk to you!"

"There's no time for that! This is the only chance you'll have to get them! Hurry."

Michele hung up and drove home to Barnstable Harbor. It was about four o'clock in the morning and still dark. The skies were beginning to turn light pink. The wind had calmed down. Their hectic night was going to be followed by a beautiful, sunny spring day.

Chapter 57

MICHELE AND ALEC had met frequently, not only to work together, but because they had both been alone and now enjoyed each other's company. They had just finished several hours of art gallery browsing in Wellfleet and were driving along Route 6 in the Rolls when Alec said: "Wellfleet is like no other place on Cape Cod. It's a town that wants to be left alone, keep its character, and stay low key and quiet. How come so many fine art galleries can survive here?"

Michele answered: "They are run by art lovers who appreciate and stimulate this atmosphere. I love this place. I love the watercolors we just saw. I love this tradition we inherited from Good Old England. Where else in the world do you find this tradition of artistic feeling and this superior skill in the most demanding and difficult painting media but in Britain and here in New England?

"We'll buy one next time we're out there."

"We?"

"Yes, we! You and I. We could hang it in our studio."

"It would fit perfectly in my studio, of course."

"Of course, it would. I'd love to see it there when I work. Mich, I have something I need to talk to you about."

He took the next exit to the Orleans Rotary where he picked up Route 6A choosing it for the drive home, preferring its scenic beauty of The Old King's Highway to the dull Mid-Cape expressway. The chestnut trees and the dogwoods were in bloom and the "Olde Cape Cod" was showing off its most charming self. He slowed down and said: "My dear, maybe it's ludicrous for an old goat like me to say this. It's hard to find the right words."

"Alec, are you trying to tell me you're in love with me?"

He nodded.

"Alec, I, too, have something serious I need to talk about first. Could we talk about love a bit later?"

She started from the beginning, telling him about her crazy adventures with Ingrid and Ted. She told about their first ambush and their robberies, about the money they had stolen and the mess it must have created among the drug dealers. In telling about Arnold, she realized she had already said too much. Cathy was going to be Alec's daughter-in-law. She stopped talking.

"I'm sorry, I didn't think of Cathy and Henry."

"You don't have to. Cathy is a great girl, just the right one for my son. I don't think her father is the only one who has fallen for the temptation of fast money. Cathy has already explained some of his problems. I understand that your temper and need of revenge made you launch an attack against Arnold Sprengler and those crooks. But risking your life, fighting ruthless gangsters, doing policemen's job, is simply stupid."

"Ingrid and I," Michele said, "have decided that the Osterville job was our last one. The other day I saw Cathy pushing Arnold in his wheelchair. She is a remarkable young woman. I'm afraid the hoodlums might be after Arnold. If they get him, it will be my fault."

They drove under a canopy of fresh green foliage on old knotty trees.

"Mich?"

"Yes?"

"Would you ever consider marrying again?"

She had sensed that he might ask her this. "I don't think I could ever grow together with a man again, the way I did with Rich. When he died, half of me died. My joy in living was gone"

"I think you have recuperated brilliantly. You seem to be brimming with life and energy."

"Thanks to Ingrid and Ted I am not alone any more, and because of you life begins to smile again."

"I think meeting you has changed me, too. Do you think that you would care…? Do you think we could have a life together?"

"I think it's worth trying," she said almost demurely.

"Let's work together and be together all the time. Do everyday things together and have fun and talk about everything, and see if we can stand each other. If we can, we'll decide on it then."

After the stop sign in Barnstable Village Alec did not turn right down to the harbor, but continued straight ahead along 6A.

"You forgot to turn to the right. I live down there, you know!" Michele reminded him.

"How about dinner at the Regatta in Cotuit? Alec suggested. "It's excellent with all the old gourmet traditions and a perfect place for a very special occasion."

"Yes, let's celebrate and get secretly engaged!"

They had a nice table near the open fire. Alec ordered champagne.

"May I kiss you?"

"You may," she said pouting and closing her eyes. He held her face between his palms and gave her a long kiss, touching her lips lovingly and tenderly.

"You won't regret it," he said.

"I'll be good to you," Michele said. "We will have a good life together, you and I."

She looked into his eyes and she slowly caressed his cheek. It felt good to be close to him.

"Now," Alec said, "let's talk money! That money is bothering you!"

"Ingrid and Ted really should be here."

"We might offer them the following suggestion," Alec said. "The money will stay in your possession. Invested it would generate 15 to 20 percent interest. One-third of the revenue could be used for expanding the fund, one-third for taxes and expenses and the remaining third part, I think, should be used for one single project each year. You should avoid splitting it into several small donations. We'll have to find out where money is needed and where it can be placed and used with a minimum of bureaucracy and administrative costs. Once a year we will decide which project will get the donation. The fund itself should never be touched.

"This is drug money, so I think we should channel it to drug victims—care for babies, education of kids and illiterates, health education for adults, job training, housing for victims, shelters for the homeless, activities keeping youngsters away from drugs, helping them find jobs and move out from the ghettoes. There are organizations where this money would make a real difference."

"You don't think we should hand it over to the authorities?" Michele gave him a provocative smile.

"Are you kidding?" Alec laughed.

"Washington has to learn that the most precious capital in the US is its people. The day your president and his supporters become role models and show they care more for common Americans than they care for rich peoples' money and profits, only then will I trust Washington. We have to follow our own common sense. We will give this money back to society in our own way. I belong to a privileged upper class, yes, but I can still see that work created wealth before wealth created work. That's why income from wealth should be taxed the same way as income from work. We, labeled 'the elite', have a responsibility not only to ourselves or our own children but to our society and the new generation."

"You are a British Lord, aren't you?"

"Yes, my dear. I am a nobleman and I am proud of the influence my American wife had on me. I am a member of the House of Lords. 'Noblesse oblige', or as you say in the American vernacular, 'nobility obliges'!"

They had fresh halibut supplied by a local fisherman and for desert a refreshing key lime pie. Michele amazed herself finding pleasure just in looking into his eyes and seeing him smile at her with affection. If she could ever be happy living with a man again, this was what she wanted…this correlation of ideas and responsibilities for others, this comfortable feeling of trust and togetherness.

"Here I am sitting just enjoying every single moment without saying a word," she said. "What I really feel like doing is jumping up shouting out my joy and happiness. Please take me home and give me a big, big hug. I'll be the best friend you've ever had. I love you, love you, love you!" Her eyes filled with tears. Resting her elbows on the table she covered her face with her hands and cried silently.

"I love you," he said, "you're a terrific little fighter and the greatest girl I know. Let's go to your place. You've told me about wonderful evenings in front of the fire at Ingrid and Ted's. Now it's our turn to invite them for that kind of a get-together. Come, let's go!"

Michele dried her eyes and held Alec's handkerchief tightly in her hand. The hostess, an aristocratic looking lady, put her hand sympathetically on Michele's arm whispering: "Madame, may I offer you a glass of sherry?"

"Oh, thank you very much it's very kind of you but no thanks. I'm all right. We're leaving right away. It's just that I am very, very happy."

The two women smiled at each other.

Alec built a fire while Michele went next door to the Hallbergs' house and asked her friends to join them. Ingrid and Ted were delighted.

Lighting some candles Michele said: "Alec has come up with a plan for using our drug money. I think it's great and we would like to know what you think about it."

Ingrid stared at Michele: "What has happened to you? You've been crying, but you look

so happy! You know, I felt it right away. You radiate happiness. Have you two…?"

"Ingrid," Ted said, "Really, you shouldn't be so…Oh, yes! If Michele and I had been alone I would have asked her straight out if Alec and she were going to…"

Alec interrupted her: "Yes, we are going to marry, Michele has agreed to be my wife. Haven't you, Mich?"

"Yes, darling."

"Congratulations, Alec. You've made a choice you'll never regret. I'm going to run home and get a bottle of Mum."

Ted was back in a flash and they cheered when the cork popped up to the ceiling leaving a deep mark as a constant reminder of a happy moment. Alec had Michele on his lap when he told them his plan. They decided to go along with it. Michele ran her fingers through his white hair again and again. Old memories flooded up as she thought about sitting in Richard's lap in the past.

"I am sure Rich wouldn't mind my caring for his best friend, and his best friend taking care of me, loving me the way he would have," she said to herself. She knew that when she and Alec would make love, their thoughts and dreams would drift to somebody else—in her dreams she would be with Rich, and Alec with Elly.

But it would be right all the same, and their dreams would be dreams molding harmony and peace, refreshing their souls, creating an appetite for life and work.

"We will grow together in a new life with a new kind of love," she assured herself. "Hopefully, it will be a process without the pain young lovers go through forming a strong, harmonious unit."

Her inner monologue made her unaware for the moment of the present and she did not hear what her friends were talking about. But when she caught Ingrid's eye she whispered: "Thanks for bringing it up."

Chapter 58

MICHELE AND ALEC met Ingrid and Ted at Los Angeles international Airport.

Driving south on Route 405 on their way to Alec's summerhouse in Newport Beach they discussed the private war the three Cape Codders had been fighting against drug dealers. Alec was excited to hear about the adventures of Michele and her Swedish friends, and he wanted to hear more. Especially about the coup in New York when Michele and Ingrid robbed the two drug dealers of more than two million dollars, stunned the gangsters, stole their money and ran away on a motorcycle.

I have for a long time been convinced that the owners of the house over there are drug importers," said Alec and pointed. "And I really think it would be very interesting to use Micheles equipment to find out if it is so, and to pay them a good joke."

"I brought my usual equipment," said Michele, "just in case we would found some unusual birds."

"Unfortunately that kind is no longer rare", said Ingrid, and continued, "Haven't we had enough of this kind of entertainment? I do not like to play games with ruthless killers and money mad big shots."

Ted knew his wife did not like their private police activity even if it had rendered them several million dollars last summer.

"Robbing crooks is lucrative, but not risk free. But, Ingrid, you have to admit it was exciting and sometimes even fun. Much more fun than running a couple of fashion and gift stores and a lot more profitable," said Alec.

"Originally we went into this crazy game because we wanted to blow the nose of some greedy drug dealers…" Ingrid talked like to herself.

"That is a jolly good reason, my friend," said Alec, and continued:

" There is a man in Louisiana, a self made multi millionaire, who pays the college education for every kid in his hometown, who fulfills four demands: one, to stay away from liquor and drugs, two, to stay away from crime, three, to maintain an average of B at school, and four, that girls not to become pregnant."

"If we use the stolen money like that, I'll join the club," said Ted.

"Very good," said Alec. "Let's set up a fund that can promise the same thing to every kid to a poor single mother in a real hopeless slum area! Preferably to someone who is a victim of drug abuse!"

***

Michele mounted her parabolic microphone and aimed it at the suspected house. It didn't take long listening to the conversation taking place there to understand that Alec's observations and suspicions proved to be correct; a big deal was eminent. Compared to the Cape Cod transactions this was much, much bigger business. Eleven million dollars worth of cocaine was expected with a truckload from the Mexican border. A truck from one of America's biggest and most well known transport companies was rented for the transport. The three men on the roof terrace did not at all look like crooks. One was a blond, muscular and sympathetic looking man in his lower twenties dressed in shorts and a golf shirt. One was a feminine looking, handsome man, also just over twenty, with crow black hair, shingled and short cut like a woman's. He was dressed in swim trunks and a T-shirt. He spoke with a Mexican accent. The host seemed to be a white, tanned, middle aged man all dressed in white. His dark hair had sprinkles of snow on his temples. His blue eyes were sparkling and alert. None of the three looked like they could be involved in any criminal activity.

The parabolic mike registered every word and everything was recorded. The men sealed their agreement with a couple of drinks and handshakes. Then, the young man in swim trunks, they called him Roy, walked down to the dock where he set out on a wind surfing board, balancing and slowly sailed into the stream of passing sail boats and power cruisers. The other visitor, the host called him Leo, walked out of the villa. Moments later the sound of a starting car was heard and between the houses he was seen driving off in a white, two seated Jaguar.

The man still on the terrace grabbed a cell phone and in a brief conversation with the cocaine supplier he confirmed the place and time for the exchange of money and goods.

Two men in a open sports car would bring the money in an aluminum trunk this Thursday at noon sharp on the Pacific Coastal Highway at Wilshire Boulevard. The supplier's truck would be there at the same time to hand over the truck to the buyer's driver. Later that same night the emptied truck should be returned to the parking lot just off the San Diego Freeway in Huntington Beach..

"Well, Ingrid," said Alec, after they had heared the taped conversation. "If you think we ought to stay out of this, let's drop it. But, if you think that eleven million dollars and a good punch in the crook's belly is worth the risk, let's go ahead and make up a detailed plan."

Ingrid looked down concentrating and thinking. After a long silence she looked up and said: "Lets discuss the whole scenario, every detail, every minute of our plan. We need several alternative escape routes and after that we should decide how to spend the money."

Alec smiled and nodded at the smart, organized, sharp and fast-thinking Swedish woman.

Dinner was seved. Grilled tuna with pinaple rice and baby veggies. For dessert they were served prune suffle with chocolate chip ice cream and small almond pastries. The coffee after dinner was served with Strega and an aged Remy Martin cognac. A superb gourmet menu! When it was dark and the moon shun over the glittering water, they were still talking, planning the coup. The boat traffic in the harbor just outside Alec's waterfront home was still intence and everywhere you could see people sitting on their balconies, decks and docks at candled flickering lights, talking, enjoying the balmy, beautiful night.

Ingrid and Michele spent all next morning planning every minute of the coup and buying the equipment they would need for a fast, sophisticated, secure blow and an even faster escape in unexpected ways.

***

Sitting in Alec's Rolls Royce, Alec and Ted saw the white Jaguar with the two men they recognized from the meeting on the roof terrace. They saw the big aluminum trunk with the money, which minutes later, should be handed over to the supplier's men in exchange for the truck with the drugs.

They saw Michele and Ingrid on their Honda motorcycle two cars behind the Jaguar. The traffic on Route 405 was intense and very slow. Bumper to bumper ten yards a minute! Ted also noticed that the same Mercedes they had seen parked beside the house of the man in the white suite, was following approximately ten cars behind the Jaguar. The man nwext to the driver of the Jaguar was talking in his cell phone every other minute. Michele and Ingrid had cell phones built in their motorcycle helmets and were in steady contact with Ted and Alec.

"This is the best place to strike", said Michele and drove up beside the Jaguar. Both Ingrid and Michele had a stun gun and in no time the two men were sitting bent forward with starring eyes and open mouths, while Ingrid in a flash grabbed the heavy trunk and jumped back up behind Michele, who pulled the throttle handle to full speed and in a few seconds were five hundred yards ahead of the Jaguar. The whole operation hadn't taken half a minute. The car with the two unconscious men brought the bumper-to-bumper line behind them to a complete stop. It took forever for the men in the Mercedes to be aware of what had happened and to get out and rush up to the Jaguar. They talked to the people in the car behind the Jag. Yes, they had witnessed it and told everything.

The Mercedes man talked in his cell phone and minutes later two men on motorcycles stopped beside the Jaguar and then drove off at an exessive speed chasing Michele and Ingrid, who by now were well over a mile ahead.

"Michele!" Ted called in his cell phone.

"We got it, we got it!" Screamed Michele.

"Michele, listen! There are two men on very fast motorcycles chasing you. You have less than five minutes lead. Get off the expressway! On those long stretches of this road they will soon be able to catch up and see you!"

A police on a motorcycle came and got the Jag to the side of the road and the traffic jam loosened up. Alec let the Rolls show its speeding capacity. It didn't take him long before he could park outside his house and he and Ted rushed through the house and down to the dock.

Michele drove full throttle, about 120 mph. They leaned in 45 degrees when they made the turn before the final stretch down into Newport Beach. The two women on the Honda were now chased, not only by two gangsters but also by two policemen on motorcycles and a couple of police cruisers as well. A wild chase followed up and down narrow streets criss-crossing downtown. The more experienced motorcycle riders were just behind Michele and Ingrid who found themselves locked in a cul de sac leading down to a fishing pier.

Alec and Ted had rushed onboard Alec's power cruiser just in time to witness their girls driving at full speed down the narrow street and out on the pier to make an enormus, well 20 yard long jump out into the harbor, finishing in a big splash!

The smiles on the faces of the chasing motorcyclists widened, when they reached their guns under their leather jackets, ready to shoot when the two heads should be visible in the water. But no little heads popped up! The men waited and waited.

Still in the air Michele and Ingrid had reached for their diving masks, opened the valves to the small oxygen tanks. They let themselves sink to the bottom. The harbor was about 30 feet deep here. They tied the trunk to the heavy motorcycle so it would not float up. In the saddle packs they had their diving equipment. Sitting on the floor the two friends put on their masks and fins. Then they swam under the water, pulling the Honda and the trunk behind themselves in the direction of Alec's house and dock.

In the middle of the waterway Alec and Ted were waiting with the anchor hanging down almost to the bottom. The anchor line was tied midship on the hidden side. On the pier lots of people were waiting for the motorcycle riders to pop up where they had disappeared. The chasing gangsters were ready to shoot. But nothing happened. The water surface became calm again.

Michele and Ingrid found the anchor and tied their load onto it, pulled the signal rope running along the anchor line. Alec and Ted got the message! They smiled at each other when their cruiser slowly passed out of the harbor.

Michele and Ingrid continued their underwater swim towards Alec's dock, where they behind the bulk walk, could come up and take off their diving gear and dress in nice, comfortable swimsuits. Relaxed they walked over to the swim platform and sat down outside the bar kitchen.

Lots of people had witnessed the dramatic motorcycle chase finishing in the long, high jump out into the harbor and a big splash. Nobody paid much attention. Everybody took for granted that the whole scene was arranged by a Hollywood film team!

When the police arrived they asked the motorcycle gangsters what had happened and soon a police diver swam out to search for the drowned. After a long time under the water, his seal like head was seen. The diver just shook his head. There was nothing to be found. The motorcycle and the two on it just weren't there.

Alec took his cruiser with its underwater catch to a place near Corona del Mar, where they left the motorcycle with a friend of Alec's. It was dark when they docked at Alec's house and were met and hugged by their laughing wives. Knowing the danger of talking outdoors nobody mentioned anything about what they just had been through. Trumpet glasses with a nice Champagne clinked in toasts and the moon was full and the water sprinkled with silver.

Chapter 59

STANDING IN THE doorway she looked lost. Arnold didn't recognize her right away, the tiny, tired-looking, little woman. Her face lacked both emotion and recognition. She studied his pale face, the gray hair, the weary eyes. His neck was wrinkled; he was not well shaven; salt-and-pepper bristles covered his chin. There were brown spots she never noticed before on his hands and temples. On his hand was the ring she had given him more than 30 years ago.

"Today is the day," she said. "I've come to take you home." Her voice jolted him into reality. This was Sara, his one and only love. The woman whose child he helped to kill; whose dreams of a good life he had destroyed; who had been faithful and given him advice that would have kept their child alive and himself an honest man.

"I want to beg your forgiveness," he spoke in a low voice and paused. "I have been a bad husband to you and a bad father to our children. I am very, very sorry for all the suffering I have caused you and Cathy."

"You deserve the punishment God gave you." Sara replied. "Our child died because of your heartlessness and greed. If I had my way everybody involved in the cocaine trade would burn in Hell. But I guess Our Lord is more forgiving than I am. It is my duty as a Christian to tell you I forgive you, but, frankly, it will take my heart a long, long time to really mean it."

She sat down on his bed and took his hands and said: "My heart will forgive you when you carry your disability without self-pity and if you work hard to make good for the evil you have done."

"I am glad you came, Sara. I'll never disappoint you again. I've been longing for you. I love you."

"You are a good lawyer, Arnold, you know all the right words. But you confuse facts. You loved me once, but it was long ago. You love yourself most of all, and you love Cathy because she saved your life from being wasted and your soul condemned. No, Arnold, you don't love me any longer. What you feel is not love. It's shame. My Arnold died with Maggie. But, I too, am responsible for our misfortune. I should have steered you away from your evil business associates. I should have said loud and clear: 'Drug money is evil money. Neither the girls nor I needed it or wanted it."

This was the woman he truly loved. He loved her determination, her clear views of right and wrong and her frankness in stating her opinion. He had never heard her talk about God like this before. But, he understood that it must have been her relationship with the Lord that had made her come back to him, making an effort to forgive him.

A nurse came into the room and explained Arnold's injuries to Sara. She identified which of his nerves were damaged beyond repair and which ones they hoped would heal. She talked about equipment needed for his care; how to bathe him, help him to the bathroom, protect his fragile skin—every detail. She had a schedule for the daily routine and care, and phone numbers to call for help and advice. With the right therapy, she assured Sara, he would be able to help himself. Together the two women dressed him and placed him in a wheelchair.

"It's a very demanding responsibility you are taking on, Mrs. Sprengler," the nurse said. "Moments will come when you regret you accepted it. We know what difficult patients are like! But Mr. Sprengler never complains, never asks for favors, never causes any problems." She talked while she rolled Arnold out to a waiting ambulance. She handed Sara a bag with brochures, medication and accessories.

"Good luck, Mrs. Sprengler! I'll call you regularly to hear how things are working out, and you can call me anytime if you get too discouraged and tired, or if you need advice. We are always here. And, Mr. Sprengler, thank you for being a wonderful patient. It has been a pleasure getting to know you. Good luck!"

Sara sat beside her husband in the ambulance.

"I am happy to be on my way home together with you," Arnold said.

Nothing else was said during their one-and-a-half-hour drive to Cape Cod. Sara didn't know what to say, but she took his hand and held it all the way home. Cathy was there to welcome them. When Arnold's wheelchair passed his parked BMW he noticed two bullet holes just behind the driver's seat. They were certainly bullet holes; he knew it right away. His car had been shot at. Only Sara and Cathy had been driving it and neither of them even seemed to have noticed it. He made no comment.

***

Cathy's and Henry's wedding took place on June 24th in St. Mary's Episcopal Church in Barnstable. The beautiful church was decorated with thousands of summer flowers. Cathy's family was represented by her parents, her Grandma from Florida, and Aunt Loulou with Uncle Maxi. Arnold's wheelchair was placed close to

Sara. Ingrid and Ted were also seated on the bride's side of the aisle together with a large group of Cathy's friends. Mike and Suzy were there, too. Henry's family was well represented by his mother's family from Osterville. A crowd of Henry's friends enjoyed each other's company with laughter and chatter. Alec and Michele were seated in the front pew.

Cathy was a beautiful bride. She was escorted down the aisle by her Uncle Maxi, elderly and silver-haired, he still had his military bearing. After the ceremony the guests went to Osterville and joined a gala party in Alec's garden. There were lots of drinks and good food and an excellent band. After Ingrid danced with Alec, and Ted with the bride, they left together with Michele and Alec in his Rolls driving behind Arnold's new van, which had a platform that could lift him on board sitting in his wheelchair. Grandma Sprengler sat quietly with her hand resting on Arnold's arm. Sara was driving. She was in a joyful mood laughing and talking constantly recalling pleasant incidents that occurred at the wedding.

"Wasn't Cathy just the most beautiful bride? When she came out of the church and saw the crowd wasn't it crazy that she threw her bouquet high in the air and it landed on our neighbor, Michele, who blushed like a schoolgirl!"

When Sara parked, Arnold waved to Ted and Ingrid, Michele and Alec to join them. Sara served drinks on their farmer's porch. It was a beautiful summer evening, clear and balmy. The air smelled of honeysuckle and pine. A salty, fresh wind blew in from the bay.

"Ingrid," Sara said, "we want to thank you for being so nice to our daughter. Cathy told us she had stayed with you and you picked her up and dropped her at the bus terminal, and you took her to see Arnold at the hospital."

"Cathy and I have become close friends," Ingrid said.

"I hope Cathy and you and I will meet often."

Sara smiled and nodded.

Suddenly Arnold announced: "I have decided to spend the rest of my life fighting drugs. Where should I start?"

His four guests exchanged glances. Michele didn't want to speak about these things. Was he playing cat and mouse with her?

"In the prisons," Ingrid said without hesitation, "Everyone in the care of our society should be protected from drugs and treated for his drug dependence. Everyone leaving a prison, should leave it drug-free. Start there!"

"Never thought of that!" Arnold exclaimed.

It was dark when they said good night and left. Arnold sat in his wheelchair alone looking at the stars. He was happy with Cathy's choice of husband. He also liked Henry's father; and he definitely liked Cathy's new home. But the bullet holes in his own BMW showed somebody was after him and his family. He shuddered with the thought his involvement with crime might once again bring death and sorrow to his family. He had to find a way out of this terror.

Chapter 60

MICHELE WAS READY for bed when her phone rang. It was Ted.

"Michele! Did you notice the bullet holes in Arnold's car? Somebody is trying to get rid of him! I saw their Lincoln coming down the alley just as we walked in. They've come to get Arnold! Get your shotgun and run to the window! Quick! Hurry, for God's sake!"

Michele, wearing her long, black nightgown, ran downstairs, grabbed her FN rifle with the infra-scope and dashed back upstairs. She fell halfway up and the cartridge box opened, spilling ammunition all over. She collected a handful and came up to the window just in time to see a man with a pistol in his hand aiming at Arnold. The man shouted to Sara to stand still or she would get shot, too.

Arnold did the only smart thing to do, he started to talk: "OK, you think it's necessary to get rid of me. Why? I don't even know your names or who you are. You could at least tell my wife and me what I have done to you. I'll tell you if you are right or wrong. I'm not afraid to die, but I want you and my wife to know the truth. And the truth is that I have not robbed anybody or cheated anybody. Somebody had been playing games with both Bolivar and Cavallo. Both of them lost money and shipments."

The man at the wheel of the Lincoln rolled down the window and shouted: "For God's sake, don't waste our time. I'm in a hurry. Get rid of him and let's go. Kill the lady, too. Who needs her? Who needs a witness? Come on! Now!"

In a loud voice Sara interrupted him: "Please! Don't shoot my husband. He won't harm anybody any longer. I was the one who master-minded it all!" She tried to sound convincing. "I'm the one you should shoot."

The man raised the long-barreled pistol and aimed at Arnold's head. A shot rang out. The echo bounced back and forth between the houses. Sara threw herself over Arnold, protecting him with her body. She held him tight, sobbing and kissing his forehead, his eyes and his cheeks. She stroked him lovingly and looked into his eyes.

"Oh, please don't die, Arnold. Please don't die! Please, my love, stay here with me. We'll have a good life together in spite of it all. Oh, dear Lord, please don't take him away from me!"

She laid her head on his chest. The sobbing paroxysms eased as she slowly relaxed, giving up all hope. Then she felt his hands holding her head. Lifting it, stroking her hair. He smiled a tired, faint smile and whispered to her: "I cannot believe this! Our guardian angels are with us tonight."

Two more shots followed. Sara shook in terror and her grip around Arnold tightened. The Lincoln with two flat tires tilted heavily to one side. From Michele's window a loud voice from a bull-horn commanded:

"You at the wheel, come out or I'll shoot you too! I've got you in the cross hair of my scope! Do as I tell you. Hurry up! You, the wounded one! If you move you're as good as dead.

Arnold was the first to realize what had happened. "Sara, please give me the gun that man dropped."

But there was no gun to pick up. Grandma Sprengler, who had heard the men and their sharp threats, had rushed downstairs when the first shot rang out. She knew Arnold had a gun in his desk drawer and she intended to take it. But, noticing a pistol with a long silencer lying on the threshold where the gangster had dropped it a moment earlier she quickly grabbed it. Holding it with both hands she aimed at the man in front of her son.

"Mother, please give me that gun?"

Grandma Sprengler hesitated but handed it to him.

"Arnold, I do not want you to take revenge or kill him. Please don't shoot," Sara said.

"No, dear. This man won't do anything to harm us now. Will you?" Arnold asked.

"No, Sir."

The man stared at his bleeding hand realizing it was he who had been shot—not Arnold. The driver had hesitated too long. Two more shots were fired shattering the car's windshield and steam hissed out from the grill. The driver jumped out of the Lincoln his hands over his head.

"Down! Down on your stomachs!" Arnold directed, aiming the gun at them. The two men hesitated a moment before giving up and lying down flat.

Ted and Ingrid came running from their house. Ted knew there must be at least one more gun in the Lincoln. He found an Uzi on the front passenger's seat. Picking it up he shouted to Michele: "OK, Mich, come down here! Arnold and I have them under control!"

Michele, still in her nightgown, walked across the open yard and up the brick path to the Sprenglers' veranda. She carried her rifle and walked up to the wounded gangster with the bleeding hand. She starred at his face, but said nothing. Already when she had been aiming at him in her telescope sight she had noticed the scars from his eyes down his cheeks. This was the man who had tried to rape Cathy. No doubt. Cathy had clearly told her she didn't want Arnold to know about the rape attack, so Michele kept silence.

Out of earshot Ted watched Michele. "Didn't Cathy say she stopped the rapist by stitching her fingers into his eyes and scratch him down his lower eyelids and his cheeks with her bent fingers using all the strength she could mobilize and that stopped him…? Did you see those scars in the face of the man, who aimed at Arnold and was ready to shoot him…? It must have been the same man."

"Yes I noticed that too. He was no doubt the rapist."

"God knows what Arnold had done, when he was aiming at that man, had he known it was the guy who tried to rape his daughter. Good thing he didn't know. Michele, isn't this a weird way to practice justice? And, what about Mike? We know he is a murderer; still, we let him go free. Is this the American way…?

The sound of police sirens came closer. Moments later a cruiser stopped near the Lincoln. Soon several cruisers with flashing blue lights and a mass of police officers were all over the place. The men on the ground were handcuffed and taken away. The Lincoln was towed. One police car remained after the others had left. The officer in charge of the investigation tape-recorded everybody's version of what had happened.

"I'll be back in the morning and ask some more questions. This is enough for now. Good night!"

"Thanks for coming so quickly, Officer!" Sara smiled. The policeman saluted and returned to his cruiser.

Arnold turned to Michele. "Thank you, Mrs. Renard, for saving my life!"

"It was pretty close, wasn't it?" Michele said in a quiet voice. "Ted saw the men coming. He called me. I am glad we made it in time. In my scope I actually saw him squeezing the trigger. That's when I shot. His hand was badly injured."

"Mrs. Renard, may I call you Michele? You are a marvelous marksman and I understand you have the right equipment for a situation like this. Your husband was Rich Renard, wasn't he? I admired him a lot. Years ago I heard him lecture about wild life protection and big game hunting with a camera." Arnold stretched and continued: "Cathy has told me about your research."

Michele was aware that Arnold had figured out she was behind the loss of drug shipments and millions of dollars meant to pay for the cocaine.

"I hear you have a personal interest in keeping this area free from drugs and drug dealers," Arnold said. Michele didn't reply and didn't meet his gaze.

Ingrid interrupted: "Michele's daughter was murdered by drug dealers,"

"So was Maggie, my daughter," said Arnold and added: "You have nothing to fear from me, Michele. I know the sorrow and the anger and I understand the relief of revenge. Besides I have no reason to squeal. It's all over now and I'll be forever grateful for what you've done."

Michele looked Arnold straight into his eyes with an intensity that made him uneasy. Her words hit him like torches of fire: "Drug running is the lowest. In the drug business you find the worst, the most heartless, the most evil, the most cynical and the totally ruthless scum. Your wife and daughters were sitting ducks. Cathy's life was in danger. We feared for her so much we kept our eyes on her. I didn't want her to meet the same fate as did my Marianne."

She continued: "Cathy loves you. You are part of her happiness so I felt responsible for you, too. Once I swore to kill drug dealers and you were one of them. I had the opportunity but I couldn't. It would have complicated things too much. Now when my life has begun a new, meaningful phase, revenge doesn't mean anything to me any longer."

Arnold looked down and his voice became a whisper. "How can I ever thank you?"

"Cathy will be my daughter-in-law," Michele said softly. "Cathy and I have become very close friends…"

Sara and Grandma Sprengler hadn't paid much attention to the conversation between Arnold and Michele. Sara standing in back of Arnold's chair, was still in shock and completely withdrawn. She ran her fingers through his hair, over and over, smiling and nodding as though answering questions no one asked.

But, Grandma Sprengler was excited. "When I held that gun," she burst out, "I said to myself: 'Emily, if they have killed Arnold, you shoot the killer dead, just like that! Not just the killer, all of them vile persons!'" She snapped her fingers several times.

"Oh, Grandma, you couldn't do that!" Sara scolded.

"You bet I could. Drug dealers don't deserve to live!"

"I think I need another Scotch." Arnold said. "Sara, please. Just a small nightcap to celebrate Cathy's new family and to say thanks to our wonderful neighbors!"

Sara went indoors still wearing an absent smile and returned with a light, soft blanket, but without drinks.

"You must not get cold, my love," she said, tucking the blanket carefully around Arnold's lame legs and kissing him.

Michele watched them, smiled and thought: "My fight for justice crushed a drug syndicate, that makes me feel good. But it makes me feel bad to see the good-hearted, totally innocent Sara be a victim. I'm glad I met her and Cathy. They really are terrific women with strong morals, forgiving, loyal and standing by their family. And, after all, was it really revenge I demanded? Or was it a need to express the qualities my ancestors, my Wampanoags, displayed in their ritual Snake Dance? Dancing with deadly poisonous snakes in their hands, juggling with them, throwing them high in the air and catching, cuddling and kissing them, playing with them in a disrespectful way and swinging them around while the hissing snakes tried to bite their adversaries.

Symbolically, these dancers humiliated the evil, demonstrating the determined warrior's superiority when facing a dangerous, sly and wicked enemy showing his ability to handle any unwanted intruder."

THE END

www.ingramcontent.com/pod-product-compliance
Lightning Source LLC
Chambersburg PA
CBHW051544250626
47157CB00001B/181